"Do you want to know what I think?" he asked.

Her gaze locked with his in the glass before them. "I'm certain you're determined to tell me."

"You were hiding behind your old spectacles."

"Nonsense." She spun around and tried to walk past him, but before he knew what he was doing, he'd grasped her upper arms.

"What are you doing?"

Good question. "This."

And he kissed her.

His lips, warm and firm against hers, somehow caused a thrumming throughout Anabelle's body, making her pleasantly light-headed. He speared his fingers through her hair, pressing lightly on her scalp. Some of the tightness of her bun was relieved, and she heard the clink of pins hitting the floor.

She'd forgotten how to breathe, or, if she was breathing, she wasn't getting enough air. It was all very strange. And wonderful . . .

When She Was Wicked

ANNE BARTON

FOREVER

NEW YORK   BOSTON

Copyright © 2013 by Anne Barton
Excerpt from *Once She Was Tempted* copyright © 2013 by Anne Barton

Forever
Hachette Book Group
237 Park Avenue
New York, NY 10017

www.HachetteBookGroup.com

Printed in the United States of America

First edition: January 2013

10 9 8 7 6 5 4 3 2 1

OPM

Forever is an imprint of Grand Central Publishing.
The Forever name and logo are trademarks of Hachette Book Group, Inc.

The Hachette Speakers Bureau provides a wide range of authors for speaking events. To find out more, go to www.hachettespeakersbureau .com or call (866) 376-6591.

The publisher is not responsible for websites (or their content) that are not owned by the publisher.

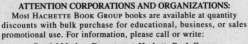

For Mike
Because when the waitress asks
if we'd like dessert
and I say I shouldn't,
you order my favorite
(hot fudge brownie sundae)
with two spoons.
And for a thousand other reasons.

When She Was Wicked

Chapter One

Alteration: (1) A change made to a garment in order to improve the fit or style. (2) A change in plans, often necessitated by misfortune, as when one is unexpectedly apprehended during the commission of a crime.

London, 1815

"Extortion" was an ugly word. It put one in mind of a villain who fleeced the pockets and slandered the names of hapless victims.

What Miss Anabelle Honeycote did to support her family was most certainly not *that*.

Perhaps her actions met the crudest definition of the word, but she preferred "accepting coin in exchange for the solemn promise to safeguard secrets." Much less nefarious, and a girl had to sleep at night.

The primary location in which Anabelle harvested secrets was not a seedy alley or gaming hell, but a small reputable dress shop situated on Bond Street where she worked as a seamstress. Mama would be appalled if she knew about the money-making scheme, but, truth be told, Anabelle would have extorted money from the Arch-bishop himself to pay for Dr. Conwell's visits. He was Mama's only glimmer of hope—and he wasn't cheap.

Someone in their household had to be practical. That someone was Anabelle.

She wiped her sleeve across her damp brow and swept aside the muslin curtain that led to the workroom in the back of Mrs. Smallwood's dress shop. Bolts of fabric stacked neatly upon shelves lining one long wall created a color-ful patchwork that never failed to tickle Anabelle's imagi-nation. While some material would become serviceable underclothes for a spinster aunt, some might be destined for the train of a duchess's gown, lovely enough to grace the Queen's Presentation Chamber. Anabelle liked thinking such a leap in social standing—from modest workroom to St. James's Palace—was possible. Not that she had grand ambitions, but being pinned to her current station in life like a butterfly to an entomologist's collection rankled.

She glided past a large table laden with dress parts set out like the interlocking pieces of a puzzle. The dis-embodied sleeves, collars, and skirt panels lay life-less, waiting for her to transform them into something vibrant—something more than the sum of its parts. After all, anyone could make a functional dress. The challenge was to create a garment that felt magical—the fabric tex-ture, the gown's lines, and the embellishments blending in perfect harmony.

Though occasionally, she mused—plucking a simple yet elegant white silk ball gown from the rack of her cur-rent projects—a dress required *less* rather than *more*.

The creation she held, Miss Starling's newest ball gown, was a fine example. Anabelle twirled it in front of her, checking for loose threads and lint. Satisfied, she walked briskly through the workroom and into the shop's sitting area with the gown draped over her arm. When she held it up for Miss Starling to see, the young woman's face lit with pleasure.

"Why, Miss... Honeycut, is it?"

"Honeycote."

Miss Starling gave a smile that didn't reach her deep blue eyes. "How talented you are. This gown is magnificent. I must try it on."

Anabelle nodded demurely and led the beautiful woman toward the dressing room located at the end of the shop away from the front door. Miss Starling's mother hopped up from the chair where she'd been sipping tea and toddled behind, calling out over her daughter's shoulder, "Is that the dress for the Hopewell ball? Gads. It looks awfully *plain*, darling. Money is no object. Have the girl add a few bows or some trim, for goodness' sake."

Anabelle opened her mouth to object but caught herself. If her clients wanted frippery, who was she to deny their wish? Mrs. Smallwood had taught her the importance of pleasing her clients, no matter how garish the outcome. At least she knew her employer valued her skill and dedication.

The problem was that even though Anabelle toiled at the shop day after day, she earned a meager ten shillings a week. If she only needed to pay for her own food and lodging at a boardinghouse, her salary would be enough. But Mama was too ill to move from the small rooms they let, and her medicine was dear.

It had been three months since Anabelle had last written an anonymous note demanding money in exchange for her silence. On that occasion, Lady Bonneville had paid thirty pounds to prevent the details of her torrid affair with her handsome butler—who was half her age—from appearing on the pages of London's most widely circulated gossip rag.

The outspoken viscountess was one of her favorite customers, and Anabelle disliked having to threaten the woman; however, the money she'd paid had seen Anabelle's family through the spring months. Mama's cough even seemed a little less violent after she inhaled the medicated vapor Dr. Conwell prescribed. But their money had run out, and a stack of bills sat upon the table in their tiny parlor.

Yes, it was time to act again. Papa, God rest his soul, had been a gentleman, and her parents had raised her properly. Though her scheme was legally and morally wrong, she wasn't entirely without scruples. She adhered to a code of conduct, embodied by her List of Nevers. She'd written the list before issuing her first demand note nearly three years ago:

1. Never request payment from someone who cannot afford it.
2. Never request an exorbitant amount—only what is necessary.
3. Never request payment from the same person on more than one occasion.
4. Never reveal the secrets of a paying customer.

And finally, most importantly:

5. Never enter into any form of social interaction
with a former customer.

This last rule was prudent in order to avoid detection but was also designed to prevent her from having to engage in hypocrisy, which she found unpalatable in the extreme.

Just running through the List in her mind calmed her. As usual, she'd listen intently this morning for any gossip that might be useful.

The most fertile ground in the shop was the dressing room, which was really just a large section of the shop's front room partitioned off by folding screens draped with fabric, providing clients ample privacy. The centerpiece of the dressing area was a round dais which had been cleverly painted to resemble a cake with pink icing. Anabelle's mouth always watered at the sight of the wretched thing, and since she'd had nothing more than a piece of toast for breakfast, today was no exception. A large, rectangular ottoman in one corner provided a perch for mothers, sisters, friends, companions, and the like. Miss Starling's mother made a beeline for it, and Anabelle helped the younger woman remove her fashionable walking gown and wriggle into the new dress.

The small puffs of sleeves barely skimmed the debutante's shoulders, showing the lovely line of her neck to advantage, just as Anabelle had hoped. Some adjustments to the hem were necessary, but she could manage them in an hour or so. Miss Starling stepped onto the platform and smoothed the skirt down her waist and over her hips.

The rapturous expression on Mrs. Starling's face told Anabelle she'd changed her mind about the need for embellishments. The matron slapped a gloved hand to her chest and gave a little cry. "Huntford will find you irresistible."

Miss Starling huffed as though vexed by the utter obviousness of the statement.

Anabelle's face heated at the mention of the Duke of Huntford. He'd been in the shop once, last year, with his mistress. His dark hair, heavy-lidded green eyes, and athletic physique had flustered the unflappable Mrs. Smallwood, causing her to make an error when tallying his bill.

He was the sort of man who could make a girl forget to carry her tens.

"The duke will be mine before the end of the Season, Mama."

Anabelle knelt behind Miss Starling, reached for her basket, and began pinning up the hem. As she glanced at her client's reflection in the dressing room mirror, she avoided her own, knowing her appearance wouldn't hold up well in comparison.

Miss Starling's blonde locks had been coaxed into a fetching Grecian knot at the nape of her neck, and her eyes sparkled with satisfaction. The white gown was beautiful enough for Aphrodite.

Anabelle pushed her spectacles, which were forever sliding down her nose, back into position. Kneeling in the shadow of the Season's incomparable beauty, Anabelle was all but invisible—highly depressing, but for the best.

Mrs. Starling was nodding vigorously. "When we passed Huntford earlier, he couldn't take his eyes off of you. There is not a miss on the marriage mart who rivals your beauty or grace, two virtues sorely lacking in his household, I might add. It was very charitable of you to befriend his sisters—and clever, too. An excellent excuse to visit and show him what a fine influence you'd be as a sister-in-law." Mrs. Starling fanned herself and rambled on. "The sisters are quite homely, are they not? Gads, the one with the freakishly enormous forehead—"

"Lady Olivia," Miss Starling offered helpfully.

"—bounded out of the bookstore like a disobedient puppy. And the younger girl with the wild, orange hair—"

"Lady Rose."

"—is so meek I don't believe I've ever heard her string two words together. Don't ask that one about the weather unless you've a pair of forceps to pull a reply out of her. What a shame! Especially since the duke is the model of graciousness and propriety."

The last comment made Anabelle stab her index finger with a pin. The devilishly attractive duke a paragon of good behavior? She'd seen the lacy undergarments he'd purchased for his mistress. They weren't the sort of things one wore beneath church clothes.

Anabelle sat back on her heels to better gauge the evenness of the silk flounced hem. It was perfect. Since the conversation was growing interesting, however, she clucked her tongue and fiddled with the flounce a bit more.

Miss Starling smiled smugly. "Huntford needs a wife who will help him ease his awkward sisters into polite society, and he shouldn't dither. When I went riding with Lady Olivia last week, she all but confided that she's developed a tendre for the duke's stable master."

"No!" Mrs. Starling sucked in a breath, and her ample bosom rose to within inches of her chin. "What did she say?"

Miss Starling pressed her lips together as though she

meant to barricade the secret. Anabelle tried to make herself smaller, more insignificant, if that were possible. Finally, Miss Starling's words whooshed out. "Well, Olivia said she'd met with him on several occasions... *unchaperoned.*"

"The devil you say!"

"And she said she finds him quite handsome—"

"But, but...he's a servant." Mrs. Starling's face was screwed up like she'd sucked a lemon wedge.

"*And* Olivia said she thought it a terrible shame that the sister of a duke shouldn't be able to marry someone like him."

The matron's mouth opened and closed like a trout's before she actually spoke. "That is *beyond* scandalous."

Scandalous, indeed. And just what Anabelle needed. She sent up a silent prayer of gratitude, even though the irony of thanking God for providing fodder for her extortion scheme was not entirely lost on her.

The duke was an excellent candidate. He had plenty in his coffers and probably spent more in one night at the gaming tables than Anabelle had spent on rent all of last year. She wouldn't demand more than she needed to pay Mama's medical bills and their basic living expenses for a couple of months, of course. Considering how damaging the information about Lady Olivia could be, the duke really was getting an excellent bargain. Better that he learn about the indiscretion now, *before* Miss Starling managed to disseminate it to every county.

Keeping her face impassive, Anabelle stood and loosened the discreet laces at the side of the ball gown. After Miss Starling stepped out of it, Anabelle gathered it in her arms, taking extra care with the delicate sleeves. As she helped her client slip back into her walking dress, she asked, "Will there be anything else today, ma'am?"

"Hmm? No, that's all. I'll just linger for a moment and freshen up. I'll need the gown by tomorrow."

Anabelle inclined her head. "It will be delivered this afternoon." She was whisking the gown into the workroom, thinking how fortunate it was that the shop was not very busy that morning, when a bell on the front door jangled, signaling the arrival of a customer.

Three, actually.

Mrs. Smallwood's shrill voice carried throughout the shop. "Good morning, Your Grace! What a pleasure to see you and your lovely sisters."

Anabelle's fingers went numb, just like the time Papa had caught her in his study taking an experimental puff on his pipe. There was no way the duke could know what she planned. Swallowing hard, she tried to remember what she'd been doing before he arrived. It suddenly seemed important that she appear very busy, even though she was out of sight.

The duke's voice, smooth and rich, seeped under her skin. She couldn't make out what he was saying, but the deep tone warmed her, so much so, she felt the need to fan herself with her apron. Perhaps Mrs. Smallwood would realize she was working on a pressing project and spare her from having to—

"Miss Honeycote!"

Or, perhaps not.

With the same eagerness that one might walk the plank, Anabelle hung the ball gown on a vacant hook and pushed her spectacles up her nose before returning to the front room. It seemed to have shrunk now that the Duke of Huntford occupied it.

Before, the two elegant wingback chairs and piecrust table had seemed to be the correct scale; now, they looked like children's furniture. The duke's broad shoulders blocked much of the morning light that streamed through the shop's window, casting a shadow that reached all the way from his Hessians to Anabelle's half boots. His thick head of black hair and green eyes made him appear more gypsy than aristocrat, and he had the wiry strength of a boxer. He wore buckskin breeches and an expertly tailored moss-green jacket, which she could fully appreciate, as a seamstress *and* a woman.

Belatedly, she remembered to curtsey.

Mrs. Smallwood shot Anabelle a curious look. "Lady Olivia and Lady Rose each require a new dress. I assured His Grace that you would work with them to design gowns that are tasteful and befitting their station."

"Of course." The sister whom Anabelle deduced must be Olivia had wandered to the far side of the shop and was fingering samples of fabric and lace. She appeared to be a couple of years younger than Anabelle, perhaps nineteen. Rose was obviously the younger sister; she played with the button on the wrist of her glove, eyes downcast.

The duke's intense gaze, however, was fixed on Anabelle. For three long seconds, he seemed to scrutinize her wretched brown dress, ill-fitting spectacles, and oversized cap. If the dubious expression on his ruggedly handsome face was any indication, he found the whole ensemble rather lacking. She raised her chin a notch.

Even Mrs. Smallwood must have sensed the duke's displeasure. "Er, Miss Honeycote is extremely skilled with a needle, Your Grace. She has a particular talent for creating gowns that complement our clients' best features. Why,

Miss Starling was delighted with her latest creation. Your sisters will be pleased with the results, I assure you."

The duke was silent for the space of several heartbeats, during which Anabelle was sure he was cataloguing the deficiencies in her physical appearance. Or perhaps he was merely debating whether a mousy seamstress without a French accent was qualified to design his sisters' gowns.

"Miss Honeycote, was it?"

He was more astute than the average duke. "Yes, Your Grace."

"The gowns must be modest."

As if she would design something indecent. "I understand," she said. "Are there any other requirements?"

More silence. More glaring. "Pretty."

"Pretty?"

He frowned and adjusted his cravat as though he couldn't quite believe he'd uttered the word. "Pretty," he repeated, "to suit my sisters."

Rose lifted her head to look at him, her skepticism obvious. In response, the duke wrapped his arm around her frail shoulders and smiled at her with a combination of pride, protectiveness, and love. It was powerful enough to coax a smile out of Rose, and in that instant, Anabelle could see Rose *was* pretty. Stunning, even.

The whole exchange left Anabelle slightly breathless. Devotion to one's family was something she understood— and respected. The duke's interest in his sisters went beyond duty, and that bit of knowledge made him seem more...human.

Oh, she still planned to extort money from him; there was no help for that. But now, she found herself anxious to design dresses that would delight the young ladies *and* simultaneously prove her skill to their brother. Perhaps, in some small way, it would make up for her bad behavior.

Miss Starling swept out of the dressing room, her mother in tow. Every head in the room swiveled toward the debutante, her beauty as irresistible as gravity. Olivia dropped a length of ribbon and rushed across the shop to join her sister. Rose moved closer to the duke.

"Good morning, once again, Your Grace," Miss Starling said, all tooth-aching sweetness. "How delighted I am to see my dear friends Lady Olivia and Lady Rose twice in the same day. *And* how fortunate that I am here to offer my assistance with their gown selections. Gentlemen don't realize the numerous pitfalls one must avoid when choosing a ball gown, do they, ladies?"

Olivia replied with an equal measure of drama. "Alas, they do not."

"Never fear. I have plenty of experience in this sort of thing and am happy to lend my expertise...that is, if you have no objection, Your Grace." Miss Starling unleashed a dazzling smile on the duke.

His intelligent eyes flicked to Anabelle, ever so briefly, and the subtle acknowledgement made her shiver deliciously. Then he returned his attention to Miss Starling. "That is generous of you."

Preening like a peacock in the Queen's garden, Miss Starling said, "You may rely on me, Huntford. A fashionable gown can do wonders for a woman's appearance. You won't even recognize your sisters in their new finery. Why don't you leave us to our own devices for an hour or so?"

The duke searched his sisters' faces. "Olivia? Rose?" Olivia nodded happily, but Rose cowered into his shoulder. He gave her a stiff pat on the back and looked imploringly at Miss Starling, who had managed to find a small mirror on the counter and was scowling at the reflection of a loose tendril above her ear. No help from that quarter was forthcoming, and Rose's cheek was still glued to his jacket. The more he tried to gently pry her off him, the tighter she clung. He turned to Anabelle and held out his palms in a silent plea.

Startled, she quickly considered how best to put the young woman at ease and cleared her throat. "If you'd like, Lady Rose, I could start by showing you a few sketches and gowns. You may show me what you like or don't like about each. Once I have a feel for your tastes, I shall design something that suits you perfectly." Noting Rose's shy yet graceful manner, Anabelle hazarded a guess. "Something elegant and simple?"

Rose slowly peeled herself off of her brother, who looked relieved beyond words.

"Why don't you and your sister make yourselves comfortable?" Anabelle waved them into the chairs beside her and winked. "I promise to make this as painless as possible."

The duke leaned forward and gave Rose an affectionate squeeze. "Very well." Anabelle endeavored not to stare at his shoulders and arms as they flexed beneath his jacket.

Miss Starling snapped her out of her reverie. "We'll need to see bolts of French pink muslin, green silk, blue satin, and peach sarsenet, as well as swansdown and scalloped lace." Anabelle had started for the back room, rather hoping all the items were not intended for the same dress, when Miss Starling added, "And bring us a fresh pot of tea, Miss Honeycut."

"Honey*cote*." In a shop teeming with women, there was no mistaking the duke's commanding voice.

Anabelle halted. She imagined that Miss Starling's glorious peacock tail had lost a feather or two.

"I beg your pardon?" the debutante asked.

"Her name," said the duke. "It's Miss Honeycote."

With that, he jammed his hat on his head, turned on his heel, and quit the shop.

A few hours later, Anabelle tiptoed into the foyer of the townhouse where she lived and gently shut the front door behind her. Their landlady's quarters were beyond the door to the right, which, fortunately, was closed. The tantalizing aroma of baking bread wafted from the shared kitchen to her left, but Anabelle didn't linger. She quickly started up the long narrow staircase leading to the small suite of rooms that she, Daphne, and Mama rented, treading lightly on the second step, which had an unfortunate tendency to creak. She'd made it halfway up the staircase when Mrs. Bowman's door sprang open.

"Miss Honeycote!" Their landlady was a kindly, stoop-shouldered widow with gray hair so thin her scalp peeked through. She craned her neck around the doorway and smiled. "Ah, I'm glad to see you have an afternoon off. How is your mother?"

Anabelle slowly turned and descended the stairs, full of dread. "About the same, I'm afraid." But then, persons with consumption did not usually improve. She swallowed past the knot in her throat. "Breathless all the time, and a fever in the evenings, but Daphne and I are hopeful that the medicine Dr. Conwell prescribed will help."

Mrs. Bowman nodded soberly, waved for Anabelle to

follow her, and shuffled to the kitchen. "Take some bread and stew for her—and for you and your sister, too." Her gaze flicked to Anabelle's waist, and she frowned. "You won't be able to properly care for your mother if you don't eat."

"You're very kind, Mrs. Bowman. Thank you."

The elderly woman sighed heavily. "I'm fond of you and your sister and mother...but luv, your rent was due three days ago."

Anabelle had known this was coming, but heat crept up her neck anyway. Her landlady needed the money as desperately as they did. "I'm sorry I don't have it just yet." She'd stopped during the walk home and spent her last shilling on paper for the demand note she planned to write to the Duke of Huntford. "I can pay you..." She quickly worked through the plan in her head. "...on Saturday evening after I return from the shop."

Mrs. Bowman patted Anabelle's shoulder in the same reassuring way Mama once had, before illness had plunged her into her frightening torpor. "You'll pay me when you can." She pressed her thin lips together and handed Anabelle a pot and a loaf of bread wrapped in a cloth.

The smells of garlic, gravy, and yeast made her suddenly light-headed, as though her body had just now remembered that it had missed a few meals. "Someday I shall repay you for all you've done for us."

The old woman smiled, but disbelief clouded her eyes. "Give your mother and sister my best," she said and retreated into her rooms.

Anabelle shook off her melancholy and ascended the stairs, buoyed at the thought of presenting Mama and Daphne with a tasty dinner. Even Mama, who'd mostly picked at her food of late, wouldn't be able to resist the hearty stew.

She pushed open the door but didn't call out, in case Mama was sleeping. After unloading the items she carried onto the table beneath the room's only window, she looked around the small parlor. As usual, Daphne had tidied and arranged things to make the room look as cheerful as possible. She'd folded the blanket on the settee where she and Anabelle took turns sleeping. One of them always stayed with Mama in her bedroom at night. Her sister had fluffed the cushions on the ancient armchair and placed a colorful scrap of cloth on a side table, upon which sat a miniature portrait of their parents. Daphne must have pulled it out of Mama's old trunk; Anabelle hadn't seen it in years. The food forgotten, she drifted to the picture and picked it up.

Mama's eyes were bright, and pink tinged her cheeks; Papa stood behind her, his love for his new bride palpable. Papa, the youngest son of a viscount, had sacrificed everything to be with her: wealth, family, and social status. As far as Anabelle knew, he'd never regretted it. Until he'd been dying. He'd reached out to his parents then and begged them to provide for his wife and daughters.

They'd never responded to his plea.

And Anabelle would never forgive them.

"You're home! How was the shop?" Daphne glided into the parlor, her bright smile at odds with the smudges beneath her eyes. She wore a yellow dress that reminded Anabelle of the buttercups that grew behind their old cottage.

She hastily returned the portrait to the table. "Wonderful. How's Mama?"

"Uncomfortable for much of the day, but she's resting now." Daphne inhaled deeply. "What's that delicious smell?"

"Mrs. Bowman sent up dinner. You should eat up and then go enjoy a walk in the park. Get some fresh air."

"A walk would be lovely, and I do need to make a trip to the apothecary."

Anabelle worried her bottom lip. "Daph, there's no money."

"I know. I believe I can get Mr. Vanders to extend me credit."

Daphne probably could. Her cheerful disposition could melt the hardest of hearts. If she weren't chained to the apartment, caring for Mama, she'd have a slew of suitors. She retrieved a couple of chipped bowls and some spoons from the shelf above the table and peeked under the lid of the pot. "Oh," she said, closing her eyes as she breathed in, "this is heavenly. Come sit and eat."

Anabelle held up a hand. "I couldn't possibly. Mrs. Smallwood stuffed me with sandwiches and cakes before I left the shop today."

Daphne arched a blonde brow. "There's plenty here, Belle."

"Maybe after Mama eats." Anabelle retrieved the paper she'd purchased, pulled out a chair, and sat next to her sister. "I'm going to write a letter this evening." There was no need to explain what sort of letter. "I'll deliver it shortly after dark."

Her sister set down her spoon and placed a hand over Anabelle's. "I wish you'd let me help you."

"You're doing more than enough, caring for Mama. I only mentioned it so you'd know I need to go out tonight. We'll have a little money soon."

Later that night, after Daphne had returned with a vial of medication as promised, Anabelle kissed her mother, said good night to her sister, and retired to the parlor.

She slipped behind the folding screen in the corner that served as their dressing area and removed her spectacles, slippers, dress, shift, corset, and stockings. From the bottom corner of her old trunk, she pulled a long strip of linen that had been wadded into a ball. After locating an end, she tucked it under her arm, placed the strip over her bare breasts, and wound the linen around and around, securing it so tightly that she could only manage the shallowest of breaths, through her nose. She tucked the loose end of the strip underneath, against her skin, and skimmed her palms over her flattened breasts. Satisfied, she pulled out the other items she'd need: a shirt, breeches, a waistcoat, and a jacket.

She donned each garment, relieved to find that the breeches weren't quite as snug across the hips as they'd been the last time. Finally, she pinned her hair up higher on her head, stuffed it under a boy's cap, and pulled the brim down low. It had been a few months since she'd worn the disguise, so she practiced walking in the breeches— long strides, square shoulders, swinging arms. The rough wool brushed her thighs and cupped her bottom intimately, but the breeches were quite comfortable once she became accustomed to them.

Her heart pounded and her breathing quickened, not unpleasantly, as she tucked the letter she'd written to the Duke of Huntford—left-handed to disguise her handwriting—into the pocket of her shabby jacket. A few subtle inquiries had yielded his address, which was, predictably, in fashionable Mayfair, several blocks away.

A woman couldn't walk the streets of London alone at night, but a lad could. Her mission was dangerous but simple: deliver the note to the duke's butler and slip away before anyone could question her. She should be quaking in her secondhand boys' boots, but a decidedly wicked side of her craved this excitement, relished the chance for adventure.

She sent up a quick prayer asking for both safety and forgiveness, then skulked down the stairs and out into the misty night.

Chapter Two

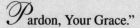

"Pardon, Your Grace."

Owen Sherbourne, the Duke of Huntford, glanced up from the ledger he'd been scrutinizing for the past two hours. Something in his books was off, and he'd correct it if it took him all night. Which it likely would. His butler stood in the doorway of the study, his bushy white brows drawn together like two damned caterpillars mating. If caterpillars even did. Good God. "What *is* it, Dennison?"

The butler presented a silver salver with an annoying flourish. "This letter was just delivered for you. The messenger said it was urgent."

"Who's it from?"

"I don't know, Sir."

"Well then," Owen said, summoning patience, "I suggest you remedy that."

The butler's jowls swayed as he shook his head. "I can't. The messenger ran off after he handed me the letter."

Owen set his pen in the center of the ledger and rubbed his eyelids to erase the numbers burned onto the backs of them. "A mysterious messenger." He poked the inside of his cheek with his tongue. Let the sarcasm fester for a while. "I thought you knew everyone, Dennison. Every bloody footman, maid, and butler for miles around. Here, I'll take it." He waved the butler in and held out his palm.

Dennison inched his way to the desk as if he were entering Medusa's cave. Everyone knew what had happened there, and although three years had passed since Owen's father's suicide, the staff still drew straws to see who had to dust the bookshelves. Owen didn't blame them.

He took the letter and placed it on the corner of his desk. The butler made a quick getaway. Determined to return to work, Owen picked up his pen and scanned the columns of numbers to find his place. Urgent, indeed. Probably another damned ball invitation. He looked at it out of the corner of his eye. Ordinary parchment, a puddle of green wax, a seal he didn't recognize.

Infinitely more interesting than a page of numbers.

Cursing, he grabbed the letter, slipped his finger under the seal, and unfolded it.

My Lord Duke of Huntford,

There is no way to pleasantly state this, so I shall be blunt. I have learned that your sister, Lady Olivia Sherbourne, is romantically involved with a servant in your household. They have met, unchaperoned, on more than one occasion. In addition, she has some rather unconventional views regarding relationships between servants and members of the aristocracy.

I regret to inform you of this news, as I'm sure you find it exceedingly troubling. I further regret to inform you that this information will be made public in the next issue of The London Tattler *unless you precisely follow the instructions given below.*

First, you must wrap 40 gold sovereign coins in a handkerchief and secure it with a string.

Second, tomorrow night, after dusk, have a servant take the coins to the stone footbridge that spans the north end of the Serpent River in Hyde Park. He must place the coins just under the east side of the bridge on the flat rock next to the riverbank.

Third, neither you nor your servant may lie in wait or attempt to discover my identity. If I detect any-one in the vicinity of the bridge, I will not attempt to retrieve the coins but will instead deliver a letter containing news of your sister's activities directly to The Tattler's *offices.*

Rest assured, however, that if you do as I've instructed, I will never reveal your sister's secret, nor will I trouble you in the future. I give you my word on this.

Sincerely yours,
A Necessarily Resourceful Citizen

Rage, pure and hot, coursed through Owen's veins and settled in his temples, pounding steadily. He skimmed the contents of the letter once more, searching for evidence that it was an idiotic prank. Though bizarre, it seemed authentic.

A threat to his *sister*. Nothing could infuriate him more. However, his curiosity had been piqued.

What, pray tell, had Olivia been doing?

He shoved his chair back, rounded his desk, and strode past the bell pull out into the hallway. "Dennison!"

The butler scampered around the corner and attempted a dignified bow.

Owen glared at him. Dennison was a dandy, in his own way. Some of the maids tittered around him. What if—Owen could not even finish the thought. The butler was thrice Olivia's age and nearly a head shorter.

Owen sneered at the man for good measure. "Tell Lady Olivia to meet me in the drawing room. At once."

The butler blinked and was off.

With brittle control, Owen folded the letter and placed it inside his jacket pocket. He marched down the corridor and considered plowing his fist into the plaster wall, but thought better of it. At times, his newly acquired restraint was damned inconvenient.

In the three years since he'd become the duke, he'd faced challenges: enormous debt, corruption among his staff, understandably disgruntled tenants, and social and political obligations that had been ignored for decades. He'd conquered each problem the same way: with a logical plan, hard work, and the sheer determination to right things. He would deal with this letter—this misguided attempt to extort money by ruining his sister—the same way.

And the miscreant responsible would rue the day he'd set pen to paper.

Owen stalked into the drawing room, but its elegant furnishings and refined wall coverings did nothing to quell the savagery inside him. He paced in front of the windows so ferociously that the velvet drapes recoiled.

Questions bombarded his mind, but he couldn't begin to answer them until he spoke to Olivia.

"Good evening." Olivia flitted toward him, the picture of innocence in a white dressing gown that covered her from neck to toes. Rose, who entered the room on Olivia's heels, was similarly dressed. Both girls had braided their hair and looked utterly incapable of a wayward thought, much less the shocking behavior described in the extortion note. His heart squeezed at the sight of them.

They were much younger than he, and ever since they'd been born, he'd adored them. Olivia was headstrong, honest, and impulsive, a baby bird eager to test her wings, oblivious to hawks who'd devour her without remorse. Rose was quiet and keen. Well, she hadn't always been quiet, but she was now. Deep as the woods and wise as the hills. And unless they changed, neither of his sisters had a chance in hell of being embraced by the *ton*.

"What are you doing here, Rose?" he said sharply. "I need to speak to Olivia." Rose's face fell.

"Goodness, Owen," exclaimed Olivia. "You needn't be such a beast. We were in my room reading poetry. When you summoned me, it seemed the perfect opportunity for a cozy family visit. You're usually so busy." She plunked herself on the sofa, tucked her feet beneath her, and patted the cushion beside her. "Come sit, Rose darling."

Owen ran a hand over his chin and glowered at Olivia. No one else would dream of speaking to him so flippantly, but he'd made allowances for his sisters ever since their parents had deserted them. He was a poor excuse for a guardian, but he was doing the best he could. He wished to God his best were better. "I have a grave matter to discuss with you. It doesn't concern Rose."

Olivia's brown eyes grew round. "Grave? What's wrong, Owen? If there's a problem, I think it best that we face it together. As a trio."

He pondered this. Although it galled him to admit it, Olivia might be right. At seventeen, Rose was no longer a child, and smarter than most of his acquaintances. He missed their talks.

"Fine." He closed the door and sat in the chair across from them. "Someone has informed me that you"—he nodded at Olivia—"are romantically involved with a member of our staff."

Rose fumbled with the book on her lap, but he would not be distracted. He studied Olivia's face intently. There was no flash of guilt, as he'd expected—just distress and mild confusion.

At length she asked, "Who told you this?"

"I can't say." He wouldn't distress them with the truth; he was distressed enough for all three of them.

"Can't or won't?"

"Can't."

"I see." Her face alight, she leaned forward. "Whom, precisely, am I rumored to be...involved with?"

"A servant. I wasn't given a name." He narrowed his eyes at her. "If I didn't know better, I'd think you were flattered."

"Being the subject of gossip is quite an improvement over being ignored. But I can honestly say I have no idea what could have sparked such talk." She tilted her head to one side as though a thought had just occurred to her. "I *did* give Newton a pair of gloves last Christmas—his old ones were in tatters. Perhaps someone misconstrued the gesture?"

"Newton? Our half-deaf footman?"

"Yes," said Olivia. "It must be him."

Owen stood and raked a hand through his hair. "No, no. We're missing something." He remembered another detail from the letter. "What are your views on relationships between servants and members of the aristocracy?"

Olivia exchanged a quick, panicked look with Rose. So. There was something to the accusations after all.

"I think," Olivia said carefully, "that as long as both parties observe social strictures, a friendship is possible."

"A friendship?" How naïve she was. "Olivia, a servant is not your social equal. That kind of *friendship* jeopardizes your reputation."

She shrugged as though her reputation was a trifling thing, something that could be sent out for repairs if the need arose.

Owen placed his hands on his hips. "Tell me who he is."

Olivia again looked to Rose; the latter gave a slight but firm shake of her head. "Why do you want to know?"

"So I can sack him."

Olivia clapped a hand to her mouth. Rose's chin puckered like a strawberry.

"Tell me his name."

With too much vehemence, Olivia said, "I have no idea whom you're talking about. And I must say, I'm surprised that you'd give credence to idle gossip."

"Olivia."

"I've done nothing wrong, and you won't badger me into thinking otherwise."

"I'm trying to protect you, and the two of you are shutting me out." Owen lowered his voice from thundercloud to gray mist. "What happened to our trio?"

Olivia stood and placed a reassuring hand on his arm.

"It's intact, my dear brother. But it's a fragile thing. You need to respect us, trust us."

"I do." He did respect them. Trust was harder. "I try."

"The world is very black and white to you, isn't it? Right and wrong. Truth and lies. Master and servant. But it's really much more complicated than that." Olivia turned to Rose and extended a hand. "Come. It's late, and I don't want to have puffy eyes at Lady Hopewell's ball tomorrow evening." She smiled wistfully at Owen. "Everything will be fine. You'll see."

Rose stood and gave him a brief, fervent hug before following Olivia out of the room, leaving him alone.

Damn. The gossip obviously held a kernel of truth, and yet, he had no more information than before. Olivia had appeared so dumbfounded by the accusation that he doubted she was guilty. But what was that nonsense she'd spouted about black and white? It was times like these that he *almost* wished he had a wife—someone who could help him understand his sisters and love them as fiercely as he did.

Exhausted, he sank onto the sofa and withdrew the extortion note from his pocket. He tried his best to analyze it objectively.

Forty pounds was a paltry sum for a man of his wealth. Why hadn't the degenerate demanded more? How had he heard the gossip concerning Olivia, and was he bluffing about going to *The Tattler*?

No answers would be forthcoming tonight. Tomorrow, however, was another matter.

Owen trudged back to his study and picked up his pen from the center of his ledger. Just before dawn, he found the culprit: a nine that resembled a bloody zero.

He corrected the error and, two minutes later, was slumped over his desk, snoring blissfully.

The time between delivering the note and retrieving the coins was always the most excruciating.

Anabelle had fretted all day Friday. She'd demanded money from four wealthy aristocrats before the duke, but he was altogether different. More austere, menacing... and sinfully attractive. Sleep had eluded her that night; no matter—it was a comfort she didn't deserve. She needed to leave the townhouse two hours early that Saturday morning so she could walk through the park, pick up the coins before the sun rose, and get to the dress shop on time.

Now that it was time to go, she was relieved to have something to do. Action was infinitely preferable to waiting.

Although the weather was mild, Anabelle draped a dark shawl over her head and shoulders. A few industrious souls populated the sidewalks of Oxford Street, but they were too concerned with their own errands to notice her. Shops and businesses were still closed up tightly; only the bakery showed signs of life. She passed Bond Street, where she normally turned to go to the dress shop, and her skin prickled. No longer could she delude herself into thinking she was simply on her way to work and not about to commit a heinous crime.

As she approached the pebbled footpath that wound through the north side of Hyde Park, her pulse skittered. The bridge she'd chosen as the drop-off location was on the opposite side of the river from Rotten Row, so she didn't have to contend with raucous gentlemen out for a drunken ride. This end of the park was almost deserted.

A haggard woman with a cane hobbled toward her on

the path. Anabelle's heart pounded so hard she was certain the woman would be able to hear it, but she merely passed with a smile and a nod.

She had just managed to catch her breath when the bridge came into view. She paused to scan the entire area. The reeds along the banks of the river were too sparse to hide anyone, and the trees were spaced too far apart for anyone to be lurking there. The dim light of the pre-dawn hour made it impossible to be certain that she was alone, but at least it extended some protection to her as well. She attuned her ears to the sounds of the park: the rustling of squirrels, the caw of birds, the gentle lapping of the river, but otherwise, silence.

Her mouth dry as the pebbles beneath her feet, she followed the path up the slight incline to the bridge. After one last sweeping glance behind her, she stepped across the grass that sloped down to the riverbank. Staying close to the stones that formed the base of the bridge, she reached blindly into the damp air underneath. She wanted nothing more than to feel the weight of the coins, slip them in her bag, and flee to the safety—and the blessed drudgery—of the dress shop.

At last, she located the flat rock, its surface cool and rough to the touch. Farther underneath the bridge she stretched, until she brushed against something lumpy and heavy. She grabbed at it and heard the beautiful, unmistakable clinking of gold against gold.

Thank God.

She crouched and opened her satchel so that she could slide the coin-filled handkerchief directly into it. But as she reached for the bundle again, a hand closed around her arm.

Anabelle cried out in surprise and tried to yank away, but her captor squeezed her wrist so tightly that her skin burned.

She couldn't budge.

Despair, cold and raw, seeped into her bones. How could she have let this happen? She'd failed Mama and Daphne. She'd probably hang, or perhaps be deported to America.

Her life was over.

The man yanked her closer, so forcefully that her spectacles toppled off her nose.

She was face to face with him under the bridge. In that instant, even in the shadows, she knew.

She'd been caught, red-handed, by the Duke of Huntford.

Chapter Three

Bias: (1) A diagonal line across the grain of the fabric. (2) An inclination, such as the irrational dislike of a servant's cap, which prevents impartial judgment.

"Stop squirming." Owen pressed the girl's wrists together and grasped them with one hand. With the other he shoved the bag of coins into his pocket. He stood bent over at the waist in deference to the mossy stones a few inches above his head. "Step back, out from under the bridge. I feel like a damned troll."

The girl ignored his command and crouched, shaking like a frightened rabbit.

Which made him think maybe he *was* a troll. Or an ogre of some sort.

Owen heaved a sigh. "I wasn't expecting a girl."

She sniffled. "Sorry to disappoint." Her voice was more mature than he'd anticipated.

"It *is* disappointing, you know. I spent all night cramped under here so I could give the man who threatened my sister a solid blow to the nose."

She cowered, and he felt another stab of guilt. Ridiculous. *She'd* attempted to extort money from *him.*

"Who *are* you?" he asked.

Instead of answering, she leaned back, planted a foot on one of his thighs, and used all her weight to try and pull her wrists free. She struggled, kicked, thrashed.

An impressive show of resistance for someone her size, but Owen had no difficulty holding on to her. He let her wriggle 'til she'd spent all her energy and was gasping for breath.

Before long, she fell to the ground in a heap, choking on a sob.

Perfect. Exasperated, he scooped her up in his arms, took a step and—

Crunch.

He froze mid-stride.

"Oh, no. My spectacles."

Cursing, he let her feet swing to the ground, but kept a tight hold on her waist. Then, he leaned over and groped around in the brush 'til he felt the mangled wire rims. "I've got them." What was left of them, anyway. He stuffed them in his pocket.

Finally, he managed to pull her out from under the bridge. They staggered onto the grassy riverbank, slick with dew. The sky had lightened from dark gray to silver, and the trees on the horizon were silhouetted by the rising sun. With the exception of a few ducks that waddled on the other side of the river, he and the woman were alone.

And Owen had absolutely no idea what to do with her.

Who was she, and how did she know about his sister's activities? Her plain, dark-colored dress and floppy white cap suggested she was a servant. A thought occurred to him. "Are you working with someone else?"

"No!" she cried. It was the first time she'd looked directly at him, and fear flashed in her eyes.

"I see. So this...scheme was entirely your own?"

"Yes." She raised her chin, and the proud gesture looked oddly familiar. He'd seen her somewhere before—he was sure of it.

"And how long is your list of victims?"

"Pardon?"

"I assume you've done this before."

She flushed. "Never." Right.

"My butler said a lad delivered the demand note." He let his gaze drift over her as though he were making a frank assessment of her build—which he was. She seemed to be of average height, but she was thin. Too thin. "I assume that was you?"

She swallowed before answering. "It was."

Interesting. With his free hand, he rubbed his lower back, which ached like the devil. "If I released you, would you promise not to run away?"

She nodded.

"I'll need to *hear* your promise."

"You have my word," she ground out.

"Excellent." He let go of her wrists. She took a step back but did not bolt. Which was fortunate, as it spared him a morning run through Hyde Park. "Your extortion scheme was *completely* fool-brained. But your letter suggests that you possess at least a modicum of intelligence. That being the case, I'm sure you realize that you've left me no choice. I must turn you over to the authorities and make them aware of your illegal activities."

She flinched as though she'd been hit. "But Your Grace," she pleaded, "you *do* have a choice. You could show me mercy—let me go. If you did, I'd swear never to bother you or your family again."

He refrained from snorting. Barely. "Maybe not. But you'd prey upon another hapless victim." She opened her mouth to deny it, but he cut her off. "I can't allow that to happen. You've committed a crime, Miss...?" The stubborn chit didn't supply her name. "There are consequences."

"True," she said softly. "There are also consequences of inaction."

What, in God's name, was that supposed to mean? Perhaps she wasn't altogether sane. The sooner he rid himself of her, the better. But he was curious about a few things. "Before I take you to Bow Street, I'll need some answers."

She swayed on her feet.

Christ. "When was the last time you had something to eat?"

She fisted her hands, and there it was again—the flash of pride. "I don't see where that's any of your concern."

He couldn't have her swooning on him. "There's a bench beneath the trees on the other side of the bridge. We'll finish our conversation there."

"Conversation or interrogation?"

"Call it what you will. Come." He took her elbow, keeping a firm hold as they walked across the footbridge toward a grove of trees. She sat on the bench and gripped the edge of the seat. The light was better here, and he was now certain that he knew this woman. Thick lashes veiled her wary, gray eyes. Her hair was of an indeterminate color—light brown, he'd guess—but it was pulled back tightly, revealing a smooth forehead and hollowed cheeks. The way she pressed her lips together suggested that the answers he sought would not tumble forth. But he had to try.

"Who are you? How did you know about Olivia?"

She stared at the ducks that had waded into the river for a morning swim but said nothing.

"I am very protective of my sisters," he said.

She glanced at him and nodded. He detected something akin to approval.

"Naturally," he said, "I'd like to ensure that the rumor you threatened to reveal is squashed. You could undo some of the damage you've caused if you were forthcoming now."

A frown marred her face, and he could tell her mind was scrambling, probably concocting an elaborate lie.

Finally, she spoke. "If I tell you who I am and how I learned the news about your sister, will you let me return to my family?"

"Do you have a husband? Children?" The possibility hadn't occurred to him.

She arched a brow. "Do we have a deal?"

"No." He raked a hand through his hair. "It would be irresponsible of me to let you go."

"And I suppose you've never done anything irresponsible," she said glumly.

If she only knew. "Not lately."

"You know," she said, "sometimes there's good cause for bending the rules."

She didn't speak like a servant. And she was much too philosophical for this godforsaken hour of the morning. "Nonsense. That's a lie people tell themselves to ease their guilt. I suppose you're going to say you had a good reason for extorting money from me."

"My mother's very ill."

He shifted on the bench. As reasons went, it was good. Of course, he had no way of knowing if it was true. "I'm sorry."

"The forty pounds would have paid for the doctor's vis-its, her medicine, and our rent. At least for a few months."

The bundle of coins weighed heavily in his pocket. To him, forty pounds was just a new jacket and a pair of boots. But it was the principle of the thing. She'd threatened to ruin his sister. "Why was it left to you to raise the money? Do you have a father or siblings?"

"My father is dead." Her voice cracked on the final word. "My sister and I take care of our mother."

"Surely you had other options. Besides extortion."

She snorted. "I could have tucked up my skirts and hung about Covent Garden."

"I meant you could have sought gainful employment."

"I *have* a respectable job. At least, I did until today. But my salary didn't begin to cover the cost of Mama's care."

Owen wasn't sure why he believed this woman when she had every reason to lie. All he knew was that the whole exchange had left him feeling depressed. And confused.

"I assume you possess a skill for something other than writing demand notes."

"Yes," she said.

"But if I were to release you"—she looked up at him, gray eyes full of hope—"you'd still be in dire need of money. You might turn to extortion again."

"I would do whatever I needed to do to take care of my family," she said unapologetically.

And there it was—the familiar, haughty look. A ray of sunshine, pure as the morning, penetrated the canopy of trees and illuminated her face. And in that moment, he was almost certain of her identity. Upon meeting her, the proud tilt of her chin had struck him as completely incongruous with her drab clothes and ill-fitting spectacles. Given her demeanor and appearance, the seamstress's name had, at first, seemed ironic. Upon further inspection, however, he'd noticed that beneath the godawful cap she wore, there were golden streaks in her hair. They started at her temples and traveled obediently to the bun at the back of her head. And then he'd thought her name suited her after all.

"Oh, here." He pulled the spectacles from his pocket and handed them to her.

One lens was cracked, and the wire was badly bent. She attempted, unsuccessfully, to twist them into their proper shape before putting them on.

The oversized spectacles perched on her sloping nose, in combination with her ridiculous cap, confirmed his suspicion.

"I admire your devotion to your family, *Miss Honeycote*."

She gasped.

He leaned forward until only a breath separated them. "And I believe I have a proposition for you."

The duke's smug smile raised the hairs on the back of Anabelle's neck.

Although her left lens was cracked, she could see him clearly through the right. His bloodshot eyes suggested he'd had even less sleep than she, and his burgundy jacket with contrasting velvet trim looked like . . . well, it looked like he'd spent the night curled up under a bridge. Even so, he was handsome as sin.

She'd never spoken so frankly with a man before. Heavens, she'd even alluded to prostitution. But she was in the frightening—and yet oddly liberating—position of having absolutely nothing to lose.

"What, precisely, do you propose?" She managed a calm, matter-of-fact tone. As though she were not utterly and completely at his mercy.

"You say you need money to support your family."

"I *do*." She prickled at the suggestion that she would lie about such a thing.

"And you work at Mrs. Smallwood's dress shop."

She thought longingly of the projects waiting for her in the cozy back room. "Yes. Mrs. Smallwood will expect me when the shop opens this morning. She'll be worried when I don't arrive for work on time."

He stroked his chin thoughtfully. "You are in the process of designing gowns for my sisters."

"True." She'd been in the process of a great many things. What was he getting at?

"The day I came into the dress shop, I had reservations about you. I mentioned them to Miss Starling, and do you know what she said?"

"I'm sure I don't." But she was sure the duke had hung on every word that the debutante uttered.

"She said you're the secret to Mrs. Smallwood's success, that there's not another dressmaker in London with half your talent. She said that the most discerning and beautiful women of the *ton* demand you make their gowns."

Anabelle shrugged. It didn't surprise her that Miss Starling would refer to herself as discerning and beautiful.

"I assume the dress shop is where you heard the gossip about Olivia."

Heat crept up her neck, and she nodded.

"And will you swear to me that you've never extorted money before?"

"I've already told you—"

"Do you swear, Miss Honeycote? It is important that I have all the facts. That I know the truth." His green eyes were skeptical. And hopeful.

Anabelle hated lying—it made her physically sick. But if she told the duke about her prior victims, he'd demand to know who they were, and she could never, ever reveal that information. She'd created her List of Nevers for a reason. It protected her clients and, more importantly, her family.

"I swear."

"Well then, here's my offer. If you'd like to avoid being brought before the magistrate . . . you may come and work for me."

She narrowed her eyes. "In what capacity?"

"As a dressmaker, of course."

Oh. Of course. "You'd want me to work at your residence?"

"Yes, my townhouse is in St. James's Square, as you're well aware. I believe you've met my butler."

She felt her flush deepen. But the duke was offering her an alternative to prison, deportation, or . . . worse. She wouldn't have to say good-bye to Mama and Daphne. Perhaps she could even keep her job at the dress shop.

A glimmer of hope burned in her chest. "It wouldn't

take me long to complete your sisters' ball gowns. I'd gladly make them in exchange for my freedom."

He laughed, a sharp, hollow sound. "The ball gowns are only a start. I want you to create complete wardrobes for each of them. They've only recently come out of mourning for my father, and Olivia tells me that all of her older things are out of fashion. Rose had just turned fifteen when he...died. She owns few gowns that are suitable for a young woman."

"But two entirely new wardrobes would take me months to complete."

"You'd rather spend those months in Newgate?"

"Of course not." She squared her shoulders. "I'm accustomed to hard work. I'll arrive at dawn each morning and work 'til nightfall."

"No."

No? "I don't understand."

"I can't unleash an extortionist on the unsuspecting citizens of London. You'll live under my roof. Where I can keep an eye on you."

Oh no. "Your Grace," she begged, "my mother and sister need me. I can't leave them for days on end."

He dragged a hand through his dark, closely cropped hair. "Your sister can tend to your mother. *If* I am able to confirm your story, I will pay your mother's medical bills and your family's rent while you work for me."

Anabelle gulped and her eyes burned. The thought of living away from Mama and Daph devastated her, and yet, it was a generous offer.

"You may send a message to your family," the duke continued. "Tell them what you will. I'll inform Mrs. Smallwood of the special assignment I have for you, and if, after you've completed your duties, I'm convinced that you're reformed, I think I could persuade her to give you back your position."

Anabelle sniffled. "Could I say good-bye to my mother and sister?"

"Why would I let you out of my sight when you've given me no reason to trust you? No. You'd have to come with me immediately." He stood, his patience apparently exhausted. "Take it or leave it."

She hesitated only briefly before rising and looking directly into his eyes. "It would appear, Your Grace, that you now employ a full-time seamstress." They shook hands to seal the deal, and the hint of a smirk hovered at the corner of his mouth. It instantly transformed him from austere duke to handsome rogue.

Anabelle's insides went soft, and an alarm simultaneously sounded in her head. Rule number five on her List of Nevers: Never enter into any form of social interaction with a former customer.

She reminded herself that this was a business transaction, pure and simple. She'd sever ties with him and his family as soon as she completed his sisters' wardrobes, and they would, no doubt, be relieved to be done with her as well. After all, she was a penniless seamstress with a criminal past. And broken spectacles.

The duke held out a palm, politely indicating the direction they should walk. "Shall we, Miss Honeycote?"

She fell in step beside him and realized—with no small amount of dread—that she'd just made a deal with the Devil.

Chapter Four

$\mathcal{O}$wen didn't speak to Miss Honeycote during the walk to his townhouse. He was much too busy trying to figure out what the hell was wrong with him.

The little miscreant at his side had threatened to ruin Olivia's reputation, and instead of turning her in—which would have been the logical course of action—he'd invited her into his *home*, giving her unfettered access to his sisters. Not to mention the silver. Good God.

He strode through the park and headed west on Picadilly, slowing now and then when she fell too far behind. He'd almost offered her his arm—out of sheer habit—but thankfully caught himself. This wasn't meant to be a pleasant stroll. He wondered what his friends and acquaintances would think if they saw him in his current disheveled state with his dreary companion. Shuddering at the thought, he walked faster and thanked heaven that no self-respecting member of the *ton* would be out at this ungodly hour.

At the sight of his brick townhouse, Owen breathed a

sigh of relief. Once he stepped through the front door, he could hand Miss Honeycote off to his housekeeper—Mrs. Pottsbury had a fondness for strays—and return to his normal duties.

He opened the door and hurried Miss Honeycote into the foyer. Dennison sauntered in moments later, his bushy eyebrows twitching at the sight of a strange young woman with the master of the house.

Owen shot the butler a warning look. "Tell Mrs. Pottsbury I wish to see her."

Dennison rushed off, and Owen paced, his boots clicking on the Venetian tile.

"I don't have any supplies with me," Miss Honeycote said. "Thread, needles, fabric, lace...I'll need a great many things just to get started."

He paused and glared at her. She must be in quite a hurry to fulfill her duties, which, for some reason, irked him. As did her cap. He pointed at her head. "Why do you wear that ridiculous thing?"

"For modesty's sake, Your Grace." Her tone, however, was the opposite of modest. Rather sarcastic, actually.

He wasn't sure why the cap bothered him so much. All the female servants wore some form of it. But it seemed too dowdy for someone as proud as Miss Honeycote. If she was capable of making such beautiful things, why didn't she make something less hideous for herself? "It makes your head look like a mushroom."

Her eyebrows shot up and she opened her mouth, but Mrs. Pottsbury teetered in and effectively cut her off. "Good morning, Your Grace," she said with a curtsey. Owen was always fascinated by how the woman managed to keep her balance. Shaped like her namesake, she was round about the middle, with spindly arms and tiny feet. Even her cap resembled the knob on a teapot's lid.

"Mrs. Pottsbury," he said, "this is Miss Honeycote. I've commissioned her to design new wardrobes for my sisters, so she'll be staying with us for a few months."

The housekeeper smiled at Miss Honeycote, but the wrinkles on her forehead signaled her confusion. "I see. Shall I put her in one of the attic rooms?"

Even his capable housekeeper was uncertain about what to do with a live-in seamstress. "I'll leave the decision to you."

Mrs. Pottsbury frowned and spoke to the newest member of her staff. "Where are your things?"

"At my home." Miss Honeycote gave him a pointed look. "I didn't have time to retrieve them."

The housekeeper clucked. "Goodness."

For the love of— He turned to Miss Honeycote. "We will send for your things. You may write that letter to your mother and sister. I will speak to Mrs. Smallwood about your assignment and ask her to send you all the materials you'll need. But before you do *anything* else, you are to follow Mrs. Pottsbury directly to the kitchen and eat a decent breakfast." He knew he sounded like a tyrant. Didn't care. "And find yourself another cap."

Both women gasped, and the housekeeper quickly ushered Miss Honeycote toward the servants' hall.

Lack of sleep must be responsible for his foul mood. He stalked off to his study, wishing it wasn't too early for a glass of brandy.

Mrs. Pottsbury escorted Anabelle to a small, tidy room that appeared to serve as the housekeeper's office. A wall of shelves was crowded with colorful jars of preserves, shiny tins of all sizes, and a variety of household books. The homey smells of coffee, tea, and spices made Anabelle's stomach rumble.

The housekeeper pointed to a ladder-backed chair that was tucked under a round table just big enough for two. "Sit. The master wants you to eat." She pursed her lips and eyed Anabelle critically before adding, "And I can see why. I'll get us each a plate from the kitchen and join you. Then we'll get you settled. I hope you don't mind me saying so, but you look like you could use a rest before you start"—she fluttered her tiny, graceful hands—"cutting, pinning, and sewing." She left, black iron keys jangling at her waist, before Anabelle could respond.

Grateful to have a minute to herself, Anabelle willed the stinging in her chest to subside. She attempted to smooth the bodice of her gown, ignoring the bumps of her ribs beneath the layers of cotton and wool.

First, the duke ridiculed her cap, and then Mrs. Pottsbury insinuated she was too thin and tired-looking. Anabelle was no beauty. She'd needed to wear spectacles soon after she'd learned to read and had always been the plain sister. If Daphne was a sunny, perfect daffodil, Anabelle was a plain, dry reed. It was just the way of things.

And quite fortunate, actually. In comparison to her, clients at the dress shop always appeared beautiful and elegant. Gentlemen rarely noticed her, so she didn't have to ward off unwanted advances.

No, she'd never really fretted over not being pretty.

But today, she wished that she were. If for no other reason than to erase the pity on Mrs. Pottsbury's face. And, possibly, the sneer on the duke's.

"Ah, here we are." The housekeeper's shoes clicked across the wooden floor with staccato steps, and she set two plates, napkins, and silverware on the tiny table.

Anabelle gazed at the food heaped upon her plate. Ham, eggs, pheasant, and pastries.

"Please, eat," instructed Mrs. Pottsbury. "I'll fetch tea."

The housekeeper toddled off again, and unexpected tears burned Anabelle's eyes. The food on her plate amounted to more than her family had eaten in the past two days. While she sat there with a feast before her, at home Mama and Daph choked down dry toast and maybe a poached egg. She would speak to the duke today and ask—no, demand—that he send them money and a delivery of some necessities, too.

As she debated how to approach the duke, Mrs. Pottsbury returned.

"What's this? Miss Honeycote, you must eat. Good heavens, child, what's wrong?"

Anabelle swiped at her face and shook her head. "Nothing. This looks wonderful—thank you." She picked up her fork and took a bite of ham. It was heavenly. She would see to it that Mama and Daph had food in their cupboards. Soon.

A quarter of an hour later, her plate was empty, her belly full, and her eyelids drooping. She took a sip of tea and sighed. Mrs. Pottsbury placed her last bite of egg in her mouth and dabbed her lips with a napkin. "Now then," the housekeeper said, "I've been thinking about which room you should use during your stay."

"Anywhere is fine, I can assure you."

"Mmm. But it occurs to me that you'll be spending most of your time with Lady Olivia and Lady Rose. You'll need room for all your supplies and sewing projects. The attic rooms are small and would not be convenient."

Anabelle shrugged. "I appreciate your concern, but I'm certain I can manage."

"No, no. An attic room won't do. I'm going to put you in the spare chamber next to the young ladies' rooms. It connects to the nursery, which will make an excellent workroom for you."

"I don't know..." It didn't seem right for her to stay in a guest chamber when she was half-indentured servant, half-prisoner. However, Mrs. Pottsbury was correct—Anabelle *would* need ample space for designing and creating.

"The duke left it up to me, and I think the guest chamber is the perfect solution." The housekeeper stood and pushed in her chair. "Come. I'll show you to your room."

Mrs. Pottsbury ushered Anabelle from the tiny office and led her down the carpeted hallway, detouring to point out the well-equipped kitchen and spacious dining room. But the opulent drawing room on the first floor took her breath away. The ceiling was comprised of hexagons that fit together like a honeycomb, and at the center a painted frieze depicted plump seraphim frolicking among the clouds. Three recessed windows framed with elegant carved paneling stretched from floor to ceiling. Several large mirrors placed at regular intervals around the room made it seem even more enormous than it was. The top half of the walls was covered in a light green brocade that tied everything in the room together: the ceiling mural, the plush carpet, and the graceful furniture.

That particular shade of green—sea foam—made Anabelle's heart beat faster. She'd often dreamed of making herself a dress of light green silk. Maybe one day, after she'd served her sentence, and Mama had recovered, and Daphne had married an upstanding gentleman—then Anabelle would sew herself a pale green gown. She sighed softly. The odds of this particular dream coming true were about as great as her chances of ascending to the throne.

But dreams were free.

On the first floor the housekeeper also proudly pointed out the duke's study, which was, of course, strictly off limits.

"And now for the second floor." Mrs. Pottsbury held a finger to her lips as she tiptoed up the stairs. "Lady Olivia and Lady Rose are still abed, which is as it should be. Such fine girls," she said. "They've been through so much."

Anabelle longed to ask what had happened to the young women and whether it had anything to do with their overbearing brother but didn't want to risk waking anyone.

The housekeeper paused at the top of the stairs to catch her breath and pointed down the hall. "To the right is the master's suite," she whispered with the appropriate amount of respect. "These two rooms"—she indicated the closed doors located side-by-side in front of them—"are Lady Olivia's and Lady Rose's bedchambers. Yours is to the left. Come."

Mrs. Pottsbury entered, waved Anabelle in, and closed the door behind them.

Anabelle caught her breath. The entire chamber was decorated in...pale green. It reminded her of the lichen that had grown on the trees in the woods surrounding her family's cottage and the new leaves that sprouted each spring. Though the room was small, the furnishings were sumptuous. The silk bedding, velvet curtains, and thick Aubusson rug were fit for a palace.

"It's terribly dusty," the housekeeper said apologetically. "I didn't have the chance to air it out."

Understandable, since she couldn't have predicted that the duke, after being out all night, would return home with a seamstress.

"It's beautiful." Much too grand, in fact. After spending each night of the last two years either in a chair or on a settee, such luxury seemed positively decadent.

"I'll have a maid bring up some water. You'll find paper, pen, and ink in the desk drawer. I know you want to send a message to your family, so make use of whatever you need."

"Thank you."

"Now. Your workspace is through here." Mrs. Pottsbury walked toward a door across from the bed and reached for a key on her belt. She fiddled with the lock until it clicked, and the door to the one-time nursery swung open. "This room's been closed up since... well, for a long time."

The large room had a picture window, and once Mrs. Pottsbury opened the drapes, Anabelle could see it overlooked a colorful garden in the back of the townhouse. A few bulky pieces of furniture were hidden by sheets, and everything in the room was covered with a thin layer of dust. Tiny motes floated in the air, illuminated by the morning light streaming through the cloudy windowpanes.

It was perfect.

The housekeeper nodded as though she concurred with Anabelle's thought. "I'll send up a couple of maids to dust and remove the drop cloths. Thomas and Roger—they're the footmen—will bring up some tables and additional lanterns." She let her gaze sweep across the room. "Is there anything else? Any questions?"

Oh, Anabelle had questions, like, when would she meet with the sisters, and did they know she'd used a secret about Olivia to try to extort money from their brother? And why had the duke taken pity on her? But she said, "No. Thank you."

"I hate to mention it, but the duke did seem rather adamant about your cap." Mrs. Pottsbury fiddled with her keys. "I have several that are quite smart and...less worn. You may pick one to use until the rest of your things come."

"Thank you, but I'll make do with what I have."

Mrs. Pottsbury deflated. "He won't be pleased. I've no idea why it vexes him so."

"Nor do I." But she was not going to let him tell her what she could and could not wear. She had precious little freedom as it was.

The housekeeper gave her a suit-yourself smile, turned to go, and then spun around like a top. "Would you like me to send your glasses out to be repaired?"

Although Anabelle would have loved nothing more, she could not afford it. She had no wish to be further indebted to the duke. "No, thank you. I have a spare pair at home," she lied.

"Oh. Very well, then." The kindly woman patted Anabelle on the shoulder. "Get some rest, and I'll see you at lunchtime. I suspect you'll have your first meeting with the young ladies this afternoon."

Anabelle waited until Mrs. Pottsbury left the nursery—er, workroom—and then walked back into her room through the adjoining door. She shed her dreary black shawl and placed it on the bed. The shawl's coarse, rough texture was distinctly incongruous with all the lovely luxury in the room. It was the only thing that didn't belong—besides her.

She walked around the four-poster and sat at the small desk below the window. Locating the paper, pen, and ink was easy. Deciding how much to tell Mama and Daphne was much more difficult.

Dearest Mother and Sister,

I'm sure you are shocked to receive correspondence from me, so let me allay your fears at once: I have excellent news. I have been commissioned by the Duke of Huntford to create entirely new wardrobes for both of his sisters. It is a wonderful opportunity, and I'll be earning much more than I did at the dress shop. In fact, the duke has generously advanced a portion of my wages so that I can pay Dr. Conwell as well as the rent we owe. I will send you money for other expenses as soon as I am able.

My only regret is that I must stay here, at the duke's residence in Mayfair, until my assignment is completed. It is no hardship, I assure you, except that I shall miss both of you dreadfully. I wish I could be there to help with household matters.

However, I expect that I will be working here for about three months. I will write regularly, of course, and you must keep me apprised of everything Dr. Conwell says and how Mama is faring. If you need me, send word to this address, and I will come as quickly as I can.

Lovingly yours,
Anabelle

Relieved to have the letter written and frustrated that there was nothing more she could do at the moment, she removed her spectacles, tugged off her cap, pulled the pins from her hair, and rubbed her aching scalp. After slipping off her shoes, she climbed onto the bed and sank into the mattress. Although she'd been awake for two days straight, she was far too anxious to sleep. She would try to rest, though. She curled up on her side and let the silky pillowcase cradle her cheek.

Although her living arrangements were more than comfortable, she would not let down her guard. Members of the aristocracy were not to be trusted. Her own titled grandparents were the perfect example. They'd disowned their son—just because he'd married a commoner.

Wealth and privilege corrupted a person, and the Duke of Huntford had plenty of both. He also had the sort of green eyes that dazzled unsuspecting women.

Which was neither here nor there.

She was thinking of those heavy-lidded, soulful eyes, when, despite her best intentions, she drifted off to sleep.

Chapter Five

*Binding: (1) A long strip of fabric used to create
a neat or decorative finish on an edge. (2) Chafing or
restricting, as is often the case with tightly laced corsets.*

After returning from Hyde Park that morning, Owen spent a few hours holed up in his study. He sent a message to Mrs. Smallwood, letting the proprietor of the dress shop know that her prized employee was on special assignment for a few months. She replied that she'd be happy to lend Miss Honeycote's services and that the dress shop would supply all the fabric and trimmings.

It occurred to him that Miss Honeycote's punishment was turning out to be a rather expensive prospect.

At breakfast he'd informed his sisters of the morning's developments. He left out the bit about the bridge and the extortion.

They'd seemed delighted when he told them that Miss Honeycote would be making each of them several new gowns, and even more delighted when he mentioned that she'd be staying with them. As if it was a damned social visit.

A fly buzzing around Owen's head distracted him from the papers that his steward had sent from Huntford Manor. He glanced at the clock on the mantel and realized that although it was almost two in the afternoon, he still hadn't shaved or eaten lunch. Deciding he needed an excuse to stretch his legs, he walked upstairs to his bedchamber and, since his valet was not hovering about, saw to the task of lathering his face himself.

The cool blade scratched over his beard, and when the task was completed, he felt a tad more civilized. Now, if he could only locate a decent sandwich, he'd be a happy man. He strode down the corridor and turned toward the stairs, then stopped. Something at the other end of the hall looked odd. Different.

The door to the nursery. It was ajar.

He walked over and pushed it open. No one was there, but someone *had* been. The sheets covering the furniture were gone, and the shelves had been dusted and cleared. Four small desks were pushed together to make a table, and two other large tables had been placed against the wall opposite the windows. The center of the rug was worn thin from all the battles he'd reenacted with his wooden figures as a boy. But now, there was a full-length mirror propped against a chair. And baskets on the floor. Upon closer inspection, he could see that they held pins, scissors, buttons, and other things he would not venture to name.

Remnants of his boyhood remained. A globe in the corner. Slates on a shelf. A volume of Homer's works, in Latin—the mere sight of which made him shudder. But it was clear that, at least for now, his old nursery would be used as a sewing room.

It was a good plan. No sense in keeping rooms closed off just because of an unpleasant memory or two when—

Interesting. The inside door that led to an adjoining guest room was open. He crossed the nursery and entered the bedchamber. Everything looked normal.

Except.

There, in the middle of the four-poster bed, a woman slept. He knew he should leave at once, before she awoke or someone saw him here. But he froze.

Her long hair flowed over the pillow in shiny, chestnut waves. Her smooth cheek was tinged with pink. As though she'd been dreaming of something wicked. Her slightly parted lips were the color of a lush peach and curled in the hint of a smile.

He moved toward the bed, pausing and holding his breath when she shifted in her sleep. When he reached her side, he realized the identity of the sleeping beauty.

Beautiful was not a word he would ever have imagined he'd apply to Miss Honeycote. Proud, devious, stubborn, and prickly—*those* words described her. But the evidence lay before him. Her features were almost perfect, save for the concave slope of her nose—the reason her spectacles never stayed put. Her body was lithe, and though he could not see her legs, he imagined they would be long.

The kind he liked to wrap around his waist. Or better yet, caress. Starting at an ankle, lingering behind a knee, grazing the skin on the inside of a thigh, and teasing the soft, swollen—

She bolted upright. "Your Grace?" It was a question and a scolding at the same time. She grabbed the pillow to her torso, as though attempting to cover her nakedness when, in fact, she was fully clothed.

A shame, that. "Good morning, Miss Honeycote."

Out of the corner of her eyes, she peered at the window. "I slept through the night?"

"No. I jest."

She scowled.

"I was in the nursery, saw the door open, and wandered in here. I thought Mrs. Pottsbury planned to set you up in the attic."

Blushing deeply, she said, "She insisted this room would be fine. But I would be happy in an attic room. Would prefer it, actually—"

"No. This is fine."

"Well, then," she said, still clutching the pillow to her chest, "perhaps you could give me some privacy?"

It would have been the gentlemanly, decent thing to do. "We still have a few matters to discuss."

"Now?"

"I assumed you'd be eager to send word—and the necessary funds—to your mother and sister." He was a true cad.

"I am," she said quickly. "I've written a letter explaining my new circumstances." Eying him warily, she eased herself off the bed and maneuvered around him toward the desk. The pillow was her shield, positioned between them at all times. She handed him the letter. "Here."

He slapped the folded parchment against his palm. "How much did you tell them?"

"Just that you hired me for three months . . . and that the salary you offered was generous."

"Indeed," he said dryly. "I think we should settle your debts immediately. I'd like some level of confidence that you won't be pocketing my priceless artifacts and hocking them at the nearest pawn shop. Who is your mother's doctor, and how much do you owe him?"

"We owe Dr. Conwell fifteen pounds, and the apothecary, Mr. Vanders, two pounds."

That must be a lot of money for someone like her. "My curiosity is piqued, Miss Honeycote. How much do seamstresses make?"

"Ten shillings a week." She jerked her chin up, and her eyes flashed. "That's why I've fallen so behind with payments."

"What other debts do you have outstanding?"

She swallowed and gazed at the floor. "The rent. We owe Mrs. Bowman ten pounds."

"Anyone else?"

"No...but my mother and sister have no money for food or any other basic things, like candles or oil for the lamps. If you could lend me a few extra shillings, I'd be grateful."

Her lips were pressed together in a thin line as she awaited his response. Asking for help couldn't be easy for her. He'd already planned to send her family spending money, but he guessed she would be uncomfortable receiving outright charity.

"I'm prepared to give you an advance on your salary. You'll be earning it over the next three months." He flicked his eyes to the mussed bedding. "Which, by the way, doesn't begin until you actually *start* working."

She threw the pillow on the bed and clenched her fists. She glanced at the dresser where her spectacles and cap lay, and then attempted to shoulder past him. But she stepped awkwardly on one of her slippers, and a leg buckled underneath her.

With a yelp, she started to fall, flailed her arms, and clipped him on the jaw.

He winced but caught her around her tiny waist. And steadied her against his body.

Her palms were pressed against his chest, where his heart beat faster than it should have. Her body felt right next to his. Surprisingly strong, yet soft. The silky ends of her hair brushed the back of his hand, and he inhaled the clean scents of soap and cotton.

When she gazed up at him, her gray eyes weren't hard and stormy, as he'd expected. They were warm and sultry. She bit her lower lip, plump and moist. His cock went hard.

God, he wanted to kiss her—had to try. He leaned in, and she raised a hand to his face. With a smooth fingertip, she slowly traced a line on his chin. His skin tingled where she'd touched him.

"I scratched you," she said.

He blinked and said nothing.

"Are you hurt?"

"No." His voice was more gruff than usual.

"You can, ah, release me now."

Christ, he was still holding her as though they were about to dance a bloody waltz. "Of course." Reluctantly, he let her go and attempted to smooth the crumpled letter in his hand. He held it up. "I will see that this is delivered to your residence along with enough money to last them several months. I don't want you to worry about your family while you're here. It would only distract you from your duties."

She nodded soberly.

"Shall I have a footman bring your things here?"

"Oh yes, please. After my sister, Daphne, reads my letter, she'll know what to pack for me."

"Very well. I shall inform my sisters to meet you in the workroom"—he nodded toward the nursery—"after you've eaten your lunch, at say, three o'clock. They know nothing of your extortion scheme, by the way. I'd prefer to protect them from that bit of ugliness."

She hung her head, her hair forming a lovely veil around her face. "I understand. I...I promise not to hurt them."

"Rose, in particular, is fragile," he said. He never knew how to explain her quirks. "She doesn't speak to anyone but Olivia—and only rarely. But she's very bright and communicates in other ways. Olivia understands her intuitively, but I..." He shook his head, unsure why he was telling all this to the seamstress. "I just want to see them happy."

"Then that will be my goal," she said, and he believed her. She'd been able to put Rose at ease at the dress shop; maybe she could work other small miracles.

They looked at each other for a long moment. Although he was a duke and she was an indentured servant, and there was a whole complicated social structure separating them, he felt an undeniable connection with her. She seemed to feel it, too.

He turned to leave through the nursery door so that no one who happened to be in the hallway would know he'd been in Miss Honeycote's room. As he passed by the dresser where her broken spectacles lay, he slipped them into his palm and deposited them in his pocket. Fortunately, she didn't notice.

He'd be damned if she was going to walk around his house wearing broken spectacles. It was the principle of the thing. She might sew a crooked seam on one of his sister's dresses or miss a step and break her neck on the bloody stairs. There was enough drama in the household already.

He paused at the doorway. "I think this arrangement may work out better than either of us had hoped."

She shot him a dubious look—he'd expect nothing less—and he shut the door behind him. When he heard the lock click, he smiled to himself.

Though he was uncharacteristically optimistic about the seamstress, he mustn't forget what she'd done or why she was here.

And he definitely couldn't kiss her. Or even have thoughts about kissing her.

Just two nights ago, he'd lectured Olivia on this very topic. Relationships between nobility and servants were forbidden—and with good reason. Those types of affairs were socially damaging for the lady or gentleman, true, but the servant had the most to lose. He would never be so callous—or desperate—as to use a member of his staff that way.

The problem was that he hadn't expected Miss Honeycote to be so beautiful. If one could get past her blasted cap and spectacles and her perpetual scowl, she was nothing short of stunning.

Fortunately, he did not expect their paths to cross very often over the next three months. She'd likely spend her time in the nursery and with his sisters. He'd be busy running his damned dukedom and attending tedious social functions featuring pampered debutantes.

He withdrew the sorry spectacles from his pocket. Only someone as stubborn as Miss Honeycote would insist that she could see perfectly well through a cobweb of cracks.

No, there was no reason to think he would see her, except in passing. But then, one never knew.

Anabelle let out the breath she'd been holding.

What on earth was wrong with her?

She should never have fallen asleep. This assignment was her chance to prove to the duke that she wasn't a lazy opportunist intent on taking advantage of others. She'd planned to impress him with her dedication and hard work but had, somehow, ended up *napping*.

But that wasn't the only reason she deserved to be flogged. Instead of throwing him out of the room the moment he'd entered, she'd engaged in conversation with him. Worse, she'd been in complete dishabille, and *that* had put her at a distinct disadvantage during their exchange. While he'd worn an impeccably tailored jacket that showed his broad shoulders to advantage, she'd been caught—quite literally—with her hair down. It was humiliating.

The way the duke had looked at her was disturbing. And heady. During the few moments in his arms, she'd behaved like a complete wanton—sinking into him and touching his face—before managing to regain her common sense. Thank goodness she had, because, unlikely as it seemed, she suspected he'd been about to kiss her.

And she'd been about to let him.

Kissing was unquestionably prohibited by rule number five on her List of Nevers.

At least his unexpected visit had saved her from seeking him out. It was a huge relief to know that Mama and

Daphne would have enough money to get them through the next few weeks. Perhaps a few good meals and additional visits from Dr. Conwell would help Mama improve. It wasn't likely, but for the first time in a very long while she had a glimmer of hope.

Deciding it was high time she went to work, she buried her worries, straightened her spine, and went to the washbasin on the dresser. The fresh, cool water felt lovely against her skin, but when she looked up at the mirror she groaned. Her hair was loose and wild, and she resembled one of those naughty woodland nymphs who were forever flitting barefoot through the forest. The precise *opposite* of the impression she'd wished to make on the duke.

Well. She would rectify that now, brush or no brush. Grabbing the handful of pins she'd left on the dresser, she began to work her tresses back into a tight coil on the crown of her head. It took some doing and was not as smooth as she'd have liked, but she managed to pull every last wave into the knot.

Now, for her cap. She'd saved the last two pins to secure it. As she reached for it, she discovered that another cap had been left on top of it—Mrs. Pottsbury's doing, no doubt. The new one was much smaller than her own, delicate, and edged in lace. Anabelle held it in her palm and admired it. It looked like a fancy little cake. The duke would find it much less offensive.

Pity, she had no intention of wearing it.

She shoved the pretty confection in a drawer and placed her own floppy cap on her head, making sure it covered as much of her hair as possible. There. She patted it down, not quite trusting the tightly coiled tresses beneath.

As soon as she put her spectacles on, she'd feel like she was back to her normal self. Only, she couldn't find them. She was sure she'd left them on the dresser, but perhaps Mrs. Pottsbury had moved them when she'd left the cap. Anabelle searched on the floor in case they'd been knocked off and checked the desk where she'd written the letter. They were nowhere to be found. She tried not to let panic overwhelm her, but without them, any object farther away than her outstretched hand looked like it was under three feet of water.

It was very unlike her to misplace them; however, all sorts of things had gone amiss today.

She suspected this latest misfortune would not be the last.

Chapter Six

$\mathscr{W}$ithout her spectacles, Anabelle bumped off walls and furniture like a child who was *it* in blind man's bluff.

Perhaps Mrs. Pottsbury would know their whereabouts. Anabelle felt her way downstairs, glad she'd paid close attention during the tour.

She found the housekeeper in her little office on the first floor. At least, she assumed the blurry figure standing next to the wall of shelves was she.

"Excuse me, ma'am," said Anabelle.

Tins clattered and the housekeeper spun around. "Ah, there you are—and looking quite refreshed, too."

Anabelle felt her face heat. "I didn't mean to sleep for so long. Would you happen to have my spectacles? I can't seem to find them."

"No, dear, but don't worry," Mrs. Pottsbury said cheerfully. "They've probably gone to the same place as missing stockings and cuff links and ribbons. They all turn up sooner or later."

Anabelle wanted to say that losing her spectacles was rather more troublesome than losing a ribbon. But the housekeeper was so kind that Anabelle held her tongue.

"Our next order of business is lunch," Mrs. Pottsbury announced. "Follow me. I'll introduce you to Cook, and we'll have a bite to eat in the kitchen."

Anabelle hoped she wouldn't trip over anything on the way. She kept one hand on the wall, stumbling behind the housekeeper like she'd had one too many glasses of wine.

An hour later, after eating a delicious meal of sliced chicken, peas, and ripe grapes, Anabelle and Mrs. Pottsbury returned to the workroom. Sheets had been removed, tables brought in, and Anabelle was keen to take up her needle and begin working.

"A large delivery came while you were resting," said the housekeeper. "I had the maids place the packages on the table there."

Anabelle squinted in the direction Mrs. Pottsbury gestured. One of the tables was, indeed, stacked high with brown bundles. They could have been sacks of grain or a mound of sleeping dogs, for all she knew. But it was more likely that they'd come from the dress shop.

"Thank you. This is a wonderful space—almost as big as the entire back room at Mrs. Smallwood's shop. I'll begin by organizing everything."

"Excellent. If you require anything else, just let me know."

"Would you please inform the staff that I've misplaced my spectacles?"

Mrs. Pottsbury patted her shoulder. "Of course, dear. Did you see the new cap I left for you on the dresser? It's quite lovely."

"I did. Thank you for offering it, but I'm content with this one. It's not nearly as elegant, of course, but it suits me." Although Anabelle couldn't make out the expression on the housekeeper's face, she imagined the woman's eyes were wide with alarm.

Mrs. Pottsbury coughed to cover her gasp. "You don't say. I'll leave it with you in case you have a change of heart." With a nervous jangling of her keys, she bustled down the hall.

Anabelle carefully navigated her way across the workroom to the table where the packages lay. Using a pair of scissors she retrieved from one of the baskets on the floor, she snipped the string off the packages and peeled away the brown paper like she was lifting the lid off a treasure chest.

Mrs. Smallwood had sent the two ball gowns that Anabelle had begun making for Lady Olivia and Lady Rose. The other bundles contained yards and yards of gorgeous fabrics, lace, braiding, ribbons, feathers, and buttons.

Anabelle's breath caught in her throat. She could hardly wait to get started. When she was absorbed in the details of a gorgeous dress, she could forget her troubles. Stacks of bills, Mama's illness, brooding dukes, and disappearing spectacles ceased to plague her.

She'd flung the curtains back to flood the room with light and was threading a needle when her clients entered the room.

"Good afternoon, Miss Honeycote." Lady Olivia practically skipped into the room. Miss Starling's mother had characterized Olivia's exuberance as unladylike; Anabelle found it refreshing.

She stood and dipped a curtsey. "Good afternoon,

ladies." She swallowed, wondering how to begin her duties on the best possible foot. *I'm sorry I threatened to spread a scandalous rumor about you, Lady Olivia. It's quite fortunate that your brother saved you from social ruin. Tell me, would you prefer the bombazine or satin for your pelisse?* Clearly, that would *not* do. If she was to work with the ladies for the next few months, she ought to develop some sort of a rapport. "I'm very much looking forward to—"

"Look, Rose, it's the beginnings of our ball gowns— the ones Miss Starling helped us choose." Lady Olivia rushed past Anabelle to the table where she'd laid out the fabric. She plucked the rich pink silk from the pile and held it against her cheek. "Ooh, it's lovely, isn't it, Miss Honeycote?" She reached out and squeezed Anabelle's hand as though she were not a servant but a dear friend.

"Quite lovely," said Anabelle. It had been ages since anyone besides Daphne had touched her like that. Guilt sliced through her, and she gently pulled her hand away.

Lady Rose glided to the table, stood beside her sister, and smiled at the sight of her gown draped over the hill of supplies. Currently it was little more than several panels that would eventually comprise the bodice and skirt. The sky blue color was perfect for her creamy skin and strawberry hair. A little safe, perhaps, but Anabelle would attempt to convince her to try a sash or shawl in a deeper shade.

"This is all very exciting," said Lady Olivia, clasping her hands together.

"Indeed," said Anabelle. These women were not at all like her self-assured clients in Mrs. Smallwood's shop. Thank heaven. "Where would you like to start?"

Lady Olivia frowned. "Oh, I don't know. What do you think, Rose?"

The question had been asked as though Rose routinely responded to inquiries with more than a nod or shake of the head. Anabelle was scrambling to think of a way to end the awkward silence when she saw Rose gesturing.

Anabelle's spectacles would have proved immensely helpful at this juncture. She moved closer and squinted. Lady Rose held a palm flat in front of her, formed a loose fist with her other hand, and rested it on her palm.

"Heavens, you're quite right," Olivia exclaimed. "Why, I have no manners at all." She stuck her head into the hallway, and called to a passing maid. "Judy, fetch us tea, please. And some rolls and butter." She rejoined Anabelle and Rose. "Let's sit and have a chat, shall we?"

Anabelle hesitated, but Rose gently pulled her hand toward the large bench beneath the window. They settled themselves on the faded but comfortable cushion, propping pillows behind their backs. Anabelle occupied a sunny spot and savored the warmth of the rays on her neck. The nursery-turned-workroom was a marked improvement over the dark, crowded back room of Mrs. Smallwood's shop. Also, vastly preferable to a jail cell. A chill skittered between her shoulders, a not-so-subtle reminder of why she was here.

Anabelle cleared her throat. "I think that my first project should be finishing the two ball gowns. Together, they should take no more than three days to complete. Although, if we decide on elaborate embellishments, a fourth day might be necessary." If she didn't find her spectacles, it could take even longer.

"I'm sure that's fine," Lady Olivia remarked in a polite

if only vaguely interested manner. Lady Rose nodded her head, so Anabelle continued.

"Thereafter, I'd like to create one dress a week for each of you. You can decide which items are most pressing, but I expect you'll need morning dresses, walking dresses, and evening gowns. And all the garments to be worn with them, of course. Spencers, pelisses, cloaks, mantles, and chemises." Just listing all that she needed to do was rather daunting. It was an ambitious schedule, but she was determined to keep to it so that she could complete the terms of her sentence and return home to Mama and Daphne. Just being around the Sherbourne sisters made her miss her own. "This will require you to try the garments on two or three times a week to ensure the best fit. But at the end of three months, you'll each have ten new gowns. What do you think?"

"Why, it sounds positively exhausting. Not the fittings—Rose and I have nothing better to do, do we, Rose? But that is an awful lot of sewing. Do you have an assistant?"

Anabelle choked on a laugh. "No. I will be busy, but I enjoy making dresses. It's actually . . . rewarding."

Rose leaned forward as though fascinated. Even in her half-blind state, Anabelle understood the question in her eyes.

"A pretty dress makes a woman feel happy. I can see it in her face, and that makes *me* feel wonderful. Don't get me wrong, the sewing is sometimes tedious—mind numbing, if you want to know the truth—but even plying a needle can be soothing—"

"Until one's thread gets jumbled in a disastrous knot." Lady Olivia shuddered, as though she'd experienced her share.

"True," Anabelle admitted. "Knots are ghastly." And they chuckled—even Lady Rose, in a silent sort of way.

A tall footman appeared in the doorway, holding a beige blob which Anabelle deduced was her shabby portmanteau. "Oh," she said, standing, "my things have arrived."

"Come in, Roger," said Lady Olivia. She turned to Anabelle. "Would you like your bag in your room?"

"I'll take it." She was eager to know if there was a note from Daphne.

Roger walked in and handed her the case. She thanked him and rummaged through her bag. Three simple dresses—one of which was Daphne's—two chemises, a corset, stockings, slippers, a hair brush and mirror...but no letter. She'd probably been too busy. Anabelle sighed.

"Where are the rest of your things?" asked Lady Olivia.

Anabelle flushed. "Besides a few personal effects, this is all that I have." She frowned as she sifted through the garments in the bag once more. "Although my night-rail does appear to be missing." She'd left it on the floor behind the dressing screen in her hurry to leave for Hyde Park that morning. It was hard to believe she'd slept on the settee in her family's parlor just last night. It seemed a lifetime ago.

Lady Olivia opened her mouth to say something but was distracted by the arrival of a maid pushing the tea cart. Lady Rose poured, and they all helped themselves to warm, buttered rolls. Anabelle couldn't recall ever having eaten so much in one day.

As luck would have it, she was popping the last morsel of the delicious roll into her mouth when the duke strode into the room.

"Owen!" cried Lady Olivia. "Come sit. You must join us for tea."

Anabelle focused on swallowing. And not choking—after having first been caught napping and now enjoying a leisurely tea during what was to be her first day of work.

He glared at the three of them, and while they waited for his response to a simple invitation, Anabelle had time to think.

His Christian name was Owen. It seemed very improper that she should know this, and yet she was amused to discover that the very intimidating Duke of Huntford was simply "Owen" to his sisters. It suited him. The brevity of it, the roundness of the vowel, the crispness of the consonant ending.

"No, thank you." He adjusted his cravat, and Anabelle's gaze was drawn to the thick, corded muscles of his neck. "The fabric and the, ah...other supplies—have they arrived?"

"Oh yes. Everything is over there on the table." Lady Olivia patted Anabelle's knee. "Was there anything else you needed, Miss Honeycote?"

Anabelle set her plate, empty but for a few crumbs, on the tea tray. "Not at the moment."

He stared at her for several heartbeats but said nothing. She realized this was something she must accustom herself to—his habit of silently appraising her.

At last, he said, "The matters we discussed earlier this afternoon have been settled."

She assumed he referred to her debts.

"This letter"—he walked closer and handed it to her—"is for you. The footman brought it after retrieving your things."

Anabelle held the letter close to her face. Her name, in Daphne's buoyant script, appeared on the outside, but the note wasn't sealed. There probably hadn't been time. Anabelle assumed the duke had read it and hoped Daphne hadn't revealed anything too embarrassing. Although, she supposed, he knew most of their secrets now anyway. "Thank you."

He grunted and jerked his chin toward her portmanteau. "You have your things."

"Yes." She forced herself to sit perfectly still, a polite smile pasted on her face, as he stared some more.

"I trust that you have another, more tasteful, cap in your bag. See that you're wearing it tomorrow." He gave a nod to each of his sisters, who stared at him slack-jawed as he stalked out of the room.

Lady Olivia cleared her throat. "I must apologize for my brother. Sometimes, he can be rather..."

"Overbearing?" Anabelle offered—though it was clearly not her place.

"Precisely." Lady Olivia sighed. "I believe he means well. He was very different before our father died. But let's not discuss such heavy matters today. We should let you unpack your things and prepare for dinner."

Dinner? Anabelle hoped she wouldn't have to eat again for at least a few hours. "Thank you. I'd like to spend some time working on your ball gowns so they'll be ready for you to try on tomorrow."

"We shall look forward to it. Shan't we, Rose?"

Lady Rose smiled, nodded demurely, and stood.

The moment the sisters had taken their leave, Anabelle read Daphne's letter. She was understandably curious about the terms of Anabelle's new employment, but made no mention of Mama's condition. Anabelle would write tomorrow and ask Daph for daily reports.

Sighing, she went to work on Rose's gown. The design Miss Starling had chosen for the young redhead in the dress shop seemed too fussy for her. Miss Starling had requested epaulettes of lace, crepe trimming, and three rows of muslin frills around the bottom. But now that Anabelle knew a little about Lady Rose, she felt certain that a simpler, more refined style would better suit.

Deciding to trust her own judgment, Anabelle adjusted the lines of the dress and set about replacing the epaulettes with cap sleeves. She would decorate them with two rows of tiny pearls that would fall from the back of the shoulder to the front of the arm. The softer, more feminine sleeves would complement Lady Rose's long, graceful arms.

Anabelle cut, pinned, and sewed until the light from the nursery window was too dim for her to see her needle, and then she lit some lamps and worked some more even though her eyes ached from squinting. Mrs. Pottsbury stopped in to remind her to come down for dinner, but Anabelle was too caught up in her project to take a break, and, besides, she wasn't hungry in the least.

Several hours later, she was done—at least all that she could do that evening. Tomorrow morning, she would wake up early and begin working on Lady Olivia's gown. She had put away the pale blue gown and was crawling on the floor, feeling for loose threads and tiny scraps of silk, when she heard a knock at the doorway. Her heart pounded. Surely the duke wouldn't seek her out at this time of night.

She scrambled to her feet and faced the doorway.

Without her spectacles, she couldn't tell who her visitor was, but since she wore a dress, Anabelle felt she could confidently rule out the duke. The red hair, however, was her best clue.

"Lady Rose! It's so late. Is everything all right?"

The girl nodded and smiled, then produced a white bundle from behind her back. She placed it in Anabelle's hands.

"What's this?" The soft white garment was folded in a neat square and smelled of crisp, clean cotton.

Lady Rose said nothing, so Anabelle unfolded it. Waves of white lawn billowed to the floor.

A nightgown.

"Is this for me to sleep in?"

Lady Rose raised her eyebrows and smirked, as though she'd have thought the answer would be obvious.

A lump formed in Anabelle's throat. "Thank you. It's lovely."

The girl smiled and glided from the room.

"Good night," Anabelle called. She wasn't sure why a simple act of kindness had almost moved her to tears.

But she *was* sure of one thing. She was going to make Lady Rose a ball gown sure to bring every handsome bachelor in the *ton* to his knees. After the Miss Starlings of the world saw Lady Rose in her finery, they'd never again look at her with pity or condescension. In fact, the only emotion they'd feel toward her would be hot, desperate envy.

Chapter Seven

*Bolt: (1) An amount of fabric wrapped around
a cylinder. (2) To flee; one's natural inclination
after behaving like a lightskirt.*

After getting off to a slow start, Miss Honeycote *finally* seemed to be earning her keep. Owen had last seen her taking a leisurely tea with his sisters in the nursery, of all things. But in the three days since, he'd received impressive reports of her industriousness from Mrs. Pottsbury and Olivia. If one believed the housekeeper, Miss Honeycote rarely slept and had to be reminded to stop and take her meals. Olivia gushed over the seamstress's sketches as though she were an artistic genius—nothing short of Gainsborough with a needle and thread. Most surprising, though, was that Rose—who was an excellent judge of character—was purported to like Anabelle immensely.

Anabelle.

The extortionist-turned-seamstress had a name. Olivia had reasoned that since the three women would be spending the next several weeks together, they should be less formal.

Owen grunted to himself. He didn't give a damn what Olivia called her. As far as he was concerned, she was Miss Honeycote. Or, better yet, *the seamstress*. And she always would be.

The odd impulse to kiss her after finding her sleeping was nothing more than a bizarre aberration. His mistress had left him two months ago, and he'd tired of their arrangement three months before that. He couldn't explain why, except she was so damned eager to please him all the time. She lacked spirit and... authenticity. His friends were convinced he'd gone mad.

They were probably right.

Miss Honeycote's unexpected loveliness had caught him off guard in the bedroom that day. It was like discovering that an ugly stalk in one's garden had managed to bloom into a rare flower. Interesting at first, but once the novelty wore off, it was just a pretty flower in a garden chock full of them. No, the intense physical pull he'd felt toward the seamstress was clearly due to lack of sex, sleep, and, possibly, his sanity.

Owen walked from the window of his study to his mahogany desk and opened the top right drawer. He removed a small parcel and tossed it onto the desk. "Dennison!" he called.

The butler appeared, standing just outside the threshold. "Yes, Your Grace?"

"Inform Miss Honeycote that I wish to see her at once."

"Shall I have her meet you in the drawing room, Sir?"

Owen looked the butler up and down. Either Dennison was attempting to spare Miss Honeycote from entering the study where the unspeakable had happened, or he deemed the drawing room a more genteel setting for their meeting. Everyone in the household seemed convinced she was a naïve young miss when she was an *extortionist*, for God's sake. "I'm not in the drawing room, Dennison. I'm *here*."

The butler's bushy eyebrows rose a fraction of an inch, and he hurried off.

Owen had had her spectacles repaired so that she'd be able to see properly when she was hemming hems or trimming trim or whatever the hell it was that seamstresses did. He couldn't have one of his employees going about her duties with a cracked lens. It would reflect poorly on him even if no one else knew that he'd been the one to trample them.

He didn't want Miss Honeycote's gratitude. He just wanted her to be able to do her damned job.

She arrived at the study still wearing that blasted cap. It really was an atrocity.

However, there was a pleasant fullness to her cheeks that hadn't been there before. Her features looked softer and her gray eyes brighter. The ghastly brown dress had been replaced with an unsightly green one that could not be considered pretty by any stretch. But it was a slight improvement. At least he could tell that she did, indeed, have a figure. Her breasts, while smallish, were high and nicely shaped. The swell of her hips, just visible beneath her skirts, made his blood thrum in appreciation.

But that cap. It was an insult to all other caps. He decided to let it go—for now.

"You sent for me, Your Grace?"

"Come in."

She approached slowly and stood in front of his desk. He picked up the package, walked around his desk, and handed it to her. "Here. This is for you."

Delight and then curiosity flitted across her face. "Is it from my sister?"

"No."

"Then, who?"

"No one."

She shot him a dubious look. "I have received a package from *no one*?"

Only she would be suspicious of a simple gift. "Just open it. You'll see."

She untied the string and unwrapped the paper. "Spectacles," she said, frowning at them. Like a mermaid who'd been given slippers.

"I assumed you'd be glad to have your spectacles back."

She shook her head slowly. "These aren't *my* spectacles. Mine were larger, and the rims around the lenses were round. These are oval. I don't know who these belong to, but they're not mine." She handed them back to him, and turned as though she'd leave.

"Wait."

She halted and slowly faced him again.

Owen raked a hand through his hair. "I took your old spectacles to be repaired, but the jeweler said he couldn't fix them."

"You *took* them? You had no right." She planted her fists on her hips. "I want them back."

Damn, but this was turning into a disaster. Some ancient but trustworthy male instinct warned him of an impending scene, so he walked to the door, shut it, and returned. "Your old spectacles were not salvageable. They're gone."

Suddenly, he felt like the ogre again. He supposed this was what happened when one tried to do something nice for a criminal with an overblown sense of pride.

"What do you mean, *gone*?" Her voice had an edge to it. "My father had those made for me."

He recalled her telling him that her father had died. The jeweler had offered to wrap up the old pair, but Owen instructed him to destroy the mangled things. He never dreamed he'd regret it. "Do you honestly believe your father would want you to wear broken spectacles?"

"That's not the point," she spat.

Of course it wasn't. But there was nothing to be done for it now. "The jeweler said these would be lighter, more comfortable. The lenses are brand new. I don't know how you could see out of the old ones, as scratched as they were. I took a chance and had the prescription made a little stronger. Just put them on." He held them out to her, but she crossed her arms in front of her chest.

Obstinate little wench. "Fine. Stand still."

He half-expected her to bolt, but for once, she did as he asked. He approached her as he would have a wild horse; from the side, his palms out. In two cautious steps, he closed the space between them.

"Try them."

She made no move to accept the gift.

"Look. Do you see how thin the temples are? They're curved to fit snugly around your ears." He rotated the spectacles around so she could examine them. "And the lenses are smaller to better fit your face." Wonderful. He sounded like a damned sales clerk.

Her gaze flicked to the spectacles, betraying her curiosity.

Slowly, he raised them in front of her face. "Don't move. I've no wish to poke out your eye. Messy, that."

This drew the slightest smirk. Encouraged, he carefully positioned the rims on the bridge of her sloping nose, then slid the temples around her ears. When his fingers traced the delicate pink shells, she drew back. He dropped his hands to her shoulders and cupped them lightly to steady her. The scents of linen, wool, and soap filled his senses, and although he didn't want to let her go, he did.

"Well?" he asked.

She blinked twice behind the crystal-clear lenses, and then opened her eyes wide. "Amazing."

"How so?"

"I've never seen the world in such focus—even with my old spectacles." Her gaze flicked to the window. "The clouds outside—they're the gray, wispy kind that means it shall likely drizzle all day. It's . . . it's wonderful."

"Drizzle puts me in a bloody foul mood."

Ignoring him, she looked intently around the room. "Your desk is magnificent—I can see every striation in the wood grain. Did you know there are three drops of blue sealing wax caked on it?

He leaned over her shoulder to confirm the presence of the wax. Damned if she wasn't right. "Impressive."

She turned and startled slightly, surprised to find herself wedged between him and the desk. Her gaze locked with his, the dark centers of her eyes drawing him in like fire on a bitter cold night. And he wasn't inclined to move.

Behind the new spectacles, her eyes sparkled with wonder and intelligence. The delicate muscles in her throat worked as she swallowed, and her chest rose and fell with each shallow breath. Too quickly, she cast her gaze downward.

He would have given her some space then—truly, he would have—if she hadn't leaned in to examine his chest. "The texture of your waistcoat is fascinating. Why, it's a fleur de lis." With a fingertip, she traced the brocade pattern, making his heart beat faster. "I can almost see the individual threads."

He resisted the urge to lace his fingers through hers and pull her closer. Her interest in his damned waistcoat was purely academic. For all he knew, seamstresses were required to study such things.

"You can see threads? This is alarming," he said. "Next you'll tell me you can see *through* my waistcoat."

She raised her eyebrows wickedly. "They're quite powerful."

He laughed, for the first time in maybe a month. "My turn." Miss Honeycote's eyes widened and her hand dropped to her side. "Did you think you were the only one who could play the game?" He cleared his throat. "Your skin is smooth like…" Damn it, what was something smooth? "Silk. Yes, silk." A cliché, but he mentally congratulated himself regardless. "And your hair…" In one fluid motion he snatched off her cap and flung it at the shelves behind his desk. It landed on his antique clock at a jaunty angle.

Miss Honeycote gasped and stared at him as though he'd stripped off her corset instead of her bloody cap. But since there was no going back, he forged ahead. "Your hair cannot decide whether it wants to be brown or red or gold. It's fickle, but…lovely."

He'd lost his senses. If the puzzled expression on Miss Honeycote's face was any indication, she agreed. But she did smile shyly, making the whole awkward moment worthwhile.

"Thank you. Er, for the spectacles, that is."

He grunted. She hadn't even looked at the bloody things yet. Grasping her shoulders, he positioned her in front of the large mirror resting on the mantel. "What do you think?"

Wrinkling her nose, she said, "They feel more secure than my old ones. Perhaps they won't slide so much."

She was missing the point, damn it. "Do you like them?"

"I suppose they'll take some getting used to. They're rather odd, aren't they?"

Odd? "No." He moved closer, and his chest bumped against her back. Their gazes met in the mirror. "Look again."

Miss Honeycote sighed as though completely uninterested in her reflection. How different she was from most females. Original, real…and practical to a fault. Thus, the extortion note.

"Do you want to know what I think?" he asked.

Her gaze locked with his in the glass before them. "I'm certain you're determined to tell me."

"You were hiding behind your old spectacles."

"Nonsense." She spun around and tried to walk past him, but before he knew what he was doing, he'd grasped her upper arms.

"What are you doing?"

Good question. "This."

And he kissed her.

His lips, warm and firm against hers, somehow caused a thrumming throughout Anabelle's body, making her pleasantly light-headed. He speared his fingers through her hair, pressing lightly on her scalp. Some of the tightness of her bun was relieved, and she heard the clink of pins hitting the floor.

She'd forgotten how to breathe, or, if she was breathing, she wasn't getting enough air. It was all very strange. And wonderful.

She'd hoped to have a proper kiss one day. She and Daphne had discussed the possibility at length and agreed that they should each prefer to be kissed by a gentleman who was kind, gentle, and not particularly demanding.

Not in a thousand lifetimes would Anabelle have dreamed that she'd be kissed by the same wickedly handsome duke from whom earlier that very week she'd attempted to extort forty gold coins.

Part of her wondered if she were imagining the entire thing—all the hours spent on intricate beadwork the last few days had no doubt addled her brain. She opened her eyes to take a peek and saw the dark lock of hair over his brow.

This was no dream.

Although hard to fathom, he was the same formidable duke who'd captured her under a bridge. His elegant clothes couldn't disguise the wiry strength and sheer intensity beneath. And the object of his intense focus at the moment was *her*.

The stubble on his chin prickled and tickled her cheek. His mouth covered hers in the most intimate way, his lips molded seamlessly to hers. He tasted like a spicy tea—tangy and masculine. She savored each sensation like a traveler in a foreign land filled with exotic textures and scents.

His hands drifted down her spine and settled at the

small of her back, where he rubbed intoxicating little circles that turned her legs to jelly. He kissed her harder, coaxed her lips apart, and traced them with his tongue. The pressure, warm and wet, made her heart beat wildly, and she understood.

She understood *why* so many of the women in Mrs. Smallwood's dress shop were willing to risk their reputations for a kiss.

And then, the duke's forehead bumped into her new spectacles.

Her eyes fluttered open, and for a moment she was confused by the fog covering her lenses. She doubted there had ever been a more obvious metaphor for clouded judgment. God was giving her a sign. A divine slap in the face.

"Let me take them off," the duke said smoothly, reaching for the rims.

"No." If she let him, before she knew it he'd be asking to remove *other* personal articles. She'd rather not subject her own willpower to such a rigorous test.

"I think," she said, taking a step back, "that I should go." She took off her spectacles, carefully wiped the lenses with her pinafore, and replaced them. Her heart still beat wildly, but the simple habit of putting on her spectacles helped compose her.

Heavens. This encounter would lower his opinion of her character even further. In his mind she'd probably gone from being an extortionist to an extortionist with loose morals—a label which seemed unnecessarily redundant.

He moved toward her, and then stopped as though torn. "Anabelle, er, Miss Honeycote, I should apologize for my actions."

She shook her head. If he was wrong, she had been, too. An apology wouldn't make her feel better.

The duke moved closer and cupped her cheek in his palm, forcing her to meet his gaze. "I'm sorry if I've made you feel uncomfortable. But I'm *not* sorry I kissed you."

Oh. Anabelle was not used to such declarations, so she tried to remember what Daphne normally said to her swarms of suitors. "I, ah, am very flattered by your attentions. I do think, however, that I should go and that we should put this behind us," she said firmly. "I'm sure the spectacles must have been dear, and I don't know how or when I shall be able to repay you, but I shall." The only thing she could do was make dresses. "Have you any other female relatives for whom I could create wardrobes?"

"I have fourteen great aunts, ranging in age from fifty-nine to eighty-two."

She blinked slowly, wondering just how much the spectacles had cost. "You jest."

He grinned in answer. Of course he'd been teasing. But she sighed in relief just the same.

His smile faded and the dark slashes of his brows drew together in a slight frown. "You don't owe me anything for the spectacles. I broke your old ones."

She raised an eyebrow so he'd know she was aware of the major flaw in his logic, namely that he would never have stepped on her spectacles if she hadn't written him a rather nasty demand note.

Exhaling, she attempted to restore herself to some semblance of respectability. She smoothed her skirts and tucked loose wisps of hair behind her ears, all the while ignoring the duke's amused glances.

"Good afternoon, Your Grace," she said and, with as

much dignity as she could muster, walked toward the door. He backed up, blocking her path, and scooped up one of her hands in his. With a wicked smile, he said, "Good afternoon, Miss Honeycote," and seared the back of her hand with a kiss.

She tried her best to appear unaffected but marched out of the room on shaky legs. The import of what she'd done was sinking in. She'd kissed her employer, who happened to be a duke *and* the man she'd tried to extort money from. A clear and blatant violation of her own rules of conduct. She was scurrying down the hallway and heading for the staircase when she stopped in her tracks.

Dash it all, she had to go back.

Full of dread, she spun around and returned to the scene of the kiss—er, the study. When she arrived at the doorway, the duke was staring out the window rather contemplatively. She wasn't sure what she'd expected him to be doing but was vastly relieved to see that he wasn't, oh, banging his forehead on his desk in regret or tossing back a large glass of gin.

When she cleared her throat, he looked at her, surprised. And, perhaps, a little hopeful.

"I came to retrieve something that belongs to me." Without waiting for permission, she crossed the study, plucked her cap off the clock, and jammed it on her head.

It occurred to her she should amend her List of Nevers to include rules governing her unusual relationship with the duke. The first addendum would be "Never remove one's cap—or allow it to be removed—in the presence of the duke, as it may well be the only impediment to wanton behavior by both parties." Yes, now that she thought on it, rules were definitely necessary.

She dared not look at him as she exited the room—for the second time. She was fairly certain he'd be mocking her; but of course, he'd been mocking her since he'd met her.

The problem was, she now cared far more than she should.

Chapter Eight

The next day as Owen sat in his coach, rumbling across Town to an appointment, he was still trying to come to terms with what he'd done. At first he told himself that he'd kissed Anabelle because he felt sorry for her. That was laughable. She wasn't the kind of woman one pitied—she'd never permit it.

He then wondered whether she'd somehow seduced him with coy looks and subtle invitations. But that, too, was ridiculous. It was impossible for a woman to be coy in a huge floppy cap.

One could argue that in the absence of a mistress, he'd lowered his normally high standards for feminine companionship. But...no.

The truth was he'd admired her since the first morning he'd met her. He'd desired her since the evening she'd tripped and fallen into his arms. She was clever, proud, beautiful, and loyal.

A damned arousing combination.

Just this morning, he'd found himself concocting excuses to walk by the workroom where he knew she'd be. That's when he'd realized he needed to get out of the house. Determined to turn his mind to business—contracts, estate matters, and finances—he leaned back against the velvet squabs in his coach and dragged his hands down his face.

Maybe once he'd finished his meeting with James Averill, Owen could convince the solicitor—also a trusted friend—to head to Bond Street for a boxing match.

Owen was a decent fighter. He'd been in his share of tavern brawls, and although he rarely escaped unscathed, the other chap usually looked much worse. But Owen was no match for Averill in a boxing bout. A few solid punches to Owen's head might help him forget about Anabelle. Or at least knock the good sense back into him. The thought cheered him.

His coach came to a halt in front of Averill's office on Chancery Lane. Owen strode up an ancient-looking stone walkway and entered Averill's office, which was cluttered with an odd collection of exotic furniture that he had purchased on his travels. The solicitor was bent over a stack of papers on his desk looking thoroughly perplexed—like a frustrated archeologist trying to decipher hieroglyphics.

Without preamble, he glanced up at Owen and said, "The allowances you've set up for your aunts are extremely generous, Huntford. Are you sure you didn't write an extra zero or two here?" He spun a paper around for Owen's examination.

Owen checked the figure and grunted. "They're sweet old ladies. And they've known me since I was in nappies."

"Ah. In that case, their allowances can't be too large."

Averill grinned. "After seeing these numbers, I'm thinking I should raise my fees."

Owen picked up a dreary-looking urn and inspected a crack near the rim. "So you can buy more ramshackle furniture and chipped vases?"

Averill sprang from his chair, snatched the vase from him and cradled it in the crook of an arm like it was his firstborn. "This is a relic from ancient Greece. I paid almost as much for it as you did for your gelding last spring."

"If that's your idea of an investment," said Owen, "I must be insane to entrust my business affairs to you."

"Not insane. A bit naïve, perhaps." He grinned, set the vase on a stack of dusty tomes behind him, and returned to his chair.

Chuckling, Owen picked up a white marble statue of a cross-legged man occupying *his* chair. "Sorry," he said to the Buddha, placing him on the floor. To Averill, "How was the opera last night?"

"Dreadful. My sister, however, was mesmerized by the performance. She declared herself forever in your debt. Thank you for giving us your seats."

Owen held up a hand, happy to have been spared.

"Miss Starling, however, was disappointed to discover that we were in your box…and you weren't." Averill raised a cocky brow. Owen would enjoy taking a few punches at him later. "Her dowry would pad your coffers nicely."

"My coffers are doing just fine."

"True, but if you keep giving those aunts of yours huge allowances—"

"Damn it, Averill, just give me the bloody papers to sign."

One hour and a couple of drinks later, Owen's business

was concluded. He loosened his cravat as Averill poured more brandy into their glasses.

"What you've managed to accomplish in a little over two years' time," Averill mused, "is nothing short of miraculous. I wish my other clients took their responsibilities half as seriously as you do."

Owen stared into his glass. Rather than deal with the unpleasant realities of an adulterous wife and a dwindling fortune, Owen's father had pointed a gun at his right temple and squeezed the trigger. A cowardly, selfish act if ever there was one. As a boy, Owen had wanted nothing more than to be like him—riding fine horses, hosting lavish parties, and drinking expensive brandy.

But Owen was *not* like him. He would never let down his family, never shirk the responsibilities of his title.

Oh, he'd resented being thrust into the role of duke so suddenly, but righting the affairs of his estates was giving him more satisfaction than he'd thought. It took a hell of a lot of time and energy, and it was worth it. His *sisters* were worth it.

The meeting with Averill had been productive, and yet, Owen still hadn't managed to banish Anabelle from his mind.

It occurred to him that her allure could stem from the mystery surrounding her. Miss Starling, for example, although undeniably beautiful, was not appealing. Owen had the misfortune of sitting next to her during a musicale last week, and during the course of the twenty-minute performance, he'd learned that she'd spent the day embroidering birds on a handkerchief and purchasing a new hat. She'd waited for him to compliment the latter, and he did, even though, to him, it looked unremarkable. Miss

Starling was like every other young miss on the marriage mart: intent on snaring a titled gentleman by any means possible.

But Anabelle was an enigma, and therein lay her charm. If he knew more about her, he would certainly lose his fascination with her.

Even within the confines of his own mind, the theory sounded thin.

He swirled the liquid in his glass, studying the sloshing waves he created. Anabelle had tried to extort money from him. He'd trusted that the story about her family's dire circumstances was true, but what proof did he have? Perhaps she'd lied about her mother's condition to gain his sympathy. It couldn't hurt to investigate.

"Ever heard of a Dr. Conwell?" he asked Averill.

Concern registered on his friend's face. "Are your sisters well? No one is sick, I hope."

"Olivia is fine, and Rose...well, she's the same. I asked because the mother of one of my servants is ill. Dr. Conwell is treating the woman, and I'm curious. Er, to know how serious her condition is."

Averill stared suspiciously, damn him. "Is the servant requesting too much time off, shirking duties and the like?"

"Nothing like that. But I do wonder if her mother is as sick as Miss Honeycote claims."

"Would Miss Honeycote happen to be young and beautiful?"

It was no use lying to Averill. "Yes. But she's also stubborn and conniving."

His friend nodded sagely and tented his fingers. "Are you thinking mistress or marriage?"

"Good God. She's a seamstress. She dresses like a

spinster who's been on the shelf for a couple of decades. Hardly duchess material."

"Mistress, then."

"No." Owen seethed. How he longed to punch the smirk off Averill's face. Instead, he stood and said, "This bloody inquisition is over. I'm going to ride across Town and ask my physician about Conwell. Why don't you come, and afterward, we can box a few rounds?"

Averill stood, flexed his hands, and looked at Owen as if he'd gone mad. "If you're sure."

Owen glared at him and headed for the damned door. "You coming, or not?"

Anabelle was nearly finished with Olivia's ball gown. It was white sarsenet, with a bodice and sleeves of blue satin that set off Olivia's light green eyes. The sleeves, slitted in the front, were held together by gold clasps matching a Grecian border. Anabelle planned to stitch the border in gold thread but needed Olivia to try on the dress one more time before she did so.

Since Olivia was shopping and wouldn't be available for at least a half-hour, Anabelle ventured downstairs to ask Mr. Dennison about the post. Two days had passed without a letter from Daphne. Never having been apart from her family for so long, Anabelle missed them. She was accustomed to coming home from work, sitting at Mama's bedside, and telling her and Daphne all about the quirky patrons at the shop. Silly things, like the countess demanding five ostrich feathers on her hat or the debutante wanting padding sewn into the breast area of her corset.

Since Anabelle had arrived at the duke's house, a mere five days ago, she'd seen and experienced so much.

Mama would love to hear about the crystal chandelier in the duke's foyer, and Daphne would love to hear about the kiss in the duke's study. Anabelle supposed she could describe the chandelier in a letter, but a kiss like that... well, it defied description.

In the absence of a letter from her sister, Anabelle imagined all sorts of tragedies. Perhaps Daphne had fallen sick, or Mama's health had taken a worse turn, or they'd used up the money the duke had sent and would starve in their apartment rather than worry Anabelle. She desperately hoped for word from them.

When she located the butler at his usual station in the pantry, his white eyebrows rose halfway up his wrinkled forehead. "Miss Honeycote," he said kindly. "How may I help you?"

"Good afternoon, Mr. Dennison. Could you tell me whether the post has arrived?"

"It has." He hoisted himself off his stool and beckoned Anabelle to follow him. After sifting through a stack of letters sitting on a table in the foyer, he handed an envelope to her. "It arrived just a few moments ago."

She glanced at the envelope, relieved to see Daphne's handwriting. "Thank you." She tapped the envelope against her palm and headed for the privacy of her bedchamber to read her sister's note. After slipping off her shoes and climbing onto the bed, she tucked her feet under her and opened the letter.

My Dearest Belle,

I'm sorry I haven't written for a couple of days. You must be anxious for news of Mama. I wish I could tell you that her condition is improving, but, unfortu-

nately, it grows worse. Her cough is persistent, and she eats very little. It is not for lack of food. Thanks to the generous sum you sent, I've been feasting like the Queen herself, but not even the finest cuts of meat tempt Mama.

She is so weak that all she wants to do is sleep. I let her, for the most part, since she seems so exhausted. At least her frequent naps give her some peace from the coughing. Dr. Conwell visited yesterday and has prescribed more medicine. He promised to check on Mama early next week.

In the meantime, I'm doing everything I can to make her comfortable. Yesterday, Mrs. Bowman came to sit with Mama while I ran some errands. I stopped by the lending library and borrowed several books. I've begun reading one of Mrs. Radcliffe's novels to Mama, and she seems to enjoy it, until she nods off. It helps us pass the time.

How I wish I had better news to share. I know you are working hard to provide for us, and I am so grateful for all you've sacrificed. However, I can't help but wish you were here. I feel certain you would know what to do to help Mama.

I will, of course, let you know if there is any change in her condition. In the meantime, take proper care of yourself and do not let this news distress you too deeply.

Lovingly yours,
Daph

Pressing the letter to her chest, Anabelle choked on a sob. Mama was getting sicker, and she had been frighteningly sick to begin with. If Daphne, the eternal optimist, was concerned, the situation must be dire.

Anabelle sprang off the bed and paced the length of her room. She needed to see Mama for herself. The duke, however, had made it clear that visits would not be permitted during the term of her indenture. Although he'd been fair in most respects, he'd been adamant that she was a prisoner in his house. She couldn't blame him for not trusting her. He probably feared she'd head out of Town, leaving his sisters with nothing more than half a ball gown each. She had no intention of reneging on her end of the deal, but she couldn't abandon her family.

She'd have to sneak out in the middle of the night. Tonight.

"Good afternoon, Anabelle!"

The sight of Olivia standing in the doorway of her bedchamber made Anabelle jump and give a little shriek.

"Oh dear, forgive me for startling you. Are you all right?"

Anabelle smiled, though her hands still trembled. "I'm fine." She folded Daphne's letter and tucked it in the pocket of her pinafore. "I'm glad you're here. Do you have time for one more fitting?"

"I was hoping you'd ask," Olivia said cheerfully. "I'm eager to try it on."

"Then you shall." Anabelle led the way into the workroom and helped Olivia change into the dress, relieved to have a distraction from the news in Daphne's letter. Although there was nothing she could do at the moment, she comforted herself with the knowledge that she would visit Mama and Daphne that night. The trick would be getting out of the duke's townhouse. And then getting back in.

Olivia stood still while Anabelle laced up the gown. She watched as Olivia placed her palm flat over her stomacher and preened in the long mirror in front of her. "This plum silk cord is lovely," she said. "I look almost..."

"Beautiful?" offered Anabelle. "Most definitely. Your dance card will be full at Lady Milverton's ball."

"I don't know how to thank you. Neither does Rose. She adores the dress you made for her. But mostly, I think she adores you."

"I can't imagine why." She was not the sort of person young ladies admired. Sometimes matrons did, like Mrs. Bowman—maybe because they favored the same type of cap.

Anabelle had grown fond of Rose and enjoyed her visits to the workroom. But the conversation was mostly one-sided. Although Rose communicated using gestures and occasionally writing, Anabelle would have loved to hear her voice and to have an honest-to-goodness chat.

"I'm glad Rose is pleased with her gown," Anabelle said, stooping to pin Olivia's hem. "Someone with such a kind and generous nature deserves every happiness." She paused. "Forgive me for asking a personal question, but why doesn't she talk?"

Olivia sighed. "She did once. She was a loquacious little thing up until about three years ago."

Anabelle's stomach clenched. "Was she injured?"

"No. That is, we're not entirely certain." Olivia frowned and lifted the hem of her dress so as not to trip on it, walked to the window seat, and sat on the faded cushion. Anabelle followed and sat beside her. "Rose was a lively, spirited girl. But then, when she was fifteen, our mother left."

"For where?"

"We think she had a lover on the Continent." Olivia stated this matter of factly, but the fine creases on either side of her mouth betrayed her pain.

Anabelle knew something of the duchess's scandalous reputation and wished she didn't. "Is she still...living?" Although it was impolite to pry, Olivia seemed relieved to be talking about it.

"I haven't heard any reports to the contrary, so I assume she is. However, we haven't received any letters from her."

"I'm sorry."

Olivia traced the silk cord of her stomacher, criss-crossing, back and forth. "I wasn't particularly close to her. She left without so much as a good-bye, destroying my father. He killed himself a few scant weeks later."

Anabelle gasped. She'd heard rumors that the former duke had killed himself, but, of course, the authorities had called his death an accident so that he could have a proper burial. "Oh, Olivia. I don't know what to say."

"Owen took care of us, took care of everything. But he hasn't been able to fix Rose. Nothing pains him more."

Anabelle's heart ached. "I don't think Rose is broken. She seems happy, and she obviously loves you and your brother."

"Rose and I have very few secrets, but even I don't know what happened that day—the day my mother left. We were all at Huntford Manor, our country estate, where my parents were hosting a house party. On the fourth evening after the guests arrived, Rose went missing. People searched for her all night. The next morning, my mother was gone and Owen found Rose sleeping in the stable. Physically, she seemed to be fine, but she hasn't spoken a word since."

It wasn't Anabelle's place, but she had to ask. "Have you tried to talk to her about that night? To find out what happened?"

"Yes, Owen and I have tried. We don't know why she left the house or what upset her so. Whenever we bring it up, she simply stares straight ahead—as if we aren't there." Olivia heaved a deep sigh. "Owen felt she should not come out this year, even though she's seventeen. He worried that people would ridicule her, mistake her silence for lack of intelligence. Worse, he was concerned an unscrupulous gentleman would try to take advantage of her condition."

"I can understand his reservations. He's very protective of both of you."

"*That's* an understatement." Olivia smiled wanly. "I convinced him, however, to let Rose make her debut at a few smaller balls. She has greater strength of character than anyone I know. Insulating her from society would be unfair and insulting in a way."

Anabelle was impressed. And ashamed she hadn't recognized that truth on her own. "She's lucky to have a sister like you."

"I'm lucky, too."

They sat in companionable silence for a few moments, and then, as though the thought had just occurred to her, Olivia asked, "Do you have a sister?"

Anabelle touched the letter in her pocket. "I do. She's a few years younger than I and much more beautiful."

Olivia reached over and squeezed her hand. "I doubt that. That is, I'm sure your sister is lovely, but so are you. Perhaps in a different way."

The duke had called her beautiful also. Apparently the

whole family had odd ideas about the nature of beauty. But Anabelle had bigger concerns. She was already a day behind on her self-imposed dressmaking schedule and needed to finish Olivia's gown tonight. Then, after everyone had gone to bed, she had to figure out how to sneak out of the townhouse, visit her family in the dead of the night, and get back to Mayfair before dawn. She wished she had her boy's clothes with her, but Daph hadn't sent them. She'd just have to stick to the shadows and walk briskly.

It was going to be a long night.

Chapter Nine

Buckle: (1) A clasp used to fasten. (2) To crumple or collapse, as is often the case with one's knees during a kiss with a dashing duke.

At two o'clock in the morning, Anabelle threw back the covers and sprang out of bed, fully clothed in a dark gray dress she hoped would blend in with the night. She pulled on her boots, lacing them tightly as though doing so would provide some protection from the ruffians who roamed the streets of London. Perhaps she'd be able to run faster, if necessary.

But she prayed it wouldn't come to that.

The house was as quiet as a church. Anabelle exited through the workroom and then made her way into the dim corridor. She tiptoed past Rose's door, then Olivia's, and down the staircase to the second floor. As she passed the duke's study, her pulse quickened. Last night hardly seemed real. She'd never forget the feel of the duke's body, warm and solid, behind hers or the wonder of discovering how perfectly his mouth fit to hers. Her face flushed, and she walked faster, as though removing herself from the scene could erase the imprints on her mind. Foolish, but worth a try.

Silently, she glided toward the servants' narrow staircase at the back of the house and descended the creaky steps, treading as lightly as she could. Upon reaching the back door, she paused and caught her breath. She'd considered leaving the house through this door, but a servant might discover the door had been left unlocked and correct the oversight, preventing her from being able to re-enter. Furthermore, the back door led into the garden, and from the upper-story windows, Anabelle had noted the gate on the tall, black iron fence, which was, no doubt, locked. Mr. Dennison slept near the front door, making it out of the question.

She needed an alternate escape route, and so, after much deliberation, she settled on a library window. The library, located on the ground level at the front of the house, had windows facing the street. It was a simple matter of opening the sash and climbing out onto the sidewalk.

She hoped.

With deliberate steps, Anabelle weaved her way around cabinets, arm chairs, and piecrust tables until she reached the huge center window of the room. The heavy velvet drapes were drawn closed, and when she slipped behind them a cocoon formed around her, allowing her to work on the sash without fear of detection. The lock stuck at first, but she eventually slid it to the side and heaved open the window several inches. Warm, humid air kissed her face, and she inhaled deeply. She could do this. Daphne and Mama needed her.

After making sure that no one walked in front of the

townhouse, she stuck her head out the window and surveyed the ground below. The drop looked farther than she'd imagined—perhaps four feet off the ground. With a quick but fervent prayer, she hoisted a leg over the sill, squeezed through the window, and hopped to the ground—and freedom.

Owen decided to walk home from White's. He'd enjoyed an excellent dinner and several excellent drinks afterward. A brisk, head-clearing stroll was definitely in order.

Earlier that afternoon, he and Averill had paid a visit to Owen's physician and made some inquiries. His doctor had never heard of Conwell. Owen then instructed his driver to take them to the address where he'd sent the money for Anabelle's mother's treatment. The house, located in a rather shady part of Town, looked abandoned.

It seemed his seamstress was more manipulative than he'd given her credit for.

Anabelle had probably fabricated her mother's illness, made up the doctor's name, and given him the address of an accomplice—possibly her lover. Owen ignored the sick feeling in his gut.

If she was involved with someone, that was no concern of his, but he wouldn't tolerate her deception. What a fool he'd been to believe her—sending money to doctors, apothecaries, ailing mothers, and helpless sisters. He'd obviously been blinded by lust. Tomorrow morning he'd summon Anabelle to his study and make it clear that—

What in the *devil* was going on at his townhouse?

He halted at the corner of his street and squinted at what appeared to be a woman's shapely bottom hanging out of a window.

His window.

He stayed close to the brick façade of the house he was passing but continued walking toward the woman. As she wriggled her way over the sill, her skirts hitched on the sash. Owen caught a glimpse of lithe legs in the lamplight before she plopped unceremoniously to the ground and tugged her dress down. She glanced around, so he pressed his back against the rough brick and waited to see which direction she would head.

It had to be Anabelle. Even without the offensive cap, he recognized her efficient movements and the lean lines of her body. His heart beat faster at the sight of her. Perhaps because a confrontation was imminent.

But then, being near her always made his blood heat.

What the hell was she doing sneaking out of his house? For one thing, it was damned dangerous for a woman to walk the streets of London at night. But something else vexed him.

She wanted to escape.

He'd thought that they were all getting on reasonably well. His sisters liked the dresses Anabelle made for them. She liked her new spectacles. He liked the way she kissed.

But now she was leaving, and at this time of the evening the only possible explanation was a romantic tryst.

Owen swallowed the bile in his throat and skulked along behind her. She headed east, marching down the sidewalk like she owned it, but he guessed her bravado was a front. Any sane woman would be terrified. He curled his fists. What kind of man must her lover be if he let her roam the streets, unescorted, in the middle of the night?

By God, Owen would soon find out.

Gas lamps illuminated the deserted neighborhood. The occasional owl hoot or coach rumble on a nearby street punctuated the silence. Anabelle hurried, pausing now and then to listen—as though she suspected someone followed her.

He retreated farther into the shadows, and she increased her pace for the next few blocks as she left the relative safety of Mayfair for a less savory part of Town. As she reached the corner of Holborn and Red Lion Streets, a howl echoed. Anabelle froze, and the hairs on Owen's arms stood on end.

From out of the shadows, a pair of huge dogs charged, aiming straight for her. Their eyes glowed white in the darkness, evil as the hounds of Hades. The beasts barked and bared their teeth as they closed the distance at a run. He'd expected thugs or drunken dandies, for God's sake— not dogs. From the collar encircling each dog's thick neck, a frayed rope dragged, undulating behind as it ran.

If their jutting ribs were any indication, the beasts were hungry.

"Anabelle!" She turned toward him, and in the eerie yellow light of the street lamps he could see her terror. "Run!"

He scooped up a stone and ran toward the dogs, hoping to draw them away from her. But he couldn't throw the rock and risk hurting her.

She looked left, toward a deserted square, then right, down an alley. Hiking up her skirts, she sprinted for the alley and disappeared between two buildings.

He hurled the stone at the mangy pair, but they just snarled and bounded after Anabelle down the alley, close on her heels.

Owen gave chase, running for all he was worth. He rounded the corner, and—*Damn!* The alley ended at a brick wall. "I'm coming," he shouted. *Hold on.*

She whipped her head around, saw him and the dogs, and kept running. He wanted to tell her to watch where she was going, but she seemed unable to take her eyes off the vicious dogs.

Still several yards away, he called, "Look out!" Too late. She slammed into a wooden crate and tumbled over it, landing sprawled on her back. One of the hounds pounced, capturing her skirt in his jaws and shredding it in a mere second. She tried to scoot backward on her bottom, but the dogs circled her.

"Help!" she cried.

Owen raced down the alley, slippery with grime, grabbing the crate as he passed it. He dashed between the dogs and stood over Anabelle, using the crate to shove at the hound gnawing on her skirt. It yelped, backed off, and the other dog growled, pinning Anabelle with its fierce glare. Owen swung at its head, knocking it off its feet. As he did, the first mutt launched at him, locking its jaws around his forearm.

Pain buzzed up his arm and into his shoulder. Anabelle shrieked and stumbled to her feet.

"Run!" he called to her. While one dog whimpered and the other used his arm as a toy, she could escape.

He tried to free his arm by swinging it, but the dog only clamped down harder. Brandishing the crate, he kept the other dog at bay.

Anabelle ignored his order—hardly surprising. She fumbled around on the ground and rushed to his side.

He tried again. "Go."

As though she hadn't heard him, she raised a long wooden plank above her head. With a primal scream, she slammed the board onto the head of the dog on Owen's arm.

Instantly, the dog released him and cowered; the other followed suit. Owen jabbed the crate at them a few more times, and at last, they ran away.

He stood there, trying to catch his breath, for several moments. Realizing he no longer needed the crate as a weapon, he tossed it aside. Blood trickled down his arm and soaked his sleeve.

"Are you hurt?" he asked, taking in her torn clothes and smudged face.

"I…I don't think so." She leaned against the wall as though her legs might not support her.

Without thinking, he pulled her to him and wrapped his good arm around her. He inhaled the clean scent of her hair—a haven in the dankness of the alley—and savored the pressure of her body against his. There were questions he needed to ask, but for now, it was enough to hold her.

He kissed the top of her head, and she lifted her face to look at him. "I see your spectacles are still intact."

She gave him a weak smile. "Yes."

With one hand, he carefully removed them and tucked them in his pocket. Then he kissed her forehead, her eyes, her cheeks, and, at last, her mouth. Cradling her face in his hands, he parted her lips with his tongue and tasted her. He didn't attempt to keep his desire in check. Instead, he kissed her as he'd longed to—hungrily, feverishly, possessively.

As though she were actually his.

Anabelle responded. She clung to him, and her tongue

tangled with his in an imitation of something more intimate. When he deepened the kiss, she moaned and speared her fingers through his hair like she wanted him closer still.

His heart ached with the irony of it all, because he knew that what she really wanted—what she'd been attempting to do that very night—was to run away.

Owen lost track of time. He didn't want to let her go, or stop kissing her, or scold her for trying to leave him in the dead of the night. If they hadn't been standing in a damp dark alley, they might have shed their clothes and explored each other. God knows he would have liked to. Instead, he contented himself with running a hand over the front of her dress, brushing the undersides of her breasts and teasing the peaks into hard little nubs. He imagined himself unbuttoning the back of her dress, slipping the sleeves off her shoulders, and loosening her corset. He would hold the perfect weight of her breasts in his hands, draw a rosy nipple into his mouth, and suckle her till she—

"Your Grace," she said, breaking off their kiss.

Damn it. Her formal manner of address froze him like a dip in a frigid lake. "Owen. Or Huntford, if you can't bring yourself to say my Christian name."

She swallowed and worked her throat, but no sound emerged.

He muttered a curse, grabbed her hand, and pulled her along to the street. As they walked beneath a lamp, he saw that the lower half of her skirt was missing, but at least her chemise covered her legs.

"I'm sure you must think the worst of me, and I wouldn't blame you if you did," she said. "But, please, let me explain."

God, she looked earnest, trustworthy. Her wide eyes and forthright expression chilled him to the core. What kind of person could be so deceptive, so skilled at lying? And what kind of fool was he for harboring a sliver of hope that she could explain away payments to doctors who didn't exist and clandestine meetings in the middle of the night?

"I'm not interested in your excuses. We had a deal. Your dressmaking services for three months in exchange for your freedom. You were attempting to renege on that."

"That's not true. I would have returned before dawn."

Her words almost made him double over, like a punch to his gut. He wondered on how many other occasions she'd snuck out of his house for a rendezvous, risking her life to meet with someone. He tried to squash the jealousy that made his blood simmer. "My, but you are a conscientious employee."

She recoiled as though he'd cracked a whip. "You don't believe me."

"Whether or not you were going to return is immaterial. You violated the terms of our agreement."

"I had a good reason for leaving. And I *would* have come back," she said, stomping her foot for emphasis.

"I don't think you would have. Do you know why?" He closed the distance between them, leaned over, and spoke into her ear. "You wouldn't have been able to. You'd be bleeding to death in a godforsaken alley while those dogs feasted on your flesh."

Anabelle choked on a sob and tears began to trickle down her cheeks. "I know. But I had to see them. I still need to."

Them, not *him*—? "Who?"

"Mama and Daphne. I received a letter from them today, and Daph said Mama's gotten worse. My sister is impossibly cheerful, so when I read the dire news I had to see Mama for myself."

"If that's true—"

"It *is* true."

"—then why wouldn't you have just asked me to visit them?" He added, "During a civilized hour of the day?"

"I *did* ask you," she retorted. "On the first day, I asked if I could say good-bye to them. You refused. You don't seem like the type of person who changes his mind."

He vaguely remembered the conversation. In retrospect, it was not well done of him. Although in his defense, he'd been livid because of the threat to his sister. And after spending the night under a bridge he hadn't been inclined to grant Anabelle any favors.

"Things have changed since then." It was true. He still didn't know if he could trust her or even if her mother was truly ill. But now, he wanted to know. He *wanted* to believe her.

"Is your sister expecting you tonight?"

She shook her head. "She would have been furious with me for taking such a risk."

"Your sister and I are of the same mind. Even if you'd managed to arrive safely, chances are your sister and mother would have been sleeping. We'll return to my house now. In the morning, I'll escort you on a visit to your family. We have other matters to discuss also, but at the moment, my primary concern is getting you home in one piece."

Belatedly, he remembered her spectacles were in his pocket and gave them to her.

She settled them on her little nose and narrowed her eyes. "Your arm," she said, taking his wrist. "This gash needs to be cleaned and dressed quickly."

Actually, it felt as though the bleeding had slowed. He would survive, but he couldn't say the same for his jacket. His sleeve was in tatters and pitted with puncture marks. "I'm all for getting home quickly. And avoiding dogs of all breeds."

"What if the dogs are...that is, could they be...?"

"They looked more hungry than rabid."

She reached and traced his eyebrow with an index finger. "Your eye is cut and swollen. You were more badly hurt than I realized."

Owen touched the heel of his hand to his bruised eye and winced. "This isn't from the dogs. My friend, Averill, did it."

"Your *friend* did that to you?"

Owen smiled. "Yes, but he walked away with a fat lip." He wasn't sure why he felt obliged to mention it. Cursed pride, he guessed.

"How charming."

"You'd like Averill." Owen snorted. "All the ladies do."

"Yes, well, I've never been one to blindly follow the pack."

Her response pleased him. She inspected his arm more closely before releasing it. "You should send for a doctor."

"Probably," he admitted. "But all I really want to do right now is find my bed."

She nodded and yawned. "An excellent idea."

He quirked a brow at her, and even in the darkness, he could see the flush creep up her cheeks.

They walked side by side, in silence, down the deserted

streets until they reached his house. As he ushered her up the steps toward the entrance, he said, "The front door isn't nearly as adventurous a means of entry as, say, a window, but at least one can walk upright through it."

She blushed again. "How'd you know about that?"

He thought fondly of her bottom hanging out of his library window, and leaned close to her ear. "I saw you. I saw everything."

Her mouth opened, and he had the fierce and sudden urge to kiss her again, but from the dark foyer he heard a throat clear. Dennison. The butler rounded the corner holding a lantern aloft.

"Is everything all right, Your Grace?" Dennison's eyes took in his and Anabelle's tattered clothes before flicking to the grandfather clock against the wall.

"Perfect," Owen answered cheerfully. He enjoyed tormenting his butler. To Anabelle, he said, "Good night, Miss Honeycote. Rest up so that you'll be fresh for our outing in the morning." She fled to her room like the wild dogs still snapped at her heels.

Chapter Ten

The next morning, Anabelle dragged herself out of bed. Her legs were leaden and her eyes puffy. All night long she'd been haunted alternately between visions of Mama coughing into a blood-splattered handkerchief and the duke being eaten alive by ferocious dogs. On top of that, she anxiously awaited her visit to Mama and Daph.

On one hand, it was generous of the duke to escort her. She'd see for herself how Mama fared. On the other, the thought of him seeing their humble living conditions made her stomach knot like a novice's embroidery thread. It wasn't precisely embarrassment that made her reluctant to show him their rooms. It was more than that.

Introducing the duke to her sister and mother was tantamount to inviting him into her other life—her *real* life. The one she'd return to after serving out her term working for him, and she didn't like the idea of him briefly stepping into it to satisfy his curiosity—or worse, to cater to them as though her family were some sort of charity project.

They might not have much, but they had pride. And, more importantly, they had each other.

After hastily washing her face and dressing, she went downstairs, ate breakfast, and returned to the workroom. She had much to do, and since she suspected the duke would sleep for a few more hours, she intended to make as much progress as she could.

Today she was starting a new walking dress for Olivia. Each dress she completed brought her closer to freedom, but she still had eighteen to go and would not compromise her high standards of quality no matter how much she longed to be home. She would make the walking gown itself from white India muslin, but the pelisse would be a lovely gold color, trimmed with a broad band of lace. The rich color matched the golden strands in Olivia's hair, and Anabelle could hardly wait to show it to her.

As Anabelle measured amber silk for the pelisse, Olivia entered the nursery for her usual mid-morning visit.

"Good morning," she said, looking slightly puzzled. "I passed my brother on my way back from breakfast, and he asked me to fetch you."

Anabelle swallowed. "He did?"

"Yes, and he looked ready to pay a call on someone. Have you any idea what he is up to?"

"I think so. Excuse me a moment." She set down her measuring tape and retrieved her reticule from her bed-chamber next door.

When she returned to the workroom, Olivia was staring at her. "Why do you and Owen both look so tired this morning?"

Anabelle laughed—a bit too loudly—in response. "I'm

afraid I stayed up late last evening. It won't affect progress on your new dress, though. I shall return in a few hours and spend some more time on it."

Olivia smiled as though amused. "Excellent. I'll stop by and perhaps we can have a nice chat."

"I'd like that." Anabelle hurried past Olivia and down the staircase to find the duke waiting in the foyer. Dennison stood at his side, holding the duke's hat at the ready.

"Shall we go?" the duke asked her.

She patted a hand to her head, relieved to find her cap securely in place. "Yes."

He took his hat and jammed it on his head before ushering her out the front door. The gray sky hung low and heavy, and cool raindrops pelted Anabelle's face. She wrapped her shawl more tightly about her and hoped she wouldn't resemble a wet rat by the time they reached her home.

But instead of setting off down the street, the duke shepherded her toward the most elegant coach she'd ever seen. It waited just a few steps away, the shiny black finish of the cab so polished she could see their reflection in it. A painted gold "H" decorated the door of the cab, marking it as the duke's. In case there'd been any doubt.

"We're riding in *this*?" she asked.

As if to answer, one of the footmen stepped forward and opened the door, revealing plush black velvet seats and squabs. Anabelle couldn't wait to run her fingers over them and test whether the nap of the fabric was as thick and soft as it looked.

The duke helped her in, and when she would have chosen the rear-facing bench, he guided her to the forward-facing one before joining her there. The moment the footman shut the cab door, the duke banged the roof with his fist and the carriage rolled into motion.

The cab was more cozy and intimate than Anabelle would have expected. With the shades lowered to half-mast, the dreariness of the day outside remained at bay. Although the interior was spacious, the duke's long legs sprawled across the floor, and the top of his head nearly touched the ceiling. She could smell his shaving soap, and heat emanated from his body. His dark hair was damp from the rain, and his eye had turned a rather nasty shade of purple. Though the line of his mouth was grim, his lips were full. The feel of that beautiful mouth on hers—warm, wet, and insistent—came flooding back to her.

Just then, out of the corner of her eye, she noticed a basket tucked under the opposite seat of the coach.

The duke's gaze flicked from her to the basket and back. "Cook sent along some fruit, bread, cheese, and God knows what else for you to take your mother and sister. Cook is certain everyone is one scone away from starvation."

Perhaps. But Cook couldn't have prepared anything unless the duke had made it a point to inform her…or even ask her. The gesture touched Anabelle even more than the spectacles had. He seemed reluctant to take credit for the idea, but he didn't fool her. He was more generous than he liked to let on.

He peered at her from beneath his dark lashes. "Why, in God's name, do you insist on wearing that hat?"

She blinked, startled by the blunt question. The answer was complicated. The cap marked her as a servant and was a physical reminder that in spite of her silly dreams in the workroom of the dress shop, she'd probably never be anything more. Oh, she might sleep on silk sheets and dine on roast beef for a few months. She might even be the current object of the duke's desire. There was no harm in enjoying the fantasy while it lasted, but none of it was enduring or real. Her reality was the daily struggle to put food on her family's table and keep her mother alive. Removing the cap couldn't change that no matter how badly she wished it would. And if her dowdy cap helped remind the duke of her servant status, so much the better.

But it seemed pointless to share these thoughts with him. "How is your arm today?" Not a soul would know by looking at him that a wild dog had had his arm in a death grip several hours before. His jacket was impeccable, and he'd moved without a hint of pain, but she'd seen the gash in his flesh and his blood-soaked shirt last night. It had to hurt.

"It's fine," he said tightly.

"May I?" Without waiting for his response, she reached for his arm and, as gently as she could, pushed first his jacket, and then his sleeve up to his elbow. The duke rolled his eyes but did not pull away.

His wound had been bandaged with strips of clean linen, but a crimson stain had already begun to soak through the layers. His skin near the edges of the bandages looked swollen, pink, and hot to the touch. Guilt niggled at her conscience. If she hadn't snuck out… "I thought you were going to have a doctor look at this."

"Maybe I did."

She shot him a skeptical glance and leaned closer to have a better look at his eye. The lid had swollen, but instead of detracting from his good looks, it merely lent him a dangerous and brooding air. She opened her mouth to tease him about the lavender color when the coach lurched, throwing her off balance.

Anabelle clung to his broad shoulders; he grasped her by the waist and sat her firmly on one of his thighs. The sensation was odd, not unpleasant. However, sitting on a gentleman's lap was beyond the pale, even for her. The situation probably demanded a new rule: "Never sit beside the duke in a jostling coach." Pity she didn't have her List and a pen handy.

She squirmed in an attempt to return to her seat, but he held her tightly. His leg felt hard and solid beneath her bottom, and his large hands almost spanned her waist.

The tenderness in his eyes melted her like so much wax. Her heartbeat sped up, and when his gaze drifted to her mouth, she didn't wait for him to kiss her. Instead, she slid a hand around the back of his neck and kissed him softly.

They seemed to be making a habit of this—cap, or no cap.

He didn't take over as she'd expected him to, but let her explore at will. She trailed her hand over the slight stubble on his jaw as she brushed her lips over his. When she teased his lips apart with her tongue, however, he groaned and pulled her closer, deepening the kiss.

Her body instantly responded to the now familiar taste of him. Moist heat gathered between her legs and, instinctively, she rocked against him. A pulsing started, and though it felt very good, it was not quite enough. She moaned and pressed herself closer to him, annoyed at the layers of her skirt and petticoats.

"Anabelle," he gasped. "Christ." He appeared breathless, dazed.

She leaned back, feeling slightly awkward and ashamed. She didn't *think* she'd done anything wrong, but this business of kissing was all quite new to her.

"I'm sorry," he said with exasperation. "I find it hard to control myself around you."

Unsure whether she should be flattered or insulted, she scrambled off his lap and scooted to the far end of the bench seat. Meanwhile, he yanked down the sleeve of his jacket and dragged a hand through his hair.

Anabelle looked out of the window, surprised to find they were only a few streets away from her home. "We're almost there." The worry she felt for Mama, forgotten as long as she'd been kissing the duke, now weighed on her chest like a heap of bricks.

"I'll wait in the coach," he said, "and let you visit with your family in private."

She considered this for a moment. "If you didn't intend to come inside, why did you come with me? A footman could have brought me." She'd been certain that his motivation for bringing her here was to find out if she was telling the truth about her family's dire situation.

"To make sure you got here safely."

"And to make sure I came back?"

He threw her a level stare. "Yes." Honest, to a fault.

"I made a promise to you and your sisters," Anabelle said. "I intend to keep it. But I also need to make sure my family is all right."

"I know." As he handed her the basket from under the seat, she realized that, of all people, he *would* understand. He loved his sisters the same way she loved Mama and Daph. It was a thread between them, and in that instant, he looked so sure of himself—and at the same time, so vulnerable—that she wanted to launch herself at him and kiss him again.

The coach drew to a halt alongside Anabelle's building and passersby who were running for cover from the rain stopped and stared. She would be the subject of much gossip in the local taverns that evening—although not as much as if she'd still been seated on the duke's lap when the coach rolled up. The rain came down in sheets, so she pulled her shawl over her cap and prepared to make a run for the door.

"Wait." He withdrew an umbrella from beneath the seat and disembarked first, opening the umbrella and holding it over her solicitously. Countless times, she'd trudged up this sidewalk, and never—ever—imagined a scenario such as this.

"Take your time," he said, holding open the door of her building. She stepped inside and turned to thank him, but he'd already shut the door behind her.

Anabelle inhaled the smells of home—yeasty baked bread, the acrid odor of the ointment that Mrs. Bowman used for her aching joints, and the mildew that seemed to linger in the worn carpet runner on the stairs. It was all so familiar, as though she'd just walked home after a long day in the dress shop. She traipsed up the stairs, eager to see Mama and Daph, and yet worried—that Mama would be thinner than before, that Daph would be pale with exhaustion. Anabelle straightened her shoulders. Whatever the problem, she'd fix it. Same as she'd always done.

When she reached the landing, she placed her hand on the doorknob and hesitated. She had her key but didn't want to startle Daph, so she gave a quick rap before letting herself in.

The parlor was immaculate. A vase on their tiny table held freshly cut flowers, and the room smelled lemony, as though every surface had been recently dusted and cleaned. The large tray they used to transport bowls and cups for washing was empty—hadn't they been eating? She set the basket down beside it. "Daphne?" she called.

"Belle!" Daph rushed into the room and the two of them collided in a fierce, tearful hug. Until that very moment, Anabelle hadn't realized how much she missed her sister. Without her, she'd been off-kilter—but now everything seemed right. Embracing Daph was like holding a ray of golden sunshine in her arms, warming and healing her soul.

They were both soggy by the time Daph finally let go and held her at arm's length.

"Your spectacles!" she cried. "You're even more beautiful than before."

Anabelle had forgotten how different she looked. "I can see so much better with them." And she was relieved to see that in spite of the shadows beneath her eyes, Daph appeared healthy—and as lovely as ever. Her blue eyes sparkled with emotion and her cheeks glowed with happiness. "You look wonderful. I fear you've been working too hard, though, without me here to relieve you."

"Mrs. Bowman comes up to sit with Mama every other day so that I may go out and get the things we need. The money you sent has kept us well-fed and comfortable. I hope you're not overtaxing yourself, Belle."

She thought of the busy but happy hours she'd spent in the workroom at the duke's townhouse. "I'm not—truly. How is Mama?"

Daph bit her bottom lip. "Come see for yourself."

She took Anabelle's hand and led her into the darkened bedroom where Mama lay sleeping, her skin almost as white as her nightrail. Her hair looked grayer than Anabelle remembered, which was ridiculous—people didn't age in the course of a week, and yet, it seemed Mama had. Anabelle walked to the edge of the bed, let her hand trail across the back of her mother's papery cheek, and kissed her cool forehead. Her lips were cracked and dry.

Anabelle recalled the empty tray in the parlor. "Has she been eating?"

"Not much. I've tried to tempt her with all her favorites, but she's not interested in food."

"What does Dr. Conwell say?"

Daphne shrugged sadly. "He seemed pleased that we could afford more medicine and prescribed her a larger dose. I think it makes her more comfortable, but she's so listless. And sleeping almost around the clock."

Anabelle pressed a fist to her mouth. Even when Mama's cough had been at its worst, she'd longed for her daughters' company. She'd delighted in the songs Daph would sing and Anabelle's tales of insipid customers at the dress shop. She'd loved sharing memories of Papa and reading letters he'd sent to her years ago. She should *not* be lying in a bed, sleeping her life away.

And if Anabelle could help it, she would not.

"I think we should try to rouse her." She took her mother's hand and pressed a kiss to the back of it. "Mama, it's Anabelle," she said firmly.

Her head lolled from side to side, but her eyes remained closed.

"Mama." Anabelle gently nudged her shoulder. "I'm home."

She mumbled groggily without waking.

Anabelle looked helplessly to Daph, who reached for the glass of water on the bedside table. "Sometimes a cool drink will bring her to."

As Anabelle helped her sister lift Mama's shoulders and hold the glass to her lips, her admiration for Daphne grew. The task was difficult even with the two of them, but Daph must have done this many times on her own.

Mama choked down a little water, murmured something, and drifted to sleep once more.

Anabelle's throat constricted. Selfishly, she'd wanted Mama to hug her and tell her how much she'd missed her. At the very least, she'd hoped her visit might lift Mama's spirits. Instead, she was in an awful stupor.

Daphne tugged on her elbow. "Come. Let's go sit in the parlor and have a chat. I want to know everything about the duke and his sisters."

Anabelle had almost forgotten he was waiting for her downstairs. "I suppose we could talk for a few minutes, but then I need to return to work." They sat on the worn settee in the parlor, and Anabelle felt an unusual awkwardness with her sister. She'd kept very few secrets from Daphne over the years. As much as she longed to confide in her, however, her relationship with the duke was complicated. She'd started out as his nemesis, turned into his employee, and then, finally, become something like . . . his romantic interest.

If she mentioned the kisses it might seem like the money he advanced her was payment not for her dressmaking skills, but for something else altogether—not the case at all. Now that she thought of it, however, the line was not drawn as clearly as she might have liked.

"So," said Daphne, "tell me how you persuaded the Duke of Huntford to hire you as a seamstress. It was a brilliant idea."

"I can't take credit. It was his...suggestion." *Suggestion* sounded better than *ultimatum*, and Anabelle thought it best not to mention that he'd threatened to turn her over to the authorities. "I'd met his sisters at the shop. They're sweet as can be, and I've grown fond of them."

"I'm sure they adore you as well. But I want to know about the duke." Daph quirked a golden brow. "Is he as handsome as they say?"

Anabelle's body thrummed at the mere mention of him. "Yes. And very arrogant." Feeling a little guilty, she added, "But generous."

"Indeed. He paid for Dr. Conwell's next two visits and three months' worth of Mama's medicine from the apothecary."

"He did?"

Daph bobbed her head. "In addition to the thirty pounds that came with your letter. Don't worry, I've been frugal—I know it needs to last. But it's such a comfort to know that for the next few months we don't need to choose between buying food or medicine."

Money helped, but Mama was barely clinging to life. Anabelle stood, walked to the window, and looked out at the grimy alley behind their building. She hadn't realized the duke had sent such a large sum. It was too generous, and it would take her decades of working at the dress shop to repay him. "I wish I could stay and visit with you all day. But I really must go. The duke gave me a ride in his coach and is waiting on our street."

Daphne's eyes grew wide. "He escorted you here? May

I walk down with you and meet him? I'd like to express my thanks for all he's done for us."

"Of course." Anabelle instantly regretted mentioning that he was here. It was awful of her—petty and childish. But once the duke saw Daphne, any attraction that he felt for Anabelle was sure to evaporate. It had always been that way. Her sister couldn't help it. Her beauty and charm made men lose their minds. They wanted to be near her, protect her, provide for her. The duke would fall under Daphne's spell the moment he met her, and Anabelle would be invisible once more. Perhaps that would be for the best.

Daphne grabbed her white chip hat from a hook by the door and tied the ribbons on the side of her chin. The bonnet was old and certainly not in the first stare of fashion, but it didn't matter. She was fresh and lovely—a peach ripe for picking. Anabelle checked the pins holding her cap in place. She was a grape shriveling on the vine.

Normally, she didn't begrudge Daphne her legions of admirers. But, just this once, Anabelle had wanted an admirer of her own. She'd wanted this little sliver of happiness for herself.

They walked down the staircase to the small foyer at the bottom, and cracked open the front door. The coach stood at the curb, its gleaming black surface slick with rain. It was completely out of place on their quiet street— too polished and grand by far. The rain had turned torrential and was not conducive to even a short conversation. Daphne heaved a disappointed sigh. "Another day, perhaps."

Then the duke emerged from his coach, a closed umbrella in his hand, and marched to their door as though he didn't feel the rain. The breadth of his shoulders and the narrowness of his hips made Anabelle's toes curl in her slippers.

"Ready?" he asked, opening the umbrella.

Anabelle knew the exact moment that he saw Daphne behind her. He froze briefly, closed the umbrella, and wedged himself inside. The hallway was so small that they stood nearly shoulder-to-shoulder. Droplets of rainwater pooled at the duke's feet. His gaze flickered from Anabelle to Daphne, somewhat expectantly.

Anabelle tried to keep any trace of bitterness from her voice—maybe too hard. "Your Grace, may I present my sister, Miss Daphne Honeycote. Daph, this is the Duke of Huntford."

Daphne attempted a curtsey and her elbow jabbed Anabelle in the side. "Sorry, Belle!" she said, blushing, and all three of them laughed good-naturedly. Daphne had that effect on people. Who else could have made the most arrogant duke in England laugh during their first meeting?

He greeted her politely, but the truth was, Anabelle only half-listened. She was busy trying to convince herself that she didn't care if the duke was smitten with her sister. Anabelle had no claim to him. And yet, her chest ached.

They quickly exhausted the usual topics. Anabelle couldn't help grabbing one last hug with Daph before saying good-bye. The duke bowed formally—as though her sister were a princess and not a peasant—and held the umbrella aloft as he guided Anabelle into the dry, cozy coach.

Rain pattered on the roof. It would have been excellent weather for sleeping; during the day it was just rather gloomy. But that may have had more to do with Anabelle's mood than anything else.

He rapped on the roof and the coach started rolling.

"How was your mother?" The concern in his green eyes squeezed at her heart.

"Not well. I wasn't able to wake her, and she hasn't been eating much."

His brow furrowed. "How well do you know Dr. Conwell?"

"He was highly recommended by the apothecary we've always used."

"My physician isn't acquainted with him."

So, the duke had been checking up on her. She bristled. "London is a large city."

"Not as large as you might think." He stroked his chin and stared out of his window, which was blurred with streaks of water. "I could send my doctor over to check on your mother."

Out of sheer pride, she started to say it wasn't necessary. But it occurred to her that the duke probably had the very best physician money could buy, and Mama needed the best—pride be damned. "Thank you," she choked out. "My sister and I would be very grateful."

"I'm glad I got to meet your sister," he said. He was still distracted and staring out the window at the buildings rushing by. If she had to guess, dreaming of waltzing with Daphne.

"She is as kind as she is beautiful," Anabelle said softly. Which made it dreadfully difficult to resent her.

"Do you want to know what I liked best about her?"

No. No, she did not, but she swallowed, nodded, and

braced herself for his response. She suspected "her corn-flower blue eyes" or "her shining gold hair." Men were predictable creatures.

"I liked the way she made you laugh. I've never heard you laugh that way before." He turned to her then and cupped her cheeks in his warm hands. "And the way she called you Belle. It suits you...Belle."

Chapter Eleven

*Contour: (1) Cut on a curve, instead of a straight
line. (2) A curving shape or surface, as in: She traced
the contours of his chest with a fingertip.*

Owen wanted to kiss Anabelle. Again.

He wanted to press his lips to the creases in her fore-head and make her forget her family's problems. He wouldn't mind having her back on his lap, either, with the pressure of her soft bottom rocking on top of him. With every shaky breath she drew, she tempted him.

But she was distressed, and the thing that she probably most wanted was the thing he'd become something of an expert at avoiding. Conversation.

He stroked his thumbs across her smooth cheeks. "I'll do what I can to help your mother. I promise." She smiled, and he exhaled slowly, relieved to know he'd said the right thing. Encouraged, he continued. "I know what it's like to fret about your family. I worry about my sisters."

She frowned, and her eyebrows dipped below her

spectacles. "But, they're healthy and happy, and you've made sure they want for nothing."

His concerns must seem trite compared to hers. They weren't life or death, but with both his parents gone, he was acutely aware of his duty to his sisters. "Rose might go the rest of her life without speaking, without experiencing life in the way she should."

Anabelle stared at a spot on her skirt. "Rose is so wise and warm that I sometimes forget she doesn't really… talk."

"I do the same. The worst part is, it's getting difficult to remember what she sounded like. I don't mean just the tone and pitch of her voice, but all the things that she said and *how* she said them. She giggled when she read the scandals in the gossip sheets. Her voice cracked when she read the indulgent scene where Romeo finds Juliet in the tomb. I miss that side of her—even the way she chided me for hunting poor, defenseless foxes. Now that she's silent, I've lost a part of her."

Anabelle nodded soberly. "You want that back, you want *her* back, and yet, you feel guilty for not accepting Rose as she is now."

Exactly. He coughed into his hand. "Something like that."

This whole exchange with Anabelle felt awkward, as if he'd used muscles that hadn't been exercised in, oh, a couple of decades. But it was a relief to tell another human being the thoughts that had been knocking around in his mind for so long. Anabelle seemed to understand. He laced her fingers through his and pressed their palms together, liking the fit. "It's not just Rose who concerns me. I worry that Olivia's headstrong ways will land her in trouble. She's always been impulsive, which is my fault. After my father died, I was too lenient with her. I still don't know which member of my staff she's seeing. After I received your extortion note, I confronted her. She refuses to talk about it."

Anabelle's face flushed at the mention of the note. After a few moments of silence she said, "I wonder if I could help."

"How?"

"Well," she began, licking her pink lips, "I could try to learn more about your sisters—not as your spy, you understand—but as a concerned friend. Maybe I could persuade them to confide in you."

"You would do that?"

She gazed at their intertwined fingers. "It's the least I can do. You've done so much for my family and me. And I don't think it will be difficult to convince your sisters to talk with you about personal matters. They worship you, you know."

He arched a brow. "They have an odd way of showing it."

"When you look up to someone, you live in fear of disappointing them."

He wondered if her wisdom was hard won; not much in her life could have been easy. "You think Rose and Olivia fear me?"

"Of course not. I suspect they're among the precious few who don't. But perhaps they're afraid they can't live up to your high standards."

Ridiculous. "They could never disappoint me."

Anabelle adjusted her spectacles. "Have you told them that?"

"Not recently." Not ever.

"I see." She looked directly at him, her huge eyes shining with compassion and amusement. "I'll subtly encourage Olivia and Rose to open their hearts to you. But you…"

"What?"

"…must try not to frighten them off."

"Preposterous. I—" He paused and shot her a wicked grin. "Do I frighten *you*, Belle?"

She raised her chin in that adorable manner of hers. "No," she said, a bit too emphatically. "*You* are not frightening. The shade of green around your eye, however… *that's* rather alarming."

Owen nodded, pleased with how the morning had turned out and annoyed that it was almost over. The coach rumbled along, and fat raindrops continued to pummel the roof. Anabelle pulled her hand free from his and placed it in her lap, leaving him suddenly bereft. The closer they drew to Mayfair, the more rigid her posture became. He considered ordering the coachman to ride north for two hours until the social strictures of London were tiny dots on the landscape seen from the back window of his coach.

Their relationship—if it could be called that—did not fit into any neat category, and that irked him. Categories were useful. Living things, for example, were Animalia, Plantae, or Protista. He generally classified women as wives, mistresses, relatives, and acquaintances. His relationship with Belle was *not* an affair or a courtship, so what was it? Why the hell wasn't there a category for a not-quite-affair between a duke and an aspiring extortionist-turned-seamstress?

She sat on the same bench as he, her leg inches from his, but the chasm between them was as wide as the

English Channel. As St. James's Square came into view, he shamelessly grasped at the one thing that bound her to him. "Olivia tells me you promised her and Rose ten dresses each."

Anabelle blinked, clearly puzzled by the sudden change in subject. "That's right."

"I trust you'll be able to deliver them within the three-month period." He congratulated himself on his pompous, ducal tone. God, he was an ass.

A hurt expression flashed across her face before a mask of indifference settled over it. "Yes. I shall make twenty gowns before I leave, and each one shall be to your sisters' satisfaction. You have my word." In an acidic tone, she added, "Your Grace."

Touché. "Excellent."

According to Olivia, Anabelle had completed two and one-half gowns. He assumed the next eighteen would require a good bit of work, which meant he'd have time. Time to hammer their relationship into some identifiable, legitimate category. As the coach pulled into the Square, he said, "In the meantime, you are not to leave the house without my knowledge. If you wish to visit your family, I will escort you myself."

She narrowed her beautiful gray eyes at him. Damn, she probably saw right through him—knew how desperate he was to keep her with him. Even the visits would give him an excuse to spend time with her. "Thank you for rescuing me last night and for your assistance today."

"It was nothing. I'll send my doctor over to see your mother this afternoon."

"Maybe you should ask him to come here first and tend to your arm."

Good point. His forearm hurt like the devil. "Maybe you should remove that godawful cap."

She shot him a lethal look.

At least they were back on familiar, solid footing.

The coach rolled to a stop, a footman opened the door, and Owen stepped out. The rain had turned into drizzle. He extended a hand to Anabelle to help her step down from the cab. "Your charm knows no bounds," she said sweetly.

He chuckled. "So I've been told."

As she walked into the townhouse, he appreciated the elegant line of her neck and the gentle sway of her hips. He hoped eighteen dresses would take a very long time.

A few hours later, Owen gritted his teeth in pain. The kind of pain that makes one want to spew curses and drink copious amounts of alcohol. Nothing personal against Dr. Loxton, but Owen was leery of the medical profession as a whole. Loxton was employing some kind of sadistic torture that would supposedly help heal his arm, all the while shaking his graying head over the unlikelihood of encountering wild dogs in the capital of a civilized nation such as this. When he put down his sharp metal instruments and finally began bandaging, Owen loosened his death grip on the arm of his chair and breathed easier.

Loxton was the rare physician who didn't mind getting his hands dirty. He'd set a fracture or stitch a person up as long as the patient could be trusted not to spread the gory details about Town. Of course, he didn't want it known that he occasionally did such ungentlemanly work—his wife had been presented at Court, for God's sake.

The doctor had an opinion on everything, which didn't

bother Owen. Listening to those opinions *did* bother Owen, but he tolerated the doctor's ramblings because, well, he was the best.

"I'd like you to visit and examine the mother of·... a servant of mine." Owen held out a card with Anabelle's address on it. "The mother's name is Mrs. Honeycote. I don't know much about her condition, but her daughters are very worried. Dr. Conwell has been treating her."

The doctor stroked his bushy beard. "The man you inquired about a couple of days ago? I asked around. He's not licensed by the Royal College."

"Maybe he's a surgeon." Damned if Loxton wasn't tying the bandage too tightly.

The physician puffed out his chest. "Then he shouldn't tout himself as a doctor. None of my colleagues is familiar with him. My guess is he's a fraud."

Owen clenched his fist and tested the feel of the dressing as he considered the possibility that Anabelle had been handing over every shilling she earned—or extorted—to a quack. "Mrs. Honeycote is very sick. Don't tell her or her daughter, Daphne, about your suspicions. Just do everything you can to help her and send me the bill."

The physician raised his wiry, white brows. "You're a generous employer, Huntford."

"Actually, I'm a demanding bastard." To prove his point, he bit off the knot of his bandage and unraveled it like an irate mummy. "It's a bandage, not a tourniquet. Try again."

Later that evening, as Anabelle threaded a needle, her mind was still reeling from the coach ride with the duke. Owen. After kissing him in his carriage today—their third kiss—she'd begun to think of him by his Christian name, even if she couldn't quite bring herself to utter it.

Kissing had certainly made him seem less intimidating. He'd talked with her like she was more than a lowly seamstress—like a trusted friend.

Things between them had grown complicated, indeed, but she harbored no illusions about the true nature of their relationship. She was a paid servant…with whom he wanted to dally. The friendship aspect, which had developed of late, blurred the line, but once her debt was paid, she'd never see him again—unless he happened to return to Mrs. Smallwood's dress shop one day in the future, with his mistress in tow.

Still, she was indebted to Owen on many counts. He'd offered to help Mama, bought her new spectacles, and rescued her from vicious dogs. Although her List of Nevers forbade her from becoming involved with him, she felt obliged to help him and his sisters. She'd do what she could to make Rose less shy and to bring the siblings closer to one another.

Mama's condition was distressing, and Anabelle was eager for news from Dr. Loxton. Since she could do nothing but wait, however, she dedicated herself to making a gorgeous walking dress for Rose. She was preparing to sew some velvet trim onto a pelisse when both Olivia and Rose entered the workroom. "Good evening," Anabelle said with surprise.

Olivia smiled warmly. "I hope you don't mind some company. Rose and I thought we'd visit—unless you find it too bothersome while you work."

"Not at all." Anabelle cleared snippets of fabric and lace from the window seat and invited the women to sit.

"I'm delighted you're here. Would you like to see how your newest dresses are coming along?"

Rose shook her head, and gently nudged her sister with an elbow.

"No," said Olivia. "That's not why we came." She worried the ends of the pink ribbons that served as the sash of her dress. "We heard that Owen took you to visit your mother this morning. We didn't know she was ill. If there's anything we can do, you must let us know. We feel awful that you're here slaving over fancy gowns for us when you'd most certainly rather be at your mother's side."

Anabelle's nose stung and her eyes welled; she set the pelisse in her lap. "You're both very kind. Thank you. Your brother has generously offered to send his physician, but to be honest, I'm not sure anything can help her."

Rose reached out and clasped her hand.

"You mustn't say that," Olivia scolded. "Don't give up hope. Dr. Loxton is a learned man. He cares for all of our great-aunts."

Anabelle sniffled. So, Owen *did* have great-aunts. "How many aunts do you have?"

"Fourteen," said Olivia proudly, "ranging in age from fifty-nine to—"

"Eighty-two."

Rose clapped her hands in delight.

"How did you know?" asked Olivia.

"Your brother mentioned them once." Of course, immediately afterward he'd denied their existence.

"Did he?" Olivia asked with some surprise. "He dotes on them shamelessly."

How interesting. Anabelle turned up the lantern on the table and adjusted her spectacles before picking up her sewing. "Your brother also seems very devoted to the two of you."

"Oh, yes," said Olivia. "He means well, in any event. It is sometimes hard for him to fathom that we're no longer wearing pigtails and dresses with bloomers. He keeps us on a very short leash, and he never tells us anything."

Anabelle tilted her head. "Why do you think that is?"

Olivia sighed. "Ever since Father died, Owen's been quite protective. He'd like to shield us from all of life's unpleasantries, which, as you know, is quite impossible. Nor is it any way to live. Suffering is a part of life." She looked wistfully at Rose and then continued. "In any event, we believe that if he just found the right sort of woman to marry, she could help him be less…"

"Rigid?"

"Precisely! Of course, our brother is extremely particular when it comes to women. Everyone seems to think Miss Starling will be the miss to capture his affection."

Rose puckered as though she'd sucked on a lemon wedge.

Olivia turned to her sister. "You cannot deny that Miss Starling is beautiful. And her manners are so refined. She'd make an excellent duchess."

Anabelle considered the matter objectively, which was difficult because her stomach was twisted in knots. She chalked it up to the fish she'd eaten at dinner. But it was obvious that Miss Starling had been raised to be a duchess—or a countess at the very least. *She* certainly seemed to think so. "Does your brother seem fond of her?" It was an absurd question. Any warm-blooded male would be fond of Miss Starling.

"It is hard to say," admitted Olivia. "Owen doesn't

keep us apprised of such matters. I expect he'll call us into the drawing room one evening and announce that he's betrothed in much the same way he'd announce he's bought a gelding."

Interesting. Owen wanted his sisters to be more forth-coming, and they wished the same of him.

Rose, in particular, looked highly agitated by the con-versation. Anabelle couldn't tell if she objected to Miss Starling or to the idea of her brother suddenly announcing his engagement. Either way, a change of subject was in order. She forced a bright smile. "Well then. What kind of husbands would the duke choose for the two of you?"

The sisters exchanged a glance that Anabelle couldn't read. "Someone from a respectable family," said Olivia.

"You mean, a gentleman?" Anabelle recalled the rumor she'd transcribed in her extortion note and felt like she was treading close to the edge of a rocky crag.

"A rich and titled gentleman," Olivia clarified.

Anabelle smiled sympathetically. "Does that seem unreasonable to you? You are, after all, the sisters of a duke."

Rose tapped Olivia's shoulder and pressed her palm to her heart.

Olivia interpreted. "Rose thinks a kind and gentle nature is more important than wealth and lineage. She believes in love."

It didn't surprise Anabelle that Rose was a romantic sort. Under different circumstances, Anabelle might have been one herself. As it was, she'd given up on fairy tales. To Rose, she said, "Perhaps you'll be fortunate enough to find a man who meets your brother's high standards as well as your own."

Although Anabelle had meant to cheer Rose, the red-head's shoulders drooped as though she were...broken-hearted.

"Forgive me if I've offended you," Anabelle said.

Rose stood, gave a wan smile, and touched Anabelle's shoulder before tilting her head to the door regretfully.

"Sleep well," Olivia said to her sister. "You'll feel better in the morning."

Rose glided silently from the room, leaving Anabelle feeling wretched.

"I'm sorry I upset her. What was it that I said?"

Olivia waved away her apology. "We've both been a bit sensitive lately. You couldn't have known about—"

About what? Or whom? Anabelle waited impatiently for Olivia to complete her thought.

"I shouldn't say more on the subject."

Anabelle stifled her disappointment. "I understand."

"Although, it would be lovely to have someone to confide in. You seem so sure of yourself—and wise for someone so young."

Although Anabelle longed to know the sisters' secret, she didn't feel worthy after threatening to publish horrid gossip about Olivia. And the more she thought of it, she didn't want to be in the awkward position of keeping secrets from Owen. "You could always confide in your brother," she said.

"No, no. We most certainly cannot." Olivia began pacing, nibbling on an index finger as she wore a path in the Aubusson rug. "But I know we can trust you."

Anabelle tamped down a wave of guilt. If Olivia chose to confide in her, she wouldn't let her down again. "Yes, of course you can."

Olivia walked to the door, closed it quietly, and continued her pacing. "Rose fancies herself in love."

"Why, that's wonderful. Isn't it?"

"Yes. And no. The man she loves is not someone my brother would approve of."

"Because he's not titled?"

"Or rich," added Olivia.

"Perhaps, if your brother got to know him, he'd change his mind. Does this man treat Rose well? Does he make her happy?"

"Charles—that's his name—admires Rose greatly. And when she's with him, she's a different person. Confident, secure...and yes, happy. I don't know if my sister will ever talk freely again, but I think if anyone could help her, Charles could."

"Maybe if your brother could see for himself how happy Rose is with Charles, he'd be more willing to entertain the idea of a match." For some reason, Anabelle desperately wanted to believe he would.

Olivia rolled her eyes. "Did I mention that Charles is the stable master at our country estate? Owen has very strict rules regarding friendships with servants." As though the thought had just occurred to her, she asked, "Is this uncomfortable for you to discuss? That is, I don't think of you as a servant, but I suppose you are in the strictest sense of the word. And yet, we've become friends, have we not?"

Anabelle swallowed the knot in her throat. "I would say that we have." And then, although she suspected that the answer would be painful, she was obliged to ask the question. "What *are* your brother's rules regarding friendships with servants?"

"They are strictly forbidden. The worst part is that he's threatened to fire any member of the staff he suspects could be involved. Of course, he's convinced *I'm* the one who's been having clandestine meetings, when, in truth, it's been Rose all along."

Anabelle digested this news. She was tickled to learn that Rose had a slightly rebellious nature. At least she wasn't afraid of defying her brother. How had someone of her mettle remained almost completely silent for close to three years? A thought occurred to her. "You said Rose disappeared at that house party the night before your mother left."

Olivia nodded. "We were terrified that some harm had befallen her. But when we found her the next day, she seemed fine, by all appearances. Only ... she wasn't."

"Perhaps if we could find out what happened that night, we might be able to help her find her voice again."

Olivia gave a weary smile and shrugged. "I have asked her. Whatever happened, Rose does not want to talk about it."

"Maybe someone else at the house party knows. Do you recall who was there?"

"My mother and father, Owen, Rose, and I..." Olivia counted the guests on her fingers. "...Lady Fallon, Sir Howard, Lord and Lady Winthrope—"

At the mention of that last name, Anabelle's heart seized. "Did you say Winthrope? As in the earl?"

"I did. Are you acquainted with him?"

Anabelle was not. But she knew more about him than did most of the *ton*. And she wished she didn't. "No, I don't know the earl. I know a little *of* him."

"Oh, well, there's not much to know. He's a dreadfully boring sort. He's mostly bald, but he tries to hide it by brushing a few strands 'round the top of his head. He doesn't say much, and he wears a perpetual scowl."

"Really?" The earl's mistress had painted an altogether different picture of him in Mrs. Smallwood's dress shop. She'd alluded to his sexual prowess and his fondness for tupping two women at the same time. Anabelle repressed a shiver.

On that momentous, gray morning in Hyde Park when Owen had caught her, he'd asked about previous extortion schemes—demanded truth. Even at the time, she'd known the lie that crossed her lips would haunt her. But she'd never fathomed that she'd feel so wretched about her deception.

It seemed her first extortion scheme had improbably collided with what would have been the fourth.

Chapter Twelve

$\mathcal{L}$ong before the sun rose, Anabelle squirmed on her feather mattress, her legs tangled in the silky sheets. She told herself there was no harm in dreaming of Owen's heavy-lidded gaze or his warm, large hands skimming over her hips and bottom. Wanton fantasies—the sort she'd never before imagined—played out in her mind.

He crawled into bed behind her, pressed the hard wall of his chest to her back, and murmured her name into her ear. His breath, hot and moist on her nape, shot longing through her limbs. He slid a hand beneath her nightgown, caressed the length of her side, and cupped her breast. Pleasure radiated throughout her body before settling into a hypnotic pulsing rhythm between her legs.

She never wanted to wake.

As dawn began to break, however, she could no longer feel Owen's warmth or hear his gravelly voice. The lovely dream receded like the tide, leaving her cold and alone on the shore. She squeezed her eyes closed, desperate to return to that place where she could give in to her deepest desires, where the threats of scandal and ruin did not suffocate her.

Instead, distressing memories of the Earl of Winthrope knocked on the door of her consciousness. Reluctantly, she threw back the covers, padded to the washstand, and splashed chilly water onto her cheeks. She had the strong feeling that the earl was somehow connected to Rose's sudden loss of speech. Anabelle could clearly remember the things that the earl's mistress, Miss Peckham, had said about him. And if they were true, it was no wonder Rose had sentenced herself to a life of silence.

After patting her face dry, Anabelle looked at her blurry reflection in the mirror and let her mind wander back to the day she'd first heard of the Earl of Winthrope. It was also the day she'd first stooped to extortion.

Miss Peckham and her friend had walked through the door of the shop that December morning, bringing with them a gust of frigid air.

And opportunity.

The memory of that day, almost three years ago, would forever be intertwined with physical discomfort. Hunger so sharp she would have sold her soul for an apple; cold so penetrating her fingers could scarcely hold a needle; despair over Mama's illness so deep Anabelle could hardly breathe.

The frosty weather had kept most people at home in front of their cozy fires, and the shop was abnormally peaceful. Mrs. Smallwood had taken to the back room with her ledgers, leaving Anabelle in charge of the front room. Miss Peckham and her friend, Miss Devlin, had come into the shop barking demands.

"The milliner's shop is quite inconveniently closed. I'd like you to make this hat"—Miss Peckham plopped a plain white chip hat on the counter—"look like this one." Beside the hat she laid a wrinkled copy of *The Lady's Magazine*, showing a woman wearing an ornamented headdress. It appeared to have grapes or berries attached to one side, which, of course, made Anabelle's stomach growl.

She attempted a bright smile. "I can show you a variety of trimmings. We have artificial roses, sprigs of myrtle, ermine, ostrich feathers, and lace and velvet in every color. Where would you like to start?"

Miss Peckham smiled in amusement. "I haven't the faintest, darling. Hats aren't my specialty."

Miss Devlin giggled. "Peignoirs, on the other hand..."

"Pardon?" Anabelle asked.

"Never mind," said Miss Peckham. "Would you be a dear and sew something onto this for me while I wait? I'll be riding in the park later—with a gentleman."

"How lovely," said Anabelle, although frankly, a ride in the open air on such a bitter cold day sounded anything but. "I think we should use the ermine to take away the chill. And perhaps a blue ribbon to contrast with it?"

"That's fine," Miss Peckham said, pulling up a chair. "I don't expect the earl will be very interested in my hat."

Miss Devlin raised an unnaturally arched brow. "Men have no appreciation for hats. Garters, however, are another matter entirely."

Anabelle felt herself flush. She tried to steer the conversation to less risqué territory. "If you'd like, I could add a bit of ermine trim to your tippet as well."

"As long as you can finish in an hour or so," Miss Peckham said.

Miss Devlin poked an elbow into her friend's side. "A fur-lined stole presents all kinds of interesting possibilities."

Since the women seemed intent on discussing the earl's proclivities and, perhaps, their own, Anabelle said, "You'll be here for a bit, so I'll put on some tea. Excuse me."

She breezed into the back room and passed Mrs. Smallwood on her way to the tiny kitchen.

"How is everything out front, Anabelle?" the shop owner asked distractedly. Her eyes were almost crossed from staring at the book in front of her.

"Quiet," she called. "I'm making over a hat for Miss Peckham." Anabelle wanted to prove that she could handle greater responsibility. Maybe Mrs. Smallwood would give her a modest raise; God knew her family desperately needed every shilling they could get.

"Let me know if you require assistance, dear."

"I have things in hand." Anabelle put a pot of water on the stove and retrieved a few more supplies from the back room. Then, bracing herself for further embarrassment, she marched into the front room.

"...no wonder the duchess left," Miss Peckham was saying. "She chafed at the rules of polite society. Did I tell you about her house party last month?"

Miss Devlin looked up from the fingernail she'd been examining. "No."

"She invited the earl and me into her bedchamber. Huntford would have skewered Winthrope on the spot if he'd discovered all three of us romping in his wife's bed. As it turns out, we *were* discovered." Miss Peckham had her friend's attention now. She had Anabelle's as well.

Miss Peckham smoothed the bodice of her very snug pelisse, and her eyes flicked to Anabelle, who busied herself searching through various drawers behind the counter. The earl's mistress shrugged and continued her story. "The three of us were having a perfectly lovely time when we heard the door to the duchess's bedchamber slam. The earl pulled on his breeches and poked his head out into the hallway, but by then, the intruder was gone. The duchess said it had probably been her lady's maid and that she knew better than to tell tales. She convinced the earl to come back into bed."

"I had no idea the duchess was so depraved." Miss Devlin's voice held a touch of awe.

"She is beautiful as well. I wouldn't have minded a repeat performance, but rumor has it she's fled to the Continent."

Anabelle listened with prurient interest. The women's conversation flitted from the lewd to the mundane and back again, and the dress shop remained otherwise empty. When at last she'd finished the modifications to the bonnet and the tippet, she held up the articles for Miss Peckham's inspection. "Will this do?"

Miss Peckham raised her brows. "It looks better than the one in *The Lady's Magazine*. Well done, Miss...?"

"Honeycote."

"I predict that the earl will find me irresistible in them," she said.

Miss Devlin grunted. "Perhaps, if you wore nothing else."

Miss Peckham paid for the items, and Anabelle wrapped them, grateful to see the women leave. It wasn't until much later that evening when she returned to the freezing rooms they rented, heard Mama's hacking cough, and opened a barren cupboard that a thought occurred to Anabelle.

The information she'd gleaned at the shop might be valuable.

Two days later, after much deliberation and drafting her List of Nevers, she composed her first extortion note, demanding thirty pounds from the earl in return for her silence concerning his romantic involvement with the Duchess of Huntford. The money had kept Mama, Daphne, and her from starving, and so she'd never really thought about who else might have been impacted by the events of that night.

Years later, she now knew, and it made her heart ache. The person who had stumbled into the duchess's bedchamber on the night of the house party had been the duchess's innocent fifteen-year-old daughter.

Rose.

Anabelle put on her spectacles. The freckles on her nose came into focus in the mirror. It was too early for anyone but the servants to be stirring, so she didn't bother to change out of her nightrail or brush out her braid before creeping into the workroom and pulling back the drapes to let in the morning light. If stitching the embroidery on Olivia's dress made her drowsy, she'd be able to slip back into bed for a nap.

But the task of embroidering scallops along the hem provided a welcome distraction. As long as she worried about keeping her stitches even and the spacing of the half-circles consistent, there was little time to worry about other things, like her mother's health, Rose's fragile state . . . or Owen's kisses.

She'd made it most of the way around the hem when she heard a knock at the door. Heavens. She'd no idea how much time had passed, but the sun was high in the sky, and she still wore her nightgown. It was probably Rose or Olivia, and she hoped they had some news of Mama. Now that they knew she was ill they both seemed determined to help. Anabelle set down the dress and her needle and thread, padded across the room in her bare feet, and stood close to the door.

"Who is it?" she called.

The door swung open and Anabelle took a quick step back to avoid being hit by it. Owen strode into the room looking almost as surprised as she.

"I didn't give you permission to enter," she said with exasperation.

"I grew tired of waiting. And this isn't a bedchamber." He raked his gaze over her. "For God's sake, why are you dressed like that?"

Anabelle bristled. It seemed he was always criticizing her manner of dress. Although, she thought, glancing down at her nightrail, this morning he actually had a point.

"Never mind," he muttered. He walked to a corner of the workroom where much of the nursery's furniture had been piled to make room for the tables. He opened a trunk and withdrew a blanket which he wrapped around her shoulders.

The gesture was sweet, more so because of the desire that simmered in his eyes.

"How is your arm?" she asked.

"It's fine." Odd; she'd expected a clever retort. Something along the lines of "still attached to my shoulder."

"Are you certain? I have a needle and thread here," she teased.

"We need to talk," he began, gesturing toward the window seat. "Please. Let's sit."

His civility in itself was rather alarming, but when she noticed the pinched lines on his face, the hairs on the back of her neck rose. She was certain this had to do with Mama, and that the news wasn't good. "What?" she demanded. "This is about my mother, isn't it?"

"She's fine. At least, Dr. Loxton thinks she will be." He grasped her upper arms, gently guided her to the bench seat, and sat beside her. "He examined her last night and spoke with your sister at length about the course of treatment Conwell has prescribed. Your mother is a very sick woman."

"I know that." She battled back tears of frustration. "Can Dr. Loxton help her?"

"Maybe. He's instructed Daphne to wean your mother off her medicine."

"What? That is ridiculous." Anabelle stood, threw off the blanket, and headed toward her room to dress. Clearly, she needed to go home and see to matters herself. She was not going to sit idly by while some strange doctor withheld the medicine that was keeping Mama comfortable. And alive.

"Anabelle." Owen was two steps behind her. "Let me explain."

She turned to face him, hands fisted at her sides. "She *can't* stop taking the medicine. You should have seen what she was like before. She coughed so violently that I feared her ribs would crack; every breath was torturous, and she was delirious with fever. I won't subject her to that again. I won't!" Her voice screeched, even in her own ears. Why couldn't he understand?

She would have closed her door, shutting him out, but he grabbed her shoulders. "The medicine that Dr. Conwell prescribed may have helped her in the beginning. Now it's doing nothing but sedating her. The dosage is much too strong. Not only is it taking away your mother's appetite, she's become dependent on it."

Panic thudded through Anabelle's veins. She pressed her fingertips to her lips to keep the scream in her throat from escaping. She wanted to trust Owen and knew he had nothing to gain by lying to her. Except, perhaps, to exact revenge for her extortion attempt. But she didn't think he would do that. Through the thin fabric of her nightgown, his hands felt warm and firm. His steady and solid presence calmed her.

"Are you saying," she said slowly, "that the medicine she's been taking isn't making her well? That it's doing her more harm than good?"

He hesitated for a fraction of a second. "Yes."

"Then . . . then why did Dr. Conwell keep prescribing it?"

"I suspect he figured that as long as your mother was sick, you'd keep paying for his visits."

Now her head was really spinning. "No, that's not possible. Dr. Conwell was highly recommended by our apothecary, Mr. Vanders."

"It's likely the two of them conspired to swindle you. I do know that Conwell isn't a licensed physician. I haven't even been able to track him down at his address. Odds are, he heard I was looking for him and left Town."

Anabelle went still. Blood pounded in her ears.

She'd believed that Conwell was the thin thread keeping her mother alive. She'd put all her trust and hope in the man and risked everything she had—her life, in fact—to pay him. If her mother never recovered, she would find him and strangle him with his own stethoscope.

But he wasn't the only one to blame. She'd been a fool, blindly accepting his falsehoods.

"Are you all right? I think you should sit down." Owen clasped her hand and led her back to the window seat. "You couldn't have known he was a fraud. This isn't your fault."

She blinked and adjusted her spectacles. "How did you know I was thinking that?"

With a sheepish smile, he said, "Because if I were in your position, I would have thought the same thing."

She dragged her eyes away from his handsome face and studied the dappled sunlight dancing on the drapes. "I suppose the real question is how to make Mama better."

"Exactly. I've asked Dr. Loxton to check in on her every day and monitor her health. He wants Daphne to slowly cut back on the amount of medicine and tell your mother that she must eat at least a little broth before she gets another dose. Loxton thinks she'll improve rapidly."

The optimistic prognosis was almost cruel. Anabelle wished it were true, had prayed for it every day, but wishes and prayers were futile. "She has consumption. If she seems better, it's likely because the disease is in the final stages. It would take a miracle for her to recover."

Owen encased her hands in his and forced her to look into his eyes. "Loxton isn't convinced she has consumption. It may take a while for him to properly diagnose her. But she may have had the croup or scarlet fever instead."

Anabelle wrangled with the idea that her mother might not be dying after all. Croup and scarlet fever were not trifling illnesses, but they were vastly preferable to consumption. It was just too much to hope for. She laid her head against Owen's chest and burst into tears. Not the pretty, feminine sort of tears one cries after hearing a moving bit of poetry, but the awful, body-wracking sobs that blindside a person when emotions are too raw for anything else.

Owen didn't shush her or tell her not to cry. Maybe he knew it wouldn't have done a whit of good. To his credit, he gently pried off her spectacles so she could cry that much harder. She clutched his shirtfront and sobbed until the fine lawn was soaked with tears. He didn't seem to mind.

He rubbed her back and arms, ran his hand down the length of her braid, murmured little things that sounded sweet even if she couldn't make out the words over her own pitiful howling.

She cried until her body was limp with exhaustion and then sniffled and hiccupped for a few more moments. When at last she felt she could sit up without clinging to him, she did, instantly missing the starchy yet masculine smell of his shirt.

Owen withdrew a handkerchief from his pocket and offered it with a heart-stopping smile. She gratefully dried her face.

"I don't want to raise your hopes too high." He took her hands in his, making her stomach flutter happily. "But Dr. Loxton has tended to me since I was a boy, and to my father before me. I'd trust him—*have* trusted him—to care for my own sisters. Maybe he can help your mother."

"I feel like such a fool for taking Conwell at his word. I'm not sure what to say . . . except thank you."

They gazed at each other for several moments, not saying anything. His thumbs made sweet little circles on her palms, and desire welled up inside her. Her nipples tightened, and she was suddenly very aware that she wore no corset, no chemise, nothing beneath her thin nightgown. And although it was very wanton of her, she didn't care.

She liked being the object of his attention, and she would enjoy it for as long as it lasted. With boldness she hadn't known she possessed, she raised herself onto her knees so that her face was level with his, took his scratchy cheeks into her palms, and kissed him.

Not out of gratitude, or obligation, or to prove something.

She kissed Owen simply because . . . she wanted to.

Chapter Thirteen

*Darts: (1) Tucks used to remove extra fullness from
a garment. (2) A sharp projectile similar to an arrow,
employed by Cupid to induce wanton, foolish behavior.*

*O*wen vaguely recalled a promise he'd made to himself before looking for Belle to tell her the news he
knew would unsettle her. He was fairly sure the promise
involved kissing. Or not kissing. Right. Under no circumstances was there to be kissing.

It wasn't that he was opposed to the idea—quite the
contrary.

But he'd suspected that she was going to be upset, and
he didn't want to take advantage of her distress. Only
a scoundrel would try to seduce a woman who'd just
received momentous news.

He supposed "scoundrel" was an apt description for
him. In his defense, she'd started it...and his body had
thought it a capital idea.

When he'd tasted the salt of her tears on her cheeks
and lips, he'd wanted to wash away her sadness. Even

with her puffy eyes and pink face, she was utterly irresistible. He couldn't imagine that she showed this vulnerable side very often, but she had for him, and he was strangely humbled.

Telling Belle she'd been swindled had been harder than he'd thought. It *shouldn't* have been. After all, her mother was going to receive proper care now and could conceivably recover. But Belle's family was everything to her, and, ridiculous as it seemed, she felt she'd let them down. He'd seen it in the shock and anger that flitted across her face. He'd seen her normally proud shoulders slump in defeat.

And he wanted to make her feel good again, to remind her that she wasn't just a daughter, sister, or seamstress. She was all of those things and more—a woman, young and vibrant, with dreams and desires of her own.

He wanted to make them all come true.

Her lithe body pressed against him, taunting and torturing his senses. Her tongue teased the corner of his mouth, and for a brief moment, Owen considered laying her back against the soft window seat cushions and seducing her until she begged him to take her—honorable promises be damned. The sight of her pebbled nipples jutting toward him made him want to lay claim to every inch of her until she was crying out his name.

"Owen," she murmured.

At last. She'd said it. Not "Your Grace" or even "Huntford," but *Owen*.

He let one last sweet kiss linger before he pulled away. "You are so beautiful," he said, smoothing a few wisps of hair away from her face, "that I forget myself. You don't know how badly I want you."

She blushed. "I like kissing you."

Since the current conversation was not cooling his ardor, he needed to do the sensible thing and put some space between them. He stood, raked a hand through his hair, and walked to his old globe on the shelf where he'd abandoned it decades before. He spun it and let his fingers trail over the oceans and continents until it slowed to a stop.

"There's something else I need to tell you, Anabelle." Upon seeing the stricken look that crossed her face, he quickly added, "I think you'll be pleased."

She looked rather doubtful but smiled bravely.

"Circumstances being what they are," he said, "I'd like to propose that we amend the terms of our agreement."

"I don't understand."

He shrugged, a feeble attempt to appear casual when he felt anything but. "I'm sure you'd like to be with your mother right now, and though Olivia and Rose will be sorely disappointed, I can have someone else make their gowns. If you'd like to go, you're free to do so."

He held his breath as he awaited her response. He'd hoped for at least three months with her, but that was selfish. For some time now, he'd known that she presented no threat to society, and yet, he'd wanted her to stay. To help him understand his sisters; to challenge him when he behaved badly; to brighten the whole damned house.

But he couldn't keep her here like she was some prisoner. He spun the globe again.

She nibbled on her bottom lip. "You're releasing me from my debt?"

It sounded so final. "Yes."

"That's very generous, but...I can't allow you to do that."

"I already did."

"I owe you too much. It wouldn't feel right after all you've done for my family and me. I know I'll never be able to repay you—not unless I discover that I'm an heiress to a long-forgotten fortune."

"Duly noted. However, if you should become an heiress, I'll come to collect your debt. With interest."

"That seems reasonable," she said seriously.

He was teasing, for God's sake. "Anabelle, there is no more debt."

She strode toward him and placed her palm on the globe, stopping it on its axis. "I won't accept outright charity."

He snorted. Couldn't help it. "You were willing to extort money from me. How can you object to charity?"

Her gray eyes flashed at him, and he had his answer. Pride.

"We made a deal, and I intend to honor it. It's the least I can do."

She stood so close that he could smell the soap she used to wash her hair—citrusy and sweet—and her hand lay next to his, somewhere near the North Pole. "Fine." He managed a light tone, as though he couldn't care less one way or the other.

She'd made it clear she was only sticking to their agreement out of a sense of obligation, but at least he knew she wouldn't disappear from his life altogether. Not yet. He exhaled, took her hand from the globe, and held it lightly in his. He had one other option to offer.

"If you'd like to return home and be with your family,

you may. You could work out of your apartment or Mrs. Smallwood's shop, finish Olivia's and Rose's wardrobes, and fulfill your end of the bargain."

He held his breath and waited for her answer.

She let go of his hand and drifted around the room, pausing now and then to inspect various items. Ethereal in her pale nightgown, she ran her fingers over the fabric piled on the tables, ribbons strewn across an old desk, and a yardstick leaning against the window seat. When at last she'd circled the room and stood in front of him once more, she said, "Would you prefer it if I left?"

"No."

She nibbled the tip of her index finger. "There's little I'd be able to do for Mama at home, and I know she's in excellent hands with Dr. Loxton. Daphne can keep me informed of her progress, so... I think I'd like to stay."

"You would?" He dared to hope he was the reason. Or, at least, *a* reason.

"This room is so spacious and bright, and everything I could possibly need is here. If I were to work at the shop, I'd be distracted by customers and other projects. It could easily take me a year to complete the assignment. If I stay, I'll be able to make the dresses more quickly and confer with Rose and Olivia whenever I need to."

"It's settled then. You'll remain here." He spoke quickly, before she had the chance to change her mind. It pricked a little that she was only staying for the conveniences and not because she'd miss him, but at least she was staying. "You may visit your mother and sister whenever you wish."

She beamed. "Thank you, Owen."

"However," he said sternly, "you will *not* walk there unescorted."

"But I am accustomed to walking alone to the dress shop each day. I promise not to attempt another evening visit."

"That is comforting," he said wryly. "I must have your word that you will not go anywhere, especially to your home, unescorted. You may take a footman or, if you can bear it, you could take me."

She opened her mouth to object, but then appeared to stop herself. "You'd walk me to my house?"

"I'd prefer to take the coach. But yes."

"I'm sure you have many more important matters to tend to."

"Not really." Most days he didn't even have time to read a newspaper, but he had time for her.

"I'd love to visit Mama this afternoon," she said timidly. "Just to see how she's getting on without her medicine. But there's no need to rearrange your schedule. I could ask Roger or another footm—"

"How is four o'clock?"

She blinked. "That would be wonderful. Thank you."

"I'll see you then." He gave a cursory bow and turned to leave. If he had to stay in that room alone with her for one more minute he might lock the door, strip off her nightgown, and show her there was much more between them than a simple business arrangement. She was more than his employee, and he was more than a deal to be fulfilled.

He just needed the chance to prove it to her.

Much later that evening, after most of the household had been in bed and dreaming for hours, Anabelle was back in the workroom. One of the sleeves on the dress she was making for Rose had turned out to be puffier than its partner, and she'd decided the only hope of correcting it was to remove the flawed sleeve entirely and start over. Normally, fixing her own mistakes put her in a surly mood.

But as she carefully snipped the threads along the shoulder seam she was unusually content.

She liked the coziness of the night—the inky sky hanging outside her window, the silence that had settled over the house like a warm blanket, and the solitude that gave her imagination free rein. Thoughts of Owen had occupied her all evening. She knew she was foolish to daydream about him, but she gave herself license. Dreaming was less dangerous than doing, and the day had been too magical to stick it in the back of a drawer like a pair of torn stockings and forget about it.

Owen had taken her home for a visit, as promised, and had been most gracious from start to finish. After they'd ridden across Town in his coach, he'd surprised her by escorting her upstairs. He sat patiently in the parlor while she chatted with Daphne in Mama's room, waiting for her to wake. When she did, Anabelle brought Owen into the bedroom and introduced him. Mama kept saying that she must be having visions if there was an honest-to-goodness duke—and a handsome one at that—in her bedchamber. Owen laughed good-naturedly and presented Mama with a gorgeous bouquet of flowers. The smile on her face had melted Anabelle's heart like a pat of butter on a hot plate.

There'd been no more kissing since that morning, but there had been moments of . . . giddiness. Mortifying as it was to admit—even to herself—Owen could make her belly turn a somersault without even saying a word. All it took was his heavy-lidded stare, his hand on the small of her back, or the ironic smile he shot at her when no one else was looking.

Despite her intent to keep their relationship on a purely business level, she couldn't deny that it had evolved into something more complicated. She wouldn't delude herself that he'd offer marriage—the very idea of a duke courting a seamstress was laughable. And yet, the unfairness of it all made her want to scream. Or hurl a porcelain vase at the wall. Why was she less worthy of Owen's love than a gently bred lady? She might not be perfectly at ease in the company of titled lords and ladies, but she had good manners, which was more than she could say for Miss Starling.

Anabelle sniffled and swiped at her eyes. The anger and sadness gnawed at her insides like a rat chewing through a rope. She mustn't let the hurt fester, turning her relationship with Owen into something rotten and putrid. She'd rather enjoy the tenuous truce they'd achieved— and the occasional kiss—for a bit longer.

She'd removed the offending sleeve and was preparing to reduce its puffiness when she heard something in the hallway outside the workroom. Footsteps.

Her breath hitched in her throat. Luckily, she was still dressed. After Owen's unexpected visit this morning, she'd surmised that working in her nightgown was not prudent. Her plain, yellow gown was comfortable enough, and her usual cap kept wisps of hair from falling into her eyes as she worked. The only concession she'd made to the late, or actually, early hour was kicking off her slippers.

She put them on now. And pinched her cheeks for a little color.

She'd heard Owen was attending a ball tonight, but maybe he'd—

"Anabelle?" Olivia whispered through the crack of the slightly ajar nursery door. "Are you still working?"

She rushed to the door, tamping down her disappointment and eyeing the clock as she passed it. "I am," she said, waving Olivia in. Rose tiptoed behind her; both girls were clad in their nightgowns. "What are you two doing up at this hour?"

"I couldn't sleep," Olivia said with an impish grin. "So I checked on Rose, and she was awake, too." Rose rolled her eyes and Olivia quickly added, "Well, she was sleeping so lightly she may as well have been awake. We decided we'd sneak down to the kitchen and help ourselves to a snack. When we noticed your light, we made a detour. Let's go, shall we?"

"What?" Anabelle glanced over her shoulder at the one-sleeved gown, a pitiful sight if ever she saw one. "Oh, no. I can't. I'm in the middle of fixing a—"

Rose grasped Anabelle's forearm and pulled her firmly behind as she began walking down the hall. For a quiet, subdued girl, Rose really was very strong. Anabelle stumbled a little as they rounded a dark corner, and Olivia giggled.

On the way down the stairs, Anabelle whispered, "Do you do this often?"

"More often than Owen knows." Olivia led the way to the kitchen, and when they entered the dark room that still smelled of savory stewed vegetables Anabelle realized she was, indeed, hungry.

Rose lit a drip-covered candle in a rustic pewter holder and set in on the sturdy kitchen table. Copper pots gleamed above the range, a teapot dangled at a jaunty angle over the fireplace, and clean white aprons hung from nails beside the door. No grand paintings or silver-plated serving pieces in sight, thank goodness. Every item in the room was blessedly utilitarian. Anabelle approved.

She sat on a bench beside the table and watched as Olivia and Rose scoured the pantry and raided the shelves. They returned with appetizing bits of cheese, grapes and berries, and an assortment of dainty cakes left over from tea that afternoon, all arranged haphazardly on a large plate. Olivia set the food in the center of the table and poured generous amounts of wine into three glasses. "This should help us sleep," she said, topping off the last glass.

The girls' enthusiasm was infectious. The only thing that could have made the escapade more perfect was if Daphne had been there, too. She would love Olivia and Rose, and of course, the girls would love her—everyone did. Owen had found her delightful without falling the least bit under her spell. Anabelle sighed contentedly.

The sisters sat on the bench opposite her, but as she and Olivia reached for a morsel from the plate, Rose swatted their hands away and raised her wineglass.

"Why didn't I think of that?" Olivia said. "We need to make a toast. Anabelle, would you do the honors?"

She thought of the girls' kind, sweet nature and all they'd had to endure. They'd been abandoned by their mother, left heartbroken by their father's suicide, and unappreciated by the *ton*.

"Yes, I would." Anabelle raised her glass. "To the ones who pulled our hair and braided it at night, the ones who borrowed our dresses and lent us theirs, the ones who read our diaries and kept our secrets. To sisters."

"To sisters!" said Olivia, clinking her glass to Anabelle's.

Rose tapped Olivia on the shoulder, pressed a hand to her chest, and pointed to Anabelle.

"Right," said Olivia. "To sisters *and* sisters of the heart."

Anabelle's eyes stung, and, fearing she'd be reduced to a puddle of tears, she took a gulp of her wine and smiled brightly. "I'm famished. Shall we?"

"It's every woman for herself," announced Olivia. She popped an impressive wedge of cheese in her mouth.

Rose was slightly more timid but did not hesitate to go directly for the sweets. Anabelle followed suit, sampling tarts and little pies. Before long, they'd devoured everything on the platter. Only crumbs remained. Anabelle's eyelids grew heavy, but she so enjoyed the girls' company that she continued sipping her wine and chatting. When the conversation eventually turned to Owen, as she'd hoped it would, she endeavored not to appear overly interested.

But she hung on every word.

"He's at the Milford ball this evening," said Olivia. "Miss Starling mentioned it when I saw her at the musicale yesterday. She was kind enough to sit next to Rose and me. She must have had a dozen admirers trying to curry her favor. But she discouraged them all—politely of course. I wish I had a smidgen of her beauty and grace."

Anabelle wanted to tell Olivia that Miss Starling was

not really a friend and that she was using her and Rose to snare Owen, but she feared Olivia would be devastated to hear it. Instead, Anabelle latched on to Olivia's other comment. "You are every bit as beautiful as Miss Starling. More so, if you ask me."

Olivia erupted into peals of laughter, surely loud enough to awaken the servants. Rose put a finger to her lips to shush her sister.

Anabelle was insulted by Olivia's skepticism. She'd always had an eye for beautiful things; it was part of what made her a talented designer of gowns. She could see the potential in fabrics, frippery, and people. "You don't believe me?"

"Miss Starling is a diamond of the first water," Olivia said. "I'm paste jewelry."

Rose frowned and shook her head. At least she was on Anabelle's side.

Her lips loosened by the wine, Anabelle said, "Miss Starling is the cumbersome train and feathers one must wear before the Queen at Court. You are the stunning silk gown made for whirling around the dance floor in a candlelit ballroom."

Olivia actually blushed. "I liked the whirling part. I shall try to remember your kind description next time I'm tripping over my own feet. Now, what kind of dress is Rose?"

Anabelle thought for a moment. "Rose is a light, shimmery summer frock made for chasing butterflies in the meadow."

Rose smiled and Olivia sighed happily. "Well, it seems Miss Starling is destined to become our sister-in-law," Olivia said. "I, for one, couldn't be more pleased."

Anabelle's heart thudded in her chest. "Why do you say that? I mean, the part about her being destined?"

Olivia leaned forward as though about to impart something salacious. "Just yesterday, Owen told me it was high time he did his duty and married. When I asked him if anyone had captured his fancy he gave me a dark, disgusted look and said he'd probably do as our father would have wanted and shackle himself to Miss Starling. Papa and Mr. Starling were quite chummy before...In any case, Owen said he supposed marrying Miss Starling would be the most expedient course."

"How utterly romantic." Anabelle tipped her wineglass back and swallowed the last drop.

Olivia giggled and then went silent. She and Rose were both focused on something behind Anabelle.

And then she *knew*.

"What's romantic?" Owen's deep, rich voice sent shivers down her spine.

She turned and saw him leaning casually against the doorjamb. His hair was mussed and his shirttail was showing on one side. Anabelle couldn't recall him ever looking as handsome.

"Well?" he asked, scowling at her. Or perhaps he was scowling at her cap. Either way, Anabelle had no intention of answering his question.

Olivia, however, managed to find her tongue. "Ah, we were just having a girls' chat. How was the ball?"

"Splendid." He plopped himself down on the bench next to Anabelle and eyed her empty wineglass. "Why are you three sitting in the kitchen at this hour of the morning?" She detected the hint of a slur to his words.

"Probably the same thing you are," Olivia said. "Shall I round you up a snack?"

He raised his brows and looked pointedly at the empty plate in the center of the table. "Is there anything left?"

"Oh, I'm sure I can find a stale crust of bread." Olivia began to rise from the bench but Rose motioned for her to stay and headed to the pantry herself.

"So, tell me," Olivia said gleefully, "which ladies did you dance with tonight?"

"If you're so bloody curious, you should have come."

"Owen!" Olivia shot a pointed look in Anabelle's direction.

"Sorry," he said. "If you're so *damned* curious."

Olivia rolled her eyes. "Forgive my brother," she said to Anabelle, "I fear he's foxed."

He grunted but did not deny it. Perhaps that was why he seemed even more attractive than usual. Although he could not be called charming by any stretch, he was not as firmly in control as he normally was.

His sister prodded him some more. "If you tell me your dance partners I shall fetch you a glass of brandy."

Anabelle did not think it wise to bribe him with more drink, but she had to admit she was oddly curious about his dance partners. She supposed it wasn't unlike a starving person asking for a description of each course of a feast. It would be torture, but at least she'd know what she'd missed.

"Lady Portman, Miss Morley, and Miss Starling. There's a decanter on the sideboard in my study."

"How many times with each?" Olivia pressed.

"Once, once, and twice. Don't be stingy with the stuff."

Olivia flipped her thick brown braid over her shoulder

and sighed as she rose from the table. "Behave yourself while I am gone."

The moment she left, Owen reached under the table and squeezed Anabelle's hand. In a gruff whisper he said, "I missed you."

Her face grew hot. Although she longed to believe him, she sincerely doubted that he had spared her a thought while drinking champagne and spinning beautiful women around the ballroom dance floor. "You didn't miss anything. It was not an especially exciting evening in the workroom."

"No?" He leaned closer, warm breath tickling her ear. "It *could* have been exciting."

She bit her bottom lip and tried to scoot farther away from him on the bench. His teasing was exquisite torture. "Not now."

He would not let go of her hand. Instead, he traced little circles on her wrist. "When?"

"I don't know."

"I thought about you all night. Give me a time."

Anabelle craned her neck to see where Rose was. The pantry door was still ajar. "Later."

"Fine. I'll come to the workroom in an hour."

She opened her mouth to tell him that under no circumstances should he venture anywhere near her end of the corridor, but at that very moment, Rose returned carrying Owen's snack. Anabelle kicked Owen's shin—hard—but not before Rose's keen gaze flicked to their joined hands beneath the table. She gracefully set the plate on the table, sat, and smiled like a cat presented with a saucer of warm milk.

Anabelle sprang off of the bench. "This was delightful," she said to Rose. "But I'm afraid I must turn in." She swallowed and turned to Owen. How her fingers itched to slap the smirk off his face. "Good night..."—she couldn't imagine how she'd choke out the words—"...Your Grace."

Chapter Fourteen

Anabelle fled the kitchen, and in the hallway almost bumped into Olivia, returning with Owen's brandy.

"Where are you going?" Olivia called.

"To bed. Thanks for a wonderful evening." Anabelle was already halfway up the stairs. "I'll see you tomorrow." When she reached her room, she locked her door, splashed her face with cool water, and took several deep breaths.

Owen wouldn't risk coming to the workroom in the wee hours of the morning.

Would he?

Beyond tired, but doubtful she'd be able to sleep, she forced herself to change into her nightgown, brush out and braid her hair, and climb into bed. If he came to her door, she'd simply pretend to be asleep.

Half an hour later, she heard the girls shuffle upstairs and settle into their rooms. Another half hour passed. Perhaps he wasn't coming after all.

He probably viewed their earlier conversation as playful flirtation and would have no recollection of it tomorrow. Ignoring the stab of disappointment in her belly, she fluffed her pillow, flipped to her side, and squeezed her eyes shut. Thank heaven he had the common sense to go to his bed and stay away from hers. No good could come from his silver-tongued compliments and knee-buckling kisses. Dwelling on the duke's broad shoulders and smoldering eyes only distracted her from her objective: fulfilling her end of the deal so she could return home.

To make herself drowsy, she counted stitches in her head—the simple, boring kind that wound round and round. Her breathing slowed, the wine relaxed her muscles, and sleep beckoned.

The soft knock on her door nearly made her jump out of her skin.

"Belle."

Foolishly, her heart leapt at the sound of his voice. He was in the workroom, thankfully, and not in the hallway where his sisters might hear him. Covering her head with a pillow, she reminded herself of the plan. Ignore the knocking. Feign sleep.

But the next sound was more of a thumping. "Anabelle, I know you're not asleep."

He could not possibly know that. She buried her head deeper and hummed softly to drown out his voice.

When the thumping turned to pounding, she bolted out of bed, dashed to the door, and hauled it open. "Are you trying to wake the entire household?"

"Just you." His boyish grin melted the edges of her resolve. "It would take a thunderbolt from Zeus himself to wake my sisters, and the staff has retired for the night. I would never take foolish risks with your reputation."

The soft sincerity of his tone warmed her.

"Now," he said wickedly, "come out and play."

She shook her head firmly. "I can't."

"Want me to come in?"

"No!" She closed the door all but a crack and spoke through it. "I have to work tomorrow, and seeing as how you're a duke, you must have responsibilities as well. Go to bed."

"Do you know what your problem is?"

How dare he imply she was the one with problems? "Enlighten me."

"You work too hard." He reached through the crack and tugged playfully on her sleeve. "Come with me. I want to show you something." Mischief gleamed in his eyes, and candlelight glowed in the workroom behind him.

"What have you done? Please tell me you haven't moved the panels that were laid out on the long table or touched the fabric on the shelf because I had it arranged just so, and—"

"Trust me." He gently but firmly pushed the door open and pulled her into the workroom.

Only, it didn't feel like the workroom.

The soft quilt that he'd wrapped around her shoulders the morning before had been spread in the center of the floor. A large candelabrum rested on a stack of atlases to one side, and pillows from the window seat were strewn around the blanket. Without her spectacles, the whole room was blurry and pleasantly dreamlike. The window sash was raised, the night breeze sweetening the air with grass and honeysuckle. Outside, leaves rustled, insects chirped, and the occasional bird trilled in a natural, soothing cadence.

Anabelle's breath hitched in her throat. He'd done this for her.

"See? I didn't disturb anything," he said proudly.

"What is all this for?"

He led her to the blanket. "Sit and I'll show you."

Although she was suspicious, she did as he asked, drawing her bare feet beneath the hem of her nightgown. Owen shed his jacket; his dark green waistcoat was unbuttoned, revealing a fine white shirt, untucked from his breeches. He sat behind her, so close that his warm breath fanned her neck.

"I have noticed," he said, placing his hands on her shoulders, "that you are constantly holed up in this room, working. You spend too much time hunched over ball gowns. Too little time wearing them."

She stifled a laugh. He should know that seamstresses didn't own ball gowns.

"At the ball earlier, I kept wishing you were there. I imagined you in blue silk, chestnut tresses cascading over your shoulders, gray eyes sparkling. Every man would want you for his dance partner, Belle, but *I'd* be the one holding you, twirling you around the floor."

Ridiculous. She opened her mouth to tell him so, but—

Oh my. His fingers kneaded the tight muscles just below her neck and around her shoulders, slowly, with just the right pressure to ease out the tension without causing pain.

Her eyes shut, her shoulders relaxed, and her head lolled forward. Heaven.

He tended to every spot that yearned for attention. She had only to wish for him to caress her neck and scalp, and he did. She merely thought it might feel nice if he were to massage the length of her spine, and he did. He lingered in the sensitive places, like the small of her back and the nape of her neck.

"Loosen this," he whispered, plucking at the neck of her nightgown.

As though in a trance, she obeyed. Cool air roved over her exposed shoulders, and she shivered, craving the touch of his hands on her skin.

"God, Belle." He skimmed his fingers down her neck and across her shoulder, and, with his mouth, traced the same path, wet and hot.

She fell further under his spell.

"Take out your braid," he murmured against her skin.

She did his bidding, eager to prolong this pleasure. The ribbon slipped off easily, and she raked her fingers through her plaited hair until it flowed in soft ripples.

Owen buried his face in it, inhaling deeply. "You smell good. I wish you would wear your hair like this all the time."

She chuckled. "And here I thought you were fond of my cap."

"I'm fond of taking it off."

"Mmmm."

He pushed her hair in front of her shoulders and continued to stroke her back. His fingertips trailed over the thin fabric of her nightrail, across her shoulders, down her arms, up her sides, and down her spine again, leaving delicious goosebumps in their wake. In utter satisfaction, she arched her back and prayed he wouldn't stop touching her.

"You are beautiful." His hands drifted lower then, cupping her bottom and kneading it until she feared she'd melt into a puddle right there on the quilt.

He was so close to her, yet she could not see him, could only feel the heat from his body behind hers and his hands, which seemed to roam everywhere. "This feels... nice," she breathed.

"Think of it as an appetizer, the soup before the roasted duck." His hands skimmed across her hips, then around to caress the tops of her thighs. Moisture gathered between her legs, and tiny pulses of pleasure beat there. "I highly recommend the roasted duck. Will you try it?"

She leaned her head back against his shoulder. Here in the candlelight it was easy to forget the difference in their stations. They were just a man and a woman who liked each other and who, naturally, wanted to be together. The consequences of lying with him, however, were too great. Not only did she have to work for him for the next several weeks, but there could be a baby. And she did not wish to give her virginity to a man who would never consider marrying her. She had her pride.

With a sigh, she reached back to caress his neck as he nuzzled hers. "I can't make love with you, Owen. It's too risky."

"I know. Just let me touch you and make you feel... amazing." He kissed a spot under her ear that shot shivers through her limbs.

She didn't want to say good night to him. Not yet. Trusting him to keep his word, she relented. "I suppose we could have one more course."

With a growl of approval, he tugged the hem of her nightgown up and exposed the tops of her thighs. She wore nothing at all underneath her nightrail, and cool air kissed her skin, lingering on the damp curls between her legs. His fingertips caressed her thighs lightly, then slipped beneath her nightgown and around to her back. As though they had all the time in the world, he slowly rubbed her shoulders, back, and bottom. This time, no fabric separated him from her, and she knew the bliss of his hands on her skin.

"My God, you're perfect. I want to explore every inch of you." He slowly swept a hand up her side, grazing her breast. "Do you like this?"

Her breath hitched. "Yes."

"Just wait." He shifted closer until she was nestled between his thighs, her arms wrapped around her bent knees. Gently, he stroked her sides, coming closer and closer to her breasts, teasing her, until she thought she'd die if he did not caress them.

At last, he slipped his hands around and took the weight of her breasts, gently tweaking her erect nipples with his thumbs. All the while, he nibbled on her ear and shoulder.

A small cry escaped her. This exquisite pleasure, this lovely intimacy, was new to her. Oh, she would regret this in the morning, but it was impossible to do so now. Owen was completely intent on pleasing her, and she gave herself up to the moment. To him.

Her breasts had grown fuller during the two weeks she had been here. Delicious, plentiful meals and less walking had restored her natural curves. Owen seemed to approve.

The pulsing at her core demanded more, but she didn't know what. She tried to turn and press her body against his, but he stilled her.

"I want to kiss you," she said.

He let out a low, sultry chuckle. "Oh, there will be kissing. Later. Lean back against me."

She did as he asked, sighing deeply and reveling in the hard warmth of his chest.

"That's good. Now, keep your eyes closed, and think only of how good this feels—how good we are together."

He hiked her nightgown up farther, so her legs were completely exposed. Slowly, he traced a path from her knees to her inner thigh, drawing little circles that made her muscles clench. With his other hand, he lightly squeezed her breast, teasing the nipple with his palm.

"Part your knees," he said gruffly.

Anabelle swallowed. She had never let anyone touch her there. She didn't even touch *herself* there. But she'd already crossed many lines tonight. What was one more?

Opening herself to him was akin to walking into a lion's cage. But he'd never hurt her. More importantly, he'd stop the instant she asked him to—assuming she had the presence of mind to ask him.

He gently stroked her legs, his hands warm and soothing. When he ventured close to the curls covering her entrance, her muscles tensed.

"It's all right," he said. "You don't need to be afraid of me. Of this."

"I know."

"Though it might seem strange, there's something very right about you and me. Together. Do you feel it, too?"

The sincerity, the vulnerability, in his voice touched her soul. But he was wrong about this. They did not belong together—not truly. They were from different worlds, and when she was done with her job, she would return to hers.

His hands stilled as he awaited her answer.

She had to be truthful. "I don't know if being with you is right. But I like it. I like you."

He chuckled softly again. "I suppose that will have to do. For now."

A breeze swept through the window, making the flames of the candelabrum flicker wildly. Shadows danced about the room, a cozy and rather perfect setting for an indiscretion of gigantic proportions. The house was so still she could imagine they were its sole inhabitants; so quiet that her soft sighs echoed in her ears. She lowered her eyelids and willed herself to relax as Owen did wicked—and wonderful—things to her body.

With deft, experienced fingers, he explored her slick folds and found the sensitive spot where all her yearning centered. She lost track of time as she surrendered to the desire that smoldered inside her, ignored for far too long. For once, she did not dwell on Mama's health or paying their rent or having enough to eat. She only focused on Owen and the way he made her feel.

In his arms, she was no longer a seamstress, but a seductress.

The lovely things he murmured in her ear were as arousing as his touch. With him, she felt beautiful, desirable, and more. She felt cared for.

The room grew warmer and the musky scent of her body enveloped them. Her hips rose off his lap as she pushed against his hand, increasing the pressure on the nub that he expertly teased. He eased a finger into her, filling her, coaxing her closer to the edge. She moaned softly, desperate for release.

"I knew this passion was inside you," he whispered. "You are everything I'd hoped."

His words confused her. She wanted to turn around. Straddle him. Kiss him. But she balanced on a precipice so high that the tiniest movement could send her hurtling over. He seemed to understand.

He stroked the sweet spot faster and harder. Her heartbeat thudded in her ears and the muscles in her stomach clenched in wonderful anticipation. She cried out as her climax neared, unprepared for the strength of it. At last it overpowered her, wave after wave shuddering through her. She bucked against his hand as her pent-up passion found release.

She had never known it was possible to feel so powerful yet vulnerable, so corporeal yet ethereal, at the same time. And long after she returned to her real life, she would remember this night, and be grateful to Owen for showing her a side of herself she never knew existed.

Owen kissed Anabelle's neck, inhaling the citrusy scent of her hair and savoring the taste of her satin skin. God, she was beautiful.

And he wanted her.

Beyond tonight.

Watching her climax had been the single most erotic experience of his life. She'd not only given herself up to pleasure, but actively pursued it.

Nothing could have aroused him more.

He held her close as her body relaxed and her breathing slowed. She wriggled around to face him, her hair a cloud of wild curls. Her cheeks glowed pink in the light of the candles, and her nightgown hung off her shoulder. As she smiled shyly at him, his already rock-hard rod twitched.

She'd beguiled him. In two weeks she'd evolved from a pale, bespectacled, tightly pinned-up seamstress into a siren capable of seducing any mortal. Or immortal.

Capable of seducing him.

Their budding relationship defied both convention and explanation. The only thing he knew with certainty was he didn't want her going anywhere anytime soon.

She slipped her hands inside his unbuttoned waistcoat and pressed her palms against his chest. "That was... amazing. Completely ill-advised and worthy of regret tomorrow morning... but amazing, nonetheless."

He loved that she said exactly what she was thinking. And that she'd called the experience amazing. He puffed out his chest and grinned. "Regrets are forbidden."

She shot him a sultry, heavy-lidded look that made his breeches even tighter. "Fine. Then I guess I shall have no regrets about this." She dragged the hem of his shirt up and raked her fingernails lightly over his chest. In one graceful motion she sat astride him, kissing him like her appetite had merely been whetted.

Good God.

He was sorely tempted to whisk her off to his bed and keep her there for the better part of a week. However, dawn would soon intrude and servants would roam the halls. He'd promised to protect her from any whisper of scandal. Gradually, he lowered the intensity of their kiss and pulled away, cupping her smooth cheeks in his hands. "The sun will be up within the hour, and you need to sleep."

She smiled sheepishly. "I am tired—in a good way. I'm fond of the roast duck."

He chuckled softly and kissed her forehead. How he'd love to sleep with her curled up next to him. He normally avoided cuddling, which was an obligation—like wearing stiff, formal breeches to a ball or attending the funeral of a little-known acquaintance. Yet, tonight, he felt cheated that his time with Anabelle was cut short.

He helped her stand, then, without warning, swept her up in his arms.

Laughing, she nestled into his chest as he carried her into her bedchamber. He laid her on the thick mattress, pulled the covers over her, and gave her one last long kiss.

"Owen, I meant to talk to you earlier about Olivia and Rose."

"They're not in imminent danger, are they?"

"Oh, no," she reassured him.

"Then let it wait until later. Good night. You're not to rise before eleven o'clock—understand?"

She yawned. "I'll sleep for a couple of hours, but I don't want to miss breakfast."

"Good thinking."

He laced his fingers through hers, and they gazed at each other for the space of several heartbeats. This was the moment when he should say how lovely she was or how much he cared for her. Although, he would think both things were painfully obvious by now, even if he was not the most demonstrative person.

He'd never met a more beautiful woman, and although he'd never been in love, it might be easy to love her. She was feisty, loyal, and honest—if one discounted the occasional extortion scheme.

It was on the tip of his tongue to tell her all that. Instead, he wrapped one of her tresses around a finger. "I'm not sure I'll recognize you at breakfast with your spectacles and cap. I don't suppose I could convince you to burn the cap?"

Her tired smile was tinged with disappointment. He felt like a cad.

"I'll see you tomorrow," he said. "Or, rather, later today."

"Good night, Owen."

He left through the door adjoining the workroom and set everything to rights before extinguishing the candles and skulking back to his room.

After shedding his clothes, he stretched out on his bed and closed his eyes, but the hurt look on Belle's face haunted him.

He'd done the right thing. Hadn't he?

Misleading her was the worst thing he could do, and their relationship couldn't be anything more than stolen moments of pleasure and companionship. All in all, a much better arrangement than marriage. They'd never become bitter or grow tired of each other's company. They'd simply enjoy their time together while it lasted.

But sleep didn't come quickly. He kept counting damned dresses in his head, growing agitated each time he reached fifteen, the number Olivia had informed him Belle had yet to complete.

His time left with Belle was measured not in years or months or weeks.

It was measured in dresses.

Chapter Fifteen

Embellish: (1) To add special stitching or other items of a decorative nature to a gown. (2) To exaggerate the truth slightly in order to spare one's pride.

Anabelle missed breakfast in the morning. Although she woke in time, she ignored the gnawing sensation in her belly. She wasn't ready to face Owen, his sisters, or Dennison just yet. Instead, she tightly coiled and pinned her hair and covered the bun with her cap.

Thinking about the night she had shared with Owen made her flush hot all over. Her introduction to pleasure had been natural and beautiful and every bit as lovely as she'd hoped. If only she could bask in the glow without the intrusion of reality a bit longer.

But she and Owen had crossed a line. How was she supposed to behave toward him now? When others were present, she'd have to pretend nothing of an earth-shattering nature had transpired between them. The idea of keeping their relationship a secret felt wrong, like keeping a beautiful songbird covered in a cage.

However, she was not naïve. She and Owen each had roles to play—that of seamstress and duke. And she would do well to remember that. She mentally added the item to her List of Nevers: "No matter how tempting it is to dream, one must never forget the boundaries of one's station in life."

The thought tangled up her insides, and she wondered how they might act toward one another in private. She had no experience to guide her. Flirting might be in order *if* she were the flirting type. Alas, she'd never developed the skill. They might talk, but she doubted he was interested in news that satin spencers of gray or orange trimmed with buttons *à la militaire* were all the rage. Likewise, she could not comment intelligently on the latest maneuverings in Parliament. There must be *something* they could discuss besides servants' caps and doctor's bills. But what?

She didn't anticipate flowers or a declaration of any sort, but some acknowledgement of their friendship might be nice. Something to make her feel like more than a drunken night's diversion.

Anabelle sighed and threaded a needle. In the harsh light of morning, the workroom was hardly the romantic retreat it had been last night. Mounds of fabric covered every surface in the room, reminders of the many dresses she still had to complete to fulfill the deal. She might have believed the prior evening had been a dream if one of the atlases resting on the bookshelf didn't have several drops of cooled wax on its cover. She had checked it—just to be sure.

A tap at the door sent her heart into her throat. "Come in," she called, heat creeping up her neck.

"Good afternoon, dear," said Mrs. Pottsbury. "Dennison said you had a message delivered this morning but that you hadn't risen yet." Wonderful. If the butler hadn't already thought Anabelle was a lazy opportunist, he must be convinced now. "When you didn't come down for breakfast I feared you were sick. You know, I believe you are a little flushed."

"I'm fine," Anabelle said, certain she was becoming redder by the minute. "Sorry I worried you. Since I overslept, I wanted to get to work as soon as possible."

"It's not like you." The housekeeper eyed Anabelle critically, as though she might be harboring a ghastly illness. "In any case, I told Dennison that I would deliver your message and check on you personally."

Anabelle took the letter, which was addressed in Daphne's handwriting, and frowned. If Daphne had paid for a messenger instead of using the Post, the contents must be urgent. Her fingers trembled as she unfolded the note.

"Are you sure you are all right, dear?" the housekeeper asked doubtfully.

"Yes. Thank you for bringing this."

"Ah, that's fine, then. See that you make it down for lunch, and be careful that you don't take a chill." With a jangle of her keys, Mrs. Pottsbury swept out of the nursery.

The moment she was gone, Anabelle said a quick prayer that Mama had not taken a turn for the worse. Taking a deep breath, she read the note.

Dearest Belle,

    I simply could not wait for your next visit to tell you the events of this morning. I awoke in my chair as usual, and when I looked over at Mama's bed, she was

*not in it, but instead, standing next to it. I was horri-
fied, at first, to find her there, wobbling on unsteady
legs—I was certain she'd fall and hurt herself and
scolded her for trying to go somewhere without me.*

*However, I then realized that, for the first time in
several weeks, she was out of bed, and she'd done it on
her own. When I asked her what had possessed her to
try to walk by herself she sheepishly told me that she
was hungry and didn't want to wake me. She was hungry! Her appetite is returning—a miracle to be sure.
Even better, though, is her eagerness to rejoin the world
of the living.*

*You are forever teasing me about being too cheer-
ful and optimistic. I think you will agree, however, that
Mama's progress is cause for great celebration. We
have your generous duke to thank, as well as Dr. Loxton. I hope I can forgive Mr. Conwell one day but fear
that day is a long way off. In the meantime, I will focus
on Mama's recovery.*

*I know you will want to see Mama and witness her
transformation for yourself, but you may believe me—
she is vastly improved from her grave condition just
two days ago.*

*It is only because of your valiant efforts and sac-
rifices that Mama has survived and none of us has
starved. I hope you are well and look forward to seeing you so that we may rejoice together.*

Your loving sister,
Daph

Anabelle read the letter again to make sure she'd
understood correctly.

Mama had gotten out of bed.

She was improving.

The note slipped from Anabelle's hands and fell to the floor; hot tears sprang to her eyes. Her heart was so full of joy, she feared it might burst. As she looked out the window at the dark gray clouds, she thought she'd never seen such a beautiful overcast day. Who needed the glare of a brilliant sun or the incessant chirping of happy birds? There was much to be said for the quiet, unassuming calm that accompanied a perfectly dreary day.

"Anabelle?"

She turned from the window to see Olivia and Rose standing behind her, concern creasing their brows. She must look a wreck. Tears streamed down her cheeks, and although she wanted to reassure them, her throat was too tight to speak.

"What's wrong?" Olivia asked.

Anabelle shook her head, picked up Daphne's letter, and handed it to Olivia.

Rose looked over her shoulder, and when both girls finished reading, they smiled. "Your mother is improving?" Olivia asked. "You're crying because you're happy?"

Feeling foolish, but not really caring, Anabelle nodded.

Rose clasped her hands under her chin, and her eyes glistened. Olivia bounced happily. "This is wonderful!"

The girls joined Anabelle on the window seat, wrapped their arms around her, and began crying, too. There was not a handkerchief to be had among the three of them, so much sniffling ensued until the tears finally petered out.

A rather violent hiccup escaped Anabelle's throat, sending them all into fits of giggles. "I think that one or both of you ought to try on a gown so I can keep up the pretense of working and avoid being sacked."

"Oh, yes," Olivia said. "Being sacked would definitely spoil your day, and that would be a shame after the wonderful start."

Anabelle hugged each sister fervently before picking up her needle again.

If last night had been magical, this morning had been miraculous.

She couldn't wait to see what the afternoon would bring.

Immediately after tea, Anabelle met Owen in the foyer for his promised drive across Town to visit Mama. He stood next to a gilt table, rifling through notes and calling cards left on an ornate silver stray, and her breath caught at the sight of him. His dark hair hung over the slash of his brows, and the angles of his face were somehow both harsh and beautiful. Though he barely moved, a vibrant energy flowed out of him and seeped under her skin.

Olivia had informed Owen about the wonderful change in Anabelle's mother and insisted that he escort her home for a visit. Although she really shouldn't take off another afternoon or monopolize Owen's time, she told herself the visit would be quick. She'd use the coach ride to figure out the rules of their unlikely but very real relationship. Her pulse skittered at the thought of broaching the subject, but broach it she would. And she still wanted to bring up the matter of his sisters. The lines she'd practiced in the workroom had sounded very diplomatic to her own ears. Pity she couldn't remember a word.

He turned as she approached, a smile stretching lazily across his face. "Are you ready?"

She'd thought she was. But with him standing so close it was impossible to appear cool and unaffected. Dennison rolled his eyes as he handed Owen his hat.

"Yes." She felt slightly cheated that she couldn't take his arm as they walked outside, but that was silly. A few moments later they were ensconced in the private luxury of his coach and could speak freely.

Owen sat on the bench opposite her. "I'm happy to hear your mother is improving. I've asked Dr. Loxton to meet us at your home so he can give you his professional opinion as well. I thought it might give you some added peace of mind."

"Thank you." It was an undeniably kind and thoughtful gesture, but his manner was polite and distant—at least compared to last evening. Her earlier joy wilted.

"Last night..." he said.

"Yes?"

"...you mentioned that you wanted to talk with me about Olivia and Rose."

"Yes." She swallowed her disappointment and straightened her spectacles. "Your sisters are curious about your life. They want you to confide in them more."

He took on the dazed look of a boxer who's received a blow to the head. "What?"

"They'd like to know more about you. What you do during the day, your views on various subjects, your marriage plans—"

"Christ, Belle."

She shrugged. "They seem to think a wife would soften some of your rough edges."

"Is this about—"

"No! I'm simply trying to help you. You wanted to

understand your sisters better. They want the same thing. Only, the three of you need to talk with each other."

"I sincerely doubt Rose and Olivia are interested in my daily activities. Why would they care about tenant problems and taxes and sheep?"

"Maybe they wouldn't. I cannot say, but I don't think you should underestimate them."

He raked a hand through his hair. "My private life is none of their concern. They don't need to know the sordid details."

She flinched. Last night had not seemed sordid to her. "You're embarrassed."

Regret washed over his face. "Not of you, Belle. But of some of the things I've done. I haven't always set the best example."

"I'm not suggesting that you discuss *those* types of details with your sisters. Rose and Olivia are interested in knowing about the proper young women that you may one day marry—those who could be their sister-in-law."

He stroked his chin as he gazed at her for several moments; the rumbling of the coach's wheels over cobbled streets was the only sound. "I just want to know what Olivia and Rose are plotting. They're keeping something from me, probably because they fear I'll lock them in their rooms for the next two months—an idea with significant merit. I don't see how talking about my bloody dance partners will make a difference."

"Well," she said dryly, "when you have a conversation, you share some information, and then the other party shares. If you want to know more about Rose and Olivia, you have to reveal more of yourself. They'll follow suit. When they *do* talk to you, you must listen without issuing judgment."

"I knew it." He leaned forward, elbows on knees. "They confided in you, didn't they? Are they involved in anything that could hurt them? Tell me that much."

"No." Although Rose's budding romance with the stable master could be problematic in many ways, she didn't think Rose could get hurt. For the time being, at least, there was no opportunity for her to be with him, so... "If I believed either of them was in physical danger, I would tell you."

He nodded, but had the cynical expression of an older brother worried about myriad misfortunes befalling his sisters.

They had almost reached Anabelle's street. "There's one more thing." She had debated whether to say anything about Lord Winthrope to Owen. She could never reveal the earl's secret. But if Owen could figure it out without her help, then she wasn't violating her List of Nevers. "I think I may know what happened to Rose the night that she disappeared at the house party."

His eyes focused sharply on her. "You know what changed my sister?"

"Not for certain. I need to find out a bit more. But, in the meantime, she needs to feel safe. She needs to know that you'll stand by her no matter what."

Owen lifted his chin as though mildly insulted. "She already knows that."

The coach pulled up in front of her building. Anabelle reached across the cab and laid a hand on his knee. "But she—and Olivia—might like hearing it once in a while."

His beautiful mouth was closed in a tight, thin line. Finally, he said, "I don't see Loxton's coach yet, but I'm sure he'll be here soon. I'll send him up."

"You're not going to come upstairs?"

"No. I thought I'd give you and your mother and sister some privacy. Please give them both my best."

"Of course." Despite the warm sentiment, his distant manner gave Anabelle a chill. Wobbly and confused, she gathered her reticule, patted her cap, and edged toward the door where a footman waited outside.

Owen reached out and squeezed her arm, stopping her. "You're different today." His tone walked the line between hurt and accusatory.

She was different? She shook her head, trying to dislodge the cobwebs which were surely there. Sitting back against the velvet squabs, she raised a brow and smiled. "I suppose I am different. I'm wearing several more articles of clothing today. My nightgown didn't seem appropriate for a cross-town coach ride. Also, I'm making a valiant attempt to adhere to basic social strictures."

"That's better." He grinned, and her traitorous heart skipped a beat. "I didn't mean to imply that you should traipse around in a filmy nightgown. I wouldn't object, you understand, but I appreciate the need for clothes, on occasion. After last night, though, it was a shock to see you in your cap, spectacles, and drab gown."

"Careful, Your Grace, you'll turn my head."

He grimaced. "Don't call me that."

"Why not? Last night didn't change who we are. You're still a duke. I'm still a penniless seamstress."

"That's *not* who you are."

She leaned forward and enunciated carefully, willing him to understand. "Yes, it is. I work for a living and earn a deplorable wage making beautiful gowns for wealthy, privileged ladies. I am a seamstress."

He shook his head as though disgusted and gazed outside.

She tried a different tack. "You aren't the same as last night either. Today you are in utter control—a duke from the toes of your polished boots to the folds of your starched cravat. This is who you are. A member of the *ton*'s upper crust. A dashing aristocrat."

With a hollow laugh he said, "I pray to God I'm more than that." Stiffly, he opened the door, stepped out of the coach, and helped her down, leaving her wondering what on earth she'd said wrong.

Owen watched as Anabelle walked inside and up the stairs toward her rooms. He waited another minute and then went inside, knocked on the landlady's door, and heard her shuffle toward it.

"Who is it?" she called through the scraped and paint-chipped door.

"The Duke of Huntford."

After a beat of silence, "Sure, and I'm Marie Antoinette."

For the love of—"Mrs. Bowman, I apologize for coming unannounced. Miss Honeycote is upstairs visiting with her mother and sister. Could I please have a word?"

She opened the door a crack. "Hmm. I'd heard you'd escorted Anabelle to visit her mother." Her wise old eyes traveled the length of him as though he were a ruffian straight off the streets. "Very well. Come in."

The landlady's apartment was stuffed with furniture, and almost every surface was covered with knickknacks and decorative objects. He felt cramped the moment he entered.

She pointed to the portrait of a stern-faced man above her mantel. "When my husband passed—God rest his soul—I decided to rent out the rooms upstairs. I had to clear out those rooms, of course, but I couldn't bring myself to sell the things we'd accumulated during our wonderful life together. So it's a bit crowded."

Owen doubted she'd disposed of a single item since the reign of George the First.

She waved him toward a faded green sofa, where he sat between a tabby cat and a silver antique that looked part candlestick, part serving platter. The cat was sleeping. At least he hoped it was sleeping.

"Shall I prepare tea, Your Grace?"

"Thank you, no. I won't take much of your time. As you may know, Miss Honeycote has been working for me."

Mrs. Bowman arched a sparse white brow. "I'd heard."

He shifted on the couch, and the cat's tail twitched.

"Actually, she's making gowns for both of my sisters."

"I see." Mrs. Bowman laced her arthritic fingers with unexpected grace and scrutinized him as thoroughly as any queen might.

He'd better get to the point. "I'd like to pay the Honey-cotes' rent, in advance, for the next year." He handed her a pouch of coins. "I've included a sum for you as well—all I ask is that you not mention anything to the Honeycotes."

"You don't want them to know that you're paying their rent?"

"Not yet."

"And why not, Your Grace?"

Anabelle was too proud to accept an outright gift. She'd insisted on staying to complete the dresses for his sisters even after he'd released her from their agreement. "I would prefer to be discreet."

Although the woman's eyes were cloudy with age, they pinned him to the sofa. She clinked the bag of coins against her open palm. "Miss Honeycote is a fine girl who was taught the manners of a lady—her grandpapa was a viscount, you know."

"*What?*" His heart thudded against his ribs. Why would she keep that from him?

"He wasn't happy when his son married a common sort of girl and refused to support them. Anabelle's father made ends meet somehow, but after he died, her family fell on hard times."

Owen wrestled with this knowledge. Belle was the granddaughter of a viscount, hell bent on insisting she was nothing but a seamstress.

"Anabelle is a fine girl," Mrs. Bowman repeated, "who would do just about anything for her mother and sister. I'm sure there are some who would take advantage of her dire circumstances."

The cat beside Owen stretched a paw sleepily and dug its razorlike claws into his leg; he pried the animal off and turned his attention back to the landlady. "You misunderstand. She's working for me—as a seamstress. I'm simply trying to help her family."

"And do you routinely pay the rent of your servants' families? Do you even know their families or where they live?"

He pondered this. "No. But perhaps I should." He stood and walked to the door. "I don't intend to hurt Miss Honeycote."

The gray-haired woman smiled sadly. "Your kind never does."

Chapter Sixteen

$\mathcal{O}$ver the course of the next four weeks, Anabelle's mother continued to recover. Although still thin and tired, she no longer spent the majority of time in bed. During Anabelle's frequent visits home, she rejoiced at the rosy tinge to Mama's cheeks. Even better was the return of the woman Anabelle remembered—who worried and chattered, and occasionally meddled.

During a recent visit, she'd overheard Mama talking to a neighbor in hushed tones about her plans to throw Daphne into the path of a dashing young viscount—proof Mama was on the mend. Anabelle was ecstatic, if nervous about Mama's matchmaking tendencies. At least she focused the majority of her efforts on Daphne rather than on Anabelle, whom she no doubt recognized as a lost cause.

Dr. Loxton, who now called to check on Mama only once a week, concluded that she had most likely suffered from a bad case of the croup, exacerbated by the near-fatal doses of opiates that Conwell had prescribed. Owen had notified the authorities and had gone so far as to search for Conwell himself, but the lout appeared to have left London. Anabelle was so incensed she often dreamt of subjecting the man to various forms of public humiliation. She imagined printing a large advertisement in the newspaper proclaiming him a fraud and requiring him to sell the paper on a street corner. Or, perhaps, he should have to *eat* the entire newspaper. Or parade down Bond Street wearing nothing *but* the newspaper.

She could amuse herself thus all day.

Devising means of torture for Conwell was vastly preferable to thinking of Owen. Ever since the night of their encounter in the workroom, he'd avoided her. He was rarely home, and when he was, he holed up in his study, working. He hadn't escorted her to visit Mama and Daph again, leaving the job to one of the footmen. On the rare occasion when Anabelle saw Owen—at breakfast or in passing—he greeted her like a friend of his sisters, or perhaps a distant cousin.

Each civil remark and polite comment about the weather was a little stab wound, killing her slowly and painfully. It would have been more humane had he told her outright that he never should have given in to the drunken urge to hold her, kiss her... and more.

Only the hungry looks he sometimes cast her way gave her hope. One morning last week, she'd been in Olivia's room, showing her how she could use a hot iron to curl a few tendrils around her face. A frisson of awareness skittered down Anabelle's spine, making her tingle all over. She turned toward the door and saw Owen standing there, staring at her with undisguised longing. His heavy-lidded gaze almost made her lose her grip on the iron, and her heart leapt. He was not as unaffected by her as he pretended to be.

He no doubt thought their relationship a mistake, and yet, he wanted her. It was some comfort.

At least he was making an effort to converse more with Rose and Olivia. A few days ago, he'd taken them on a picnic—just the three of them—and Anabelle had never seen the girls so happy. They returned with flushed cheeks, eager to divulge the details of their outing. Owen had told them he wanted to have a come-out ball for Rose at the end of the summer. At first, Rose balked at the idea, but when she found out it would be held at their country estate, she agreed.

Anabelle suspected she was more excited about the prospect of seeing her beau, the stable master, than in having a ball thrown in her honor.

But Owen had finally realized that Rose should have the same opportunities as Olivia and the other young ladies of their station. Being shy shouldn't destine her to the rank of social outcast. If Owen stood behind her, the rest of the *ton* would take their cue from him—hopefully.

Six gowns. They were all Anabelle had left to make. In the last month, she'd worked from dawn to dusk and beyond in order to complete riding habits, day gowns, carriage dresses, and evening dresses. Rose and Olivia were so delighted with their garments, Anabelle didn't mind the late nights in the least. She was especially looking forward to making the gowns Rose and Olivia would wear to the ball at Huntford Manor and decided to save them for her last two projects. They'd be the *pièces de résistance* of the girls' wardrobes.

And then, Anabelle would go home. She hadn't yet figured out how to make ends meet once her assignment was over, but at least Mama was well. It was a chance for a fresh start.

Anabelle sighed and blinked back the tears that constantly threatened of late. Like a teacup filled to the brim—the slightest rattling made her overflow. But she was determined to make the most of the day.

The late July morning was warm and damp, the kind that made the little wisps of hair at the nape of one's neck curl and stick to the skin. She'd opened wide the workroom window and left the door open to allow for a cross breeze, as if it were that easy to air out the anguish in her heart.

Her next project would be a morning dress for Olivia, made of fine cambric muslin. After rolling out the smooth fabric, Anabelle carefully measured the length she'd need and picked up her scissors.

The thumping of footsteps in the corridor, however, made her set them down to investigate. Before she'd taken two steps, Olivia appeared in the doorway with Rose right behind her. "Anabelle, we have news!" Olivia waved a large card in her hand and spun a pirouette across the room.

Just seeing the girls cheered Anabelle. She placed a finger on her chin. "Let me guess," she teased. "You've been invited to join the Royal Ballet Company."

"Oh, how I wish! But it's almost as grand. We've been invited to a house party at Lord Harsby's estate, and Owen said we could go."

"How wonderful!" Anabelle hoped she sounded sincere. She'd known her days with Owen and the girls were drawing to a close, but it seemed they would end more abruptly than she'd imagined. "When will you leave?"

"In just a fortnight. This has been the best summer." Olivia ticked off the reasons on her fingers. "First we met you. Then, Owen started to treat us like grown women. Next, we received an invitation to a fashionable house party. On top of that, we have Rose's ball to look forward to."

Rose's eyes shone with happiness, but she was not quite as exuberant as Olivia—no one ever was. The pretty redhead walked up to Olivia and whispered in her ear.

"Oh, yes," Olivia said. "We hoped you would come, too."

Heavens. The very idea was preposterous. "I'm certain that Lord Harsby's invitation wasn't extended to me."

Olivia studied the invitation as though perhaps she'd merely overlooked Anabelle's name, and then frowned. "True. But Rose and I would enjoy the party so much more if you were there, and we thought—"

"That no one would notice if you brought your seamstress along?"

Rose's mouth dropped open; Anabelle crossed her arms, daring her to say something.

She didn't.

"You're much more than a seamstress, Anabelle," Olivia said.

Odd; that's what Owen had once told her. Recently though, he seemed to have forgotten. "That's kind of you to say, but I doubt Lord Harsby and his wife would agree."

"That's why we thought that you could accompany us. As our companion."

Anabelle blinked. "Do you mean, as your chaperone?"

A flush crept up Olivia's neck. "I know that you aren't more than a few years older than Rose and me, but you're very wise. And you've been working so hard. Wouldn't it be lovely to have a break from Town? The three of us would have such a grand time."

"Have you mentioned this to your brother?"

"Not yet. But we feel sure we could convince him. We just wanted to make sure you wouldn't mind the companion role. It would be for show only, of course. And you'd gain admittance to all the festivities."

Anabelle suppressed a shudder. A week or more exchanging meaningless pleasantries with the other ape leaders while a parade of young beauties flirted with Owen sounded torturous. However, Rose and Olivia were clearly excited at the prospect of having her along, and their thoughtfulness warmed her.

Not in a million years would Owen agree to let her act as their chaperone. First off, he was much too protective of his sisters to entrust them to her care. Second, it seemed he could barely stand to be in the same room with her. Why would he unnecessarily subject himself to her company?

Confident that he would veto the idea, she relented. "If your brother agrees, I have no objection."

Rose clapped and Olivia squealed. "Hurrah! We shall go talk to him at once, then return directly to tell you the good news." They each gave her a quick hug before scurrying from the room.

The rustling of fabric made Owen glance up from the letter he was composing to his steward. His foolish heart beat faster on the off chance Belle had come to see him.

She hadn't, but he was pleased to see Olivia and Rose looking fresh and happy.

Until he realized they must want something. Bracing himself, he set down his quill and narrowed his eyes at Olivia's bare arms. Too much skin showed above the neckline of her dress. "Shouldn't you be wearing a shawl?"

"Heavens, no. It's warm in here."

"For modesty's sake. You too, Rose," he said.

Olivia huffed. "Anabelle made these dresses. They're in the first stare of fashion."

"Oh, people will be staring all right." He made a mental note to keep his friends away from his sisters.

"We love the gowns. They're nicer than anything we've ever owned."

"Does Miss Honeycote realize that she doesn't have to scrimp on fabric? I can afford a *complete* dress."

Olivia laughed and plopped herself into a chair opposite his desk. "This is what all the young ladies are wearing."

"I don't care what all the young ladies are wearing— just my sisters."

Rose glided into the chair next to Olivia, smiling innocently.

A chill ran the length of his spine. "I assume that the two of you are here with a request of some sort."

"We are," admitted Olivia. "We want Anabelle to go to Lord Harsby's house party with us—as our companion."

He considered the idea for the space of a heartbeat.

"No." He picked up his pen to signify the conversation was over. No matter how appealing the idea, it wouldn't be prudent. When he'd passed Anabelle in the corridor yesterday, it had taken every ounce of self-control he possessed not to press her against the wall with his hips and ravish her mouth with his. Out of respect for her, he had to avoid her.

Olivia sighed. "That's fine, then. I suppose you shall have the pleasure of escorting us to all the entertainments."

Dread perched on his shoulders like a vulture. "What kinds of entertainments?"

She waved a hand in the air. "Oh, the usual—charades, whist, shopping excursions in the village, flower gathering—"

"*Flower gathering?*"

"Of course. We'll pick them in the fields. You may carry the basket." The imp smiled smugly.

He knew what Olivia was trying to do, and he felt a stir of pride. She'd come a long way.

But she was no match for him.

"I'll be pleased to spend so much time in the company of my sisters."

Rose tapped Olivia on the shoulder and leaned in to tell her something.

Olivia nodded. "Not just our company. Lady Harsby and her mother shall be at all the festivities."

Nice move. Lady Harsby was a shrill harpie, and her mother had a habit of talking in long, winding sentences that never seemed to end. Still, he would not relent. "We shall never lack for conversation."

Olivia leaned back and crossed her ankles. "Are you aware that Lady Harsby's sister has two daughters of marriageable age? I believe you have heard them sing and play the pianoforte together. Perhaps you could sing a duet with—"

Damn it. "Fine."

Olivia tented her fingers. "Meaning what, precisely?"

"Meaning I'll talk to Miss Honeycote about acting as your chaperone."

"Oh, we've—"

Rose placed a hand on Olivia's arm, silencing her momentarily before she continued. "That would be wonderful. Thank you."

Owen glared at the pair of them, debating whether it was worth his time to question them further. The housekeeper's keys clinked as she walked down the corridor. "Mrs. Pottsbury," he called.

She teetered to the doorway of the study, the toes of her impossibly small feet touching the threshold. "Yes, Your Grace?"

"Inform Miss Honeycote that I wish to see her at once."

She scurried off, and his sisters exchanged a look. "Excellent," Olivia said. "We shall leave you to talk with Anabelle. Do try to ask nicely."

He grunted. Did she think him some sort of beast?

The girls started to leave, but Olivia halted at the door and faced him. "This room is starting to feel right again. The whole time we were talking, I never once thought about him."

Owen swallowed past the knot in his throat. It had been ages since they'd spoken of their father. Guilt niggled between his shoulders. "Don't forget him. Our father was weak, but he was a good man. And he loved the two of you more than anything."

Olivia pressed her lips tightly together, as though she were fighting back tears. "Don't worry. I remember him well. I only meant that the image of him—here, at the end—*that* is fading." Her eyes flicked to the spot behind the desk where a new carpet covered the bloodstained floor.

"I'm glad." Owen rose from his chair, walked to the other side of the desk, and put an arm around each sister. "Remember picnics by the river with him and the ponies he bought you. Forget the rest."

"What about Mama?" Olivia whispered.

The pain in her voice made fury course through him— not hot, but ice cold. For all he cared, their mother could rot in hell. But that image wouldn't comfort his sisters. "Our mother made choices that I don't understand. I doubt I'll ever forgive her for leaving the two of you. But you may choose to remember her as you wish." He squeezed their slight shoulders and then held them at arm's length so he could look into their brown eyes. "Know this. Mother may have abandoned you. In his own way, Father did too. But I never will. I'll be here for you long after you're married. Even after you have children and grand-children. We're family."

Both sisters launched themselves at him; he patted their backs awkwardly. If he'd known they were going to cry he would have changed the subject to bonnets or wall-paper or poetry, for God's sake.

Belle arrived at his study in the middle of the maud-lin scene. Owen looked at her over the girls' heads and shrugged helplessly. Anabelle would know what to do, thank God.

"What's wrong?" she asked, her face pale.

Olivia turned toward her and sniffled. "We're just happy." She blew her nose loudly into the handkerchief she'd plucked from his pocket.

Anabelle shot him a suspicious look. "Is this a bad time?"

"Oh no," Olivia answered for him. "Rose and I were

about to leave." She stood on tiptoe and planted a kiss on his cheek. Rose mirrored the action on the other cheek. Maybe—wonder of wonders—he'd finally done something right where his sisters were concerned. They linked arms and gave Anabelle a conspiratorial smile as they left.

"You wanted to see me?"

"Yes." Several tendrils had slipped free of her normally unflinching knot, and they curled softly around her face—the face that filled his mind as he drifted off to sleep each night and countless times throughout the day. He could almost ignore the cap. Almost.

Running his palms down the front of his tear-dampened jacket, he said, "I could use some fresh air." And a drink. "Let's go sit in the garden."

Although he tried to usher her out of the room, she remained frozen, her feet rooted to the rug. "Is that an order or a request?"

"I don't know. Does it matter? There's something I want to discuss with you."

She raised her chin a notch, every inch a viscount's granddaughter. "As you wish, Your Grace."

Her stiff manner seemed like a denial of everything they'd shared, and it hurt more than he cared to admit. But he couldn't blame her for hating him. He'd been the one keeping his distance, and it was for her own good.

She followed him through the library, onto the terrace, and beyond to the small, lush garden. He waved her to a bench in the shade of a dense canopy of leaves and sat beside her—at a respectful distance.

He hadn't been in the garden for months. Hadn't appreciated the vibrant blossoms up close or inhaled the unmistakably sweet scent of summer. Now, he longed to race across a pasture on his horse, the warm wind whipping at his clothes.

Although they were located in the middle of Town, he could almost imagine that Anabelle and he were in a country field surrounded by wildflowers and grass and sunshine. No one but the two of them for miles and miles.

If only it were true, he'd pick a bright yellow flower and put it in her hair. Then, after removing every stitch of her clothing, he'd lay her back in the soft grass and pleasure her a dozen different ways before plunging into her and making her his. All his.

"What would you like to discuss?" she asked, her spine as straight and unyielding as a rod. How could her poise and fine manners have escaped his notice? He should have known she was no ordinary seamstress. Had circumstances been different, she might have had her first Season a few years ago. Lovely as she was, many gentlemen—including some of his debauched friends—would have tripped over themselves to gain her favor and offer for her.

He shook off the thought with distaste. "Do you want to go to Lord Harsby's house party?"

"I beg your pardon?"

"I assume my sisters have already told you their proposal."

She chewed the inside of her cheek. "They have."

"Will you come? It was the girls' idea, but I'll admit that I like it, too."

Peering at him out of the corner of her eye, she asked, "You do?"

"You make my sisters happy."

"Though I may look the part"—she pushed her

spectacles onto the bridge of her nose—"I'm hardly a suitable companion."

He wanted to say that, as a viscount's granddaughter, she was more than qualified. But since he suspected she didn't want him knowing about her lineage, he said, "You'll do."

"Have you forgotten the circumstances under which we met? And the rather scandalous things we did afterward?"

His blood heated at the mention of their passionate encounters. He looked directly into her eyes. "I haven't forgotten."

She blushed. "And you're not worried I'll corrupt your sisters?"

"Maybe I should be," he teased, "but no."

"How would it look if I accompanied you to the house party?"

"It would look like my sisters had a companion who was far younger and prettier than most."

Her cheeks turned a deeper shade of pink. Clearly exasperated, she stood and paced in front of the bench. "People are bound to ask questions about who I am. What would you have me say?"

"The truth."

She threw up her hands, agitated and yet utterly beautiful. "That I'm a servant with whom you've taken many liberties and have recently promoted to companion?"

"You forgot to mention that you were also an extortionist."

"This will never work, Owen."

Encouraged by her use of his name, he stood and took her hands in his. His body instantly responded to the feel of her skin, and he had to think hard about what he wanted to say. "Your mother is recovering nicely. She and your sister will be fine for a few weeks. Getting away from Town would be good for you."

"I need to finish making the dresses."

Of course she wanted to be done with them. With him. "How many do you have left?"

"Six."

It wasn't much time, but maybe the house party would delay her departure. With a casualness he didn't feel, he shrugged. "Make them when we return."

"I can't. The last two are the gowns for Rose's debut ball. It's less than a month away."

She was slipping away from him, and it was his fault. Avoiding her had been infinitely easier than admitting the depth of his feelings. He laced his fingers through hers and squeezed her hands. As though holding onto her were just that easy. "Is there anything I could say that would convince you to come?"

"Yes." Her gray eyes searched his, and he knew what he had to do.

"Belle," he said softly, "I want you to go with us. Not just because I'm trying to avoid Lady Harsby and her mother, or because you make my sisters happy, or because the country air would be good for you. I want you to go because if you didn't . . . I'd miss you."

He'd spoken the truth, but it didn't make him feel any less foolish. He'd sounded like a lovesick boy.

Anabelle smiled, transforming her face. "I'll go with you." She was more beautiful than a dozen Miss Starlings, more captivating than a choir of sea sirens. Best of all, she challenged him to be a better man. Maybe he could find a way to fulfill the duties of his title and ensure the acceptance of his sisters without forfeiting a future with Belle. The odds weren't in his favor, but he clung to hope like a cardplayer who's wagered everything on a poorly dealt hand.

She pulled free and began walking to the house; he released the breath he'd been holding.

"But"—she whirled around to face him—"I'll need to bring the material and supplies for the dresses. I'll work on them there."

"Fine," he said. He could live with that.

He might be a fool, but he was a happier fool than he'd been in weeks.

Chapter Seventeen

Facing: (1) Fabric sewn on the raw edge of a garment piece.
(2) The act of addressing a situation head-on, especially
after one has been deftly avoiding it for far too long.

*I*n the days leading up to Lord Harsby's house party, Anabelle might as well have had a needle attached to her hand. She worked from dawn till after midnight; even as she slept, dresses swirled in her head like bodiless ghosts dancing the quadrille on an otherworldly dance floor. As a result, she was able to piece together all six of the remaining dresses. By no means were they done—they were little more than shells at this point, all in need of trimming, hemming, and adorning. But accomplishing those things at the house party would be fairly easy, especially during the hours everyone was resting or dressing for dinner.

The ball gowns, in particular, delighted her; the silk she'd chosen was exquisite. Rose's gown was white, of course, but would be trimmed in a light green satin perfect for her fair complexion. Olivia's gown was pale pink silk embellished in white satin. Individually, they would look lovely; together, they would be striking.

Before dawn on the day they were to leave, Anabelle carefully packed each of the gowns, along with all the lace, ribbon, swansdown, feathers, and crepe she could possibly need. The gowns and her sewing supplies occupied a large trunk, which Olivia had provided.

Her own things fit into the small shabby portmanteau that Daphne had sent from home, filled with almost all of the drab, serviceable clothing Anabelle owned. The contrast between the contents of the trunk and her bag was stark. And rather depressing.

Her dismal dresses would reflect not only on her, but on Rose and Olivia as well. Of course, companions were supposed to fade into the wallpaper, but it would never do for Anabelle to arrive at a fashionable house party wearing dresses that bordered on ragged.

Since she lacked the time and fabric to make herself new gowns, she resolved to spruce up the old ones. Rummaging through a pile of scraps from the girls' wardrobes, she plucked out several items, which she shoved into her portmanteau. Her first order of business ought to have been replacing her old cap, but for reasons she couldn't explain, she was reluctant to let it go. Just in case she changed her mind, however, she stuffed an old bonnet into her bag as well.

The packing complete, Anabelle sat on the edge of her bed. She hadn't slept all night, and the sun was already beginning to rise. Lying down now was pointless; their party was leaving for Lord Harsby's country estate in Norfolk directly after breakfast.

Owen had informed them that the journey would take

two days. At the end of the first day they'd stop at an inn, spend the night, and arrive at Lord Harsby's estate on the afternoon of the second day.

Anabelle had never been on such a long coach ride and had imagined it would be a grand adventure. After two hours of being jostled over pitted country roads and sweltering in a cramped coach, however, she couldn't imagine what had possessed her to think such a thing.

She, Olivia, and Rose sat in the coach, alternately chatting, reading, and napping. Owen rode his horse alongside them. Anabelle had never learned to ride, and she envied him. Every now and then, she caught a glimpse of him astride his fierce-looking black gelding. Already his face had turned a deeper shade of tan, and the breeze ruffled his hair, lending an unexpected charm to his normally austere appearance. With his broad shoulders and commanding air, he looked impossibly handsome.

If she could have watched him to her heart's content, time would have passed much more quickly.

However, she took care not to stare overmuch. Rose was ever watchful and astute, and must have had an inkling that Owen and Anabelle were romantically involved. Or had been.

Anabelle pulled down the window shade, cutting off her view of Owen. At Olivia's quirked brow, Anabelle said, "I am just trying to keep the sun from roasting us."

"Good thinking. Rose and I are so glad you agreed to come."

Rose nodded vigorously.

"So am I," Anabelle said, meaning it. However, the farther they got from London, the more nervous she grew. She hoped she'd comport herself properly in front of Lord and Lady Harsby and their guests. Although Mama and Papa had taught her the manners of a lady, she'd never been called upon to practice them among earls and countessess. "Do you know who else will be attending?"

"Mr. Averill, our brother's solicitor and friend, will be there," Olivia said with a shy smile. "I'm sure that's the reason Owen accepted Lord Harsby's invitation."

"What's Mr. Averill like?" Anabelle asked.

Olivia's cheeks turned pink. "He collects exotic things from foreign lands. He's very worldly."

Goodness, it seemed Olivia was rather smitten with him. "'Worldly' is often a euphemism for 'aged,'" Anabelle teased. "Am I correct in assuming Mr. Averill is an elderly gentleman in possession of a dusty collection of ancient artifacts?"

"No," Olivia countered, her feathers ruffled. "He's younger than Owen and very fit. I heard my brother say that when it came to boxing he was no match for Mr. Averill."

Slyly, Anabelle winked at Rose. "He's a pugilist, then. Scores of boxing matches must have left him with a patchwork of scars and a misshapen nose."

"Not at all!" Olivia cried. "His features are perfectly classic—like a statue of Adonis. He's one of the most handsome men I've ever met."

"Interesting," said Anabelle, smiling.

Olivia covered her face with her hands. "How mortifying! Rose already knows I have a tendre for him. But you needn't worry about my virtue. James thinks of me only as Owen's little sister. The last time I saw him—September the twenty-fifth, a Friday—he actually told me to eat my vegetables."

Anabelle raised her brows. "James, is it? And did he really?"

"Yes—I had rhubarb on my plate, and he told me that some ladies of his acquaintance swear it keeps their waists trim." Olivia sighed wistfully. "I've known him since I was wearing pigtails. Which is probably why he thinks I'm still in the schoolroom."

"Mr. Averill will not be able to ignore you any longer. And he most certainly will not think to lecture you on the merits of rhubarb. You are far too pretty, and in your new gowns you are undeniably a woman."

Olivia's cheeks flushed a deeper shade. "I hope he'll see me that way."

Anabelle exchanged a glance with Rose and made a note to determine Mr. Averill's character for herself. Olivia could be so headstrong, and though Anabelle wanted her to be happy, she also needed to act the part of chaperone. "Who else is attending the house party?"

"I confess I wasn't much interested in the guest list beyond James. But let me see...Lady Danshire, a marchioness who was widowed two years ago, shall be there along with her two sons. She's eager for the eldest to marry, but the brothers, Lord Danshire and Sir Sandleigh, are more interested in pulling pranks. Rather juvenile stunts like stealing horses from each other and placing ants in one another's boots. I find the gentlemen quite entertaining; Owen says they need to stop acting like they're still at Eton." Olivia's face lit up. "Oh, I'd forgotten that you know Miss Starling and her mother. They shall be there also. Mrs. Starling is a very close acquaintance of Lord Harsby's mother."

Anabelle stretched her lips into a smile. "I wasn't aware of the connection."

"Fortuitous, is it not?" Olivia said. "Miss Starling says Owen could very well ask for her hand over the course of the party. Apparently, for the past several weeks, he's been hinting that he intends to propose."

The coach suddenly seemed much too small and dreadfully hot. Why would Owen ask Anabelle to go to the party if he intended to propose to Miss Starling? She tried to cling to her composure, but the news that Miss Starling would be among the guests, combined with the swaying of the coach, made her stomach roil. If she'd known that the debutante would be there, she never would have agreed to come. Of course, Owen's future duchess would be someone like Miss Starling, but Anabelle didn't want to be forced to observe their courtship.

Fortunately, Olivia seemed oblivious to Anabelle's discomfort. She didn't dare look at Rose, who was too perceptive by half.

It was too late to turn the coach around. Anabelle would have to endure a fortnight of torture. Perhaps it would be good for her; if she witnessed the entire spectacle of Owen and Miss Starling flirting and eventually falling into each other's arms, she'd be cured of her affection for him once and for all.

Either that, or she'd be left utterly and irrevocably heartbroken.

"Anabelle?" Olivia looked at her, clearly puzzled.

She searched her brain for the thread of the conversation but couldn't find it. "Forgive me. What were you saying?"

"I asked if you knew how to play the pianoforte. What were you thinking about?"

"That I really should attempt to look slightly more fashionable. I don't want to be an embarrassment to you and Rose." Her pride may have had something to do with it as well. She didn't want Miss Starling to think she was some kind of charity project—even if she was.

Rose opened her mouth, aghast, and Olivia quickly said, "You would never be an embarrassment to us. You possess a timeless sort of beauty that needn't bow to convention. More importantly, your kind nature will be evident to everyone."

Anabelle swallowed the wave of guilt that rose up in her chest. She'd threatened to destroy Olivia's reputation in exchange for a few gold coins and was hardly deserving of her high opinion. "You are very kind," she said to Olivia. "However, most people cannot see past my drab appearance. I have no wish to look like a debutante or even a stylish lady, but I'd like to smarten myself up. Will you help me?"

Rose rubbed her palms together and Olivia grinned. "Oh yes. We'll help. In fact, when we stop at the inn this evening, we have a little surprise for you."

As the coach slowed and halted, Anabelle raised the shade and got her first glimpse of The Elephant and Castle. The inn was nestled in a bed of ivy that crawled up its stone walls, almost to the thatched roof where a trio of chimneys poked through. The surrounding gardens burst with colorful blooms, and the setting sun glinted off a lake in the distance with a charming effect. Eager as Anabelle was to escape the confines of the coach, however, even a shack would have looked inviting.

She watched as, outside, Owen deftly dismounted and handed the reins to a stable boy. He tossed the lad a coin and strode through the inn's front door.

"It will feel wonderful to stretch our legs," Olivia said. She nudged her sister. "Wake up, Rose. We're here."

The three women gingerly unfolded their limbs, stepped out of the coach, and breathed in the crisp air, ripe with the smell of horses, grass, and a cooking fire. Olivia whispered to the footman, who looked at the luggage strapped to the back of the coach and nodded.

"Owen must be ordering dinner and securing rooms," Olivia said. "Let's wander around the garden for a bit."

They strolled, watching as the inn bustled with servants, guests, and farmers who'd come to the taproom for an ale after a long day in the fields. After a few minutes, Owen joined them near a bed of sprawling rosebushes, his blatant masculinity a sharp contrast to the pink petals and lush greenery. His gaze lingered on each of his sisters and then Anabelle, in turn. Apparently satisfied they were none the worse for wear, he said, "We'll have dinner in a private room at eight o'clock. That gives you almost an hour to get settled in your rooms."

"Rooms?" said Olivia. "I assumed the three of us would be sharing."

Owen shook his head. "There were no large rooms left. I purchased one room for you and Rose and another for Miss Honeycote."

Anabelle slid her spectacles up her nose. "That's not necessary. I can sleep on the floor in their room."

A sour, yet incredulous, expression crossed Owen's face. "You would rather sleep on the floor than in a bed?"

"I'm no princess. I can survive a night on the floor." Although, after spending all day in the coach, a bed sounded heavenly.

He grunted. "I've paid for two rooms in addition to

mine. If you choose to use only one, it makes no difference to me."

Olivia linked her arm through Anabelle's and said, "We will sort it all out once we inspect the rooms. Shall we, ladies? I'd like to freshen up before dinner."

Owen escorted them through the tiny front room of the inn and up the narrow stairway. The first room had a large bed and a window overlooking a small courtyard. It smelled a bit musty, but the linens were clean and the small bedside table was free of dust. Rose and Olivia's bags had been placed against the wall; Anabelle carried her own portmanteau.

Olivia walked to the window and lifted the sash. "This will do nicely."

Owen shrugged. "The room next door is yours as well." He took Anabelle's hand and dropped a key in her open palm. "I am at the end of the hall on the left if you need me. Otherwise, I shall return at eight to escort you all to dinner."

Rose smiled sweetly at him as he walked out and shut the door behind him.

"I thought he'd never leave," Olivia said, reaching for one of her bags. She and Rose perched on the edge of the bed, the large bag between them.

"What's going on?" Anabelle asked with some alarm. "Please tell me you don't have an animal in there."

Rose shook her head and turned to Olivia, who spoke. "Rose and I think you're lovely just as you are. But we've noticed you do more for others than you do for yourself."

Anabelle opened her mouth to protest—Heaven knew she was no saint—but Olivia held up a hand.

"You work very hard, and that leaves precious little

time to sew for yourself. That's why we thought you might take these gowns. They're not nearly as wonderful as your creations, but they're made of fine material, and you could modify them to suit you."

Olivia lifted a pale sea-green gown out of the bag and held it up by the petite puffed sleeves. The waist was lower than was currently fashionable, but the workmanship was exquisite and the fabric shimmered in the waning light. The shade of blue-green made Anabelle's heart beat faster.

"I couldn't," Anabelle said. Even if she *could* bring herself to accept such an extravagant gift, when would she wear it? As she traipsed down the dirty London sidewalks to work at the dress shop?

"Why not? Of course, they may not be to your taste. Rose and I picked out several we thought would suit you. They're not the current fashion, but you could work wonders with them. We've wanted to offer them to you for some time but feared you'd be insulted. When you told us in the coach this morning that you wished to dress more fashionably, we were ecstatic." She pulled another gown—this one in a deep rose silk—from the bag and held it beneath Anabelle's chin. "I was right, Rose. This color *is* perfect with her complexion."

She gently pushed the gown away. "I don't mean to sound ungrateful, but it wouldn't be right for me to accept these."

"Nonsense. They were collecting dust, and they're much too small for Rose and me."

"Where did they come from?"

Olivia and Rose exchanged a furtive glance. "They belonged to our mother," Olivia said. "She left suddenly, and much of her wardrobe remained in her armoire. The gowns are three or four years old, but Mama always had a wonderful sense of style."

The way Olivia spoke—as if their mother were dead—was chilling. And the idea that a lowly seamstress would wear gowns designed for a duchess was ludicrous. Utterly preposterous.

"The dresses are beautiful but much too fine for me. Thank you for your thoughtfulness, though. I'm touched that you would think to do this for me." To show the matter was settled, she set down her own bag and squeezed past the sisters as she walked to the washstand. As she tipped the pitcher, cool water splashed into the basin. Though she wasn't quite sure what companions did, she needed to begin acting like one. "Would you care to wash up before dinner?"

Rose's brow creased and Olivia quickly extracted another gown from the bag as though she hadn't heard Anabelle's question. "They're not all so impractical," she said. "This walking gown is modest and rather understated, don't you think?"

Full of skepticism, Anabelle turned to look at the dress. The light yellow sprigged muslin was pretty but not ostentatious, and the low neckline could be remedied with a fichu or a shawl. It was ten times nicer than her nicest dress. But the gowns were not Olivia's and Rose's to give away. "What if...that is, your mother could..."

"Mama's not coming back, if that's what you're worried about," Olivia said. "And believe us, if she did, she'd never deign to wear gowns a few seasons old."

Anabelle swallowed. She had one other reservation. "What about the duke?"

"Owen?"

"He might not like you giving away your mother's things."

Rose bit her lip, and Olivia huffed. "He doesn't care in the slightest. For him, Mama ceased to exist the moment she left us."

Anabelle swallowed. "I'm sorry."

Olivia wrapped an arm around her shoulders. "It would make Rose and me happy to see you making use of these dresses. But it's your choice."

Anabelle considered this. "Perhaps I could use a couple."

Rose clapped her hands, and Olivia said, "Excellent. Now that we have that settled, I intend to wash off this road dust." She tried to maneuver past the bed on her way to the washstand and bumped her hip on the footboard. "Gads, this room is dreadfully small."

"Here," said Anabelle, "I'll move the bags to the other room."

Olivia shook her head. "Later. Let's take a look through the rest of the dresses before dinner."

The girls took turns washing up, and were ready— and hungry—by the time Owen came to retrieve them. When they went downstairs, the innkeeper ushered them past the taproom to a private dining area. The cozy room was so dark that it was difficult to see the oil landscapes hung three high on the walls. A lantern in the center of a rustic square table set for four flickered invitingly. Owen held out a chair for each of his sisters in turn and scowled at Anabelle when she seated herself. She ignored him. Heavens, she'd been pulling out her own chair for as long as she could remember.

Once they were seated, the innkeeper's wife carried in

a savory cottage pie and warm, crusty bread with butter. Owen grumbled to himself about the beef being practically nonexistent, but Anabelle relished every bite of the crispy potato crust. After a glass or two of ale, everyone was full and content.

Rose yawned and Olivia followed suit. "I don't know how sitting all day can be so exhausting, but I vow my head is about to hit my plate. Are you tired as well, Anabelle?"

Too excited to be sleepy, she forced a yawn. "Quite."

Owen shot her a skeptical glance. "I'll take you to your rooms. Room. Whichever."

"Will you turn in as well?" asked Olivia.

"Ah…eventually. I think I'll find a card game. And something stronger than ale to drink."

He walked them upstairs and bid them good night with a stern warning to lock their doors the moment he left. "You needn't fuss over us so," teased Olivia. "We have a companion now."

He shot her a long-suffering look before closing the door.

Rose and Olivia prepared for bed. They donned their nightgowns and brushed out their hair. Anabelle tried to make herself useful by folding their traveling gowns.

As Olivia began twisting her thick brown locks into a braid, she said to Anabelle, "Go, make yourself comfortable in the other room. Rose and I shall be fine."

"I'd like to be near in case either of you needs me."

"You *will* be near. And in the unlikely event that Rose and I are mauled by randy tavern patrons, I shall knock on the adjoining wall."

Rose slapped a hand over her open mouth.

Anabelle laughed. "If you're sure."

"I'm certain. I suggest you get a good night's sleep. If I know my brother, he'll have us jostling down the road at the crack of dawn."

"Very well," Anabelle said. But she'd slept several hours in the coach today and was in the habit of working into the wee hours of the morning. Sleep didn't interest her in the least. "Might I take one of the gowns you showed me earlier?"

"Of course," Olivia said, pointing to the bag. "Take them all. Rose and I can't wait to see you in them."

"Thank you. You're better friends than I deserve."

"Nonsense. Rose and I are an odd pair, and yet, you've never judged us. We're very grateful for whatever... circumstances brought you into our lives."

Anabelle suppressed a shiver. Olivia and Rose must have suspected there was more to the story they'd been told about her. But they were willing to trust her—and give her a chance. "Sleep well," she said, smiling. "You don't want dark smudges beneath your eyes when you see Mr. Averill tomorrow evening."

"Heaven forfend!" cried Olivia, and Rose pulled the sheet up over her head.

Anabelle picked up her bags. "Lock the door after I leave, and knock if you need me." She paused in the hallway, waited for the click of the lock, and walked a few yards down the dark corridor. The room was even tinier than the girls'. A narrow bed was pushed into the corner, which just allowed the door to clear the foot of it. Anabelle walked to the nightstand, nothing more than a crate standing on end, and lit the lantern atop it. A tiny washstand was the only other piece of furniture, and the room's solitary window was small and round, like a porthole. Hinged at the top and pushed open, it let in a refreshing breeze.

The idea of making over a dress—for herself—filled her with trepidation and glee.

She plucked the copious pins from her hair and rubbed her scalp until the pinching sensation faded. Too excited to take time to brush, she merely ran her fingers through the strands.

After laying the duchess's yellow gown on the bed, she shed the practical—and admittedly ugly—dress she'd worn that day. Boldly, she slipped the smooth, light fabric over her head and let it cascade down her legs.

Even without a mirror, she could tell.

It was perfect.

Chapter Eighteen

*O*wen lost a few pounds playing vingt-et-un in the smoky taproom to a blacksmith with either incredibly good luck or an incredibly slick hand. He didn't care much. He just wanted to sit on something other than a saddle, have a drink...and think about anything other than Anabelle.

She'd avoided him all day. Not that they'd had much chance for conversation, but it wouldn't have killed her to smile at him once in a while.

When the bleary-eyed innkeeper finally announced he was closing the bar, Owen trudged up the stairs, cursing under his breath at the bed awaiting him. It was so short that when he'd lain on it this afternoon, his feet hung over the end. He already missed his massive four-poster bed at home, which had plenty of room for him *and* Belle.

He stopped in the middle of the stairway and blinked.

What was wrong with him? He should *not* be thinking of Anabelle in his bed.

He was supposed to find himself a wife. Maybe if he accepted his fate and did his duty, Olivia and Rose would have a role model for ladylike behavior.

Miss Starling was the logical choice. Their families had always been close. As a schoolboy, Owen had ice-skated with her on the frozen lake at her father's country estate. Olivia seemed fond of Miss Starling, and marriage to her could only enhance his sisters' social status. Since she was widely regarded as the most beautiful woman on the marriage mart, and Owen's title made him the most sought-after gentleman, half the *ton* already assumed they were engaged. The problem was, each time he thought about her in his house, in his bed, he felt empty, and worse, indifferent.

As he walked down the corridor, he paused outside his sisters' room. Olivia had a tendency to forget things like extinguishing candles and locking doors. To put his mind at ease, he tested the doorknob. It didn't budge.

Satisfied, he proceeded farther down the hall only to discover a light shining beneath the door of the second room he'd secured. Odd at this hour of the night.

He checked the knob and it turned, damn it. Any rogue could have walked in and robbed them—or worse. And why was the lantern still lit? He pushed open the door, prepared to lecture anyone who was awake, but before he could say a word, his head exploded in pain. He fell to the floor, heard the clinking of glass around him, and then ...

Numbing blackness.

"Owen?"

Cool hands smoothed his hair away from his face. It felt good. If he focused on the gentle brush of those fingers across his skin, he could almost ignore the intense throbbing that radiated from a spot at the back of his head. Almost.

"Owen, can you hear me? I'm so sorry. I thought you were an intruder."

Belle.

Reluctantly, he opened his eyes. The light sharpened the pain, so he shut them again. "For the love of— What did you do to me?"

She moaned in embarrassment. "I bashed you with a pitcher. Can you roll toward me a little? But be careful of the sharp pieces. I want to close the door before anyone comes."

He did as she asked, and she quickly shut the door. They remained still and silent for a few moments as they waited to see if anyone would come to investigate the thud Owen had made when he hit the floor. Apparently, no one awake at that late hour was concerned enough to get out of bed.

Owen groped the back of his skull, felt a knot budding, and groaned. "Please tell me you didn't realize it was me."

"Of course I didn't," she hissed. "I never imagined you'd barge into my room at two o'clock in the morning."

"You don't know me very well."

She clucked her tongue. "Your injury cannot be that serious if you're blithely tossing around innuendos."

"I beg to differ. It hurts like hell." He opened his eyes a slit and tried to make her face come into focus. Her hair formed a cloud of chestnut waves around her head, and behind her spectacles, her delicate brows furrowed in concern. She wore a sleeveless white garment—a chemise, if he wasn't mistaken. A chemise, of all things. Unless he was hallucinating, that was *all* she wore. He swallowed, wondering if the blow to his head was more serious than he'd initially thought.

"Do you think you can sit up?"

He grunted. "Of course I can." And he could. He did. Only, it hurt so much that he immediately lay back down. His head landed in Anabelle's lap. Which was...nice.

"Goodness," she said. "I think you need to rest for a while."

Stretching out his legs and adjusting his head to a more comfortable position on her thighs, he sighed. "Definitely."

She shot him a mildly scolding glance. "I could have killed you."

"I doubt that."

"What possessed you to sneak into my room?"

"I wasn't sneaking." It was damned difficult to hold up his end of the conversation when the swell of her breasts rose above the low neckline of her chemise. "I was checking that you'd locked the door. I thought you'd fallen asleep with the lantern on." He congratulated himself on sounding coherent.

"You could have knocked."

"You could have locked the door."

She frowned. "I thought I had, but perhaps I was distracted by a...project. I need to look at the back of your head. I don't think you're bleeding, but you might have a shard of the pitcher stuck in your scalp."

Her graphic description made his stomach clench. "Fine. But be gentle."

Chuckling, she said, "I promise."

He turned his head away from her and held his breath as she carefully probed. When she found the lump, he flinched.

"Sorry," she said. "It's bigger than a quail's egg but smaller than a chicken's. No blood, but it's warm to the touch. What can I do to make you feel better?"

As he thought of all the things she might do, he grinned, and Belle blushed bright red from the lobes of her pretty ears to the hollow of her lovely throat. "If you don't mind," he said, "I'd like to lie still for a few minutes."

"Certainly." While she seemed eager to oblige him, her leg muscles tensed as though she found their current position awkward.

Maybe it was—for her. He was enjoying every moment.

As he inhaled the scents of clean cotton and citrusy soap and nestled into her soft lap, he decided he could be content right there for a very long time. If he didn't move, the pain remained at bay. And other than the sounds of insects chirping outside the open window, the room was blissfully quiet.

After several minutes, he said, "Have you lost feeling in your legs yet?"

She hesitated. "No."

"Liar." He slowly sat up and cursed.

"Maybe you should lie down on the bed."

He didn't argue.

Pushing aside a yellow garment, she fluffed a pillow and helped him ease his head down onto it. From his comfortable vantage point, he watched with amusement as she briskly picked up the broken pieces of pottery from the floor and deposited them on the washstand. The picture of efficiency, she dipped a cloth into the basin, wrung it out, and returned to his side. The mattress sank as she sat beside him. "Let me hold this to your head."

She pursed her lips as she leaned over him and tenderly checked the bump again. Her manner was exactly like that of a nursemaid, or a kindly nanny. The only difference was she was young, beautiful...and scantily clad. A circumstance that could only serve to hasten his healing.

Her shoulders and arms were so inviting that he had to check the impulse to lift his head and kiss her smooth skin. Her chemise, too loose for her thin frame, gaped between her breasts and beneath her arms. Using self-control he hadn't known he possessed, he refrained from staring. The last thing he wanted was to send her fleeing for her robe.

He risked a small peek. The sight of her high, softly rounded breasts made his mouth go dry.

"How does that feel?"

"I think it's helping."

She smiled and, with her free hand, pulled up the thin straps of her chemise. "I'm sorry I hit you."

"You did the right thing. Well, it *would* have been the right thing if it were anyone other than me. I'm glad you defended yourself."

"After Papa died, Daphne and I quickly learned to do what we must."

"How did he die?" It was a brutally forward question, but he'd always hated it when well-meaning acquaintances tried to couch their inquiries.

Belle didn't seem offended, just unbearably sad. "He suffered from a wasting disease. We lost him little by little over the course of several months. He knew he was dying and we knew it too. There was nothing we could do to help him or even ease his suffering in the end."

"I'm sorry."

"When Mama became sick, I couldn't let the same fate befall her."

"Didn't you have any other family you could turn to?" Why the hell hadn't her grandfather—a viscount, according to Anabelle's landlady—helped them?

She stiffened. "No. Believe me. Extortion was my last resort."

"Would you have done it?"

"Done what?"

"Printed the gossip about Olivia in *The Tattler*. If I hadn't caught you, or paid the forty pounds, would you have destroyed her?"

She swallowed. "That was all before I really knew her—or you."

"So, you would have." His head began to throb again.

"I can't honestly say what I would have done. There would have been nothing for me to gain at that point, so maybe not. I only know I was desperate." She placed her palm on his cheek and turned his head until they looked into each other's eyes. "And I'm truly sorry. I pray they never learn of my wickedness."

"As do I." Deciding the mood was too somber, he changed the subject. "Are you trained in the use of other weapons? Besides a pitcher, I mean?"

She pressed a finger to her chin. "I'm quite skilled with a parasol, but my weapon of choice would have to be . . . a candlestick."

He winced. "I should count myself lucky."

"Perhaps you should," she agreed. They sat in companionable silence for several minutes before she stifled a yawn and gazed longingly at the pillow.

Although he hated to leave, she needed her sleep. He

sat up and swung his legs to the floor, pleased to find that the room had stopped spinning. "What were you doing up so late?"

She blushed. "Working on a dress."

"The yellow one that was on the bed?"

"Yes."

"You shouldn't be working this late, no matter how eager you are to fulfill your end of our bargain."

"This one isn't for Rose or Olivia," she admitted shyly. "It's for me."

He blinked. "That's wonderful," he said, meaning it. He was so used to seeing Anabelle in dark colors it was hard to imagine her wearing sunny yellow. "May I see it?"

She chewed on the inside of her cheek as she slowly walked to the foot of the bed and held the garment beneath her chin.

It was familiar. Pretty. And yet something about it felt oddly . . . sinister. He must be drunk *and* dazed. "Did you make it?"

"No. Olivia and Rose gave it to me." She cast him a wary look, as though he were a lion about to pounce.

"My sisters haven't been that small since they were twelve. Where did they get it?"

"Actually," she said, her voice tremulous, "this gown used to be . . . your mother's."

He remembered. His mother had breezed into the nursery during his lessons like a bright butterfly and inquired about his progress. His Latin tutor had looked more than a little lovestruck as he gave a glowing report. Mother announced that learning a dead language seemed a terrible waste of time, slammed shut the book of Ovid's poems, and left.

He remembered the dress well.

And he didn't want Anabelle wearing it.

The edge of the mattress bowed under Owen's weight; he rested his hands on his knees as he grappled with the fact that Anabelle had pilfered his mother's dress. His dark brows slashed across his unusually pale face. Though injured, he still exuded power and vitality, and the room seemed infinitely smaller with him in it. With a scowl he said, "Why would my sisters think it appropriate to give you our mother's dress?"

Before now, she'd been too concerned he might keel over and die to give much thought to her state of undress. But his brooding stare made her drop the dress and cross her arms in front of her chest. She'd been afraid he'd react this way. She never should have accepted his sisters' gift.

"Don't blame Olivia and Rose. I mentioned that I'd like to become more fashionable." It was lowering to admit.

He lifted an eyebrow and then winced as though the tiny movement had caused him pain. "I see. You want to make a good impression at the house party."

She shrugged. "I suppose I do."

"In order to catch the eyes of the eligible men there?"

Nothing could have been further from her mind. "Perhaps."

A muscle in his jaw twitched, and he sat up straighter. "You'll have many admirers."

With a sigh, she said, "Actually, my primary motivation was to avoid embarrassing your sisters. As their companion, my appearance reflects on them." Of course, she'd also hoped Owen would notice her, but she'd cut her tongue out before telling him.

He seemed to ponder what she'd said. "Whatever your reasons, I think it's high time you stopped hiding your beauty. But you should *not* be wearing my mother's dress."

Anabelle sank to the corner of the bed farthest from him. "Fine. I'll tell your sisters I can't accept them."

"There are more?"

"They brought a bag full of gowns. Most of them were entirely too elegant for me, but I thought I might make use of a few."

"I'd rather you didn't."

"Yes, you made that clear." She felt hollow inside, like all the hope in her chest had rushed out. She didn't know why, when Owen only confirmed what she already knew in her heart. She didn't belong in his world.

He slowly turned to her, reached out, and laid his hand over hers. "I don't think you understand."

She yanked her hand away. "Oh, but I do." Anger and despair battled for the top spot in her whirling, tangled emotions. "I'm good enough to amuse you. Not good enough to wear your mother's cast-offs."

"No," he said adamantly. "That's not it at all. You're too good to wear her cast-offs, Belle. You're everything she wasn't. Loyal, warm, sincere."

Oh. Her eyes grew moist. "They're just dresses, Owen. Fabric held together with thread. Wearing them wouldn't change who I am."

"Promise?"

She smiled in spite of herself. "Promise."

After taking a deep breath, he said, "Then I won't forbid you to wear them. I still don't like the idea, though."

"How about if I just wear them during the house party? Nothing else I have is appropriate."

"That seems reasonable." He paused and then tilted his head. "I don't suppose you'd let me buy you new dresses?"

"I would not."

"Damn." He stroked his chin thoughtfully. "Could I convince you to forego dresses altogether? You look very fetching in your chemise."

His smooth words rolled over her, soothing the hurt. She looked into his eyes and saw not the arrogant duke, but *him*. Heat flared between them, and like a fool, she walked into the fire.

"I've missed you," she said.

"I've missed you, too."

Leaning across the bed, he carefully removed her spectacles and placed them on the bedside crate. In one swift motion, he captured her cheek in his palm, drew her face toward his, and gently kissed her lips. Desire coursed through her body, tingling her scalp, tightening her nipples, curling her toes. She kissed him back, reveling in the perfect melding of his lips to hers. Whatever their differences—and there were many—their connection felt right and true.

She pulled back slightly. "Are you sure you're feeling well?"

"Improving by the second." He grinned and leaned in for another searing kiss. With each thrust of his tongue, each touch of his hand, he brought her further under his spell. She wanted to stay like this, cocooned in their private, simple world forever.

This time, however, she was determined to give pleasure as well as take it.

Brushing a few stray locks away from his face, she said, "Remove your jacket."

The corner of his mouth curled in a heart-stopping smile as he shrugged off the jacket and handed it to her.

"Thank you." With relish, she tossed it over her shoulder. Then she loosened his cravat, tugged it off, and sent it sailing across the room as well. "Lie back."

Green eyes full of anticipation, he did as she asked. When he placed his hands behind his head, the muscles in his arms flexed, making her mouth go dry.

"What next?" he challenged.

"I shall attempt to remove your boots." Although difficult, she managed the task with a minimal amount of grunting.

"I have to confess I found that oddly arousing," he said.

"That's good," she said, feeling quite the seductress. "We're just getting started." She turned the lantern down low and stretched out beside him on the soft mattress. The hunger that shone in his eyes was so fierce she could see it even without her spectacles. She could feel it. Taste it.

She needed to tell him how she felt about him, needed to know if he felt the same. "Owen, when I first met you, I thought you were arrogant and stubborn. But now I see a different side of you, and I . . . I care for you. Deeply. I love the way I feel when I'm with you."

There. She'd said it. And now she held her breath.

He cursed softly—not the reaction she'd hoped for.

Picking up a tendril of her hair and winding it around his fingers, he said, "You are amazing. But despite our connection, I don't know what the future holds for us. You deserve marriage, which I can't promise."

Anabelle already knew this, but hearing him say the words aloud was rather crushing. She leaned over him, placing a palm on his chest. "I'm not seeking marriage. I just want to feel that there's something real between us."

"There is, Belle." He dragged her head down and kissed her until she was dazed with longing. "Don't doubt it. I care a great deal for you."

As declarations went, it wasn't the grandest. But for him, she suspected it was extraordinary. With her index finger, she traced small circles on the hard planes of his chest. "When I'm not with you, I start to wonder if this is all a figment of my imagination. If it only exists in the dark, when we're alone."

"It's always there. I'll show you that what we have is very real . . . and erase the doubts from your mind."

He flipped her over so she was beneath him and kissed her hard, proving his point with every thrust of his tongue. And it *was* convincing.

As though removing the bow from a long-awaited present, he slipped the straps of her chemise off one shoulder, then the other. He lowered his head to suckle her breasts and kiss her belly, dragging her chemise lower and lower, until she wore nothing. He gazed at her with unabashed appreciation, and her body tingled in response.

Eager to see more of him, Anabelle lifted his shirt over his head. His chest and abdomen were so sculpted and hard they could have been made from marble. But unlike stone, his skin was warm and smelled faintly of brandy, cheroot smoke, the starch of his shirt, and *him*. She explored the cords of his neck, the expanse of his shoulders, and the ridges of muscle beneath his skin. When she touched his flat nipples, he kissed her even more deeply. She moaned from sheer pleasure.

Curious to know how his naked body would feel against hers, she pulled him closer. How different they were, and yet, they fit perfectly together. His arms felt strong and secure around her; the light sprinkling of hair on his chest tickled the sensitive skin of her breasts, teasing the tips to rigid peaks.

"Do you believe yet?" he asked.

"Hmmm?" Her head spun with desire.

"Do you believe in us?" He sucked lightly on her neck. "Do you believe in this?"

"I believe that you make me feel very good."

He went still for a moment. "You may be even more of a cynic than I am."

"What do you mean?"

"Nothing. Just close your eyes and enjoy. We have a few hours before dawn—I don't intend to waste a minute of it."

True to his word, Owen made excellent use of his time. He didn't make love to her but taught her new things about her body—what felt good, what felt amazing, and what felt utterly divine. He talked to her about his sisters and his vast assortment of great aunts and asked about her family and her childhood. She almost told him about her grandfather, the viscount, but couldn't choke out the words. Instead, she tried to explain that dressmaking was more than a profession to her; it was also her passion. They shared their silliest secret fears—hers was spiders and his was Latin translations.

Sated, she snuggled into the crook of his arm. Almost instantly, sleep began to descend upon her. Valiantly, she fought it, knowing it would end her time with Owen. But she was too content and comfortable to resist closing her eyes for a few moments. She drifted off in his arms.

Some time later, the sun's golden rays, refracted by the porthole window, warmed her cheek in a celestial kiss, and she awoke. Alone.

Chapter Nineteen

Fleece: (1) The wool coat of a sheep, which is useful for lining items. (2) To swindle persons out of their money through dishonorable means such as extortion.

With every jarring step his gelding took, Owen's head throbbed. The coach carrying the women rumbled along beside him, creating a ruckus that set his teeth on edge. His headache was on par with the worst hangover he'd ever had. Times two.

And yet, the night he'd spent with Anabelle— everything *after* the conk on the head—made him smile like a sotted fool. Which, he supposed, he was.

He'd left Belle's room as soon as he heard the birds chirping outside her window. After covering her with the blanket she seemed determined to kick off, he picked up his clothes and boots from the floor where she'd flung them—God, he'd loved that—shoved his arms into his shirt, and snuck down the hall to his own room.

At breakfast, she sat quietly, but her skin was rosy and she looked...happy. Best of all, she'd traded her usual cap for a simple bonnet that tied beneath her chin. A few wisps of hair grazed the lovely column of her neck. Though the shapeless gray dress she wore hid most of her charms, he'd committed her sweet curves and long limbs to memory. All the dismal gray fabric in London wasn't going to make him forget.

Owen insisted that his sisters and Anabelle get an early start, in spite of the girls' grumbling. After spending five hours on the road, they were almost to Lord Harsby's estate and would arrive in plenty of time for dinner.

The shade inside the coach had been drawn most of the day, leading him to wonder what the women—and Belle in particular—were doing. Sleeping, probably.

Each time he recalled the previous night—how he'd claimed every inch of her with his mouth, her hands exploring every part of him, the soft moaning sounds she made as she came—his blood heated. Resisting temptation and refusing to make love to her had required willpower he hadn't known he possessed.

Being honorable was damned difficult.

Over the last five hours he'd examined the problem from every angle. No matter how much he cared for Anabelle, there was no bridging the difference in their stations.

He needed a duchess. Though Belle was the granddaughter of viscount, she hadn't been raised as one. She'd never been to Court, Almack's, or the opera.

No woman had ever challenged him the way she did or made him feel as complete, but with his title came responsibility. His future wife needed the upbringing, social standing, and the experience necessary for the role of duchess.

Anabelle had never attended a ball—how could she be expected to host one?

From the time he was in leading strings, he'd been primed to be a duke. Before he'd even learned his sums, he understood the importance of the title he'd one day hold. And everyone in his family, his circle of acquaintances, and London society understood it, too. It was a foregone conclusion that he'd take his seat in the House of Lords and run the Huntford estates. Most importantly, however, he'd ensure the well-being of a multitude of people, including everyone from family members to tenants.

Honor and duty trumped everything.

Three years ago, marriage to Anabelle may not have been impossible. But then his mother had had an affair and deserted her family, giving the Huntford name a black eye. And his father had committed suicide—although no one outside of his household could confirm the fact, it was widely suspected by the *ton*—leaving the family name further bloodied and battered.

If he were to marry a seamstress, it would be the knock-out punch.

And he couldn't do that to his sisters. Couldn't do it to the title.

A lonely cloud drifted in front of the sun, casting long shadows beside him, and he clenched the reins in his fists. They'd enjoy a few weeks of stolen moments, clandestine meetings. After that, they'd say good-bye, and he'd pretend she wasn't the best thing to ever happen to him. He'd make sure she and her family never wanted for anything, if her stubborn pride would let him. And in time, she'd meet a kind man, get married, have children, and forget him.

But never, ever, would Owen forget her.

For his sisters' sakes, he'd marry someone with an impeccable lineage and the finest reputation—probably a pampered, delicate hothouse flower who knew nothing of life's struggles and accepted every bit of drivel he spouted like it was divine truth. The prospect left him unenthused.

Harsby's manor house came into view at last. The late afternoon sun glinted off the windows as though the stone structure were winking, aware of some private joke. A large fountain in the center of the circular drive shot foaming mist several feet into the air, creating a gauzy veil in front of the stately red brick home. Copses of birch trees dotted the gently rolling lawn surrounding the manor, which was shaped like a giant "T."

Although impressive, it had but a fraction of the grandeur of Huntford Manor. What would Belle think of this house—or of his, if she ever saw it? He shrugged off the thought. Chances were, she'd never lay eyes on his beloved estate. The golden afternoon lost some of its shine.

The coach pulled up the gravel drive and his horse trotted alongside. Owen couldn't wait to dismount, help the women out of the coach . . . and see Belle.

A stable boy raced across the lawn to meet him, and Owen hopped off his horse, grateful to hand over the reins. He strode to the coach, waved the footman away, and opened the door himself. Olivia bounded out almost before he could lower the stairs; being trapped in a coach for most of the day must have driven her mad.

"Thank goodness we're here," she cried. "I felt like I was in a crypt."

Owen raised a brow. Coaches didn't come any more luxurious or spacious than his. "You look none the worse for wear."

She sucked in her cheeks. "You are ever charming, dear brother."

Rose emerged next, her blue eyes twinkling and full of trepidation.

Owen helped her alight. "You needn't worry about meeting everyone. Olivia, Miss Honeycote, or I will be with you at all times."

She seemed to release a breath she'd been holding. Attending this house party was marked progress for Rose. She'd made her presentation to the Queen a few months ago, at his insistence. But she'd yet to obtain vouchers from the patronesses at Almack's or attend a ball. She rarely left the house—when she did, it was to run quick errands or to pay calls with Olivia, only to close friends. However, Rose enjoyed visiting the tenants who lived near Huntford Manor, taking food to the sick and gifts to the children. While she normally avoided social functions, here, at the house party, there'd be no escaping them.

She glided to Olivia's side and linked an arm through hers. Both girls looked expectantly at the coach. Like they knew a secret he didn't. Minxes.

He peered inside. "Are you coming, Miss Honeycote?" The sun behind the coach momentarily blinded him, but at last Anabelle emerged.

At least he *thought* it was Anabelle.

She looked vastly different from the woman he'd seen when they stopped briefly for lunch. Gone was the gray, shapeless dress. In its place was a gown the color of daffodils and full of the same promise—warmer, brighter days ahead. It was the dress she'd been working on last night. His mother's dress, only different. Green ribbon sewn around the sleeves and neck matched the green trim on her new bonnet. She'd added lace above the neckline, covering much of the soft, sweet skin he'd kissed last night. Given that there'd be other men at this house party, he approved of the alteration.

Unfortunately, it would take more than a bit of lace to keep men from noticing Anabelle.

The dress showcased her high breasts and her long, kissable neck. What was more, she no longer looked like a lower servant. She could easily pass for a governess or a companion. Even a lady.

She licked her lips nervously, awaiting his reaction.

He wanted to tell her how beautiful she was and that he'd been wrong about the blasted dress, and that, of course she should take all the dresses and wear them, his issues with his mother be damned.

Moreover, he longed to haul her into his arms and kiss her senseless.

He almost did, before recalling that his sisters stood just behind him.

"You're looking very well." He hoped his eyes said everything he couldn't.

"Thank you, Your Grace."

It occurred to him that she must have changed her clothes during the ride. The thought of her undressing in his coach made his whole body thrum.

"Doesn't she look positively lovely?" Olivia cried.

"I believe I just said something to that effect," he said dryly.

Olivia grunted. "Men can be so vexing, can they not, Anabelle?"

She smiled shyly. "On occasion." Quickly, she added, "I don't mean to imply that the duke is vexing."

"I'm not implying," said Olivia. "I'm stating. I do believe—"

He was spared from having to hear his sister's beliefs when Lord Harsby opened the front door of the manor house. "Huntford! So glad your party has arrived. My wife is anxious to see these sisters of yours—grand plans and all that." Harsby had the stocky build of an avid sportsman who'd enjoyed too many rich dinners. He eyed the stone steps leading to the gravel driveway with distaste, placed his fists on his hips, and remained by the front door.

Owen waved. Their trunks hadn't even been unloaded, and already Harsby was hinting that his wife intended to play matchmaker for Olivia and Rose. Anabelle had better be up to the task of chaperone—he'd need all the help he could get. "I look forward to seeing Lady Harsby." He guided all three women up the gleaming white steps leading to the house. "I believe you know my sisters, Lady Olivia and Lady Rose." The girls curtseyed prettily. "And this is their companion, Miss Honeycote."

Harsby bowed and searched Anabelle's face. "Honeycote," he mused. "The name's quite familiar."

"It's a common family name," she said smoothly. "Hundreds of us Honeycotes are scattered across England, but I've lived most of my life in London. It's a treat to visit such a grand estate—your home is most impressive."

Owen had to give Anabelle credit. She'd effectively but politely evaded Harsby's unspoken question about her family background and, in the same breath, issued a compliment. She'd topped off the whole exchange with a demure smile, and Harsby was halfway to charmed.

"Do come in," he said. "Lady Harsby will want to see the lot of you with her own eyes before we get you settled in your rooms. Won't take long, but she'd skewer me if I sent you up without letting her greet you." He closed the front door behind them and bellowed, "Neville!" His voice echoed off the high ceilings and marble floors. Even the crystal chandelier above them trembled.

A butler emerged from a doorway below a sweeping staircase.

"Tell Lady Harsby more guests have arrived."

"Here I am," came a sing-song voice, and their hostess glided into the foyer, high-heeled slippers clicking. Lady Harsby was a sparkly, rotund woman. Jewels glittered on her fingers, neck, and ears. Her dress had gold ribbon all over it, and even her hair was silver. "At last, you are here! Neville, have the footmen bring in their things."

Introductions were followed by a great deal of chatter, which caused the bump on Owen's head to throb even more than it already did.

As if he sensed the effect of his wife's voice, Lord Harsby said, "My dear, our guests will want to rest before dinner. Shall we show them to their rooms?"

"Yes, yes, of course. That's where everyone is, you know—resting in their rooms. You'll see them all at dinner."

"Has Miss Starling arrived yet?" Olivia asked. Owen had forgotten that the debutante would be there. With any luck, he could convince Averill to occupy her for the duration of their visit.

"Oh, yes. She and her mother arrived this morning. The marchioness and her two handsome sons"—she gave a not-so-subtle wink to Olivia and Rose—"came shortly after. Mr. Averill arrived last night, as did the earl and his wife and daughter."

"The earl?" asked Olivia.

"Winthrope," Lord Harsby said. "If you don't know him, you'll meet him at dinner. Good chap. Knows his horses. And a few other things." He jabbed Owen with a meaty elbow, in case there were any doubt as to what the other *things* were. Owen didn't know Winthrope well, but the old earl had a reputation for womanizing and drinking.

Rose must have known something about him, too, because her face paled and she swayed on her feet. He immediately moved to her side to steady her; Anabelle shored up her other side. Owen didn't give a damn what entertainments the earl enjoyed, as long as they didn't involve his sisters. At least with his wife and daughter in tow, the old earl would have to behave himself.

Lord Harsby slapped Owen on the back. "Care to stop in my study for a glass of brandy?"

Tempting as a drink sounded, he didn't want to leave Rose just yet. "Thank you, but I want to make sure my sisters are settled."

"We'll be fine," said Olivia. "Won't we, Rose?"

She nodded, encouraging him with her eyes.

"Yes," Anabelle chimed in. "I'll be with them."

Feeling extraneous, Owen capitulated. "Very well. Brandy is an excellent idea." Maybe it would help him relax. Ever since he'd stepped foot in the marquess's house—and for reasons he couldn't quite explain—he had the feeling that he was going to regret bringing his sisters and Anabelle to this house party.

Anabelle grappled with the news that the Earl of Winthrope was also a guest. Although her heart thundered in her chest, she managed to keep her composure while Lady Harsby showed Olivia, Rose, and her to their rooms. They were in the west wing of the manor, as were Miss Starling and her mother, Lady Harsby informed them. She had prepared three separate bedchambers. Each appeared small, but lovely, and was accessed through a larger, common sitting room.

"When I heard you were bringing a companion, I knew this suite would be perfect," Lady Harsby declared. "You have your own bedchambers but can chat to your heart's content out here in the sitting area."

"How thoughtful," Olivia said sincerely, and Anabelle smiled to herself. Lady Harsby needn't have bothered with separate rooms; Rose would probably curl up in bed next to Olivia, as she did most nights.

"Pshaw. It's nothing." Their hostess beamed. "I'll have a maid bring up some light refreshments. Dinner shall be served at eight. You'll want to rest your eyes so you look your best for the gentlemen." With a girlish giggle and a waggle of her jeweled fingers, Lady Harsby left.

Anabelle guided a pale-faced Rose to the blue settee. She was clearly distressed at the news that Lord Winthrope was here, probably reliving the day she'd walked into her mother's bedchamber to find her frolicking with the earl and his mistress. But Anabelle only knew about the incident because she'd extorted money from the earl—and Rose didn't know she knew. And Olivia, who was normally completely in tune with her sister, was oblivious.

The situation was so confusing.

As were Anabelle's emotions. The heat in Owen's gaze as she'd exited the coach had made her stomach flip. The gleam in his eyes said he approved of her new gown. *And* that he'd take immense pleasure in removing it from her person.

The moment she'd put on the altered dress—quite a feat in the rocking coach—she'd felt infused with confidence. Ridiculous, but it almost seemed as though the dress had absorbed the duchess's poise and transferred it to Anabelle.

If no one at the house party had ever met her, she might have felt comfortable acting as the girls' chaperone and even mingling with the other guests, when necessary. But Miss Starling and her mother *did* know Anabelle. And they knew she was no companion.

"Look," said Olivia, wandering into one of the bedchambers. "Our bags are already here. And from our windows, we can see miles and miles of green forests. How wonderful it is to be away from Town!" She rushed back into the sitting room and planted her hands on her hips. "Don't the two of you want to see?"

Rose shook her head and wrung her hands. Anabelle sat beside her and Olivia rushed to her other side. "What's wrong?"

Although Anabelle knew the cause of Rose's distress, she couldn't say so. "You seemed fine in the coach. Was it something Lady Harsby said?"

Olivia waved a hand in the air. "Don't fret over the countess's matchmaking efforts. I assume you noticed she's trying to pair us up with Lord Danshire and his younger brother. If she's going to expend her energy pushing a gentleman my way, why can't it be the *right* gentleman?"

Rose gave a weak smile, and Anabelle endeavored to

reel Olivia back to her sister's problem. To Rose, she said, "Is there a particular guest she mentioned that you wish to avoid?"

Rose's head snapped up.

"I don't understand," Olivia said. "You knew everyone who would be here, except for...Lord Winthrope?"

After several moments, Rose gave a slow nod.

"Winthrope is a harmless old codger," Olivia said dismissively. "Why, we barely know him. I've seen him at the occasional ball, but you couldn't have seen him since..." Understanding dawned. "Oh."

Anabelle took Rose's trembling hand in hers. "Would it help if I promised to go with you whenever you leave our rooms? Between Olivia, your brother, and me, we can make sure you're spared the earl's company as much as possible."

Rose pulled a handkerchief out of the pocket of her pinafore, dabbed her nose, and nodded.

"There," Olivia said. "That was easy enough. Now, come have a look at the view."

Rose and Anabelle joined her, and Olivia was correct—the view of the landscape from the second-story room drew a collective sigh. The air was so clear and the sky so blue, even Anabelle's poor vision seemed acute. If not for all the trees, she fancied she'd see all the way to the English Channel.

A knock on the sitting room door drew them away from the window. Anabelle admitted a maid carrying a tray of tea and pastries. "Where would you like this, ma'am?"

Anabelle blinked. *Ma'am?* Her new dress must have elevated her status in the eyes of servants. "The table next to the settee, if you please."

"It's been hours since we ate lunch." Olivia poured tea into dainty cups and passed them to Anabelle and her sister. "I intend to eat a scone—or two—and close my eyes for a bit. I suggest you ladies do the same."

"I have a few things to do," Anabelle said. A glance at the clock on the escritoire tucked in the corner of the room showed she had barely three hours until dinner.

Three hours to unpack all of their things, begin embellishing one of the dresses she was making for Olivia, help the girls dress for dinner, style their hair, and make herself presentable.

Most importantly, however, she had to figure out how on earth she'd manage to watch Miss Starling flirt outrageously with Owen and refrain from ripping her eyes out. It would require a bit of thought.

Chapter Twenty

*O*wen rubbed his freshly shaven chin and glanced toward the door of Harsby's drawing room.

James Averill tipped his glass and drank. His friend was a chameleon, equally at ease chatting in an opulent drawing room, fighting in a gritty boxing ring, or digging at an exotic archeological site. "Relax, Huntford. Your sisters will be here soon. And so will their companion. I confess I cannot wait to meet her for myself. I don't think I've ever seen you so—" He gave his cocky smile, the same bloody one that made debutantes fan themselves.

"Watch yourself, Averill."

"—distracted."

An apt description—and not the worst his friend could have used. "Rose seemed troubled when we got here. I just want to see whether she is recovered."

"Well then," James said, raising his glass toward the door, "you can put your mind at ease."

Rose and Olivia walked into the room, turning heads

in pale green and pale pink gowns, respectively. They wore their hair pinned up, with loose curls around their foreheads and faces, just like the Season's beauties did.

"Your sisters look so..."

Owen growled but didn't wait for Averill to finish his thought. He strode to his sisters and Belle and bowed deeply. "Pardon me, ladies," he began with uncharacteristic formality, "I wonder if any of you has seen my sisters and their companion."

Olivia grinned. "Can you describe the young ladies in question?"

"They're remarkably like yourselves, only not as well-dressed. And I'm accustomed to seeing them in braids and"—he turned to Anabelle and swallowed—"caps."

Tonight, Anabelle's honey-streaked brown curls were bound with a pretty green ribbon. Her yellow dress—the same one she'd worn this afternoon—was the plainest in the room, and yet, she stood out like a pretty wildflower in an otherwise predictable garden.

Dragging his gaze away from her, he said to Rose, "Are you feeling better?"

She nodded bravely.

"Good. Take my arm. We'll make our way around the room, and I'll show you off to everyone."

Although Rose kept her expression serene and her steps graceful, she clutched his forearm as if he stood between her and a colosseum full of lions. Olivia, on the other hand, seemed eager to meet all the other guests. Her gaze darted around the room, landing on each guest in turn like a fickle butterfly. She was looking for someone. When she sucked in her breath and fluttered her lashes,

Owen knew she'd found whomever it was. He looked over his shoulder and saw the rogue. Averill.

Olivia fancied *him*? Better than being in love with a servant, true, but *Averill*? The man was Owen's best friend, for God's sake. Correction. He *had* been.

Averill bowed smoothly. "Good evening, ladies."

Olivia blushed three shades of red. "How lovely to see you, James."

When they were lads and Olivia little more than a toddler, "James" had sounded charming coming from her lips. Now it set Owen's teeth on edge like a screeching violin.

He placed Olivia's hand firmly on his free arm and glared at Averill. Hard. "I'm about to take my sisters and Miss Honeycote to meet everyone."

"Excellent. I'm honored to be the first." He leaned over Olivia's hand and then Rose's. "You're a far cry from the little urchins who carried frogs in the pockets of their frocks."

Olivia blanched. "Er, that must have been Rose. She's much fonder of animals than I. Not that I dislike animals. Just the kind that hop or slither. And beetles. Anything with more than four legs, now that I think on it."

"Have you no mercy for the octopus?" Averill's damned eyes twinkled. At his sister.

Owen cleared his throat. He might as well get the next part over with. "Averill, this is Miss Honeycote. She is a companion to my sisters."

Olivia scowled. "Anabelle is much more than a companion. She's a dear friend."

"It's a pleasure to meet you, Mr. Averill."

"The pleasure is all mine, I assure you. It seems unjust that Huntford has a beautiful woman on each arm while both of mine are empty. Would you allow me to escort you around the room, Miss Honeycote?"

Owen clenched his fists, wishing they weren't in a genteel drawing room where brawling would be frowned upon. "She doesn't need an escort."

"Unless you've sprouted a third arm, I believe she does."

Anabelle pushed her spectacles higher up on her sloped nose and shot Owen a pointed look. "Thank you, Mr. Averill. I'll happily avail myself of your kind offer."

Hanging on to his temper by the thinnest of threads, Owen led the way around the room, stopping first to greet Lady Danshire, an elderly widow with a penchant for purple, and her irresponsible sons, Danshire and Sandleigh. Both gentlemen sported bloodshot eyes and rumpled cravats—and reeked of brandy. After exchanging a few pleasantries, Owen steered his sisters toward Mrs. Starling and her daughter.

Olivia and Rose were at ease in Miss Starling's company, but he was not. During their brief conversation, Mrs. Starling managed to mention no less than five different virtues her daughter possessed. Miss Starling said little but gazed at Owen with an expression that was both demure and expectant. It made him want to saddle a horse and ride hard in the opposite direction.

He contented himself with crossing the room to where the Earl of Winthrope, his wife, and their daughter sat in a group of chairs beside the dormant fireplace. Rose clutched his arm harder when they approached the earl. Odd; nothing about the man struck Owen as intimidating. A few greasy strands of hair covered his shiny head, and he was thin if one discounted the paunch that looked like he'd hidden a cat in his waistcoat.

The old earl stood and smiled broadly, showing teeth tinged from tobacco. "Good to see you, Huntford, and your lovely sisters, too."

"Winthrope." Owen nodded congenially. "Lady Winthrope and Lady Margaret, you're both looking well."

The countess fanned herself and her daughter turned four shades of red.

The earl coughed, rattling phlegm in his throat. "Margaret is seventeen—of an age with your sisters, I presume."

Olivia bobbed her head. "I am nineteen, and Rose is seventeen."

Winthrope brushed idly at the sparse strands covering his head. "Rose. A demure name for a demure young lady. I hope you don't mind me saying so, but you have your mother's eyes."

Rose's hand trembled on Owen's arm. He leveled a glare at the earl that was half-question, half-warning. The gentleman should have known better than to mention their mother, even in the most innocuous manner, and yet, Owen couldn't detect the slightest hint of malice. Mystifying, but he'd make sure she was never left alone with Winthrope—or anyone. Being so painfully shy put her at a distinct disadvantage, in even the most nonthreatening social situations.

When the butler finally entered, announcing that dinner was served, Owen was relieved to escort his sisters into the dining room. A minute later Averill entered, Belle on his arm. She listened intently as he waxed on about some bloody fossil; Owen endeavored not to snap the stem of his wineglass in his fist.

While Averill got to sit beside Anabelle, he was

sandwiched between Lady Danshire and Lady Harsby. Although neither had daughters of a marriageable age, it seemed they had many friends and close relatives who did.

They prattled on, finding no shortage of topics, in spite of the five-course meal. All he could think about, though, was holding and kissing Anabelle last night. The hours in her cozy room at the inn were worth the conk on the head, the lack of sleep, and the miniature bed. He hadn't felt that happy in a long, long time.

He needed to find a way to be alone with her again. Soon.

Anabelle had fretted over the seating arrangements at dinner. Rose would be most comfortable sitting between her and Olivia, but protocol had to be followed, and since Anabelle was at the bottom of the pecking order, she should have been seated farthest away from the head of the table.

Fortunately, Mr. Averill was near the bottom of the pecking order as well, and he did a little shuffling, which resulted in Miss Starling sitting closer to Owen and Anabelle remaining beside Rose.

Never had Anabelle experienced a dinner such as this. Eating was something she did out of necessity, to nourish her body. This meal, on the other hand, was an event in and of itself, involving a dizzying number of dishes and a parade of servants—three did nothing more than attend to half-empty wineglasses. Although Mama had taught her all the social norms and manners, they were dreadfully complicated, and Anabelle could barely recall which utensil was used for each course.

She received curious looks from several of the other

guests. Mr. Averill asked probing questions which she deftly dodged; Miss Starling glared at her like she'd spilled soup on her bodice. Owen stared at her as though he wanted to kiss her.

She'd have to speak to him about that.

After being invisible for so long, the scrutiny of the strangers around the table made her want to hide under it. Although she managed to remain in her seat, she ate very little. And imbibed more wine than she ought to have.

By dessert, the dining room was thick with the smells of rich foods and overly warm from the multitude of candles and guests. Upon noticing her napkin had slipped off her lap, she leaned down to pick it up. When she righted herself, however, bright spots danced in the corners of her vision. The room tilted like a rowboat broadsided by a wave.

She gripped the edge of the table to steady herself and blinked, vaguely aware of Rose gesturing to Olivia. Her brows furrowed in concern. "Are you in need of fresh air, Anabelle? Rose and I could walk in the gardens with you."

What kind of companion required assistance from her charges? She inhaled deeply. "I, ah..."

Mr. Averill stood and gently pulled on her elbow. "Lady Olivia and Lady Rose, please stay and finish your cakes. I'll escort Miss Honeycote to the terrace."

"You needn't trouble yourself." She reached for her water glass and almost knocked it over; Mr. Averill caught it before handing it to her as though she were a child. It seemed other conversations at the table ceased and everyone watched to see if she would fall face-first into the pears on her plate.

Owen stood and walked around the table to stand behind her. "Sit, Averill. I'll take care of this."

Anabelle bristled at being referred to as "this"—like she was a rather embarrassing mess to be swept under the rug and covered with a potted palm. However, she couldn't afford to be thin-skinned—she needed to escape the dining room. Quickly.

With an amused smile, Averill sat.

Owen helped her up and guided her toward the drawing room. As he whisked her past the guests, he said, "Excuse us." It was less entreaty than order. "Keep breathing," he whispered to her, his palm firm and steadying on the small of her back. When at last they reached the terrace, cool air whirled around her face, neck, and chest. The peaceful, low humming of insects soothed her frayed nerves.

She braced her arms on the wrought-iron fence that bordered the flagstone terrace leading to the gardens. The ground beneath her feet seemed blessedly still. "That's much better."

"You should sit." Owen pointed to a stone bench.

"Would you mind if we walked, instead? I feel as though I've been sitting all day. A stroll would help clear my head."

"As you wish." The cut of his jacket showed the breadth of his shoulders, and the stark black made his eyes look greener. Riding for the better part of two days had burnished his skin gold, and he could have passed for a dashing pirate—if his clothes hadn't clearly been the handiwork of Weston.

She took the arm he offered, and they wandered down the pebbled path, the bushes flanking them so tall they resembled leafy walls. The canopy of stars and a half moon—so much brighter here than in Town—cast a benevolent glow over everything.

"Are you feeling better?" Concern etched his face.

"Just embarrassed. I'm sorry for causing a scene."

He smiled and shrugged. "It added excitement to an otherwise boring affair."

Her heart leapt at his admission. During dinner, Miss Starling appeared captivated by every word he uttered. If Owen hadn't found the conversation nearly as titillating, Anabelle was secretly pleased.

"I don't like leaving Rose to fend for herself," she said.

"Olivia and Averill are with her. You are officially off-duty." He took her hand and laced his fingers through hers, making her stomach flip. Before she lost her head completely, she needed to talk to him about Rose.

"Have you noticed Rose is very much at unease around Lord Winthrope?"

His dark brows drew together. "She became agitated when she found out he was here. Why would she be nervous around him? He's no paragon of virtue, but Rose hardly knows him."

Anabelle suppressed a shiver. The earl was probably responsible for the drastic change in Rose's personality over two years ago. Being in such close proximity could only bring painful memories to the forefront of her mind. Whatever healing had begun might be undone. How she wished she could tell Owen what she knew. It would explain so much to him . . . the change in Rose's nature, his mother's desertion, his father's suicide.

But she couldn't.

The earl had paid her to keep his secret. Honor prevented her from revealing the truth.

Beneath a vine-covered trellis, Owen tugged her toward him. "Do you know how delectable you look tonight?"

Anabelle swallowed. Although she lacked Miss Starling's stunning silk gown and precious jewels and perfect eyesight, she had Owen all to herself. For now. "Thank you."

"I want to spend more time with you, Belle."

She resisted the urge to fall into his arms. "What does that mean? Precisely?"

He lifted her hand and pressed his lips to the back, his warm, moist breath melting away her reservations. "I care about you. I don't want you flirting with Averill. Or anyone else."

"I wasn't flirting with Mr.—"

"I know." He leaned in, kissed her neck. "I want more of this—of you."

As he traced the shell of her ear with his tongue and squeezed the curve of her bottom, her eyes fluttered shut. He skimmed his hands over her dress and down her arms, as though desperate to claim every inch of her. Desire, hot and potent, swept through her body, leaving her pleasantly woozy.

"Come with me," he said. A plea and promise.

"Where?"

"I'll take you somewhere we can be alone—with no chance of being discovered."

Although she'd been about to capitulate, his last words sobered her. She took a small step back. "What if we *are* discovered?"

"I won't let that happen," he said, reaching for a tendril that hung from her nape.

She placed a palm flat on his chest and straightened her arm, putting more distance between them. "But what if it did?" It was suddenly very important that she knew the answer. He wanted to be with her, he didn't want her to be with another man—that much she understood. But he wasn't openly courting her. If they were discovered in a compromising situation, her reputation would be forever ruined. Unless he was willing to…

Frowning, he grasped her hands and pressed them between his. "I know what's at stake for you. We'll be very careful. No one will suspect we are seeing each other. Trust me."

As she gazed into his beautiful eyes, it was easy to ignore the alarms sounding in her head. His mouth curled in a wicked smile, and he pressed his hips to hers, letting her feel his own desire. Moisture gathered between her legs, and she knew Owen could ease the need spiraling there. He could touch her until she writhed with longing, sweetly torment her until she exploded in hot white light. Even better, he could make her believe she was the only woman he'd ever care about.

"I can't be with you." She knew it with the same certainty that her worn half boots didn't suit a frothy ball gown. It was an utter and final truth.

"What? Why not?"

Because I love you too much to settle for less than all of you. She choked on a sob, wishing she weren't such a coward. "It's hard to explain."

He cupped her cheek with tenderness that made her knees go weak. "Try, my love."

The endearment, so casually spoken, squeezed her chest. She *couldn't* tell him the truth—that she wanted more from him than a series of clandestine trysts. She had her pride. Once she returned to her real life, it would be all she had.

Expecting anything more than a secret affair with Owen was foolish, but her silly heart didn't seem to realize the hopelessness of it all. So she grasped at the obvious reasons, the ones that would make sense to him. "I can't take the chance that someone will see us. I'd lose my job at the dress shop. I'd bring shame upon my mother and sister."

He exhaled loudly and ran his hands through his hair. "There are risks to anything worthwhile. What we have, Belle"—his voice cracked as he spoke her name—"is rare. Like an eclipse of the sun, everything in our respective worlds aligned, bringing us together under that godforsaken bridge in Hyde Park. And now that we're together, I don't want to let you go."

"It's difficult for me, too," she admitted. Her throat convulsed as though a noose had been placed around her neck. "But I've made up my mind. There's too much at stake. My virtue, my livelihood, my family's good name…" *My heart.*

He stared at her for several excruciating seconds while he seemed to wrestle with her decision, and Anabelle knew the exact, awful moment that he accepted it. His shoulders slumped, and the air between them grew heavy and sad. "It was selfish of me to ask you to risk so much. I'm sorry." He gazed at the ground and crossed his arms. "I still want you, Anabelle. I always will. But out of respect for your wishes, I won't press you or make advances again. I promise."

She wanted to scream that she hadn't meant what she said, that she'd take any small part of him that he was willing to give and be happy. "I think that's for the best."

"Well then," he said grimly. Anabelle hated the sudden awkwardness between them. "We'd better return to the house. If I stay out here with you for another minute, I might break my promise on the same night I made it."

Side by side, they walked toward the terrace, without touching. This was the right course of action. But in case they never spoke in private again, she had to let him know what he'd meant to her; she had to say good-bye.

At the wrought-iron railing, she stopped and faced him. The darkness softened his features and masked his usual intensity, making it easier to say the words. "Thank you for giving me a chance and trusting me to work with your sisters. Their friendship is more than I deserve. And thank you for seeing me as more than a seamstress."

He gripped the railing and looked down at her with a sad smile. "Thank for you helping me understand my sisters and for making them happy. If you'd told me a month ago that Rose would willingly attend a house party, I'd never have believed it. And thank you for seeing me as more than a duke."

Her nose stung as though she might cry. "You're welcome."

They stood in silence while Anabelle tried valiantly to compose herself. "We should go in."

Owen nodded and they slowly crossed the terrace and entered the brightly lit drawing room. Anabelle walked toward Owen's sisters.

"Oh, thank Heaven!" cried Olivia. "How are you, Anabelle?"

"Fine, thank you. Sorry I worried you."

"Don't be silly, my dear," Lady Harsby clucked. "Swooning is a fact of life. I myself have fainted twice in the last fortnight."

Miss Starling, who sidled up to Owen the moment

he walked in, muttered under her breath, "Perhaps she should try a larger-sized corset."

"How gallant of the duke to rescue you," Lady Harsby said to Anabelle, but her tone hinted that she considered the task quite beneath him.

"Indeed," she replied. "Thank you, Your Grace."

"I'm glad I could be of assistance, Miss Honeycote." He spoke so coolly no one would suspect that mere minutes ago he'd been nibbling on her ear. "If you ladies will excuse me, I believe I'll join the gentlemen."

"They're in the billiards room," Lady Harsby said. "I hope my husband isn't playing too deep. It's not his game, you know—but then, I'm not sure what is." She burst into peals of laughter as Owen thanked her and quit the room.

Olivia yawned loudly and addressed Lady Harsby. "Forgive me, but Rose and I are exhausted after our wonderful meal. Would it be terribly rude if we retired early?"

"Of course not, dears." Lady Harsby gave a brittle smile. "We'll have a grand time tomorrow, won't we, ladies?" The women responded with a halfhearted chorus of affirmative replies.

Grateful for an excuse to leave before charades commenced, Anabelle followed Olivia and Rose to their lovely suite. As soon as Anabelle closed the door behind them, Olivia asked her, "What happened at dinner? Are you sure you're improved?"

Anabelle sank into an armchair, feeling wretched. "I was just overheated. Once I escaped the dining room, I was immediately set to rights." She smiled to reassure them. "I didn't realize you were so tired, Olivia. Shall I turn down your bed?"

"Heavens, no. I pleaded exhaustion so I could finish

my book. I'm almost to the end. And I could tell Rose was eager for a little peace and solitude."

Rose nodded vigorously.

Anabelle arched a brow at Olivia. "The gentlemen would have returned for charades. You didn't wish to stay and converse with Mr. Averill?"

Olivia folded her hands and pressed them to her chest as though in rapture. "Of *course* I did. But Miss Starling told me that I should be coy and refrain from bumping into him at every turn—which gentlemen find annoying in the extreme."

Odd; Miss Starling didn't seem to follow her own advice when it came to her pursuit of Owen.

"I'm fortunate to have her advising me," Olivia continued. "When we spoke after dinner, I admitted I was fond of James, and she seemed surprised. She was under the impression that my affections were otherwise engaged."

The hairs on the back of Anabelle's neck stood up. The conversation had veered perilously close to the extortion note. Owen wouldn't mention her extortion attempt to anyone, least of all Miss Starling. Would he? If she knew, Miss Starling would no doubt leap at the chance to inform Olivia and Rose of her wickedness, and they would be devastated. They'd detest Anabelle. And she wouldn't blame them.

Her throat tightened. If her scheme was exposed she'd lose two cherished friends in one fell swoop.

"Why don't I help you out of your gowns so that you can be comfortable while you read?"

"Excellent idea," Olivia said, lifting her arm so Anabelle could undo the laces. "Did you hear all the compliments we received? Everyone adored our dresses. I wanted to give you credit but wasn't sure how you'd feel about everyone knowing you created them. You've been elevated to companion now, after all."

"I don't wish to hide what I do or what I am. I'm a seamstress and a dressmaker. I'm also your companion and friend. Proud on all counts."

Rose rushed toward Anabelle and hugged her tightly.

"It's been an emotional day for all of us, hasn't it?" Anabelle said, sniffling. "Let me finish with Olivia, and then I'll help you get settled."

A half hour later, Olivia and Rose were ensconced in one of the bedchambers. From the settee in the adjoining sitting room, Anabelle could hear Olivia reading aloud with all her usual verve. The girls invited her to join them, but Anabelle had much to do before she could sleep.

She needed to select and modify another of the duchess's old gowns to wear tomorrow. After donning the pretty yellow dress today, she hated the thought of reverting to her dark, rougher ones.

More importantly, however, she needed to make headway on the six gowns she had left to finish for Olivia and Rose. Only then could she leave Owen's household, pick up the pieces of her life, and move onward.

The day couldn't arrive soon enough.

Chapter Twenty-one

*Nap: (1) The raised part, or pile, of a fabric such
as velvet. (2) What one requires after a long night
of criminal or otherwise nefarious activity.*

Over the next four days of the house party, Owen
respected Anabelle's wishes. He did not seek her out.

Which may have been the most difficult, selfless thing
he'd ever *not* done.

Each day, she grew more confident, more beautiful. She played the part of companion perfectly, keeping a close watch over Rose and Olivia while deflecting
attention from herself. At the picnic this afternoon, she
chatted with the older women, fetched drinks and fans,
and attempted to blend in with the shrubbery. But Owen
noticed her.

And he wasn't the only one.

"It's very odd—is it not?" Miss Starling asked. She
clung to the sleeve of his jacket as they walked a trail
that bordered the lake and meandered through a series of
miniature temples. She took excruciatingly small steps. If

Owen's calculations were correct, maintaining their current pace on the footpath would ensure their return to the picnic in the fall of 1820. "Miss Honeycote sits at the dining table with us as though she is a lady born and bred. But she is far from a lady, Huntford. Two months ago she was hemming my gown."

Owen counted to three, drew up short, and faced her. "It almost sounds as though you're questioning my choice of chaperone for my sisters."

Miss Starling tossed a few tresses of her blond hair. He'd admit she was beautiful—in a cold and predictable sort of way. "I am merely suggesting that perhaps you should find out more about the mysterious Miss Honeycote. You've entrusted your sisters' welfare to her. What do you know of her background or family?"

He glared and remained silent for several seconds. "Plenty." Miss Starling overstepped her bounds.

"Then I'm sure you know best," she pouted. "I just can't help feeling that she's hiding something."

"Aren't we all?" he challenged.

Her blue eyes opened wider. "I've nothing to hide. If there's anything you wish to know about me, you need only ask."

She gazed at him expectantly, but no burning questions came to mind. About her.

Smoothly, she said, "Perhaps you'd be interested in a bit of gossip I overheard."

Dread slithered down his spine. Rumors had led to his mother's desertion, his father's suicide, and a certain extortion note. In a tone as uninterested as he could muster, he drolled, "Gossip?"

"Concerning Olivia and Rose."

He abruptly stopped again and raised a brow.

To Miss Starling's credit, she didn't cower. "Yester-day, while your sisters were in Lord Danshire's boat out there"—she nodded toward the lake—"his brother said that your sisters, though lovely, seemed to lack the grace and bearing required of a countess."

Owen growled. Tossing Danshire and his idiotic brother into the lake would give him great pleasure.

As though privy to his thoughts, Miss Starling patted his arm and said, "A display of your temper would only make matters worse. You cannot bully those gentlemen into accepting your sisters."

Couldn't he? He pictured the cretins trodding onto the shore of the lake, their fine jackets tinged green from algae, their expensive boots covered in silt…"I sup-pose not."

"Likewise, you cannot buy their acceptance. I assume you have spent a small fortune for Miss Honeycote's exclusive dressmaking services. What has it gotten your sisters? The enviable wardrobes they gained are offset by their odd friendship with the seamstress. The more time they spend with her, the more people talk."

Owen seethed. "My sisters are happy."

Miss Starling clucked her tongue. "The poor dears don't know any better. Now, I could see that your sisters are truly embraced by the *ton*. Under the right set of cir-cumstances, that is. My influence is limited now, but…"

Owen did not miss her meaning. She could help his sisters—*would* help them—if she became his wife. He didn't normally tolerate attempts to manipulate him, but Miss Starling was a shrewd woman clearly intent on becoming the Duchess of Huntford. He might have admired her dogged determination—if he hadn't been the object of it.

It was high time he married. He supposed he should summon a modicum of enthusiasm for the task, but he couldn't. Now, if he could marry someone like Anabelle... but that was not even within the realm of possibility.

He might as well marry someone who could help his sisters. Miss Starling possessed the necessary qualifications, and half the *ton* already seemed to think they were betrothed. He would probably offer for her.

But not yet.

Not here, at the house party, in front of Anabelle. He couldn't do that to her. Or himself.

"Huntford?" Miss Starling tapped her toe and pulled him toward the mock ruins on the sloping shore of the lake. The artfully crumbled columns and the flawless lawn surrounding the folly left a sour taste in his mouth. What was the sense in erecting a new structure that looked ancient? And what was the point of plopping it onto a perfectly manicured lawn? Wouldn't a real ruin have a few weeds sprouting up around it, for God's sake?

Precious little in his world was genuine and true.

"We should return to the picnic," he said.

"I only wanted to explore a little." She boldly placed her palm on his chest. "Are you worried my reputation will be sullied by a few minutes inside the ruins?"

"Of course I'm concerned for your reputation. And I'd like to check on my sisters as well." He offered his arm, but she folded hers.

"Will you answer one question?" she asked.

"If I can."

"Am I foolish to discourage other suitors? Am I wasting my time with you?"

"That was two questions."

Her blue eyes narrowed to slits. "I deserve answers."

Owen gazed across the glinting water to the dots of color darting back and forth across the lawn. The stationary light blue dot on the edge of the gathering was Anabelle, cheering on his sisters as they played cricket. He'd tried to persuade her to join in the game, but she declined, saying it wouldn't be seemly. For a companion.

"I'm waiting, Huntford."

He swallowed and forced himself to look at her. "The answers are"—somehow, he forced the words past the chokehold around his throat—"no and . . . no."

After dinner that evening, all the guests gathered in the drawing room for musical entertainment. Several young ladies—and not-so-young ladies—were called upon to play the piano and sing. Anabelle pasted on a smile and clapped politely after each performance. She was delighted to discover, however, that Rose was quite talented at the piano keys. When she perched herself on the piano bench in front of everyone, accompanying Olivia as she sang a few lively ballads, Anabelle's heart beat fast with admiration and wonder.

Owen, who was seated between Miss Starling and her mother, had looked miserable during the earlier performances, but when he heard his sisters, he leaned forward, mesmerized—and looked proud enough to pop a button off his jacket.

Unable to contain her own joy, Anabelle smiled at him. He smiled back.

Her entire body tingled.

While she and Owen sat stiffly in a drawing room crowded with ladies and gentlemen, she imagined their souls floating above the room, in perfect harmony with the music, connecting them on a higher plane. She felt so close to him in that moment that they might have been embracing, skin to skin. The frisson that ran through her was frightening in its intensity, making her blush from the roots of her hair to the hollow of her throat. How she missed him.

Owen swallowed, and his green eyes took on the hue of a turbulent sea. He wanted her, too.

How foolish of her to think keeping her distance from Owen would banish him from her heart. They may have avoided conversation with each other, but as long as he was in the same house, she couldn't help but be aware of his every move, or, indeed, his every thought.

It was torture to be so near him and not be *with* him.

And so, she'd stayed up late working the past several nights. She had to finish embellishing the dresses before the conclusion of the house party. She'd completed work on all but two—the gowns for Rose's debut ball. They'd be Anabelle's most stunning creations, more beautiful than Olivia and Rose had even dreamt.

When Anabelle and the girls finally retired to their rooms that evening, she helped ready them for bed. Olivia, in particular, was animated after their performance. "Was James looking at me while I sang?"

"Of course he was," Anabelle assured her, hoping it was true. She'd been preoccupied with Owen. "Everyone was quite impressed with the pair of you."

"I don't care about everyone," Olivia said petulantly. "Just James. Did you hear him talking about taking a trip to Egypt? He's so worldly, and I know practically nothing about the country. Other than it's the location of dusty pyramids housing dead people. I must find a book and learn all I can so I can speak intelligently on the subject."

Rose nodded in agreement, and Olivia rambled on about Mr. Averill, examining every tilt of his head, every casual comment. At last, she climbed into bed, yawning. Rose lay sprawled across the counterpane beside her, reading a book of poetry.

Anabelle hung their dresses in a small armoire, walked to the window, and pushed back the heavy drapes. Pressing the tip of a finger to the cool pane, she traced the haphazard paths in which rivulets of rain trickled on the other side.

"It's been raining for hours," Olivia said. "It will make for a muddy walk to the village tomorrow."

Anabelle let the curtain fall back into place and wrapped an arm around a post at the foot of the bed. "I love the soothing patter of rain at night."

"You should turn in early," Olivia said. "Forgive me for saying so, but you look rather tired."

Despite the weariness that made her limbs feel heavy and uncoordinated, Anabelle had work to do. "I won't stay up too late," she lied.

"Oh, you're working on our ball gowns, aren't you?" cried Olivia. "Do you think we could have a peek?"

Anabelle laughed. "No, you may not. You will not see them again until every embellishment is complete and every thread has been trimmed."

"You are cruel beyond measure!"

"Yes. Be careful, or I will cover the bodice of your gown with a dozen ostrich feathers." She pressed a finger to her chin, as though she were considering something. "You don't suppose Mr. Averill is allergic, do you?"

Rose laughed, a wonderful sound. Olivia hurled a throw pillow in Anabelle's direction, which she easily dodged. In all her pillow fights with Daph, Anabelle had yet to lose.

"Do you need anything before I go?" Anabelle asked.

Olivia pulled the coverlet up to her chin, nestled her head into her pillow, and smiled. "No, thank you. I intend to close my eyes and dream about a certain handsome solicitor."

Rose, who was braiding her glowing auburn hair into a thick rope, rolled her eyes and shook her head.

With a chuckle, Anabelle said good night and walked to her bedchamber. She penned a quick note to Daphne, taking care not to let her heartache spill onto the page. Instead, she inquired after Mama and wrote how glad she was to be coming home soon.

After finishing the letter, she closed the door leading into the suite. She planned to add crystals to the sleeves of Olivia's gown and would not put it past her to saunter by an open door in order to catch a glimpse.

Anabelle couldn't wait to see the looks on Olivia and Rose's faces when the finished gowns were unveiled.

It would be a day full of joy... and sorrow, because she'd say good-bye.

Afterward, they might exchange the occasional letter or converse in Mrs. Smallwood's dress shop, but they wouldn't be able to visit or socialize. Even if the difference in their stations didn't prohibit it, seeing Olivia and Rose would be much too painful.

They would only serve to remind her of Owen and of the life they might have had if she'd been more like Miss

Starling. If Mama hadn't been from a common family—or if Anabelle's paternal grandparents could have overlooked Mama's humble origins—Anabelle might have been raised as a true lady. She would have spent leisurely summers at her grandfather's country estate and made her come-out in a lovely white gown when she turned sixteen. Best of all, she'd have sewn for the pure pleasure of it—not because she needed to put food on her family's table.

Silly, stupid, pointless thoughts.

And they ran through her mind, tormenting her, into the wee hours of the morning.

Chapter Twenty-two

Rose Sherbourne listened to her sister's even, peaceful breathing. She was probably already dreaming about James. Rose envied her, in a way. Olivia, who expended every ounce of energy she possessed during the day, always fell asleep soon after laying her head on the pillow. Rose tossed and turned, her head full of what ifs, whys, and hows.

At least every night brought her closer to seeing Charles. She'd be at Huntford Manor within the week; they'd be together again. Her heart tripped lightly in her chest.

Until then, she could occupy herself with helping Olivia. Taking care not to bounce the mattress, she slid off the bed and slipped into her robe. Quietly, she padded across the bedchamber, entered the sitting room, and found it empty. Perhaps Anabelle had taken Olivia's advice and had gone to sleep early. No, a soft light shone beneath her door. She must be working on the ball gowns.

Rose raised a fist to knock on Anabelle's door, but hesitated. It was only a trip to Lord Harsby's library. He'd told the girls to avail themselves of all the dusty tomes they wanted. They'd already borrowed several items from his collection, and Rose knew the exact shelf where the travel journals were housed. It would be a simple matter to return the volume of poetry she'd borrowed and select a book or two on ancient Egypt for Olivia.

The house party represented a week of firsts for Rose, and in spite of the awful sense of foreboding she'd felt upon learning that the Earl of Winthrope was a guest, nothing untoward had occurred. The earl had been the model of civility all week long, doting on his wife and their daughter, Margaret.

So much time had passed since the fateful night Rose stumbled into her mother's room. Sometimes she wondered if her overactive, adolescent mind had imagined the whole sordid thing.

But every couple of months, she awoke in the dark of night, fists clutching the sheets. In her nightmares, she relived every awful detail: the earl's flabby, pale chest, glistening with sweat; his mistress's head, bent over his lap; her mother lying prone as the earl pawed at her breasts. The spectacle was all the more shocking because Rose had believed her mother the perfect lady. Never before had she seen her mother with her hair down. The air was thick with their bodily scents. And no wonder they hadn't heard Rose's gentle knock—the bedchamber had echoed with the primitive moaning and grunting of wild beasts.

The most haunting part of the dream, however, was when Mama turned her head, opened her heavy-lidded eyes, and stared directly into Rose's. Alarm, denial, and self-loathing flicked across Mama's face in quick succession. She must have known there was no way to explain her behavior. Before she could try, Rose fled. She left the house and the estate and ran and ran, as though running could erase the horror of the scene from her mind and perhaps undo it completely.

That image of her mother was the one she remembered most clearly. There'd been happier times—walks in the park, ices at Gunter's, and skating on the river. But those memories were colorless and unfocused, like she was viewing them through gossamer. No, the sharpest recollection Rose had of her mother was from that terrible night.

The last time she ever saw her.

Rose shook her head to clear it and breathed deeply. She was no longer a green girl but a woman, and it was time for her to face the truth. Life was sometimes ugly and unpleasant. But she didn't have to dwell on those bits.

Instead she imagined how delighted Olivia would be to see a book on James's favorite subject—Ancient Egypt— beside her bed when she woke.

Rose quietly retrieved her slippers, clutched the book of poetry to her chest, and headed for the library. The corridor was dark; one lamp flickered halfheartedly on a small table at the top of the landing. She picked up the lantern and tiptoed downstairs, grateful that the entire household seemed to be asleep.

Running into someone when she was alone was... awkward. They would politely greet her, and she would murmur something unintelligible, smile, and nod.

Her sudden withdrawal from the world over two years ago was a source of grave concern to Olivia and Owen, and she regretted worrying them. But something inside her had fragmented that night.

She vaguely recalled having been a happy, whole person before. Sometimes, in her dreams, she was transported to a time when she'd laughed with Olivia and Owen, hugged Papa, and played the piano for Mama. But the memories were murky and distorted—as though she gazed at her reflection in a muddy, swirling lake.

She hadn't yet figured out how to put herself back together again. Some days, when her emotions were calm and quiet, she felt certain it was only a matter of time before she'd be able to fill the cracks and return to the person she'd been before. Other days, it seemed there wasn't enough paste in the world to mend her, especially without either Mama or Papa there to help her.

She entered the second-floor room, inhaling the familiar musty smell all self-respecting libraries possessed. Lord and Lady Harsby's collection was impressive, and the room was well-appointed—thick carpets begged one to walk barefoot and plush armchairs invited one to test their soft cushions.

The travel guides stood in militarily neat rows on a bottom shelf, ready to serve. Finding a couple of books about pharaohs and mummies was an easy matter. Tucking them under an arm, she proceeded to the large bookcase dedicated to poetry. She returned the volume she had and plucked another—a rich leather volume of Donne's.

The lush imagery and angst drew her in, and before she knew it, she'd settled into a cozy wingback chair, taken off her slippers, and tucked her feet beneath her. Torrents of rain occasionally blew against the large windows, and lightning flashed, providing brief glimpses of the room's treasures. The minute hand on the grandfather clock made a revolution, or perhaps two. Rose savored the peace and stillness that were so scarce during the daylight hours.

Eventually, however, her eyes blinked in protest. She closed them—just for a moment. After a quick rest, she'd finish the page and sneak back to bed.

But the chair was so comfortable, sleep so seductive.

A tickle on her neck interrupted her slumber. She brushed a hand across her throat, but the sensation persisted. She ignored it.

When a clap of thunder rattled the windows, however, she opened her eyes and bolted upright.

Lord Winthrope leaned over her, his foul breath hot on her face.

A scream rose up in her throat and stuck there. She cowered against the back of the chair and pulled her robe tightly around her. The book of poetry fell off her lap, thudding to the floor.

"So much like your mother." His words slithered across her skin. "Stunningly beautiful and aloof. But underneath your superior façade lies a woman with a predilection for...naughtiness." He grasped the base of her throat, putting pressure on her windpipe. Air became terrifyingly scarce.

Trembling, she shook her head. He didn't know her at all. She was *nothing* like Mama.

"Oh, but it's true. She resisted at first, too. Once I introduced her to the more sophisticated pleasures"—he rubbed his crotch—"she couldn't get enough. You saw us that night, didn't you?"

She stared blankly, refusing to give any indication of the truth. Inside, though, her heart beat wildly. He knew.

"Your mother worried that you'd tell your father about us. What a ridiculous notion!" He snorted and pointed at the poetry book on the rug by his feet. "You're reading about sex when you should be trying it. Aren't you curious to know what all the fuss is about?"

Disgust and the pressure on her throat made her gag.

"You have much to learn, my pretty lass."

The vein in her neck pulsed frantically beneath his clammy hands. Her feet itched to kick him, but in her vulnerable position, she couldn't afford to anger him. She pounded the arm of the chair with her fist, desperately hoping a stray servant would hear it and investigate, but the corridor outside the library was void of light or movement.

Frustration welled inside her. A normal girl would scream and awaken the household.

Curse her stupid voice for deserting her. And curse the wretched weakness that prevented her from reclaiming it.

Lord Winthrope leered with undisguised lust and straddled her on the armchair, pinning her to it. He leaned in closer, the rum on his breath stinging her eyes.

She would *not* be a victim of this grotesque excuse for a human being. Summoning every ounce of courage, she opened her mouth, took as deep a breath as she could, and—

Nothing.

She tried again. Inhaled, and tried to let loose a yelp, a squeal, a grunt. Anything to alert someone to her predicament.

But her windpipe constricted, and the only audible sound she made was a faint gasp—worthless and futile. Oh, why hadn't she asked Anabelle to accompany her? Tears burned at the backs of her eyes.

Winthrope raised a brow and smiled smugly. "It must

be awful for you, being a mute. All kinds of thoughts run through that sweet little head of yours, but you're reduced to primitive hand signals, much like an ape. I could do anything I wanted to you." As if to prove his point, he stuck a hand inside her robe and grabbed a fistful of her nightgown. She heard the wrenching of the fabric, and cold air rushed over her shoulder and arm.

Stop. She pleaded with her eyes, but he didn't look at her face. His lecherous gaze slid over her exposed skin and down her body.

"I believe I shall give you your first lesson. It is called 'How to Please a Man.' If you tell anyone of this little encounter, using your odd gestures and pitiful looks, they'll think you insane. Even if your brother and sister could understand you, which is doubtful, they'd never believe me capable of such atrocities." He laughed cruelly. "They don't know the half of it."

Keeping one hand on her neck, he groped at her breasts, squeezing painfully. She tried to heave him off, but her wriggling only incited him further. He thrust his hips toward her, and his arousal poked her belly, making her want to retch.

If Charles were here, he'd surely snap the earl's neck. But he wasn't, and she had to be strong. She couldn't allow the earl to violate her. Not without a fight.

He lunged forward, his tongue sliding over his teeth like a ravenous wolf.

Blindly, she reached for the table beside the armchair. She knocked over a small trinket; it fell to the rug soundlessly. The earl tightened his hold on her neck, and bright spots shot across her vision like warning flares off the bow of a ship.

She reached again and this time grasped the base of the lantern she'd brought with her. It had some weight to it, and the metal edges were sharp. It was her one and only chance to escape, and unless she acted quickly, blackness would descend. She clutched the thin iron handle and, using all her might, swung the lantern at the earl's head.

Chapter Twenty-three

*Needle: (1) A sharply pointed, slender
instrument used for passing thread through cloth.
(2) To prod or tease, as in: The insensitive heiress
needled the seamstress about her dowdy clothing.*

"Wake up." Olivia's voice held a note of urgency that made the hairs on the back of Anabelle's neck stand on end.

Prying open her eyes, she groped for her spectacles on the bedside table. After sliding them onto her nose, she glanced at the clock. Barely seven in the morning—very early for Olivia. "Is something wrong?"

"I can't find Rose."

Anabelle threw back the covers and reached for her robe. "Did she sleep in your room last night?"

"I don't think so. She wasn't there when I woke, so I checked the other bedchamber." Anabelle followed as Olivia walked into that room and gestured to the made-up bed. "No one's slept here. I have an awful feeling, Anabelle."

So did she, but she pasted on what she hoped was a reassuring smile, wrapped an arm around Olivia, and gave her a squeeze. "I'm sure she hasn't gone far. Perhaps she woke up hungry and wandered downstairs for breakfast. Or decided she needed some fresh air."

"No, that can't be it." Olivia pulled Anabelle by the hand into her bedchamber. "Look, her robe and slippers are missing."

"Maybe she changed in the other room." But a quick check of the armoire disproved the theory. Each of the two dozen gowns Rose brought to the house party hung there, just as they had the night before. Where on earth could she have gone in her nightgown? "Have you ever known Rose to roam the house in her sleep?"

"Never." Olivia bit her lip. "We need to wake Owen. He'll know what to do." She started toward the door, but Anabelle grabbed her wrist.

"Not yet. Let's change quickly and check a few rooms. If we haven't found her in the next quarter hour, we'll alert your brother."

Each of the women threw on a morning gown and some slippers, then dashed out of their suite without bothering to pin up their braids. They took the back stairs to the breakfast room, nearly bumping into an upstairs maid carrying a pitcher of water.

"Did you pass Lady Rose this morning?"

"No, ma'am," the maid said. "But some early risers are already in the breakfast room."

"Thank you." Anabelle waited for the maid to scurry off and then whispered to Olivia, "You see? Rose probably borrowed one of your dresses and went downstairs."

Olivia's eyes lit with hope. When they reached the

breakfast room, however, its lone occupant was Mr. Averill, who sat reading the newspaper, a cup of steaming coffee before him. Olivia flushed bright red. "Good morning,
James," she said. "Was Rose just here, by any chance?"

He stood and although his eyes widened slightly at
their state of dishabille, bowed politely. "I haven't had the
pleasure of her company. I hope you'll join me, though."

Olivia took a step toward him. "That would be—"

"I'm sorry, but we're just passing through," Anabelle
said, nudging Olivia out into the hallway.

"We must have appeared rude," Olivia fretted. "If Rose
is playing some sort of trick, I shall not be amused."

"I don't think she'd do that."

Olivia turned remorseful. "Neither do I. Let's go find
Owen."

Anabelle's stomach flip-flopped. "I suppose we must."

As they hurried back upstairs, she looked in every
open doorway and around every corner, hoping to catch a
glimpse of Rose's auburn hair or white nightgown. Each
time, she was disappointed.

Upon reaching the door to Owen's bedchamber, Olivia
knocked and turned to Anabelle. "Allow me to do the
talking."

She nodded, more than happy to defer.

Owen opened the door a crack and peered out. His eyes
were glazed with sleep and his hair was more disheveled
than usual. "Olivia? Belle—er, Miss Honeycote?"

Too preoccupied with the news she had to deliver to
notice his slip, Olivia blurted, "Rose is missing."

"What? Damn it. Wait there." He slammed the door.
Thumps and muffled curses sounded on the other side
before he opened it once more. With his shirt untucked

and cravat absent, he strode down the hallway firing questions. Olivia answered as best she could; he found none of the answers satisfactory.

When they reached the first-floor landing, he gazed directly at Anabelle, his fear for Rose flashing in his green eyes. "How could you let this happen? I trusted you to watch over her. And you're telling me she's gone?"

She closed her eyes and choked back a sob. She'd asked herself the same questions ever since she woke this morning.

Owen pressed his palms to his temples. He had to think.

Rose had seemed perfectly fine last evening. Happy even. It was completely out of character for her to run off and not tell anyone where she was going. Olivia was the impulsive one, with the outspoken nature and radical ideas about servants. Wasn't she?

He put a hand on Olivia's shoulder. "Where did you last see her?"

"She was reading beside me in bed last evening. She was dressed for bed."

"What were you talking about?"

Olivia worried the end of her long brown braid. "I don't remember."

"Egypt." Anabelle stepped forward. "We were saying it might be nice to learn more about ancient Egypt."

Olivia's mouth formed an "O." "That's right—we were."

He started walking again. "Let's check the library." It seemed a benign place, but what if Rose reached for a book and a shelf collapsed, or something fell on her? He walked faster, and Olivia and Anabelle scurried to keep pace with him.

He rounded a corner and pushed open the heavy, paneled door of the library, half-afraid Rose would be there, half-afraid she wouldn't. At first glance, everything appeared to be in order. The long rows of books were undisturbed; no furniture was toppled. Instead of feeling relief, however, he fought a wave of panic. Where the hell could she be?

"Look at this." Anabelle stooped beside a shelf to the left of the room's large window. He went and crouched next to her. "This is where Lord Harsby houses his volumes on ancient civilizations." She pointed to a couple of gaps in the otherwise neat row of books.

"She was here," Owen said. He looked into Anabelle's somber face and knew she was hurting, probably as much as he was. "We'll find her. I was a boor earlier. This isn't your fault."

She nodded, but doubt clouded her eyes. He'd make her understand, later. After he'd found Rose.

Olivia examined the spines of books on a shelf on the opposite wall, pulled a volume from a set, and flipped through it. "This is the poetry book she was reading last night. I'm sure of it."

Owen walked across the room to inspect the book, and—

Crunch.

The rug was soft beneath his feet, and yet the sole of his shoe ground something into it. He stopped, knelt in front of an armchair, and found a small shard of glass—several, once he looked more closely—glinting in the sunlight.

The color pattern of the rug caught his eye. Though the

yarn was mostly cream and blue, crimson spots dotted the rug near the chair. He swallowed past the huge lump clogging his throat.

Please, God, no.

On his hands and knees, Owen searched for more glass, prayed he'd find no more blood. He didn't.

But under the chair were a pair of women's slippers. When he held them up, Olivia gasped. No need to ask if they were Rose's.

"I found a few pieces of glass on the carpet." He refrained from mentioning the blood. "I need James's help."

"We saw him in the breakfast room, not long ago," Olivia said. "Shall I get him?"

"Please. But don't alert anyone else yet." James was the only one here whom he trusted completely. Somebody in the household knew what had happened to Rose last night. And if that person had hurt her, he'd pay with his life.

Olivia hurried from the room, leaving him alone with Anabelle.

"I'm so sorry," she said.

He wanted to haul her into his arms and tell her everything would be all right. But he wasn't sure that was true. "Let's search the room for anything else we may have missed."

Anabelle nodded, went to the window, and swept aside the heavy drapes. "The glass panes are intact, and the window is locked. I don't think anyone left through here."

Something silver flashed near her feet, barely visible below the curtains. He walked over and picked up a lantern off the floor. The glass casing was cracked and jagged shards jutted from the base.

"Oh my," Anabelle breathed. "Why would anyone want to hurt Rose?"

"I don't know." But this had been Owen's fear ever since his sister had withdrawn into her shell. Her silence not only made her an object of curiosity, but also an easy victim.

"Owen," Anabelle said softly, "there's something I—"

Olivia and James rushed into the room; whatever Anabelle had been about to say died on her lips.

After conferring with James, Owen decided they should split up, search all the public areas in the house, and note anything that looked suspicious. Olivia and James would take the west wing; Anabelle and he would take the east. They'd meet back in the library in a half hour. If they hadn't found Rose by then, they'd notify their host, enlist the help of other guests, and form search parties.

James and Olivia left; eager to begin his search as well, Owen turned toward Anabelle. She was kneeling on the carpet near the crimson spots.

"This is blood, isn't it?"

He nodded, and the color drained from her face. The terror he saw there mirrored his own.

They moved toward each other with the force of waves crashing on the shore. He folded her into his arms, savoring the feel of her head on his chest and the rightness of them, together. Although she must have been as frightened as he was, she lifted her chin and gazed directly into his eyes. "We'll find her," she said.

He believed they would. But hoped they wouldn't be too late. "Let's go."

Anabelle grabbed Owen's wrist as he started to walk away. "I know something."

He faced her, clearly puzzled.

"About Rose."

"What?"

She flinched at his imperious tone. "It's not that simple." She'd made a promise to keep Lord Winthrope's secret, and she'd accepted payment in return. Telling the secret was tantamount to stealing, but if the information could help them find Rose, the choice was simple. She had to reveal what she knew. It was an awful thing to have to tell a person, and it should have been done gently. But there wasn't time. As if she needed reminding, Owen paced the bloodstained carpet.

Clearing her throat, she forged ahead. "Two and a half years ago, at your parents' last house party, I think Rose saw something that caused her to run away. It may be the cause of her drastic personality change."

Owen grabbed her upper arm, pulled her to the settee, and sat beside her. "Tell me."

"One day at Mrs. Smallwood's, I overheard Lord Winthrope's mistress talking about their affair."

"What does this have to do with Rose?"

Anabelle swallowed. There was no way to sugarcoat the truth. "The earl was also seeing your mother."

Owen grunted. "It's no secret that my mother was unfaithful to my father. I never sought to discover the identities of her lovers—I'm sure there were several. I don't much care whom she consorted with, although this knowledge lowers my opinion of Winthrope considerably. He was a supposed friend of my father's."

"I'm sorry," said Anabelle. "According to the earl's mistress, someone walked in on Lord Winthrope and her during the house party and caught them in bed together."

Understanding sharpened his gaze. "You think that was Rose?"

"Yes. Though I can't be certain."

"You're acting as though you have more to tell me."

"I do." She could feel heat creeping up her neck and wished she could spare him this. "On that day, when Rose walked into the bedchamber, the earl and his mistress weren't alone. Your mother was with them."

Owen stared straight ahead, his face devoid of emotion. "Rose was only a girl."

Anabelle's heart broke for him. "I know."

He stood and paced again as he wrestled with her revelation. "She was so horrified that she ran away."

"I think so."

"Her silence is a protection of sorts." He rubbed his forehead, working through the facts. "It prevents her from having to discuss that day...from having to admit what she saw."

"That's why she was so agitated when she learned Lord Winthrope was a guest here," Anabelle said. "She'd been trying to forget the past, but each time she saw the earl, there was no escaping it."

He turned to her and pointed accusingly. "You knew about this, and you kept it from me."

Anabelle's nose stung. "I had to. I'd...I'd made a promise."

"To whom exactly?" The force of the question made her step backward.

"Lord Winthrope."

Owen blinked and shook his head. When he spoke, the anger was gone. In its place was disbelief and devastation. "You extorted money from the earl. You lied."

"Yes." Such a small word, barely audible. And yet, it threatened to topple the tentative trust they'd built.

"Why? You could have told me the truth."

"If I'd told you about my previous extortion schemes—"

He snorted. "Just how many were there, Anabelle?"

"Three. Don't you see? I knew you'd ask more questions. As ironic as it might seem to you, I had a code of conduct, and that code prevented me from saying—"

"That's horse shit." His voice was low and even, but his eyes simmered with anger. "You had a choice. Your damned pride was more important to you than my sister. It was more important to you than *us*."

"That's not true," she choked out. "I adore Rose. And I...I care deeply for you. But I'd made a promise." It sounded hollow, even to her own ears. "And I did tell you, just now."

"You told me." He gave a disgusted sigh and flicked his eyes at the crimson spots on the rug. "But you waited too long."

Before she could respond, he turned on his heel and strode out of the room. Anabelle trailed behind. There must be something she could do, some way to repair the damage.

"Averill!" Owen yelled.

Mr. Averill and Olivia hurried down the corridor, breathless. "Did you find something else?" he asked.

"No," snapped Owen. "But I need to speak to Winthrope. Have you seen him?"

"The breakfast room. He's there with Lord Harsby."

"Olivia and Anabelle, you will remain here." If anyone besides Anabelle noticed the use of her given name, they didn't remark on it. To Mr. Averill, he said, "Come with me."

Anabelle watched helplessly as the men marched in the direction of the breakfast room. Olivia planted her hands on her hips. "Why would he command us to stay here? I've no intention of twiddling my fingers while my sister is missing." She bolted down the corridor, and Anabelle followed. When they drew nearer to the breakfast room, Olivia turned to Anabelle and lifted a finger to her lips. They remained in the hallway, listening intently.

"Good morning, Duke," Lord Harsby said.

"Fine morning, indeed," the earl commented cheerfully.

"No," Owen said. "No, it is not."

"Pray tell, what's the matter?" asked the earl, all concern.

"Where is my sister?"

"Good Lord, man," Lord Winthrope blustered. "I have no idea. Which sister are you speaking of?"

A cacophony of silverware clattering and china breaking made Olivia and Anabelle jump; they peeked around the doorjamb and saw that Owen, whose back was to them, had reached across the table, grabbed the earl by the lapels, and hauled him onto the breakfast table. Eggs and jelly smeared the front of his waistcoat, and his face turned a ghastly shade of purple.

The earl wriggled futilely in Owen's grasp. "How dare you. Release me at once."

Lord Harsby stood and held up his palms. "Look here, Huntford, whatever the problem, why don't we discuss it like gentlemen?"

Owen ignored both requests and opted to shake Lord

Winthrope, rattling a few more plates and shattering several glasses. "What happened in the library last night?"

The earl licked his lips; his sloping forehead was slick with sweat. "Nothing, really. A bit of a misunderstanding. But no harm was done, I assure you."

"I suggest you tell me what happened," Owen said, "before I pry it out of you with that candelabrum."

"Fine, fine," gasped the earl. "I'll tell you. I wandered into the library late last evening and found your sister, Lady Rose, there, sitting and reading. I tried to make a bit of small talk, just being polite, but it's not as though she can hold up her end of a conversation—"

Owen twisted the older man's lapels until he was coughing and sputtering for air. "Watch it, Winthrope. What happened next?"

"Nothing. It was clear she didn't want my company, so I left her in the library."

"Where'd you get the nasty cut above your ear?"

"Oh, that." The earl laughed nervously. "It was in the stable yesterday. I leaned over to check my saddle and whacked the side of my head as I stood up. Bloody clumsy of me."

"Liar." Owen's fury was barely contained. His face was mere inches from the earl's, and every muscle in his body tensed as though eager to attack. "There was an altercation in the library."

"Is that true, Winthrope?" Lord Harsby walked around the table to stand beside Owen. His gaze flicked to Anabelle and Olivia, but he didn't shoo them away.

The earl closed his eyes briefly. When he opened them he sighed and said, "Yes, yes. It's true. But *I* was the one who was injured. She swung a lantern at my head. The blow knocked me out. When I came to, she was gone. I assumed she'd returned to her room."

"My sister is not prone to violence. I will find out what you did to provoke her, and you will meet me on the dueling field."

Without warning, Owen dropped the man. His face smacked into a plate of kippers.

He deserved worse.

Not that Anabelle could throw stones. If she'd told Owen the truth earlier, he would have confronted Lord Winthrope and the earl would have kept his distance from Rose.

Before, Owen had ignored her; now she'd given him cause to hate her. The very idea made her stomach clench, her hands tremble. She had to help him find Rose and pray that she was uninjured.

After that, Anabelle would pack up her sewing basket and say good-bye to Owen and his sisters forever. She'd caused them too much pain already.

Chapter Twenty-four

Lord Harsby clasped Owen's shoulder. "My staff is at your disposal. Just tell me what you need, and you shall have it."

Owen wiped his palms on the front of his jacket. After throttling Winthrope, he felt the need to scrub his hands clean. Jerking his chin toward the earl, writhing on the table, Owen said, "Have someone escort him to his room and see that he stays there."

"Allow me," Averill said wryly. Let Winthrope try to resist. Averill was itching for an excuse to punch the depraved bastard in the face.

"Anyone who's available to help search for Rose should meet in the drawing room in ten minutes," Owen announced.

"Of course," Harsby said. He shot Winthrope a loathing glance and quickly walked into the corridor to confer with his butler.

Owen did some quick calculations in his head. If the

search teams left soon, they'd have twelve hours of daylight. God, he hoped they found Rose before nightfall. When he thought of Winthrope attacking her and how terrified she must have been, blood pounded in his ears.

Damn Winthrope, and damn his mother, who was as much to blame as the depraved earl.

"We can help, Owen." He turned, surprised to see Olivia behind him. Anabelle stood at her side, pale yet defiant, daring him to send her to her room.

He wouldn't.

Oh, he was furious with her. After all they'd shared, she'd kept a secret from him. An insidious thing that had slowly poisoned his family. He'd never forgive her for that, no matter how contrite she professed to be.

But he understood her need to do something, to contribute in some way. He'd go insane if he had to stand by idly while someone he cared for was in trouble. Besides, he needed every set of eyes, ears, and hands. "Fine," he said. "Help gather guests and servants in the drawing room."

Anabelle's shoulders sagged in relief. "We think Rose is still wearing her nightgown and robe. Since her slippers were in the library, she's probably barefoot too. I'll fetch a blanket and a pair of shoes to take along when we search."

He nodded. Warmth, shoes—men didn't think of such things. At least, he didn't.

"She could be hiding somewhere in the house," Olivia said skeptically.

God, he hoped so. "I'll have a group check every room and crevice." But his gut told him Rose had fled—that she'd wanted to put as much distance between her and the lecherous earl as she could.

As he strode to the drawing room, a plan formed in his mind. The women could search every room in the house, the gardens, and the grounds nearby. The men would pair up and head out in different directions on horseback. Harsby's estate was vast; there was an enormous amount of ground to cover.

Without slippers and proper clothes, Rose couldn't have gotten very far. But she wouldn't have had much protection from the elements, either. He clenched a fist and walked faster. *Hold on, Rose. I'm coming.*

Anabelle sat beside Olivia in the drawing room, listening carefully to the instructions Owen issued to the concerned guests. The older women *tsk*ed and murmured to one another, while Miss Starling and Lord Winthrope's daughter, Margaret, raised their brows haughtily. Of course, Margaret had no idea that her father was implicated in Rose's disappearance. If she had, she might have at least feigned concern. The men wore grave expressions but did seem rather excited at the opportunity to be the hero—the one who discovered fair Rose's whereabouts. Or perhaps they were just grateful for an excuse to avoid grouse hunting for the third straight day.

For her part, Anabelle couldn't abide much more talk. She resisted the urge to run out of the house and frantically search for Rose behind every bush, tree, or statuary. Olivia's leg bounced rhythmically as though she, too, were eager to begin *doing* something. Thankfully, she wasn't the type to become hysterical. Panicking wouldn't help matters.

On her lap Anabelle held a bundle—she'd wrapped a pair of Rose's boots in a lightweight blanket and tied it with twine. When at last everyone had their orders, Anabelle stood. The other women formed groups and divided up the various floors and wings of the house, but she hung back with Olivia. "There are plenty of women to handle the house. I want to search outside."

"I do, too." Olivia had wound her braid around her head and quickly pinned it up. Anabelle knotted a light shawl around her shoulders. "Unfortunately, I never learned how to ride. I'll have to set out on foot."

"You could share a horse with me," Olivia said.

"No." Owen's declaration, in a tone that brooked no argument, startled them.

"Fine," Olivia said, stiffly. "Anabelle and I will walk together."

However, when they would have departed, Owen blocked their way. "You"—Owen pointed to Olivia—"will take your mare and ride with James. You can show him the paths where you and Rose have ridden and walked. You"—he inclined his head toward Anabelle—"will ride with me. Come." He strode from the room without waiting for her, clearly expecting her to follow. What choice did she have? Tucking the bundle under her arm, she hurried after him.

They left the house through a side door and headed toward the stables. The gray sky hung so low that the trees seemed to hold it up. A pair of dogs bounded up to Owen, nipping at his heels and clamoring for a pat on the head. He walked on, oblivious to both the hounds and the raindrops plunking onto their heads and faces.

Owen shouted to the stable boy, who led out a massive black horse, already saddled.

Now that Anabelle saw the animal up close, she

doubted her ability to balance on top of it. Her hesitation had nothing whatsoever to do with the fact that her back would be pressed against Owen's chest.

"Are you coming?"

She looked up, surprised to see him already astride, holding his hand out impatiently.

Swallowing, she moved nearer to the horse, which pranced and behaved rather uncooperatively. She tentatively reached up to Owen, and, in one swoop, he hoisted her off her feet and planted her in the saddle before him.

"Have you ever ridden?"

"No."

"Hold on."

He wrapped one arm firmly around her middle, shouted, and kicked his horse into motion; Anabelle clung to the saddle horn with both hands.

"We're taking the northern section of the estate. We can move quickly across the meadows. If Rose is here, she'll be easy to spot. Once we reach the woods, we'll have to slow down and search more carefully."

Anabelle nodded. The ride jarred her teeth at first, but once she relaxed, her body rocked in rhythm with the horse's movements. Perhaps she wouldn't topple off and be trampled. The rain diminished to a mere mist; the wind blew softly in her ears. Since she rode sidesaddle, her shoulder rested against Owen's chest—a warm, hard wall of muscle. She squinted toward the west, searching the horizon for any sign of Rose; Owen looked east where the sun struggled to break through stubborn clouds.

After a half hour, they approached the edge of a forest. Owen slowed the horse to a trot and guided it along the tree line, first in one direction, then in another. Anabelle removed her spectacles, and with the sleeve of her gown, wiped tiny beads of water from the lenses.

"Damn."

Anabelle's heart sank, and she shoved her spectacles back on her nose. "What is it?"

"These woods are so thick and deep, I'd need a dozen men to properly search them."

He was right; the trees were so dense sunlight barely penetrated the canopy of the forest. "If anyone can find Rose, you can."

He grunted, unconvinced. "I barely know her. We haven't had a real conversation in years."

"That's not fair. You know her better than you realize." She looked up at him, even though gazing into his intense green eyes was disarming. "Why did you decide to search this direction?"

He shrugged. "It seemed logical. If Winthrope's story is true, Rose would have fled the library and house as quickly as possible. The nearest exit would have been the French doors in the drawing room leading to the terrace. If she ran from the house and continued in a fairly straight line, she'd have gone in this general direction. But there are acres and acres of forest. The foliage is so thick I can't see more than a few yards ahead."

Anabelle couldn't let him despair. She placed her palm on his chest, and he jerked his gaze to hers.

"Rose was in trouble," she said. "Where would she feel safe?"

"She loves nature—surrounding herself with plants and animals would comfort her. But if she were barefoot, she'd have looked for some semblance of a path. I spotted a few places along the edge of the woods where the underbrush looks trampled. The boughs hang too low to ride into the forest, so we'll dismount and walk in, looking for clues."

He deftly swung himself off the horse, grasped her around the waist, and helped her to the ground. His casual touch made her whole body tingle.

"There's a trail," he said, pointing into the woods. "We can start there." After tethering the horse to a tree, Owen led the way.

Although they worked as a team, Anabelle realized it was merely for Rose's sake. A great chasm gaped between them, and she had no hope of mending it. He behaved indifferently, as though they shared no history—no visits with her family, no nights of pleasure, no trading of secrets.

Owen might have forgiven her for extortion, but he'd never forgive her for lying to him. Not when she'd endangered Rose.

Anabelle doubted she'd ever forgive herself.

They wandered deeper into the woods. Dappled light danced on the forest floor, and the air hung moist and verdant. Though the rain had ceased, Anabelle's boots sunk into the soft ground. She kept to the primitive trail, as Owen instructed, looking for signs Rose had gone there earlier. They shouted her name into the otherwise peaceful forest, but their voices bounced back, unheard by anyone, save a few startled birds. Owen occasionally veered off the path to investigate, but returned looking grim, his mouth drawn into a thin line.

After a few hours on the trail, Owen shook his head. "We're on the wrong path. Let's return to the edge of the woods and try another." Out of the corner of his eye, he glanced at Anabelle. "Is the pace too grueling?"

"Not at all. I just want Rose to be all right."

He stared at her long enough to make her cheeks hot. "As do I. Come, Miss Honeycote."

Anabelle swallowed. So, she was back to being Miss Honeycote, even when the only creatures within earshot were squirrels. Not surprising, but it stung.

They backtracked to the edge of the woods and Owen rummaged through a bag tied to his horse. He withdrew a canteen, unscrewed the lid, and held it out to her. "Drink some water."

She sipped, savoring each cool, refreshing swallow. Owen shared some nuts and bread too—not much, but enough to take the edge off their hunger.

Owen selected another path, and they followed it as it sloped into a valley where a stream trickled over mossy rocks. Here, where the trees were less dense, thick shafts of sunlight penetrated the foliage. As Anabelle glanced up to admire the sight, the glinting sun momentarily blinded her. She raised an arm to shield her eyes and teetered on the heels of her boots but could not quite regain her balance.

Splat.

She landed hard on her bottom. Humiliating enough; however, she proceeded to slip and slide down the muddy hill, barreling into Owen's legs and taking him down with her.

They tumbled several yards before he grasped the trunk of a sapling and halted their plummet down the embankment.

Momentarily, anyway.

The sapling popped out of the ground—roots and all—and they slid again, all the way to the edge of the stream before stopping.

Heavens. With Owen's help, she sat up, none too gracefully.

He cupped her chin in his hand, undoubtedly smearing mud on her face. Not that she minded. "Are you hurt?" Though she was perfectly fine, the concern in his eyes made her throat constrict. She shook her head.

After exhaling loudly, he looked down at his clothes. "Christ." His jacket and breeches, blue and buff colored this morning, had turned brown. His hands and one cheek were also covered with mud. Anabelle was similarly afflicted. Her spectacles still clung to her face, thankfully, but her new yellow dress was plastered with muck, and the end of her braid looked like a rope dragged through a cow field.

Owen helped her to her feet, then leaned over the stream and cleaned his hands as best he could in the thin ribbon of water. She did the same, but all they succeeded in accomplishing was smearing the dirt around. Owen looked fierce, a warrior ready for battle; Anabelle was certain that she resembled a street urchin.

Planting his hands on his hips, he surveyed the area around them. "Rose isn't here. Let's go back up the hill and take a different path."

He turned to go, but Anabelle stayed. That spot, with the cheerful gurgle of water at her feet and the birds fluttering overhead, seemed precisely the sort of spot Rose would be drawn to explore. "Wait."

Facing her, he raised a brow. "What's wrong?"

"We should stay on this path for a little longer."

"It ends at the stream, Miss Honeycote," he said dryly.

"True. But Rose could have crossed it. I think she'd like this place."

Owen gave her a ducal look only mildly compromised by the clump of dirt in his hair. "Another half hour at the most," he said. "Then we turn back."

Anabelle led the way this time, easily hopping the stream at its narrowest point. She kept a brisk pace, propelled by an odd certainty they were on the right track.

They trudged up a hill, taking care to avoid mud this time. Soon, she became winded; Owen became frustrated. "The sun's already sinking in the sky. We can't waste any more time," he said.

"Please. A few minutes more." She couldn't explain why she felt they should keep going. She just knew they should. Attempting to distract Owen as they hiked, she said, "Mr. Averill and Olivia—or one of the other search parties—could have already found Rose. At this very moment, she could be safe and sound in her bedchamber sipping a cup of hot tea."

He didn't respond, but his bleak expression told her he didn't believe Rose was at the house any more than she did.

Was she a fool to follow her intuition? If she led Owen on a wild-goose chase, he'd have one more reason to resent her. Defeated, she said, "I suppose you're right. Let's turn back."

"Wait." He sprinted ahead of her and crouched beside a fallen log. Over his shoulder he called, "Come look at this."

Anabelle hurried toward him. "What is it?"

He held a scrap of white fabric, torn at the edges. "It was stuck to this log. Could it be from Rose's nightgown?"

"Yes," she said, her relief at finding the small remnant so great she might cry. "It looks like the hem. She must have rested here, and when she left, her nightrail snagged on the bark. She can't be far."

Owen stood and scanned the woods with renewed purpose. From their higher vantage point, they saw much of the surrounding landscape. Anabelle's gaze roved over the leaf-covered ground, seeking glimpses of white, but when Owen touched her arm, she froze. He pointed at a patch of sky peeking between the tops of the trees where dusk had muted the bright blue to a purplish gray.

Squinting, she held her spectacles slightly away from her face till white puffs came into focus. "Smoke?"

"If we find the source, we may find Rose."

He shot off ahead of Anabelle, trampling through the underbrush. As she swiped a sleeve across her moist forehead and breathed in gulps of air, she called, "Do you see anything?"

Nodding, he pointed to a hill in the distance. A tiny cottage with a thatched roof sat in a clearing, a wisp of smoke curling from its stone chimney. "It's probably a woodcutter's cottage. Maybe Rose took refuge there."

Anabelle desperately hoped so.

"Wait here," he ordered. "I'll go see."

Chapter Twenty-five

Net: (1) An open, woven fabric that is transparent.
(2) A device used to snare unsuspecting men
into the institution of marriage.

Owen hadn't really expected Anabelle to obey him. Would have been disappointed if she had. At least she hung back slightly.

The occupant of the cottage could be a woodcutter or poacher. If any sort of confrontation erupted, he didn't want Anabelle in the middle of it.

Upon reaching the clearing, he approached the cottage from the side and peered into a window too clouded with dirt to let him see inside. The front door his only other option, he walked around the corner and knocked.

No one answered.

He rammed the door with his shoulder, but the heavy wooden planks didn't budge. Banging harder, he called out, "Rose? It's Owen."

A scratching that might have been a sliding bolt

sounded on the other side. He pushed on the door again; this time it slowly creaked open. "Rose?"

From the dark interior of the cottage, a shape emerged. Rose staggered toward him, wild-eyed, a huge iron skillet raised over her head.

Thank God.

If Winthrope had hurt her, so help him.

Holding out his palms, Owen soothed her. "It's just me. Are you all right?"

The skillet clunked to the floor, and she crumpled into a heap, crying silently.

He scooped her up and carried her to a pallet on the floor by the fire. Although overwrought, she seemed to be in one piece. He took one of her small hands and laced his fingers through hers.

Anabelle rushed into the cottage. "Thank God." She knelt beside them and placed her hands on Rose's cheeks. "Let me see your face. Are you hurt?"

Rose shook her head and embraced Anabelle tightly. Although he felt rather entitled to the first hug, he overlooked the slight, much too relieved to mind.

"We were worried sick about you," Anabelle said.

She lowered her gaze, remorseful.

"We know about Winthrope," he said.

Rose snapped her head up and paled.

"I think I'll wait outside," Anabelle said, but Rose grasped her wrist. Anabelle's gaze flicked to Owen's as though seeking guidance.

"You may stay if you wish, Miss Honeycote." He turned to Rose. "Winthrope gave us his version of events in the library last night. We were able to read between the lines. You defended yourself?"

She nodded.

"Did he . . ."

Choking on a sob, she shook her head.

Owen's blood pounded, pulsing hot in his temples. "Regardless, he will pay. You won't have to worry about him again." Sighing, he considered how to broach the next topic and decided on directness. "I also know about his affair with our mother."

Rose's eyes widened.

"I only found out recently, but it all makes sense. You walked in on them—at our house party almost three years ago?"

Rose's face contorted into a mask of pain.

He folded her into his arms and pressed her head against his chest.

"I wish I could have spared you that. And I wish you hadn't been the one to find Father after . . ." No point in dredging up that memory. "I'm here now. You're safe with me."

He rocked her in his arms. When, at last, her trembling ceased, Anabelle inspected her feet, which were scratched and cut. "We need to clean and bandage these."

Rose pointed to the pot hanging over the fire.

"Ah, you were about to do that," Anabelle said. "You must be hungry also. Is there anything to eat here?"

Owen rummaged through the pantry and found a couple of mugs and some tea leaves but nothing else. Damn.

Darkness was quickly descending, and the other search parties, including Averill and Olivia, still looked for Rose. He needed to get her back to the house and call off the search, but with only one horse, he couldn't take Rose and Anabelle at the same time.

Anabelle finished winding a strip of white fabric around Rose's foot and sat back on her heels. Admiring her handiwork, she said, "I can't help thinking how frantic Olivia must be."

Owen murmured his agreement and knelt beside Rose. "I need to let her and the others know you're safe. You must eat something and have a doctor tend to the cuts on your feet."

Anabelle squeezed Rose's hand. "The two of you should return to the house. I shall be perfectly fine here for the night. Someone can come fetch me in the morning."

Rose shook her head vehemently.

"Don't be silly, Rose. I am a grown woman, perfectly capable of spending the night in a cottage. You've had a harrowing experience, and Olivia is no doubt sick with worry. No matter how many reassurances Owen gives her, she won't rest easy until she sees you with her own eyes."

Although grateful for Anabelle's convincing speech, Owen saw the flicker of fear on her face when she mentioned spending the night alone.

"We should set out soon, before it becomes too dark to find our way out of the woods," he said to Rose. Then to Anabelle, "There's some tea in the can on the shelf, and the trunk in the corner contains a blanket, a lantern, and some matches. I'll come back at dawn."

"No need to rush back; I'll be fine," she assured. The cozy cottage would shelter her from the elements, but the straw pallet and dusty, pitted floor were a far cry from her plush bedchamber at Harsby's house.

Although still hesitant, Rose hugged Anabelle good-bye and allowed Owen to pick her up. There was just enough light left that, with a little luck, he and Rose should be able to make it out of the forest before night fell.

Before leaving, he looked over his shoulder at Anabelle. The mud that covered her dress had dried a light tan. Her hair was tarred and feathered with mire and bits of leaves. Raising her chin, she gave a slight smile.

Never had he seen a more beautiful woman.

Pity he couldn't trust her.

After Owen and Rose left, Anabelle had nothing to do but think. There were no dresses to sew, no chores to do, no books to read. Being alone with one's thoughts was disconcerting—especially when one wasn't very proud of one's actions.

Oh, she was a horrid person.

Thank heaven they'd found Rose safe, but what if they hadn't? What if Rose had tripped, hit her head on a rock, and perished in the woods? Or been discovered by gypsies and kidnapped?

Suppressing a shudder, Anabelle checked that the door was securely bolted.

Perhaps she should attempt to wash her dress in the bucket of water she'd retrieved from the stream. No, there wouldn't be time for it to dry. Instead, she stripped down to her chemise and scrubbed her skin clean before turning her attention to her hair. Not nearly as soothing as lingering in a steaming bath, but at least the mud was gone. The best thing for her to do now was sleep.

After stirring the logs in the fire, she pulled the quilt from the chest. It couldn't rival the velvet counterpane on the bed where she'd slept the past week, but it smelled clean. Suddenly quite homesick, she wrapped it around her shoulders and lay down on the pallet. Closing her eyes, she imagined how happy Mama and Daph would be to have her back.

She'd missed talking with Daph into the wee hours of the morning and reading to Mama. By now, Mama would be sufficiently recovered to take walks in the park and carry on real conversations. How Anabelle longed to hear her laugh again.

For so long, she'd dreamed of Mama getting well. But now that she was better, Anabelle was forced to face other unfortunate realities. Her family couldn't afford to continue living in the apartment they rented. Unless she returned to her life of crime.

And after getting to know her most recent victims— Owen, Olivia, and Rose—she couldn't resort to extortion again. She wasn't the same person she'd been before.

The fire flickered for hours, leaving glowing embers, lulling her to sleep, when—

Bam. Pounding at the cottage door. She bolted upright.

"Anabelle?"

Owen. Disoriented, she looked around the cottage, where it was still dark. Could he and Rose have gotten lost and circled back?

Grabbing her spectacles, she sprang to her feet, slid the bolt aside, and opened the door.

Moonlight shone on the hard planes of his face and outlined his broad shoulders against the inky sky. Her breath hitched in her throat.

He was quite alone.

"What are you doing back so soon?"

"May I come in?"

She glanced down at her chemise and hesitated. However,

social strictures governing middle of the night meetings in woodcutters' cottages were murky at best. "Of course. I thought the plan was for you to return in the morning."

He set a drawstring sack on the floor, stirred the fire, and added a log. Flames danced once more, illuminating the harsh contours of his face. "I didn't like the idea of leaving you here alone."

Her heart leapt at his admission. Of course, he probably would have come back for a stranded puppy, too, but it was something. When she considered the consequences, however, she placed a hand on her chest. "Oh my."

In an instant he stood beside her, cupping her elbow. "What is it?"

"My reputation—though not much, it's all I have. And it will be destroyed once the other guests learn that we..."

"Spent the night together? No one knows." He guided her to the pallet, and they both sank onto the quilt. "All the search parties had returned to the house shortly after dusk. When Olivia saw me ride up with Rose, she burst into tears. Everyone was delighted to see Rose, but concerned about you. I told them that you'd bravely offered to stay at the cottage 'til morning."

She felt her cheeks warm. "You said that?"

"You *are* very brave. I suspect you've done many courageous things in the course of your life."

True, if one counted disguising herself as a lad and delivering extortion notes in the dead of night. "Perhaps. But I'm not proud of all of them."

"The truth is, I knew you'd manage just fine by yourself. But I still didn't like the thought of it. If you don't object, I'll stay with you for the rest of the night and return to the house just before dawn, with no one the wiser. I'll bring Averill and Olivia with me tomorrow morning to return you to the house."

She disliked being the center of such a fuss, but that's what she got for being unable to do something as simple as riding a horse. "Thank you."

"I almost forgot." He reached for the canvas sack he'd dropped earlier, pulled out a small parcel wrapped in cloth, and handed it to her.

The aroma of freshly baked bread wafted around her. She hadn't realized how ravenous she was. Her stomach growled as she broke off a crusty piece and ate it. "Mmm. It's wonderful."

"I brought some cheese and berries, too. I wish I had something more substantial to offer you."

"This is perfect. Here," she said, handing him some of the loaf. They finished off everything Owen brought and washed it down with water from his canteen.

Sated, Anabelle leaned back on the heels of her hands and stared into the fire. She had a few things to say to Owen, and this might be the last time she ever had the opportunity to speak with him—alone.

"I'm almost finished with the last two gowns—the ones for Rose's debut ball—and will soon return home."

"That's good," he said flatly. His ready acceptance stung a little.

"Yes. I'm inordinately fond of your sisters, as you know, but they shall be better off without me. I'm responsible for what happened to Rose last night. While I thank God she's safe and sound, I can't help thinking what might have happened."

"Don't. It's over." He poked idly at the charred log on the fire. "In spite of everything, they like you."

"They wouldn't if they knew all the facts."

"I don't intend to tell them *all* the facts."

"I appreciate that. But even if I weren't guilty of extortion and withholding secrets, I'm not the kind of friend they need. I don't come from your world, and certainly I don't understand all the rules. Rose and Olivia are the sisters of a duke. They don't need a seamstress for their friend. They need someone who's had a proper upbringing and who has the proper credentials." The food she'd just eaten settled uncomfortably in her stomach. "Someone like Miss Starling."

"Maybe. But they could also use a friend like you."

She arched a brow. "A friend who threatened to ruin their good name? And left them defenseless against an evil earl?"

He took her hand and laced his fingers through hers. Delicious shivers rushed up her arm. "They need a friend who's loyal and brave. Who loves them just as they are."

Warmth flooded her chest. "I'm sorry I didn't tell you about Lord Winthrope earlier. I should have the moment I realized the connection between him and the drastic change in Rose. You have every right to be angry."

"I was hard on you before—harder than I should have been—because I was worried about Rose." He caressed the back of her hand with his thumb. "I know you'll miss my sisters when you're gone. Do you think you might miss me, too?"

Anabelle blinked. Of course she'd miss him. She'd miss his rakish smile and his tender looks and his quiet strength. But most of all she'd miss how alive—how complete—she felt when she was with him. "A little."

The corner of his mouth curled into a smile. "I didn't come here to try and seduce you."

She believed it—after the day they'd had, she must look a fright.

"If you want to lie down here and sleep until the morning, I'll sit and keep watch on the other side of the room."

She shrugged as though her heart wasn't beating out of her chest. "Just out of curiosity, what do *you* want?"

He leaned closer, his breath hot and moist on her neck. "I want to make love to you. Like I've dreamt—a hundred times over."

The decision was not nearly as hard as it should have been. Dizzy with desire, she speared her fingers through his hair and kissed him full on the lips. "That's what I want, too."

Chapter Twenty-six

Owen trembled from wanting Anabelle so badly. And now he was holding her and kissing her...and would finally make love with her.

The longing he felt for her transcended the physical. God knew, there *was* that. But he missed her at the strangest times. While he was walking with Miss Starling a couple of days ago, a tiny duckling waddled across his path, and he thought it tragic that Anabelle was not there to see it. Likewise, while riding his horse over the fields, he wished he could capture the spectacular sunset and somehow bring it home to her. A *sunset,* for God's sake. He'd never noticed such trifling things before; now he waxed poetic like the lovesick fool he was.

Reluctantly, he broke off their kiss, removed her spectacles, and tucked them into his coat pocket. "Are you sure about this, Anabelle?" He had to ask but prayed she wouldn't change her mind. "I want you to be mine. Forever."

Tears welled in her eyes, and she twined her arms around his neck. "I am yours. For now."

A chill washed over him. "What does that mean?"

"I know how important your sisters are to you. I understand the duty you have to them and to your title. I won't interfere with that because if I did...you'd resent me forever."

"I would never resent you." Why was she talking about his sisters and duty right now? "This is about *us*."

"Hmm?" She left a trail of hot, moist kisses on the side of his neck, making it damned near impossible to think.

"I want us to be together," he managed. "Always."

"I want that, too, but I'm not willing to compromise."

"Neither am I."

With a seductive smile, she slipped her hands underneath his shirt and gently raked her nails down his chest. Pleasure spiked, and he groaned.

"Let's focus on tonight, shall we?"

In some corner of his mind, he was dissatisfied with her response, but his brain—muddled with desire—couldn't sort it out. All he knew was he'd die if he didn't have her now.

He shrugged off his coat and yanked off his boots and trousers. To his utter delight, Anabelle shed her chemise.

She didn't attempt to cover herself as she stood before the fire. Her skin glowed, and the shadows only highlighted the lush curves of her breasts and bottom. He'd never seen a more beautiful sight. "You are gorgeous."

With an apologetic smile, she ran her hand over the length of her braid and plucked a blade of grass from it. "Hardly. But thank you for saying so."

"Come here."

She knelt beside him on the pallet. He slid the knotted ribbon off the end of her braid and ran his fingers through the plaits until her hair flowed down her back. Starting at her crown, he massaged her scalp, neck, and back.

"Better?" he asked.

"Yes."

"Good." He swept her shining tresses aside and took the tip of her breast into his mouth, sucking until she moaned softly. Together, they lay back on the makeshift bed, and he covered her body with his, loving the way her hips cradled him.

Although she may have been inexperienced at lovemaking, she returned every thrust of his tongue and explored his body as freely as he did hers. She ran her hands down his back, over his flanks, raising his body temperature with every stroke. When she reached down to touch him, though, he stopped her.

Looking confused and slightly hurt, she said, "I shouldn't touch you?"

He swallowed and counted to three in his head before answering. "I love that you want to touch me. More than you know. But if you do, this will be over quickly. Too quickly."

"Then can't we just do it again?" She was impossibly beautiful lying beneath him, her hair fanned out around her. And her innocent question made him even harder—if that were possible.

"Yes," he said, kissing her on the nose. "Yes, we can."

Her face lit as though she'd been given an expensive gift, and she eagerly took him in her hands. "You're so warm and smooth." Her inexpert touch was more arousing than he'd imagined. "Show me how to please you."

"You are."

"How is this?" She grazed her thumb across the tip of his cock, and he groaned. "Bad?"

"Good." He couldn't wait any longer. He eased her legs apart, pressed himself against her, and kissed her thoroughly. She moved against him, warm and slick with her desire and his.

"You're mine, Anabelle."

"Yes."

With that, he thrust into her. She was incredibly tight, and he had to go still or risk climaxing instantly. As good as he felt, however, he couldn't bear the thought that he might have hurt her. "Are you all right?"

Her sultry eyes gleamed mischievously, and she wrapped her legs tightly around his waist. "I know it's supposed to hurt, but I like the feel of you inside me."

Owen growled. All thought was replaced with pure, hot need. He pumped into her again and again, and with his hands, his mouth, and his body, he claimed her. His.

She moved with him, matching his rhythm as though perfectly in tune.

A pulsing began in his ears—low, steady, unstoppable. It powered through him, coursing through his veins and pounding in his loins until he came. He spilled his seed into her, the only woman he had ever or would ever love, as he whispered her name and held her tightly.

He would never let her go.

Anabelle loved feeling so close to Owen, so connected. She loved the abandon with which he'd taken her and the weight of him lying on her now. Her first experience with lovemaking left her breathless and awed.

And only mildly disappointed. She'd thought she would feel the earth-shattering pleasure he'd given her before, but tonight had been different. Still wonderful, but different.

He eased himself off of her and thoughtfully pulled the quilt up to her chin. "You are amazing."

She breathed a bit easier. It was good to know she hadn't botched things completely. "You enjoyed it, then?"

"Immensely." He ran his palm up and down her bare arm, making her shiver. "And now, you shall too."

Her toes curled with anticipation. "There's more?"

He slipped a hand beneath the quilt and slid it up her leg. "Much more."

Sucking in a breath, she savored his touch. As he stroked her thighs and kissed her neck, hunger welled up inside, pulsing at her core. Her head lolled back and Owen's hand drifted higher, till he found the center of her need—and pleasure. Murmuring her name, he caressed the nub until she writhed in exquisite torture. When the mounting pressure became almost unbearable, she cried out and lifted her hips. His eyes full of understanding, Owen slid a finger into her and said, "My beautiful, my Belle." She shattered then, surrendering to the lovely spasms that radiated through her body and quelled the fire burning within.

When at last her breathing returned to normal, Owen rained light kisses over her face. "I'm sorry your first time wasn't as pleasurable as it should have been. You rob me of my self-control."

She smiled. "You accuse me of thievery?"

"Something like that. But I promise you that this time"—he rolled her hips toward his—"you won't be disappointed."

"I'm not—" Oh. Whatever she'd been about to say died on her lips. Owen thrust into her, filling her body, heart, and soul.

"You and I are meant for each other, Belle," he whispered against her neck. "I won't let anything—or anyone—keep us apart."

His words washed over her like a cool rain shower, leaving her energized, renewed, and utterly aroused. Each time he rocked against her sensitive, swollen flesh, her inner muscles clenched around him, pulling him deeper, filling her more, till she thought she'd die of sheer pleasure. Faster and faster he plunged into her, till the sounds in and around the cottage faded away, and all she could hear was their breathing, her heartbeat, and the soft slap of their bodies coming together—perfectly. Her climax built slowly and when release finally came, she pulled Owen along with her, the two of them shooting through the sky like comets, before gently, sweetly returning to earth.

Sated and suddenly sleepy, she nestled into the warm crook of his arm. "I wish we could stay like this forever."

As she drifted off to sleep, he whispered in her ear. "We will."

Anabelle's dreams were too pleasant to let reality intrude, but she'd apparently neglected to close the drapes in her bedchamber. An annoying beam of light prodded her awake in spite of her tightly closed eyelids. Thinking to combat it by covering her head, she reached for her pillow.

Only, it wasn't there. Odd.

Reluctantly, she opened her eyes, and saw the cottage.

It looked quite different in the morning light, which was unobstructed by curtains but muted due to the filth covering the window. The few items in the room—the trunk, the shelves, the pallet on which she lay—were well-worn, and a thin layer of dust covered most surfaces.

Owen was gone. He had to leave, of course, but she clung to his promise—that they could be together forever. Hope sprouted in her chest like a seedling, green and vulnerable.

The previous night rushed over her in a flood of emotion—panic, joy, loneliness, passion. She felt as though she'd lived a lifetime in one day, unsure what the new one would bring. Sitting up, she realized she was quite naked and should probably rectify the situation before the cavalry arrived to rescue her.

Before going in search of her clothes, however, she needed her spectacles. An advantage of occupying a one-room cottage should have been that it was nearly impossible to lose anything. And yet, her spectacles weren't on the shelf or the trunk or the rustic mantel. They weren't even hiding in the straw of the pallet. The last time she'd worn them had been—

Oh. Just before Owen removed them and put them in his pocket. A gallant gesture at the time; now it vexed her.

She wriggled into her shift and risked a quick walk outside in order to remove some of the dried mud from her yellow dress. Although she detested the thought of donning the soiled dress, it would never do to be caught in her chemise when Owen returned to the cottage with Mr. Averill and Olivia. At least they were too kind to fault her unkempt appearance. Before presenting herself to Lord and Lady Harsby and their guests she'd sneak to her bedchamber, bathe, and change.

Humming, she secured her hair with the ribbon at the nape of her neck, and then tidied the cottage as best she could. Before long, someone outside shouted her name.

Olivia.

Eager to hug her and celebrate Rose being found, Anabelle rushed to the cottage door, swung it open, and—

Froze. Olivia and Mr. Averill stood before her, smiling warmly. Owen was just behind them, his eyes full of tenderness and the secrets they'd shared. That bit was wonderful.

But Owen wasn't alone.

At his side, Miss Starling linked her arm possessively through his.

"I'm so glad to see you!" cried Olivia. "You poor thing! Did you have a horrid night?"

"It wasn't dreadful." Her eyes flew to Owen's, and she flushed. "That is, I was quite...comfortable." She wanted to crawl into the trunk and have someone put her on a cargo ship to Africa.

"How reassuring," Owen said with a wry smile.

Miss Starling shuddered delicately and peered over Anabelle's shoulder into the room. "I fail to see how anyone could possibly be comfortable in this pathetic excuse for a cottage. Why, I should think it barely qualifies as a shack, Huntford."

Owen ignored Miss Starling, and yet, she clung to his sleeve like a barnacle to the bottom of a boat. "Miss Honeycote, thank you again for helping me locate Rose and for volunteering to stay behind last night. It was a brave and selfless thing to do."

Although his words were merely for the benefit of the others, Anabelle flushed some more anyway. "I'm delighted I could help."

"Say," interjected Olivia, "where are your spectacles?"

Good heavens. Her face must resemble a beet. "I, er . . . seem to have misplaced them."

"Allow me to help you check the cottage," Owen said smoothly. After extracting his arm from Miss Starling's clutches, he walked in. He made a show of rummaging around the shelves, discreetly removed the spectacles from his pocket, and turned around, holding them out to Anabelle. "Here they are."

"Thank you. How silly of me."

"Not at all." He gazed at her with such heat and intensity that she thought she might melt. She did not but was quite unable to breathe for several seconds.

Miss Starling cleared her throat, and when Anabelle faced her, she took in the woman's shrewd, blue, narrowed eyes. "You must have been desperately lonely last night, Miss Honeycote. Without any sewing to occupy you."

Swallowing, Anabelle glanced quickly at Owen. He pressed his lips together tightly and shot her a warning look that said: *admit nothing.*

"Yes, I suppose." Miss Starling wasn't so intimidating— if one discounted her perfect hair, flawless complexion, and lush figure.

"You are very fortunate, you know," she continued icily. "Had a man been in this part of the woods, he might have welcomed the opportunity to ruin an innocent like you. In spite of your filthy dress and disheveled appearance."

Anabelle blinked, stunned. Olivia gasped, and Mr. Averill crossed his arms over his chest.

"Miss Starling," Owen said sharply, "that's quite enough."

"Indeed," she said, apparently inspecting the back of

her glove for a loose thread or speck of dust. There was none, of course. "I believe I see the way of things. And to think, I skipped breakfast for this."

Owen poured the last bit of water in the bucket onto the grate and the remaining embers hissed. "Let's go."

Their entire party followed the meandering path through the woods until it spilled onto the fields where the tethered horses grazed. Anabelle rode in front of Owen as she'd done before, but felt none of the exhilaration of the previous day. She was certain that Miss Starling's eyes were boring into the back of her head. And while the spoiled miss was clearly a shrew, her insinuations happened to be true.

If Anabelle had had her List with her, she'd add: "Never delude oneself into thinking love is an excuse for breaking the rules." For she had definitely broken the rules, and now, Miss Starling intended to make her pay.

The manor house finally came into view, and the group rode directly to the stable. Anabelle avoided Owen's gaze as he helped her dismount. Olivia was deep in conversation with Mr. Averill, and Owen turned to give instructions to the stable hand. To no one in particular, Anabelle said, "Forgive me, but I think I shall walk to the house and freshen up." Eager to escape Miss Starling's scrutiny, she glided out of the stable. Slipping into a steaming hot bath was going to feel so—

"Miss Honeycote!" The shrill voice rang out behind her, and she spun around.

Miss Starling walked briskly, looking perfectly elegant as she did so. "Do wait—I shall join you."

Anabelle tried to disguise her dread but feared she was not entirely successful. "Of course."

Falling into step beside her, Miss Starling gave a quick

glance over her shoulder as though making sure they were alone. A chill ran the length of Anabelle's spine.

She told herself Miss Starling couldn't know Owen had spent the night at the cottage with her.

But she was wrong.

"I confess that I may have underestimated you, Miss Honeycote."

Although this conversation was unavoidable, Anabelle had hoped to postpone it until after she'd removed the bits of leaves caked onto her hem. "In what way, Miss Starling?"

"Oh, I think you know." She absently twirled a blond strand of hair around her index finger until it formed an obedient curl. "I awoke this morning at dawn. I happened to look out the window of my bedchamber, and I saw the duke walk up to the house."

"How fascinating." She tried to sound droll, even as her pulse beat out of control.

"He was wearing the same clothes as last evening."

Anabelle raised her brows. "Your eyesight must be extraordinary."

"Quite." Miss Starling stopped at a rosebush along the path and admired a succulent, pink bloom. "I might not have given it a second thought, but when I joined him downstairs, I asked whether he'd been hunting. He said he hadn't."

"A scintillating conversation, to be sure. I'm not certain what it has to do with me."

"Patience, Miss Honeycote." She continued walking as if they were on a pleasant stroll. "Huntford also denied that he'd been out riding. I couldn't imagine what he was hiding from me, but I had a niggling suspicion that *you* were involved."

"I'm flattered."

Miss Starling glared. "So, I decided to join him on his ride to retrieve you. And I saw the most peculiar thing. Your missing spectacles were in the pocket of his jacket. How do you suppose they got there?"

"I have no idea." Her cheeks flamed. For an extortionist, she was a dreadfully poor liar.

"Well, I do. And it does not cast you in a favorable light." Her sharp tone made the hairs on the back of Anabelle's neck stand up. They were only a few yards from the house; she longed to flee to her bedchamber and slam the door. "Your actions are beyond the pale—hardly proper for a companion. If your *indiscretion* were to become known, I suspect your charges would be shocked and dismayed."

Anabelle swallowed the knot in her throat. She hated the thought of hurting Rose and Olivia.

"Such a scandal would not help ease their way into society. They're odd enough to begin with."

"They're lovely girls," Anabelle said hotly. "And better friends than you deserve."

Miss Starling raised a perfectly arched brow. "Your indignation is charming, in an unrefined way. Allow me to make my point, Miss Honeycote. You are merely a plaything for the duke. We both know he will tire of you before long, and your fairy tale will end. You'll return to your pathetic existence, hemming dresses and wearing your dowdy clothes. Meanwhile, Huntford will marry me."

Anabelle's chest constricted with anger and something else. Quite possibly fear. She tamped it all down. "This has been delightful. Now, if you'll excuse me, I'd like to go rest."

"Not so quickly." Miss Starling grabbed her arm in a viselike grip. "This afternoon, you will tell the duke that you must leave the house party immediately and that you can no longer act as the girls' companion."

"I can't do that. I—"

"You *must*."

Anabelle jerked her arm away. "I don't take my orders from you, Miss Starling."

With an amused smile, she responded, "No? Then consider this. If you don't leave—immediately—I will inform everyone that you are the duke's mistress."

"Mistress? That's a lie!"

"Is it, Miss Honeycote?" She laughed as though Anabelle had uttered the most amusing witticism. "Don't tell me you are deceiving yourself?"

Anabelle turned and strode into the house, fighting tears the whole way. Happiness, within her reach for the briefest of moments, had been snatched away.

Oh, Miss Starling was a wretched person, but her words only pricked because they held a painful kernel of truth.

Although seemingly unfair, the ultimatum—leave, or have her affair exposed—was a fitting if ironic form of justice.

Everything had come full circle.

Anabelle had started out as the extortionist—and had become the victim.

Chapter Twenty-seven

Raw: (1) The edge of fabric that is not stitched or finished. (2) The state of one's emotions when dreams—however fanciful—are dashed to bits.

You can't leave." Owen struggled to reconcile the memory of Anabelle from last night, warm and pliant in his arms, with the woman before him. She stood rigidly in front of the desk in Harsby's library where Owen had come to escape the perpetual chatter of the drawing room and think. Her skin glowed pink, and damp tendrils curled around her face, as though she'd just taken a bath. She wore a blue dress that turned her gray eyes to silver.

She clutched her bags in her hands, for God's sake.

Anabelle wasn't the sort of woman to play games, and yet he couldn't fathom the alternative—that she was about to climb into a coach and ride away, leaving him in a cloud of road dust.

"I know it seems sudden, but I've become desperately homesick. I'm worried about Mama and Daphne."

"I see." She was lying. Why else would she avoid

his gaze? "If this is about last night, I want you to know—"

"It's not about last night."

Another lie. He rose, walked past her to shut the library door, and faced her. "I didn't want to wake you before I left. But I meant what I said. I'll find a way for us to be together."

"It shouldn't be so difficult or complicated. We're not meant to be."

"Of course we are." He folded her in his arms, rested his chin on top of her head, and inhaled the fresh sweet scent of her hair. "I love you, Belle." He hadn't realized it before then, but the truth of it nearly bowled him over. He loved her.

She stiffened and pulled away, turning his blood to ice.

"I'm grateful for all you did for me and my family. You needn't worry about us. Now that Mama is well, I'm confident I'll be able to support her and Daphne."

Although he hadn't expected her to declare her love in return, she might have at least put down her portmanteau. "I don't view you as some kind of obligation, Anabelle. I *need* you in my life."

"We both know that's not true. Your life would be infinitely easier without me. But that's not the reason I've decided to leave."

"Why don't you *tell* me the real reason?" He watched as she swallowed and wished he could kiss the delicate skin at the hollow of her throat until the icy glaze coating her cracked and slid away.

"I don't belong in your world—I never have, and I never will." Her gray eyes, full of conviction, revealed she believed the words she spoke.

And that scared the hell out of him.

"You *can't* leave. You haven't finished the girls' dresses. What happened to your code of honor?" A petty question, but he wasn't above grasping at straws.

"I'll make sure their ball gowns arrive at your country estate in plenty of time for Rose's debut." Raising her chin, she said, "This is the right course of action. You must believe me."

"The hell I do. I won't let you travel alone. If you're going back to London, I'll go, too."

"I've already spoken to Lady Danshire. She's leaving for Town immediately after lunch, and I've arranged to ride with her."

The situation was quickly bucking out of his control. He pulled up on the reins. "It seems you've thought of everything. Have you told Olivia and Rose?"

She lowered her head. "No. They're napping."

"They adore you, you know. They'll be devastated." So would he.

"I hate the thought of hurting them. But, in a way, I already have. They'll be far better off without me." She squared her shoulders and turned to leave. If he were a gentleman he would have opened the library door, but he wasn't about to make this easy for her. She set down a satchel and reached for the knob.

"Wait." He went to her and cupped her face in his hands. "I need you, Belle. Please, don't go."

She opened her mouth to respond, but before she could, he kissed her. Hard.

He backed her up against the paneled door and pressed his body against hers, touching her in all the places that she liked. The bag she'd held thumped to the floor. At least she wasn't totally unaffected.

Pouring everything he felt for her—tenderness, passion, and love—into the kiss, he willed her to stay. And as he tasted her, he became more convinced than ever he couldn't live without her. Giving her little time to breathe or think, he kissed and caressed her until he was so hard all he wanted to do was lay her on the damned library floor, flip up her skirts, and pleasure her until she cried out in bliss. Until she forgot about leaving.

Somehow, he refrained from ravishing her. Checking his desire, he gently brushed his lips over hers. "I love you," he whispered hoarsely.

Her eyes filled with tears, but she sniffled and blinked them away. Placing a palm on his chest, she said, "Goodbye, Owen."

In utter disbelief and horror, he watched as she picked up her bags.

And left him.

Two days later, Anabelle arrived home so heartbroken she was numb. She felt as though she'd been hollowed out and left empty of emotion. Lady Danshire raised her brows when her coach rolled into Anabelle's sooty, unkempt part of Town. Anabelle was beyond caring; she simply thanked the marchioness and said good-bye.

She trudged up the narrow steps—the creak of the second stair so achingly familiar, she might never have been away from home.

For Mama and Daph's sakes, she summoned a smile before letting herself into the apartment. When they saw her, they jumped off the worn settee, crying out.

"Oh, you're home!" Daph hugged her fiercely. "You are lovelier than ever, Anabelle! Isn't she, Mama?"

Her mother, looking ten years younger than the last time she'd seen her, playfully pushed Daphne aside and hugged Anabelle herself. Feeling the strength and vigor in Mama's embrace, Anabelle began to cry.

Many tears were shed by all three women before Mama dried her eyes and announced she was going out to get a few items for a celebratory dinner.

"That's not necessary." Anabelle wasn't in a particularly festive mood.

"Nonsense! This is a special day, and I haven't made a mincemeat pie in ages."

Mmm. Mama's mincemeat pie tasted like happiness, family, and love. "That sounds heavenly," Anabelle said. "Thank you."

Daph clasped her hands beneath her elfish chin. "Could we also have those pastries, Mama, the ones stuffed with gooseberries and sprinkled with sugar?"

"We shall see." Eyes twinkling, Mama grabbed her shawl and reticule, pressed a kiss to each daughter's forehead, and set out.

"I can't believe how healthy and vibrant she is," said Anabelle, sinking onto the sofa.

Daphne nodded and joined her. "I can hardly believe the transformation. She's doing extraordinarily well, thanks to your duke."

The mention of Owen made it difficult to breathe. "He's not my duke. I can't deny he behaved charitably toward us, but I dislike being in his debt. I intend to pay him back."

Her sister considered her shrewdly. "I was not under the impression that he helped us out of a sense of duty or even charity. I think he cares for you."

Anabelle sighed. No sense in hiding the truth

from Daph. "I believe he *had* feelings for me. As I did for him."

A wide smile lit her sister's pretty face. "I knew it! That's wonderful. Only, something must have happened, or you wouldn't be here."

Anabelle reached for the miniature portrait of her mother and father on the table beside her and lovingly traced the tarnished frame with a fingertip. "I realized there was no future for us. He needs to marry, and it goes without saying that I am entirely unsuitable."

Daphne clenched her fists in her lap. "That's not fair. You're more refined, gracious, and kind than most ladies of the *ton*. I'm surprised the duke could not see that for himself."

For some reason, Anabelle felt obliged to defend him. "He didn't seem to mind my humble origins, but—"

"Humble? You are the granddaughter of a viscount!"

"Who wouldn't know me if he tripped over me on the street."

Daphne sprang from the settee and paced in front of it. "I don't see why any of that matters. If you and the duke care for each other, you should be together."

"He *did* want for us to be together. He told me he loved me." Anabelle choked back a sob. "He just didn't love me enough to . . . want to marry me."

"Oh, Belle." Daph hugged her until she grew sick of her own pathetic sobbing. Her sister handed her a soft handkerchief and said, "If he's too blind to see what a treasure you are, then he doesn't deserve you. But I know it stings just the same. I'm sorry."

As Anabelle hiccupped and dabbed at her face, she wondered how her sister had become so wise. "I feel like such a fool. I hoped that if I loved him enough, the difference in our stations wouldn't matter. But he never acknowledged our relationship to anyone—not even his sisters. He was ashamed of me." She set the framed picture of her parents back in its place. She'd always admired her father for his convictions, but never more so than now.

Daphne's eyes narrowed dangerously. "Why, the cad! If our paths ever cross in Town, I shall—"

"No. It is over between us, and I would just as soon forget him."

But in her heart, Anabelle knew she never, ever, would.

Two weeks later, Anabelle was once again installed in the cozy back room of Mrs. Smallwood's dress shop, working among the fabrics, sights, and smells she loved. The shop owner had been happy to take Anabelle back in spite of the hefty raise she'd requested. It seemed her previous association with a duke had its benefits.

Mama and Daphne were looking for work, hoping additional income would permit them to keep their modest apartment. Anabelle, however, doubted they'd meet with success. Though Daph would make a wonderful governess, she had no references or experience. Mama insisted she could do laundry and mending, but Anabelle worried she'd overexert herself.

Mama and Daph would most likely move to the country and rely on the kindness of distant, slovenly cousins on her mother's side while Anabelle moved into a boardinghouse and sent them what money she could.

Though her chest ached every time she thought of being separated from Mama and Daph, she couldn't resume her extortion scheme. She wasn't the same person she'd been a few months ago.

The bell on the front door of the shop had been ringing all morning, but Anabelle enjoyed the hustle and bustle. As long as she kept busy, she didn't have time to think about Owen or the magical night she'd spent with him. Or how empty she felt without him.

Mrs. Smallwood popped her head around the curtain. "You're needed out front, Miss Honeycote."

"Of course." Anabelle set down her needle and thread and instinctively reached up to pat her cap. It was smaller than the one Owen had hated, but she suspected he'd hate this one as well. No matter the shape or size, it was still a servant's cap.

Brushing off thoughts of him, she glided beyond the curtain to the front room. Ladies of all ages milled about, giving specifications to other seamstresses, selecting trimmings and lace, and admiring pictures in fashion magazines. Mrs. Smallwood had returned to help a mother and daughter with a spencer, so Anabelle searched for a customer in need of help.

"There you are!" The familiar voice made her gasp.

"Lady Olivia," she managed, barely. "How wonderful to see you."

"Just Olivia, remember?" She linked an arm through Anabelle's and strolled to the counter in the back of the shop. "I sent the gowns to Huntford Manor. Did you receive them? I hope they were satisfactory."

"They're perfect. How are you? I've missed you so."

"I've missed you too," Anabelle admitted. "And Rose. How is she?"

"Not well. That's why I'm here."

Anabelle's stomach clenched. "Not well? What's wrong?"

"Well, after the house party, we traveled directly to Huntford Manor. Rose has been sneaking away from the manor house to spend time...in the stables."

"She's still seeing the stable master, Charles?"

"Precisely. Owen knows she's hiding something and is threatening to cancel the ball unless we confide in him."

"I'm sorry. I know how much you and Rose looked forward to it."

"I was keen to see James—or more precisely, to have him see *me* in my ball gown—but canceling the ball would not be a tragedy. Rose doesn't seem to care about the ball one whit."

"I'm afraid I don't understand what the problem is, then."

"Rose refuses to eat unless Owen calls off his duel with Lord Winthrope."

Anabelle's fingers went numb. "Your brother really means to meet the earl on the dueling field?"

"He won't let the injury to Rose go unpunished. If he'd had his druthers, he'd have settled the matter at the house party, but Lady Harsby forbade any bloodshed."

Anabelle's stomach roiled. "When is the duel scheduled to take place?"

"After Rose's ball. One week hence, when we've all returned to Town. It's a horrible mess, Anabelle. I don't want Owen to duel Lord Winthrope—the earl is quite a good shot, if Lady Harsby is to be believed. But Rose must eat."

"Yes. She must." Anabelle drummed her fingers on the wooden counter. "Have you asked Charles to speak with her, to convince her to take care of herself?"

Olivia shook her head. "He told Rose that they must stop seeing each other. Although he cares for her deeply, he believes that she's too good for him. Rose, however, is more determined than ever to be with him." Olivia's voice grew shriller with each sentence. "And Owen has been a complete boor ever since . . . well, ever since you left."

Anabelle squeezed her hand. "I'm sorry I left so suddenly. It was cowardly of me to go without saying goodbye to you and Rose."

"We were upset at first. But we figured you must have had your reasons."

"Yes." She stared at the toes of her boots before looking into Olivia's kind brown eyes. "I'm sorry to hear of your family's troubles. But I'm not sure what I can do."

"Come to Huntford Manor with me and speak to Rose. Speak to Owen. Make them understand that they can't go on being so stubborn." Tears trickled down her face. "I can't bear to watch the two people I love most so upset with each other."

"Please, don't cry." Anabelle searched behind the counter and found a handkerchief, which she handed to Olivia. "They'll sort out their differences, I'm sure of it."

Olivia blotted her cheeks. "Do you think I'd be here, asking your help, if I thought they could? I know it's a terrible imposition and that you have your own family to worry about, but—"

"It's not an imposition. It's just that I have my job back here, and Mrs. Smallwood needs me." It was true and so much easier to explain to Olivia than the real reason she couldn't face Owen.

"Are you saying you can't travel to Huntford Manor for a couple of days because of your position?"

"Yes. You see, I'm supporting my mother and sis—"

"Oh, Mrs. Smallwood!" Olivia turned and marched across the dress shop toward the proprietor. "May I have a word?"

Anabelle hurried to catch up, but Olivia already had the woman's attention. "How may we help you, Lady Olivia?" Mrs. Smallwood asked.

"I require Miss Honeycote's assistance at Huntford Manor. It's a dressmaking emergency of sorts, and she is the only one my sister and I trust to help us."

Mrs. Smallwood gaped alternately at Olivia and Anabelle. "Well, I—"

"I'm aware she's a highly valuable member of your staff; however, if you could spare her for a few days, my family would be eternally grateful."

"We have a long list of backor—"

"My brother will insist on compensating you handsomely, of course."

The shop owner's eyes lit up like fireworks at Vauxhall Gardens. "I have no objection."

"But, Mrs. Smallwood," Anabelle choked out, "I'm in the middle of several projects."

The elderly woman raised her palm. "I insist that you go to assist Lady Olivia with their dressmaking...emergency. We shall manage for a few days." She brushed her hands down the front of her apron, her decision final.

"Thank goodness," Olivia cried. "Come. The coach is waiting outside. We can stop at your apartment on the way out of Town so you may inform your mother and sister and pack a few things."

Anabelle walked out of the dress shop, stunned at the day's turn of events. As she climbed into the coach behind

Olivia, she asked, "Does either Rose or your brother know you're here?"

"No," Olivia said breezily. "When Owen discovers I bullied the coachman into taking me into Town and came unchaperoned, he'll be even angrier with me than he is with Rose."

With a mixture of amusement and alarm, Anabelle realized Olivia would probably have resorted to kidnapping her if necessary. She'd never really had any choice in the matter.

It seemed she was going to Huntford Manor.

Chapter Twenty-eight

$\mathcal{O}$wen glared at Rose, who sat stiffly in front of his desk, glaring back.

He'd called her into his study two hours ago when he realized that Olivia had taken his coach—without a word to anyone—that morning. His initial shock had quickly combusted into anger, but now, as he looked out the window at the darkening sky, fear crept into his bones. Where in God's name had Olivia gone?

All Owen knew was that his trusted stable master, Charles, had seen her leave with the coachman shortly before lunch. Olivia had claimed Owen knew about her excursion—a bald-faced lie—and she'd be back in the evening.

Rose looked frailer than ever tucked into the bulky armchair across from him, her cheekbones too prominent. "If you know anything," he said to her, "you must tell me. Olivia could be stranded on the side of the road or in some other sort of dire circumstances. It's not safe for a young woman to travel alone—especially at night." Of course, she might not be alone, but with a man. That possibility was even more disturbing.

Rose swallowed as though she, too, had considered these scenarios but shook her head.

He shoved his chair away from the desk and paced. "I've been far too lenient with the two of you." He pointed at her. "You constantly disappear, refusing to tell me who you're seeing or what you're doing. And Olivia rides off in my godforsaken coach without telling a soul where she's going." He was sputtering and didn't care. "I will not abide this secrecy. If you and your sister don't tell me what's going on, I'll have to take extreme measures."

Rose sat forward in the chair, her eyes wide with alarm. Good.

"Maybe I'll lock you in your rooms for a few weeks." Except she'd probably like that, so he added, "And I'll forbid you to read, paint, play music, or even see Olivia—unless you eat."

He had not thought Rose was capable of scowling. At least he'd found a way of getting through to her.

"Dennison!" he yelled.

The butler appeared in the doorway of his study. "My name is Hodges, Your Grace. Dennison is still in Town."

Owen pinched the bridge of his nose. He'd known that, of course, but there was something inherently satisfying about yelling Dennison's name when he was perturbed. "Thank you for enlightening me, *Hodges*," he said dryly. "Tell Charles I wish to see him."

The butler bobbed his head and left.

Rose sat up straight and clutched the arms of her chair. Interesting.

Owen planned to interrogate the stable master once more, to inquire about any items Olivia may have carried with her when she left. Maybe he knew more than he let on.

To Rose, Owen said, "Charles is somehow involved in this, isn't he?"

She shook her head, but her cheeks flushed. He remembered the extortion note. "Is Olivia seeing him?"

She shook her head vehemently.

He leaned over, bringing his eyes level with hers. "I will find out the truth, Rose."

Crossing her arms, she stared past him. Good grief. What had happened to his meek and obedient sister?

Owen paced until Charles joined them. Holding his hat in his hands, the stable master bowed in Rose's direction. "You wanted to see me, Your Grace?"

"Sit down." He waved Charles into the leather chair next to Rose's. She avoided looking at him and vice versa. As though they were guilty. Keeping his tone pleasant, Owen asked, "Did Lady Olivia have any luggage when she left this morning? Did she carry a reticule or basket?"

Charles frowned. "No large bags, Sir. Just a small... thing on her wrist."

"Which suggests she wasn't planning an overnight trip. What was she wearing?"

"Sir?"

"What kind of dress?"

"I couldn't say, Sir. I think it may have been blue or green. Or maybe yellow."

"It's a good thing you know horses better than ladies' fashions, Charles."

"Yes, Sir."

A sudden commotion in the hallway halted the conversation, and Hodges ran into the room in a highly undignified manner. "Lady Olivia has returned," he shouted.

The words were no sooner out of the butler's mouth than Olivia herself breezed in.

She smiled broadly, as though she hadn't a care in the world—until she saw Charles sitting next to Rose. She clasped a hand to her chest, and her eyes flew to Owen's. "So, you know. I hope you did not completely lose your temper, Owen. Charles is quite the gentleman—"

"*What* are you talking about?"

Olivia placed a hand over her mouth.

"Olivia?"

"Never mind. I'm sure you're all wondering where I've been."

Owen gritted his teeth. "Wondering? No. Sick with worry? Yes."

"I wanted to surprise you."

"I'm in no mood for games," he warned.

"Look who I have with me!" She turned and presented her guest with a flourish.

For the space of a second, he couldn't breathe. "Anabelle?"

"Good evening, Your Grace." The sight of her was a punch to the gut. The two weeks since she'd left had felt like months. And now, she was really there, her honey-streaked hair and gray eyes gleaming, chin held high.

"What are you doing here?"

"I asked her to come," Olivia said.

"Why?"

She shrugged. "Because I didn't know what else to do. You want to risk your life in a duel with Lord Winthrope.

Rose refuses to eat. I'm scared to death I'm going to lose both of you."

"I think I should be going," Charles said, rising from his chair. He seemed to look to Rose for permission.

And suddenly, Owen put all the pieces together. Good God, he'd been dense.

"Wait," he said. The stable master sat back down. "I think you should tell me what's going on between you and Rose."

Charles gave Rose a weak but reassuring smile before slowly standing and looking Owen directly in the eyes. "I have a friendship with your sister, Sir. I know it's not fitting for someone as refined as her to spend time with a servant, and I'm sorry I deceived you. However, I promise you that I have never—*would* never—treat her as anything but the lady that she is."

Rage boiled inside Owen. He crossed his arms in the hopes that it might prevent him from delivering a blow to the man's jaw. His gaze flicked to Olivia and Anabelle. "You both knew about this, didn't you?"

Anabelle nodded, and Olivia said, "What could we do, Owen? You never would have allowed Rose to see him."

"You're correct on that score."

"I *knew* it," Olivia said. "You only care about the fact that he's a servant and Rose is the sister of a duke. You'd never notice how happy Rose is when she's with him, or how good he is for her."

"What a load of—"

"Stop, Your Grace!" Charles held up a hand. "This is upsetting Lady Rose. She loves you"—he nodded at Owen—"more than anything. The last thing I want to do is to cause strife between the two of you. I'll gather my things and leave the estate early tomorrow morning."

"A wise decision, if you value your life."

Rose stared at the floor in front of her chair, her whole body trembling.

Charles knelt in front of her and softly said, "I'm sorry, Lady Rose. Good-bye."

She began to shake more violently, looking so pale and fragile Owen wondered if she'd ever forgive him. Or ever fully recover from the blow.

As the stable master left, the only sound in the room was his heavy, rough boots treading across the floor. He'd been a hell of a stable master, and Owen had liked him. It was a shame that—

"Don't. Go." Rose's words were halting, but clear as day.

Everyone froze. Owen wondered if he was imagining things. He dropped to his knees and clasped her shoulders. "You spoke. I heard you."

She gripped the arms of the chair so tightly that her knuckles were stone white.

"Wait, Charles." Owen folded Rose into his arms. "Everything is going to be all right."

Rose spoke.

Tears streamed down Anabelle's face, not just for Rose, but for Olivia and Owen, too—they'd all waited so long for this day. Although Rose had said only two simple words, she'd broken through a barrier. Maybe her next words would come easier. Anabelle hoped.

She wouldn't have thought it possible, but Owen looked even more handsome than she remembered him. When he'd been angry, his green eyes looked as deep and turbulent as the ocean. His dark brows knit together so tightly, she itched to trace them with a fingertip and smooth away his worries. But now, in his wonder over Rose, his face transformed into that of a benevolent Greek god—patient, kind, and powerful.

Anabelle longed to throw her arms around him and share in his quiet awe of the night's events. Although she couldn't, at least she'd been able to witness something close to a miracle.

Once Rose had composed herself, Owen suggested they relocate to the drawing room, where everyone could sit and he could get some answers.

Anabelle finally had a chance to appreciate the magnificence of Huntford Manor. From the outside, the house resembled a medieval castle, but with larger windows and fewer turrets. Inside, however, the rooms were lavishly appointed and tastefully decorated. The drawing room was a combination of rich browns and deep reds, at once decadent and refined—like an exquisite tart.

She and Olivia entered the room and sat on a brocade sofa, Rose and Charles sat on the one opposite theirs, and Owen took an armchair between them—much like a judge holding court.

Anabelle felt like an intruder in the family's affairs. "I should leave so you may speak privately."

"No," Owen barked—but not unkindly. Rose's breakthrough had taken the bite out of his anger. "I want to know where Olivia has been all day. I want to know about Rose and Charles. But mostly I want an end to all the secrets."

The thread inside Anabelle, the one keeping all her sorrow and anger tied up, snapped. How *dare* Owen accuse Rose and Olivia of keeping secrets? He was the one who was too ashamed to tell his sisters about their relationship. Just moments before, he'd scolded Rose and Charles for seeing each other.

And yet, *he'd* been the one conducting an affair with a servant.

He was in no position to judge. Neither was she.

Although it was neither the proper time nor place, Anabelle spoke. "Is it your belief that we should reveal *all* our secrets, Your Grace?"

Owen yanked at his cravat. "The secrets that involve my *sisters*, Miss Honeycote."

"Miss Honeycote, is it? When you saw me a few moments ago, you called me Anabelle, did you not?"

The concerned look he shot her made hysterical laughter bubble in her throat. Was he blind to his hypocrisy? "Forgive me. I was shocked to see you. My sisters call you Anabelle, and I've begun to think of you that way, too."

"I see. So your sisters should tell all their secrets, but you should be allowed to keep yours?"

"We are all entitled to a few secrets."

"Yes, but where, precisely, does one draw the line?"

He stared at her intently. "If a secret adversely affects a member of this family, it should be shared."

"Very well." She stood and cleared her throat.

"Miss Honeycote," said Owen. "What are you doing?"

"I wish to share a secret."

"Anabelle, stop." Owen hung on the edge of his chair, and Charles looked like he wanted nothing so much as to slink out of the room.

She looked at Olivia and Rose before continuing. "Your brother and I have been hiding something from both of you. My behavior has been . . . most improper. You see, back before I knew you, I threatened to publish gossip about you in *The Tattler*."

"What?" Disbelieving, Olivia crossed her arms over her chest.

"Damn it, Anabelle." Owen rubbed the back of his neck.

"It's true. I'd heard a rumor that Olivia was seeing a servant, and I...I asked your brother for money in exchange for my silence."

"But that's..." Olivia's face contorted in disgust.

"Extortion," Rose finished for her.

Anabelle felt as big as a thimble. "I have nothing to say in my defense—except I am sorry."

Olivia fled the room in a blur of blue ribbons. Although Anabelle longed to comfort her, she was the last person Olivia wished to see. She slumped onto the sofa.

Rose stood. "I will go to her," she said quietly. Instead of walking past Anabelle, however, she stopped and squeezed her hand. "I forgive you." As she left, she gazed at Charles with obvious affection.

"Lady Rose," he said, causing her to halt. "If your brother sends some soup up, will you eat?" His eyes pleaded. "For me?"

She looked from the handsome stable master to Owen. "Only if he stays," she said.

Owen nodded. "Done. But we need to talk in the morning, Charles."

"Yes, Your Grace." He looked Owen directly in the eyes. "I look forward to it."

Rose left with the stable master, and suddenly, Anabelle and Owen were alone.

When he joined her on the sofa, she fought the urge

to lean into him, wrap her arms around him, and kiss away the tight lines around his eyes and mouth. When he reached for her hand, she snatched it away.

He raised his brows, and she scooted to the far end of the sofa.

It would be all too easy to ignore her good sense and the promises she'd made to herself. Her dignity was at stake. As was her heart. In order to stand a chance of keeping her head about her, she had to maintain her distance from him—both literally and figuratively.

"I want to go home," she said.

"How are your mother and sister?" His conversational tone raised her hackles.

"Please don't pretend that you care."

He looked puzzled. "Of course I care, Belle. You left Lord Harsby's house party so abruptly. I hoped you just needed some time to accept the truth—that we're meant to be together."

The *truth*? He hadn't come to London for her.

He hadn't told anyone about their relationship.

And he *certainly* hadn't issued a marriage proposal.

Not trusting herself to speak, she shook her head.

"Why did you tell Olivia and Rose about your extortion scheme?"

"You said there should be no secrets. Besides, they deserved to know the truth about me. The awful things I did."

"You didn't tell them the whole truth."

"No, I didn't tell them that I'd slept with their brother."

"Our relationship was more than that, Anabelle. It *is* more than that." He sighed. "What I meant was, you didn't tell them why you wrote the extortion note."

"It hardly matters. Olivia would have been the victim if you hadn't caught me."

"Horse shit."

She blinked. It was the second time he'd used the phrase with her. "I beg your pardon?"

"You never would have gone to *The Tattler*."

He had a point. However, the people she'd threatened didn't know that.

"Please. I need to return to London."

Something akin to fear glittered in his eyes. "You can't travel tonight."

"First thing in the morning, then." She avoided his gaze, too aware of the power it wielded over her.

"I'll have the housekeeper prepare a guest chamber for you and send up dinner and a hot bath. We can discuss your travel arrangements in the morning. I know you don't want to be here, Anabelle." He brushed a thumb lightly across her cheek and her stomach flip-flopped. "But I'm very glad you are."

Chapter Twenty-nine

Stole: (1) A shawl, often of fur, worn loosely around the shoulders.
(2) Past tense of the verb to steal, meaning to take something or
someone—such as a suitor—rightfully belonging to another.

Birds chirped outside Anabelle's window. Her hair, fanned out on the soft pillow beneath her head, smelled of mint and lavender. Inhaling deeply, she recalled her steaming bath the night before. She'd drifted off as the night breeze kissed her cheeks.

After a wonderful night's sleep, she awoke relaxed and content.

Not at *all* the plan.

She was supposed to be angry and hurt. She *was*, dash it all. And quite determined to leave Huntford Manor.

She groped the bedside table until she found her spectacles and slid them on. Stretching, she padded to the window—horrified to find the sun already high in the sky.

Heavens, she'd slept the entire morning away.

She snatched a peach-colored morning gown from her satchel and quickly dressed. After coaxing her hair—still damp at the roots from last night's washing—into a knot at the nape of her neck, she straightened the coverlet on the bed and stuffed the few personal items she'd brought into her bag.

How humiliating to have overslept when trying to make a dramatic exit, but there was nothing to be done for it. At least she was well-rested for the trip and could soon be on her way.

Using trial and error, she found her way around the enormous third floor and downstairs. The breakfast room had already been cleared, but Anabelle wasn't looking for food. She merely needed to find Owen and demand one of his army of servants escort her home.

She found him in the drawing room, sitting with Rose and Olivia. From the broad smiles on their faces, one would have thought that the strife of the previous night had never occurred. "Good morning," she said awkwardly.

Owen made a great show of looking at his pocket watch. "Good afternoon, Anabelle."

She remained in the doorway, clutching the handle of her bag. His attempt to charm her wouldn't distract her from her purpose, but Olivia's and Rose's disappointment might. How they must loathe her. Although they'd shown her nothing but kindness, she'd threatened and deceived them.

"Olivia and Rose," she choked out, "I must apologize once again for writing the horrid extortion note. I didn't deserve your friendship, but it meant the world to me. Olivia, you taught me to embrace every day. And Rose, you taught me true strength comes from inside."

"What did I teach you?" Owen flashed a rakish grin.

Goodness. Nothing she could mention in front of his sisters. Actually, there was something. "The importance of family."

He stood and walked toward her. "I think you already knew that."

"I'm ready to go, Your Grace, but there's one more thing I'd like to say."

"Shall I sit down? Have a drink?"

"Suit yourself. I was simply going to say that I think you should respect Rose's wishes."

He planted his hands on his hips. "What wishes?"

"Regarding the duel. She doesn't want you to challenge the earl."

His jaw twitched. "As I've explained to Rose, this is a matter of honor. I'll meet the earl...but will do my best not to kill him."

"Will you aim for his shoulder?" Olivia inquired. "You could just graze it a bit."

Rose made a face.

"I was thinking the knee, actually."

Anabelle exhaled in frustration. "I think you're missing the point, Your Grace. Rose is worried that you might get hurt."

"Are *you* worried about me, Anabelle?"

She bared her teeth in a mockery of a smile. "I'm worried you might be carted off to Bedlam."

He chuckled. "If my sisters don't fall in line soon, that's a distinct possibility. However, allow me to put your mind at ease with regard to Winthrope. Just yesterday, his seconds informed me that he's confined to his bed due to a nasty illness. I may be ruthless, but even I know it's not sporting to challenge an invalid in a duel."

"So you'll postpone it until he recovers?"

"*If* he recovers. He's rumored to have...syphilis."

Anabelle pondered this for a moment, and Rose and Olivia seemed to do the same.

"Well, that certainly seems fitting," Olivia announced at last. Which was, of course, what each of them thought but hadn't the audacity to say. Given the duchess's relationship with the earl, she'd most likely suffer the same fate. A sobering thought.

"I must seem terribly callous," Olivia continued. "But I'm not entirely heartless." She strolled to the piano in the center of the room and began randomly pecking on the keys. "I want you to know, Anabelle, that I've forgiven you. For almost shredding my reputation, that is."

Relief flooded Anabelle's chest, making it hard to breathe, much less speak. "Thank you. It's...it's more than I dared to hope."

Olivia plunked on the keys some more. Discordant notes rang out, surprising coming from a pianist as accomplished as she. "If it's not too much to ask, though, there's one little thing I'd like to ask of you in return."

"Of course. Just name it." She'd do anything to earn the sisters' forgiveness.

"No, I cannot. It's selfish of me to even ask."

"It's not. Please, I want to make this up to you and Rose somehow. I *need* to."

"Well, we were hoping you'd stay until Rose's ball this Saturday."

"But...but, that's six days away."

"I knew it was too much. It's just that there's so much to do, and we would have dearly loved your help. Don't worry yourself, however. We'll still forgive you."

Anabelle knew that she was being manipulated. And that she deserved it. "Very well," she said, setting down her bag. "I'll stay."

Guests began arriving on Thursday. Much to Olivia's delight, Mr. Averill came first; he'd barely dismounted before she boldly sought his opinion on the use of canopic jars for mummification. Lord and Lady Harsby, and Lady Danshire arrived shortly after, as did several of Owen's friends from Town. On Friday, all fourteen great aunts made their appearances, each one more charming and gracious than the next. Anabelle was certain she'd never manage to tell them apart, but Olivia drew a helpful chart for her detailing each woman's preference in hats—it proved indispensable.

Most of the ball guests, however, would come from the surrounding villages and nearby estates. Olivia assured Anabelle that the ball would be far less stuffy than those held in Town. A relief, even though she had no basis for comparison.

When she'd agreed to stay *until* the ball, she hadn't thought she'd be *attending* the ball. But Olivia could be very persuasive.

All week long, they practiced dancing reels and quadrilles and experimented dressing their hair in fetching styles. Rose and Olivia insisted that Anabelle wear another of their mother's old ballgowns. The girls claimed to have found the sea-foam green dress in an old armoire belonging to their mother, quite fortuitously, the day before the ball. After inspecting the flawless silk and the fashionable lines of the gown, however, Anabelle suspected *someone* had the dress made for her.

She didn't venture to guess who that person might be.

Olivia and Rose insisted on shopping excursions to the village, purchasing pretty ribbons and new bonnets. Rose spoke a little more each day. Anabelle treasured the idyllic time spent with the girls—all the more so because it couldn't last. Before long, she'd return to the dress shop where she'd toil over beautiful gowns for privileged ladies. Some of whom would, no doubt, wear her creations as they waltzed across ballroom floors...with Owen.

He left her to her own devices. Not that he behaved indifferently to her. The hot glances he shot over the rim of his wineglass and the wicked smiles he flashed across the chessboard suggested he still had feelings for her. Or rather, he still *wanted* her.

An emotion quite different from the real, all-the-days-of-your-life, sort of love.

Every distant, cordial word he spoke was a pinprick on her soul, but at least he respected her enough to honor her wishes. He kept his promise—and his distance.

When at last the day of the ball arrived, Anabelle's melancholy was no match for Rose's and Olivia's excitement. Infected by their enthusiasm, Anabelle arranged flowers and draped silk swags, avoiding thoughts of the farewells she'd bid tomorrow.

After a two-hour private meeting, Owen and Charles emerged from the study looking like spelunkers exiting a cave—weary, disheveled, and relieved. Owen decreed that Charles could attend the ball—a concession to the part the stable master played in Rose's breakthrough. Also, they were both keen on having her continue to eat. More importantly, Charles would keep his position, as long as there were no more unchaperoned meetings between him and Rose.

Charles swore on his life that he and Rose were nothing more than friends. Their unlikely relationship sparked from a mutual interest in animals—horses in particular. When Charles mentioned he'd been trying to teach himself to read, Rose brought him books on flora and fauna. If Rose had succumbed to a romantic infatuation, Charles was oblivious. He'd never heard her speak before the night Anabelle arrived.

But Rose grew more vocal each day. To Owen, she said, "Charles isn't inclined to dance, but I assume you'd have no objection to us taking a stroll about the ballroom this evening?"

Charles paled; Olivia and Anabelle held their breath.

Owen was silent for several seconds; a muscle in his cheek twitched. "Minx. A brief stroll, with one of the great-aunts a few steps behind."

Rose beamed.

"One more thing." Owen tweaked her nose. "Save the first dance for me."

Eyes glistening, Rose launched herself at Owen. "Of course I will," she sniffled. "But you'd better not step on my new slippers."

Shortly after tea, Anabelle began helping Rose and Olivia with their hair, corsets, and at last, their gowns—which were magnificent.

Rose wore white silk trimmed in delicate rosettes of pink. She looked so fresh and lovely that one of the great-aunts—who probably needed new spectacles—bent over to smell the silk flowers at Rose's shoulders. Instead of hiding Rose's strawberry hair under a fussy cap, Anabelle

wound pink ribbon through it and let a thick column of
curls cascade down her back.

Olivia wore light blue silk trimmed in silver lace and
crystals—a combination as striking as moonlight shimmering on a lake. Anabelle teased Olivia that with a
quiver and bow she would have resembled Artemis;
Olivia quipped that if she were going to carry arrows, one
of Cupid's would be helpful. Anabelle suspected that the
beautiful gown Olivia wore would prove more effective
than arrows.

As Anabelle curled a few tendrils that grazed Olivia's
bare shoulders, she realized dinner would be served in
less than a half hour, and she still needed to dress herself.

"Come," Olivia said, leading the way to Anabelle's
bedchamber. "Rose and I will help you."

"No! You mustn't do anything that will wrinkle your
dresses or muss your hair."

"Nonsense." Olivia laid Anabelle's gown across the
bed. "I don't wish to look too perfect. If I did, James
would never recognize me."

Rose giggled, and Anabelle savored the moment. It
seemed the girls had truly forgiven her.

Trailing her fingers over the sumptuous fabric of her
gown made her pleasantly light-headed. Never had she
imagined she'd wear something so lovely. Well, perhaps
she had, once or twice. The best bit was she hadn't had to
make it herself.

She quickly removed her day dress, slid into a fresh
chemise, and rolled on the silk stockings that Rose lent
her. Olivia carefully lifted the gown over Anabelle's head,
and as the soft waves of pale green silk billowed around
her legs, her breath caught in her throat. A few months

ago, she'd skulked through the streets of London wearing boy's clothes; tonight she'd mingle at a duke's ball wearing the finest of gowns. She blinked back tears as Olivia rummaged through the meager selection of ribbons and hairpins Anabelle had brought with her.

"These won't do. I shall see what Rose and I have that will suit." Olivia turned to leave, but Rose laid a hand on her arm.

"I have an idea." She plucked a delicate white bloom from a vase on the dresser and tucked it into Anabelle's hair, just above her left ear. Smiling, she said, "It's perfect."

"I feel like an impostor," Anabelle admitted.

Olivia shrugged. "So do I. I've no business looking this pretty, but thanks to the gown you made, I do."

"You do, indeed," Anabelle said, chuckling. "To dinner!"

"To dinner!" Olivia and Rose chorused.

They made their way to the drawing room, where Anabelle endeavored not to stare at Owen. In his black jacket, waistcoat, and breeches, he cut a dashing figure. His crisp white shirt and cravat contrasted sharply with his tanned face. Although Olivia chided him about the complete lack of color, Anabelle thought the austere look suited him perfectly.

He, Lord Harsby, and Mr. Averill dutifully made two or three trips to the dining room each—just to escort all the aunts. Owen then returned for his sisters, smiling tightly at Anabelle. He whispered to Olivia and Rose as he guided them to their seats.

Taking Mr. Averill's arm, Anabelle asked, "Is anything amiss?"

"Why do you ask?"

"Just a feeling. Probably my own nerves," she confessed.

"Understandable, but unwarranted. You look lovely, Miss Honeycote."

Although Anabelle sampled the many delicacies that were paraded before them, she tasted little. Sitting at such a grand, long table made her feel small and anxious. Turning to Olivia, who was wedged between Aunt Constance of the purple feathers and Aunt Eustace of the azure turban, Anabelle inclined her head toward two empty place settings across the table from her. "Who are the extra seats for?"

Olivia's gaze flew to Owen's. "Who are the extra seats for?" she repeated. "Well, let me think. I believe they were meant for—"

"The parson and his wife," Owen interjected. "They sent word that they were detained but will join us at the ball."

"Oh," Anabelle said. The aunts lining both sides of the table nodded, and the multitude of colorful feathers and bows waving—while dizzying—made her smile. But she couldn't help feeling as though she were an outsider. Like everyone kept some sort of secret from her.

But the ball would soon be over, and when it was, she'd pack her bags and return to her real life. Although mundane and fraught with strife, it was *her* life.

At the conclusion of dessert, the ladies freshened up and drifted toward the ballroom in a silk pastel cloud. The enormous hall boasted a high, arched ceiling that looked like it had been lifted straight out of a cathedral. Hundreds of candles in five crystal chandeliers burned so brightly it hurt to look at them. Along one long wall, three sets of open French doors invited guests to wander out onto the terrace. A soft breeze carried the scent of the rose garden into the hall, a reminder that Town and all its trappings were miles away. A string quartet played softly as ladies and gentlemen, dressed in their finery, began to mill about the ballroom.

And so the night began.

Olivia and Rose comported themselves beautifully, accepting compliments graciously, and making every guest, be they marchioness or villager, feel truly welcome. Realizing she was rather extraneous, Anabelle retreated to the chairs situated among a dozen or so potted palms at the far end of the ballroom. The aunts clustered in that general area, so Anabelle busied herself fetching lemonade for some and champagne for the more adventurous among them.

When it was time for the first dance, she excused herself and joined Olivia at the edge of the dance floor. Owen led Rose to the center of the room, pride oozing out of him. When the orchestra played the beginning chords of a waltz, he whirled Rose up and down the length of the floor, much to the delight of the crowd.

Mesmerized by his athletic grace—and the love for his sister shining in his eyes—Anabelle sighed. How she longed to be in his arms.

She wasn't the only one.

"You're a bold little chit, do you know that?" The deceivingly sweet voice behind Anabelle made the skin on the back of her neck prickle. Miss Starling.

Anabelle glanced to her right, where Olivia had stood just moments before, but now she was several yards away, apparently deep in conversation with Mr. Averill.

"Lady Olivia cannot protect you." Miss Starling's hair

was the color of golden wheat, and her blue eyes flashed dangerously. She was the most beautiful woman in the room by half. And the most spiteful. "I thought I'd made it clear that you were to stay away from the duke and his sisters. Have you forgotten that one whispered rumor from me could ruin you *and* Huntford's sisters by association?"

"I'm leaving in the morning to return to my position at the dress shop." Anabelle managed to keep the tremor out of her voice, but her knees shook.

"I'm sure you have all sorts of romantic notions about the duke, Miss Honeycote, but do not deceive yourself. You may scrub the working-class dirt from beneath your nails and wear an expensive gown, but you're nothing more than a seamstress, and you'll never be anything but. Except, possibly, a whore."

Anabelle's fear seeped out of her, making room for anger. A few weeks ago, she'd have believed every word Miss Starling said. She'd had the same thoughts herself. But now she knew who she really was—a seamstress, extortionist, daughter, sister, friend... and a woman in love.

"You're entitled to your opinion of me, but please, don't let your hatred for me spoil Rose's debut. I'll plead a headache, go to my room, and take the first coach headed to London tomorrow."

"How noble." Miss Starling affected a yawn. "Leave, before I tell the village's biggest gossip that you seduced Huntford while you were supposed to be chaperoning his innocent sisters. Go!" She might have been shooing an annoying insect.

But just then, the first dance ended. Owen walked Rose to Charles. The stable master bowed deeply, his eyes full of wonder and gratitude at the public acknowledgement.

"That man looks familiar," Miss Starling mumbled.

"Charles is in charge of the duke's stables," Anabelle said.

"The stable master? He and Rose must be the ones who— Good heavens, has the entire family gone mad? Consorting with servants is one thing. But in public? For shame." She jabbed Anabelle with her elbow. Hard. "Leave *now*. Huntford is coming this way to ask me for a dance, no doubt. I should refuse him, but I've a soft spot for rich dukes."

Anabelle looked up and saw he was, indeed, walking closer. Her traitorous stomach flipped at the sight of his half-cocked grin and confident stride. Just a couple more things she'd miss until her memories of him faded. After a while, the hurt would lessen.

But not anytime soon.

Thinking to blend into the crowd, she stepped back a few paces.

"Belle."

She froze momentarily, certain she must be imagining things.

"Miss Anabelle Honeycote."

His height allowed him to easily navigate the crowd. As he brushed past Miss Starling, her mouth fell open in horror.

And then he stood before Anabelle. "Come to the dance floor with me."

Not a question, but a command—and still, she felt she should refuse. It was a spectacle in the making. Miss Starling hung behind him, shooting poisonous looks at Anabelle. The crowd gasped, captivated by the scene playing out before them.

She should have politely declined, or better yet, fled the room.

But Owen's green eyes pleaded. *Come with me.*

So, taking the strong, warm hand he offered, she followed him onto the dance floor.

Chapter Thirty

$\mathcal{A}$s Anabelle walked with Owen to the center of the ballroom, her first thought was that the orchestra really should be playing. They'd only played a set, for heaven's sake, and already they were taking a break.

Her second thought was that while the only people actually *on* the dance floor were Owen and her, the whole population of England appeared to be circled around it.

Her third thought was that two of the women on the edge of the crowd looked remarkably like Mama and Daphne. They couldn't actually *be* her mother and sister, as the gowns they wore were much finer than anything they owned. If fact, they were almost as fine as the gown *she* wore—

Good heavens.

"Your Grace," she whispered through clenched teeth, "why wasn't I informed that my mother and sister would be attending the ball?"

"It was meant to be a surprise." His voice was so deep and smooth that she had to avoid the urge to melt into him. He cleared his throat. "Good evening, everyone, and thank you for coming to help us celebrate my lovely sister, Rose."

Tasteful clapping and cheers ensued.

"For the past few years, our family has faced our share of tragedy. But tonight we celebrate my sister's debut, and I couldn't be prouder of the woman she's become." Polite applause pattered around them. "I'm hopeful," he said, turning to Anabelle, "that we will have something else to celebrate tonight as well."

She was fairly certain that she knew what he would offer.

It could only be the position of ducal seamstress. Ever since they'd arrived, the fourteen aunts had been hinting that their wardrobes were in need of updating. Owen probably wished to offer her a permanent position.

It would mean financial security for her family.

It would mean she'd get to live with Olivia and Rose.

But it would also mean that she'd have to be near Owen without actually having him, and that was more than she could bear.

"What do you say, Anabelle?" Gads. She'd missed a few sentences, but no matter.

"I'm sorry, Your Grace. I don't wish to be your seamstress."

He held both her hands between his and went down on one knee. "I don't want a seamstress. I want *you*. Please say you'll be my wife."

"Your wife?"

"Yes. I love you, Anabelle."

The crowd fell so silent that the crackling of candles as they burned could be heard overhead.

"I—"

"This woman"—Miss Starling burst through the crowd, and all heads swiveled toward her—"was hemming my gowns a few months ago, Huntford. She was *working* for a few shillings each week. How can you possibly expect her to be a proper duchess? It's not even fair you should ask such a thing of her."

Rose stepped forward. "I think she'll make a fine duchess."

"As do I," Olivia announced, joining her.

Aunt Phyllis of the lemon-colored silk cap cleared her throat. "I happen to be acquainted with Miss Honeycote's grandfather."

Miss Starling made an unladylike sound which could best be described as a snort. With a toss of her head she said, "I presume he's a former member of your staff. An ex-footman, perhaps?"

"I should say not." Aunt Phyllis's cheeks shook with indignation. "Miss Honeycote's grandfather is the Viscount Longden. He's a bit stodgy, but as blue-blooded as they come."

Miss Starling staggered backward as though she'd taken a blow to her perfect chin.

"As Anabelle's sister and mother," Daphne said, her arm linked with Mama's, "we are probably quite partial. However, we believe she is most *definitely* duchess material...if that is what she wishes to be."

"What *do* you wish for, Anabelle?" Owen asked, imploring her with his eyes. "I want to make you happy."

"I want to be with you."

"So that's a ... ?"

Her eyes burned and her throat constricted, but she managed to say, "Yes. Yes, I'll marry you."

He let out a great shout, picked her up, and swung her around in a most garish display.

The band began a waltz, and he swept her around the floor, holding her closer than was proper and twirling her with gusto. Other couples began to crowd the dance floor, providing a cloak of silk gowns and tailored evening jackets. Owen pulled her closer, the spicy smell of him so tantalizing she just barely refrained from licking his neck.

"I knew you wouldn't say no in front of all those people."

Silly man. "It wasn't the public declaration that won me over."

"It wasn't?"

"No."

"I agreed to marry you because you love me," she admitted.

He gazed at her, his green eyes full of warmth and passion. "I do, Anabelle. Madly. Not in spite of who you are and where you come from, but because of it. Not many women—or men—would have had the courage to do what you did for your family."

"I love you, too," she said. "In spite of your title and wealth."

He chuckled deeply, sending shivers through her limbs. "If you don't love me for being a duke, why *do* you?"

There were so many reasons. But she saw the vulnerability in his eyes and knew how much her answer mattered to him. "Because you showed compassion for a common criminal. Because you shamelessly dote on your sisters and great-aunts. Because you saw me as more than a seamstress—as more than I saw myself." He looked amused and mildly confused. She thought some more and shrugged. "You're a pastry that's hard and crusty on the outside but warm and soft on the inside. I love both parts equally."

"God, I've missed you," he purred into her ear, his hand at the small of her back guiding her away from the dancers and through the doors leading to the terrace. "Promise you'll never leave me again."

The sultry night air enveloped them, and she boldly led him across the patio where they took cover behind a thick evergreen. The moment they were out of view, they reached for each other. She reveled in the scratchy feel of his chin and the solidness of his chest. He growled as his hands roamed over her bare shoulders and arms, across her breasts, and behind her bottom, claiming every inch of her. "I'm here to stay," she said. "Even if it means I must make plumed turbans for all fourteen of your great-aunts."

One week after the ball, Anabelle, Mama, and Daph moved into a charming furnished townhouse in Leicester Square that Owen had rented for them. Of course, Anabelle would only live there until the wedding, which was two months hence, but knowing that Daph and Mama would be so close and so comfortable...well, if there was a more perfect wedding gift, Anabelle couldn't imagine it.

Mama cried when they pulled up in front of the cheerful red brick house. "It's large enough for a family three times our size," she exclaimed.

WHEN SHE WAS WICKED   377

Daphne nearly swooned over the window boxes. "I can't wait to plant crocuses and daffodils."

"A lovely idea, but I think we should unpack first," Anabelle teased.

They spent a happy afternoon settling in, adding personal touches to each room, and getting to know the staff Owen had generously hired. Mama and Daph each had their own bedchamber, of course, and after Anabelle was married, there would be two guest rooms. Cook prepared a savory roast for the first dinner in their new home, and afterward Daph announced that if she ate like that every night, she would no longer fit into her new gowns.

Their improved circumstances were a drastic change from the darkness, sickness, and hunger that had plagued them mere months ago, and yet, Anabelle couldn't let go of one aspect of her former life.

She waited until Mama, Daph, and their newly hired servants were sleeping before quietly tossing back the covers, tiptoeing across her bedchamber, and rummaging through her old trunk. After shedding her nightgown, she donned the boy's shirt, breeches, jackets, and shoes. Once she'd tucked her hair under a wool cap and pulled the brim low, she went to her desk, retrieved the note and package she'd prepared earlier that day, and shoved it deep into her pocket. The familiar frisson of excitement thrummed through her body.

Tonight's mission was fraught with danger.

Being caught would bring ruin upon her—and the people she loved.

She swallowed, slipped on her spectacles, and checked the clock. The hour had arrived.

The layout of the townhouse was not yet familiar, so

she carefully navigated the stairs and made her way to the back door, adjacent to a cozy library. She opened the drawer of a hallway table, sifting through the contents till she grasped a key, cold and heavy, in her hand. Hopefully, the lock wouldn't click and the door wouldn't creak. Taking a deep breath, she inserted the key into the lock and—

"It's awfully late to be venturing out."

The deep, gravelly voice nearly made her heart jump out of her chest. She spun around. "Owen!" she chided. "What are you doing here?"

He stepped out of the shadows of the library and took her hands, lacing warm fingers through hers. "Did you think I'd let you do this alone?" With panther-like swiftness, he raised her hands above her head, backed her against the wall, and nuzzled her neck.

It was hard to think, much less speak coherently when one of his hands had skimmed her side and settled on her bottom. "I . . . I didn't think you approved."

"I don't like you taking risks," he murmured. "But I understand you need to do this. We're in this together. We're in everything together."

"Thank you."

"Don't thank me yet." His hand drifted lower, and his fingers caressed her wickedly through the nubby wool of her breeches. "Make me work for it."

Anabelle writhed against his hand, her breeches damp and her loins pulsing with desire. Breathlessly, she said, "Would you like to continue this conversation in the library, Your Grace?"

"An excellent idea." He tugged her toward him and slipped a hand under her shirt, cursing when he encountered the cloth she'd used to bind her breasts. "What's this?"

"I'm making you work for it," she teased.

He laughed as he pulled her into the library. "God, I love my work."

The next morning, the Viscountess of Bonneville was taking breakfast in her bedchamber—as was her custom—when her very handsome butler entered and handed her a small package accompanied by a note. She read it with great interest.

> *Dear Lady Bonneville,*
>
> *I am pleased to inform you that due to a change in personal circumstances I am able to make reparations for my prior bad behavior. Enclosed you will find your 30 pounds, returned with interest. Please accept my apologies for the distress my actions must have caused you.*
>
> *I wish you and your beau every happiness. Rest assured, your secret shall always be safe with me.*
>
> *Sincerely yours,*
> *A Remorseful, Reformed Citizen*

Casting an appreciative glance at her butler's backside, the viscountess folded the note and tucked it deep into the valley between her bosoms.

She'd always been partial to happy endings.

Lovely and sweet, Daphne
Honeycote is the picture
of perfection. But beneath her
innocent façade, Daphne guards
a shocking secret—and it's about
to become the scandal of
the season . . .

Please turn this page for a
preview of

*Once She
Was Tempted*

Chapter One

London, 1816

*U*pon meeting Miss Daphne Honeycote for the first time, Benjamin Elliot, Earl of Foxburn, had two distinct thoughts.

The first was that she *appeared* to be a suitable match for his upstanding young protégé, Hugh. Her golden hair was smoothed into a demure twist at her nape, and the collar of her gown was prim enough to pass muster in a convent. Her entire person radiated light, goodness, and purity.

The earl's second thought regarding Miss Honeycote was that he should probably take down the nude portrait of her hanging in his study.

To be fair—and to his everlasting regret—Miss Honeycote wasn't entirely nude in the painting. She reclined on a chaise of sapphire blue, her gown unlaced all the way to the small of her back, exposing slim shoulders and the long indent of her spine. The look she cast over her shoulder was serene and wise.

And utterly captivating.

His butler had once nervously suggested that a less titillating painting—of the English countryside or a fox hunt, perhaps—might be more befitting an earl's study. Ben had explained to the butler—with uncharacteristic patience—that since he had no intention of hosting the next meeting of the ladies' scripture study, he'd hang any picture he damn well pleased.

But now, as he watched poor Hugh fumbling over himself to impress Miss Honeycote at the Duchess of Huntford's dinner party, he realized he'd have to take down the painting. It would never do for Hugh to see the scandalous portrait and discover that the woman he was courting was not the paragon of virtue he imagined her to be.

Ben wasn't one to cast stones, but at least he didn't pretend to be anything other than what he was—a bitter, cynical bastard. *Everyone* knew what he was, and yet invitations were never in short supply. It was truly amazing what character defects people would tolerate if one had a title, a fortune, and a few interesting scars.

He preferred to eat alone but couldn't refuse an invitation from Huntford. Especially when he suspected the duchess had arranged the dinner party in order to further Miss Honeycote's acquaintance with Hugh. This dinner was the social equivalent of advancing a column of infantry and probably involved more strategy. It was the kind of maneuver that Robert—Hugh's older brother and Ben's best friend—would have skillfully countered. Ben tucked an index finger between his neck and cravat, which suddenly felt tight.

Robert was gone, killed in the line of duty, leaving

his younger brother with no one to look out for him but Ben—a poor substitute if ever there was one. The least he could do was protect Hugh from the mercenary and morally suspect Miss Honeycotes of the world.

Ben kept a wary eye on the stunning blonde throughout the evening. If he didn't know better, he'd swear she'd stepped out of the portrait in his study and raided the armoire of a prudish vicar's wife before coming to dinner. The contradiction between the oil-painted and in-the-flesh versions of Miss Honeycote kept his mind pleasantly—if wickedly—occupied during the meal, which was otherwise predictably tedious. Huntford sat at one end of the table, looking more medieval king than sophisticated duke; his pretty wife sat at the other. The duke's two sisters—Olivia and Rose—and Miss Honeycote were interspersed among the remaining men—Hugh, himself, and his solicitor and boxing partner, James Averill.

It was the sort of social affair Ben had avoided since returning from Waterloo. Cheerful gatherings, replete with inane conversation about the condition of the roads and the prospects for rain, made him feel like the worst kind of hypocrite. He sat in one of London's most elegant dining rooms enjoying savory roast beef while members of his regiment lay buried in the cold ground.

It seemed almost traitorous.

Ben's leg twitched, signaling its agreement.

Damn. That twitch was like a warning shot before cannon fire. Sweat broke out on his forehead, and he clutched his fork so hard the fine silver handle bent.

Beneath the polished mahogany dining room table, he gripped the arm of his chair while the twisted muscles in his right thigh spasmed and contracted like a vise. He gritted his teeth, keeping his breathing even. The dinner conversation became muffled, like he was listening through a door. Objects in front of him blurred, and he could no longer tell where the tablecloth ended and his plate began. Silently, he counted. *One, two, three…* The episode could last ten seconds or ten thousand, but he gleaned a shred of comfort from knowing it would end. Eventually.

He reached eighty-six before the pain subsided and the room slowly came back into focus. After a glance up and down the table, he relaxed slightly. No one seemed concerned or alarmed, so he must have gotten through the spell without grunting. As inconspicuously as possible, he swiped his dinner napkin across his damp forehead. Miss Honeycote cast him a curious look, but he ignored it, took a large gulp of wine, and tried to pick up some thread of the conversation around him.

Hugh was grinning at Miss Honeycote like an idiot. He seemed to fall further under her spell with each bloody course. At this rate, they'd be betrothed by dessert. "I understand you volunteer at the orphanage on Thursdays," Hugh said.

"Yes, I enjoy being around the children." She lowered her eyes, as though uncomfortable discussing her charity work. Little wonder. She probably wouldn't know an orphan if one bit her on her lovely ankle.

"The children adore Daphne," the young duchess said proudly. "With a smile, my sister can brighten the darkest of rooms."

"I do not doubt it," exclaimed Hugh.

Miss Honeycote blushed prettily, while Ben just barely refrained from snorting. He had to admit, she did a fair job of brightening his study.

She probably wouldn't deign to bat her lashes at Hugh if a viscount's title hadn't been tragically plopped onto his lap. Hugh was so smitten he'd already sunk to composing bad poetry in her honor, which meant Ben would have to confront her about the painting—in private, and soon. With any luck, he'd spare Hugh the humiliation of learning that the woman he fancied himself in love with was, for all intents and purposes, a doxy.

"Lord Biltmore tells us you're something of a hero." Olivia Sherbourne, the more animated of the duke's sisters, leaned forward, gazing expectantly at Ben.

He shot Hugh a scathing glance before responding to Miss Sherbourne. "Hardly. I had the misfortune of finding myself in the path of a bullet. Let me assure you—there was nothing vaguely heroic or romantic about it."

"Nonsense." Hugh sat up straighter. "The colonel himself came to visit Lord Foxburn, and he said—"

"Enough." It was a bark—harsher than he'd intended. The duchess fumbled her fork and it clattered onto her plate. Accusatory silence followed. The women stared at him with owlish eyes and, at the head of the table, Huntford glowered.

Ben set his napkin next to his plate and leaned back in his chair. If they were waiting for an apology, they were going to wait a long time. In fact, his flavored ice, which had been cleverly molded into the shape of a pineapple, was already starting to melt. Instead, he said, "I'm certain there are more appropriate topics of conversation for a dinner party."

The duke arched a dark brow.

Ben responded with a grin but didn't let it reach his eyes. "Better to stick with less distressing subjects when conversing with the gentler sex." He sounded like an insincere ass, and no wonder.

"Must we limit our conversation to weather and roads, then?" Miss Sherbourne looked like a chit who'd discovered her diamond earrings were paste jewelry.

"Of course not." Ben scooped the spike of the ice pineapple into his spoon. "There are plenty of interesting, *appropriate* topics for young ladies."

"Such as?"

He froze, his spoon halfway to his mouth. "I don't know...the color of Lady Bonneville's newest turban?"

Every head at the table swiveled toward him, and no one looked particularly pleased.

Miss Honeycote cleared her throat, drawing the attention away from him like a matador unfurling a scarlet cape. She smiled, instantly raising the temperature in the room several degrees. "Lord Foxburn, I cannot speak for my entire sex, but let me assure you that my sister, Olivia, Rose, and I are not nearly as fragile as you might think. If you knew us better, you wouldn't worry about offending our sensibilities. You'd be worried that we'd offend yours."

The ladies giggled, murmuring their agreement, and even Huntford chuckled reluctantly. Miss Honeycote pursed her pink lips and tilted her head as she met Ben's gaze. Her knowing smile and heavy-lidded eyes were an exact match to those of the woman in the portrait.

And, coincidentally, to the woman who invaded his dreams.

Daphne took a sip of wine and, over the rim of her glass, marveled at the luxury surrounding her. A fire crackled in the marble fireplace of the duke's dining room, gilt-framed pictures graced the sea-green walls, and a chandelier sparkled over the mahogany table.

Her sister, Anabelle, blushed prettily under her husband's appreciative gaze. If the new fullness in her cheeks and sparkle in her eyes were any indications, being a duchess suited her quite nicely.

Her sister, the Duchess of Huntford. The thought still made Daphne giddy.

A year ago she and Belle had been living in a tiny rented apartment wondering how on earth they were going to be able to feed themselves, much less purchase the medicine Mama needed. Daphne had spent night after night in Mama's room, watching over her, as if that would keep Death from skulking in and snatching her away. Some mornings, when the room was thick with the pungent smells of strong tea and bitter medicine, she was afraid to approach Mama's bed. Afraid that she'd take her hand and find it cold and stiff.

Daphne shivered in spite of herself. She wasn't the sort to dwell on dark times, but remembering was useful on occasion—if only to make one appreciate one's blessings.

And she had many.

Mama was now the picture of health. She and Daphne lived in a townhouse twenty times the size of their old apartment and a hundred times more beautiful. They had a butler and a cook and ladies' maids, for heaven's sake. If a gypsy had foretold it, Daphne would have fallen off her chair from laughing. And yet here she sat, in a ducal dining room of all places.

Enjoying her first Season.

Even she, the eternal optimist, never dared to dream

of such a thing. Because of her sister's marriage—a love match to rival any fairy tale—Daphne would gain admittance to lavish balls and perhaps receive her vouchers to Almack's. She might even be presented at Court. The very thought of which made her pulse race.

Yes, it was *that* thought that made her pulse race. Not Lord Foxburn, or his bottomless blue eyes, or his irreverent grin. He seemed a jaded, bitter sort, but Lord Biltmore held the earl in such high esteem that he must have *some* redeeming qualities. Something beyond the broad shoulders and the dimple in his left cheek. She endeavored not to stare, but he was sitting directly across from her, and a girl could hardly gaze at the ceiling all evening.

If she was nervous tonight, it was only because their recent good fortune seemed almost too perfect, too fragile. Like a tower of precariously balanced crystal glasses that would come crashing down from the slightest vibration. She pushed the image away, inhaled deeply, and savored her last bite of lemon ice, which was surely a spoonful of heaven.

Shortly after the dessert course, Daphne and the other ladies filed into the drawing room for tea. The moment the doors closed behind them, Belle drew her aside and, as only a sister could, began interrogating her without preamble. "What did you think of him?"

"He was a bit boorish, but I think that, under the circumstances, we must make allowances."

Belle squinted through the spectacles perched on her nose, perplexed. "Lord Biltmore?"

Oh, drat. Of course her sister was asking about Lord Biltmore—the kind, young viscount who'd sent flowers once and called twice. "I thought you were asking about

Lord Foxburn." Daphne's cheeks heated. "Lord *Biltmore* is a true gentleman. Amiable, gracious, and—"

"Did you notice his shoulders? They're quite broad."

Daphne frowned, wishing her sister would use pronouns with a bit more moderation. "Whose shoulders?"

"Lord Biltmore's!" Belle made the pinched face again then let out a long breath. "No matter. If he doesn't strike your fancy, there are plenty more eligible men I can introduce to you. I just thought he'd be—"

Daphne reached out and clasped the hand Belle waved about. "Lord Biltmore is the finest of gentlemen. Thank you for hosting this dinner. You arranged it all for me, didn't you?"

A mysterious smile curled at the corner of Belle's mouth and a gleam lit her eyes. "It's only the beginning."

Oh no. Belle didn't undertake any task halfway. Daphne had once asked her to replace the ribbon sash on a plain morning gown. Within a few hours, Belle transformed it into a shimmering confection of silk and delicate lace. If matchmaking became her sister's mission, Daphne would not have a moment's peace. "You are newly married and a duchess to boot. Surely you have more pressing matters to attend to than filling my social calendar."

"Not a one. This is your chance, Daph. No one deserves happiness more than you."

"I *am* happy." But she wasn't happy like Belle was with Owen. That was a rare thing.

"You know what I mean."

Daphne bit her lip. "Yes." If her sister was determined, why not let her do her best? There was no one in the world Daphne trusted more. She gave Belle a fierce hug and extricated herself before she turned completely maudlin.

Needing a moment, Daphne poured herself some tea, wandered to the rear of the drawing room, and sank into a plush armchair near an open window. A warm breeze tickled the wisps on her neck, and the simple pleasure of it made her eyes drift shut.

This Season *was* her chance, presented to her on a silver salver. She, a poor girl from St. Giles, would mingle with nobility. With just a smidgen more luck, she might marry a respectable gentleman. Someone kind and good. Greedy as she was, she even dared to hope she'd fall in love. With a man who would view life the same way she did—as a chance to bring happiness to others.

Lord Biltmore seemed the perfect candidate. His manners were impeccable, and he treated her like a rare treasure, or a fragile egg that might break if jostled. His boyish smile held not a trace of cynicism, and the way his russet-colored hair spiked up at the crown—much like a tuft of grass—was utterly endearing. Though he'd lost his brother barely six months ago, he managed to see goodness in the world around him and reflect it back tenfold.

The viscount could have his pick of the Season's debutantes, yet he appeared to be taken with *her*—a newcomer with few connections and no fortune to speak of. The advantage of being an unknown was that she had no reputation to speak of—so far, it was unblemished.

She could hardly believe how nicely the pieces of her life were falling into place.

A shadow slanted across the teacup in her lap, and she looked up. A torso clad in a finely tailored, dark blue waistcoat appeared, precisely at eye level.

"Miss Honeycote, might I have a word?"

Daphne blinked, tilted her head back, and directed her

gaze to the face above the snowy white neckcloth. What Lord Foxburn lacked in manners he certainly made up for in good looks. His tanned skin set off his startlingly blue eyes. The fine lines at their corners seemed to have resulted not from a tendency to smile, but rather, to glare, if his current expression was any indication. Although his mouth curved down at the corners, his lips were full. Daphne was quite sure that his smile—should she ever see it—would be dangerously charming. His light brown hair curled, softening the angles of his cheekbones and nose, but it was his eyes that left her slightly breathless and off-balance. Turbulent as a churning sea, they harbored a storm of accusation, curiosity, determination, and perhaps a glimmer of hope. And that was only on the surface. Daphne could not imagine what else lurked below, and the mere thought of exploring their depths made her skin tingle like—

Lord Foxburn cleared his throat.

She started, and her tea sloshed, forming a moat in the saucer. Hoping to remedy the small lapse in etiquette—what was it the earl had just asked her?—she smiled apologetically. "How clumsy of me." Heat crawled up her neck, probably producing more than could be considered a fetching blush. She waited for him to offer a gracious word, or at least smile back.

He did neither. Instead, he sighed as though he were already bored with their conversation. If, at this juncture, it could even properly be considered one.

Ah, well, the earl had returned from the battlefield not so long ago. One could understand how his manners might be out of practice. "Would you care to sit?"

"If you have no objection," he said wryly.

"I'd be delighted."

As he lowered himself to the settee, his lips drew into a thin line. He moved with the natural confidence of an athlete, but she'd detected a limp earlier. "Does your leg pain you?"

He narrowed his eyes. Yes, the lines reaching toward his temples were almost certainly due to this sort of squinting face. An unflattering look for most men, but it rather suited him.

"A great many things pain me, Miss Honeycote." His arched brow told her he wasn't referring to physical ailments alone.

Well. Though sorely tempted, she would not retaliate in kind. "I am sorry to hear it."

He studied her, no trace of remorse on his face. "I require a word with you, in private."

Daphne glanced around the drawing room. The closest person was several yards away, and her curiosity was piqued. "I'm listening."

The earl pinched the bridge of his nose. He was perhaps the most impatient person Daphne had ever met. "The matter I wish to discuss is of a delicate nature. I think it would be best to arrange a meeting for tomorrow."

"I confess I've never had such an odd or intriguing request." She'd received her fair share of improper advances from men, but Lord Foxburn didn't seem the type of man to force his attentions on a woman. With his striking good looks, Daphne was quite sure he wouldn't have to.

Perhaps he wanted to share some information about Lord Biltmore. The young viscount had mentioned that Lord Foxburn had been his brother's closest friend and that, after his death, the earl had helped him adjust to his new role. But what did that have to do with her?

"I realize this must seem forward. However, I think you'll appreciate the need for discretion once the topic of our discussion becomes clear. May I call on you tomorrow?"

Daphne pretended to regard him thoughtfully for several moments, in order to give the impression that a fierce debate raged inside her. In truth, she was much too curious to say no.

"I'm staying here, with my sister, while our mother is in Bath."

Concern flicked across his face. So, he wasn't as unfeeling as he'd like people to think. "Taking the waters?"

"No, Mama's surprisingly healthy. But she's not accustomed to the parade of parties and social engagements. I think she just wished to escape it all."

"Your mother's a wise woman." The earl rose and inclined his head in a manner that could be perceived as either polite or mocking. "Until tomorrow, Miss Honeycote."

Before she could ask one of the twenty questions swirling through her mind, Lord Foxburn walked away. For someone with an injured leg, he made an amazingly hasty departure. How vexing. And unpardonably rude to leave without giving some hint of what he wanted to discuss, some clue as to why he insisted on secrecy.

If he was toying with her, she did not care for the game. His brooding, cynical air might intimidate some, but a girl from St. Giles didn't survive long if she was the cowering type.

She'd never been one to shy away from a challenge.

THE DISH

Where authors give you the inside scoop

♥ ♥ ♥ ♥ ♥ ♥ ♥ ♥ ♥ ♥ ♥ ♥ ♥ ♥ ♥

From the desk of Kendra Leigh Castle

Dear Reader,

"Everybody's changing and I don't feel the same." That's a lyric from Keane, one of my favorite bands, and it could easily be applied to Bay Harper. She's the heroine of the fourth book in my Dark Dynasties series, IMMORTAL CRAVING, and she's grappling with the kind of changes that would send even the most well-adjusted people into a tailspin.

Bay is a character near and dear to my heart. In a series where just about everyone grows fangs, fur, or wings, she's incredibly human. And though I myself haven't had to deal with my best friend becoming a vampire, I found it very easy to relate to her struggle with the upheaval around her. I'm a Navy wife—it's a job that involves regularly scheduled chaos. Every few years, I pack up kids, pets, and boxes of stuff that seem to reproduce when I'm not looking. Then I move to a different part of the country and start again. It can be exciting, or infuriating, or just completely overwhelming…sometimes all three at the same time. In IMMORTAL CRAVING, Bay's going through all of those feelings. The difference is that in her case, she's not the one moving. It's everything around her that refuses to stay still. With her best friend now a vampire queen and her town being overrun with vampires and werewolves, Bay is clinging to what shreds of normalcy she can.

We all need things to hang on to when times get tough. For me, I rely on my family, my constant companions on this crazy journey. Bay takes solace in her cozy nest of a house, her big slobbery dog (I also have a pair of those, and I can attest that sometimes a dog hug makes everything better), and her job. Still, no matter how hard you fight it, nothing ever stays the same. And when lion-shifter Tasmin Singh shows up on Bay's doorstep—well, floor—she's finally forced to decide which things in her life she really needs to be happy, and which she can let go of.

Change happens to everyone eventually, whether you're a Navy wife or have lived in the same town all your life. I hope you'll enjoy watching Bay and Tasmin discover, as I have, that even when your entire world seems to have been upended, the people by your side can make all the difference in the end.

Happy Reading!

Kendra Leigh Castle

♥ ♥ ♥ ♥ ♥ ♥ ♥ ♥ ♥ ♥ ♥ ♥ ♥ ♥ ♥ ♥ ♥ ♥

From the desk of Anne Barton

Dear Reader,

Don't you just adore makeovers?

I do. Give me a dreary, pathetic "before" with the promise of a shiny, polished "after," and I'm hooked. The obsession began with Cinderella, when a wave of her fairy godmother's wand changed her rags into a sparkling ball gown. (With elbow-length gloves!) If only it were that easy.

Reality TV (which I also happen to love) serves up a huge variety of makeover shows. When I'm flipping through the channels, I can't resist them—room makeovers, wardrobe makeovers, relationship makeovers, and more. Even as I'm clucking my tongue and shaking my head at the "before" pictures, I'm envisioning the potential that's underneath, seeing what could be. Of course, every makeover show ends the same way—in a big (often tear-filled) reveal. The drama builds to the moment when we finally get to witness the person or thing transformed. And it feels sort of magical.

In WHEN SHE WAS WICKED, Anabelle gets a little makeover of her own. When we first meet her, she's a penniless seamstress with ill-fitting spectacles and a dowdy cap. She resists change (like a lot of us do) but eventually finds the courage to ditch the cap and trade in her plain dresses for shimmering gowns. But her hot new look is only half the story. Her *real* transformation is on the inside— and that's the one that ultimately wins Owen over.

Makeovers inspire us, and I think that's why we're

drawn to them. We may not have fairy godmothers, but we have hope…and reality TV. We all want to believe we can change—and not just on the outside.

Happy Reading!

Anne Barton

♥ ♥ ♥ ♥ ♥ ♥ ♥ ♥ ♥ ♥ ♥ ♥ ♥ ♥ ♥ ♥ ♥

From the desk of Sue-Ellen Welfonder

Dear Reader,

Do you ever wonder where characters go after their story is told? If the book is a Scottish medieval romance, can you see them slipping away into the mist? Perhaps walking across the hills and disappearing into the gloaming?

SEDUCTION OF A HIGHLAND WARRIOR ends my Highland Warriors trilogy, and I'm betting readers will know where Alasdair MacDonald and Marjory Mackintosh enjoy spending time these days, now that their happy ending is behind them. Their favorite "hideout" is extra-special, as I'm sure readers will agree when Alasdair and Marjory take them there.

Scotland brims with special places.

Is there anywhere more romantic? Anyone familiar with my work knows how I'd answer that question. Nothing fires my blood faster than deep, empty glens, misty hills, and high, rolling moors purple with heather.

Toss in a chill, damp wind carrying a hint of peat smoke, a silent loch, and a spill of ancient stone, and my heart swells. Add a touch of plaid, a skirl of pipes, and my soul soars.

My passion for Scotland has always been there.

So has my belief in Highland magic.

I always weave such whimsy into my books, and my Highland Warriors trilogy abounds with Celtic myth and lore. Readers will find an enchanted amber necklace, a magical white stag and other fabled beasties, and even a ghostie or two. There are mystical standing stones and enough Norse legend to lend shivers on cold, dark nights. My characters live in a world of such wonders. The Glen of Many Legends, the sacred glen shared by the three clans in these stories, is a magical place.

But at the heart of each book, it's always love that holds the greatest power.

Alasdair fought against his love for Marjory. If, at the beginning, you asked him what matters most, he'd answer kith and kin, and Blackshore, his beloved corner of the glen. He's a proud chieftain and a fierce warrior. He knows that giving his heart to Marjory will destroy his world, even causing the banishment of his people. As clan leader, the weal of others must come first. Yet for Marjory, he risks everything.

A strong heroine, Marjory is sure of her heart, refusing to abandon her love for Alasdair even in her darkest, most dire hours. She also desires the best for the glen. But as a passionate woman, she battles to claim the one man she can't live without.

As Marjory and Alasdair enjoyed the special place noted above, a bit of Highland magic entered my own world. In the story, Marjory has a much-loved blue ribbon.

The day I finished copy edits, I received a lovely, hand-made quilt from a friend. On opening the gift, the first thing I saw was a beautiful blue ribbon.

I smiled, my heart warming.

I'm sure the ribbon was a wink from Marjory and Alasdair.

Highland Blessings!

Sue-Ellen Welfonder

www.welfonder.com

Find out more about Forever Romance!

Visit us at
www.hachettebookgroup.com/publishing_forever.aspx

Find us on Facebook
http://www.facebook.com/ForeverRomance

Follow us on Twitter
http://twitter.com/ForeverRomance

NEW AND UPCOMING TITLES

Each month we feature our new titles
and reader favorites.

CONTESTS AND GIVEAWAYS

We give away galleys, autographed copies,
and all kinds of exclusive items.

AUTHOR INFO

You'll find bios, articles, and links to personal websites
for all your favorite authors—and so much more.

GET SOCIAL

Connect with your favorite authors, editors, and
other Forever fans, and share what's important to you.

THE BUZZ

Sign up for our monthly romance newsletter,
and be the first to read all about it.

VISIT US ONLINE AT

WWW.HACHETTEBOOKGROUP.COM

FEATURES:

OPENBOOK BROWSE AND SEARCH EXCERPTS

•

AUDIOBOOK EXCERPTS AND PODCASTS

•

AUTHOR ARTICLES AND INTERVIEWS

•

BESTSELLER AND PUBLISHING GROUP NEWS

•

SIGN UP FOR E-NEWSLETTERS

•

AUTHOR APPEARANCES AND TOUR INFORMATION

•

SOCIAL MEDIA FEEDS AND WIDGETS

•

DOWNLOAD FREE APPS

Bookmark Hachette Book Group @ www.HachetteBookGroup.com